# Game Ten

# GAME TEN

## James Long

SIMON & SCHUSTER

LONDON·SYDNEY·NEW YORK·TOKYO·SINGAPORE·TORONTO

First published in Great Britain by Simon & Schuster Ltd, 1994
A Paramount Communications Company

Copyright © James Long, 1994

The right of James Long to be identified as author of this work has been
asserted in accordance with sections 77 and 78 of the Copyright Designs
and Patents Act 1988

**Simon & Schuster Ltd**
**West Garden Place**
**Kendal Street**
**London W2 2AQ**

Simon & Schuster of Australia Pty Ltd
Sydney

A CIP catalogue record for this book is available from the British Library.

ISBN 0–671–71808–8

This book is a work of fiction. Names, characters, places and incidents
are either the product of the author's imagination or are used fictitiously.
Any resemblance to actual events or locales or persons, living or dead, is
entirely coincidental.

Typeset in 11.5/14 Sabon by
Hewer Text Composition Services, Edinburgh
Printed in Great Britain by
Butler & Tanner Ltd, Frome and London

*For Ben, Harry and Matilda*

# Prologue

## Monday June 24th

Paul Wade, flying on wings of Ecstasy, convinced of his invulnerability by an extra snort or two of the purest coke he'd ever got his hands on, thundered into the early Kentish dawn.

The other side of Caterham, he was killed by a small lump of concrete but he didn't know it at the time. The speeding car, Shamen blaring from the tape player, got away from him on a bend as his chemically modified brain completely misunderstood the evidence of his eyes and simply failed to tell his hands to turn the wheel fast enough. A broken building block, hidden in the long grass of the verge, bounced the rear tyre back into line with a violent jolt.

The car lurched back on to the road in a cacophony of noise from ancient suspension bushes, its glove-box lid dropping open and a cloud of dust, which would have delighted any drugs squad analyst, rising from the floor. Inside the radio-cassette player, the brittle filament of a tiny pea-bulb had broken under the transmitted shock. Within an hour, that tiny piece of broken wire killed him.

Paul's friends had cheered him on his way, the Lone Ranger of the satellite screen, when they'd surfaced from the warehouse rave in Catford. Blown along by the magic powder in his veins, he'd set off to breach the dark citadel and bring his long investigation to a close.

The Ecstasy, taken before midnight, wore off before he came to his destination, allowing a little blackness back into his soul. He coasted, pulling the wheel over to let gravity take the car down the lane with a dead engine. The high wire mesh of the scrapyard fence was black against a lightening pink and yellow eastern sky. He sprinkled a small heap of coke on to the back of his hand and sniffed deeply, feeling clarity burst upwards through his brain like cold, running water.

Closing the car door silently, he checked the windows of the caravan for signs of life, just as Monkey had told him to.

Normally the little red light would have warned him that, with the tape ejected, the radio was still switched on, but now its filament was hanging limply inside the bulb. It was shortly before 5.50a.m. when he found a way through the wire into the scrapyard. It was just a minute or two later when the transmitters came on all over the country and a Radio 4 announcer in the basement of Broadcasting House put on the opening medley that heralds the network's daily awakening.

The volume control had been turned right up for the rave music, and the six speaker array – possibly the most valuable part of the whole car – pumped out 'Rule, Britannia!' for all it was worth. A light came on in the caravan.

# Chapter One

## Saturday July 13th

The Gulfstream whispered its way on to the apron, joining a row of megabuck corporate jets, and dwarfing the ranks of Cessnas which were the little airfield's more usual inhabitants. The heat of Sonoma County, California hit them as they walked down the steps, but not for long. A stretch limo waited just yards away beyond the wingtip. The two men weren't dressed in the usual corporate jet and limo style. Both in their forties, they wore soft sports jackets, expensive plaid shirts, slacks and Timberland boots. Only the colours differed. The shorter man had an expression of pure glee on his face and he stopped on the tarmac, opened his arms wide, then did a little pirouette, sniffing the air appreciatively, loving it.

'Final leg, Hacker,' he said. 'Gonna be great. Bet you can't wait, huh?'

The other man looked more at home in casual clothes. He glanced around at the fields and the distant woods. 'I can't say, Ed. I hope it's not a waste of time,' he replied shortly.

'Bohemia's never a waste of time. You wait. You never saw anything like it.'

The driver opened the rear door of the limo for them. 'Good to see you, Mr Butzer. Welcome to the Grove.'

In the back, Ed pulled open the burr walnut door of the cocktail cabinet and whooped with glee. 'All right. Here we go. This'll get you started.'

He poured a large measure of brown liquid from a decanter into one of the lead crystal tumblers which nestled in padded sockets inside the cabinet, and passed it over.

'What is it?'

'Rusty stovebolt. Go on, knock it back.'

'Rusty what?'

'Scotch, Drambuie and Kahlua. Great detailing, eh? They even get the booze in the limo right. It's the camp drink for Bone Yard. That's my camp.'

The other man took a sip and made a face. 'Kind of sweet, isn't it?'

Ed Butzer, head of one of the meanest mergers and acquisitions law firms in Manhattan, looked at his old college pal and giggled. 'Sure it's sweet. Got to get into the vacation mode, Hacker. This is the biggest vacation of them all.'

'Ed, I wasn't planning on coming for a vacation. You said . . .'

'I said, you want to meet the guy, you come with me. I know where he'll be with his pants down and his schlong in his hand pissing on a tree. Doesn't mean you can't have fun.' He'd finished his drink already and his cheeks had taken on a warmer glow. 'Listen,' he said, 'you didn't used to call me Ed when we were at Harvard. You're Hacker and I'm Teddy, right? Like the old days.'

'Whatever you say . . . Teddy,' the other man said with a slight sigh.

They crossed a bridge, left a little town behind and the road began to wind through small trees. Detecting even through a mounting fog of rusty stovebolts that his companion was having second thoughts, the lawyer tried again. 'Got to appreciate the tradition here to understand it right, Hacker. The Bohemian Club's been coming to the Grove for over a hundred years. Jim Baker, Cas Weinberger, Kissinger, all those guys. Reagan spent his formative years bunking at Owl's Nest camp. Nixon was at Cave Man. Schultz, Nick Brady, Gerry Ford, they were all at Mandalay. That's a pretty special camp, Mandalay; you want to take a look in there. Luxury.'

'I thought it was all one camp.'

'Hell, no. The Grove's one big redwood forest, but over the years all these separate camps got set up. Lotsa different styles and customs. Makes it sort of exclusive but together at the same time.'

'What about George Bush?'

'Sure. Bush, now, he joined Hill Billies, with Cronkite and Tom Clausen, people like that.'

'Clausen the banker?'

Teddy nodded. 'Bankers, defence industry, construction, electronics, lawyers, the works. If it's Republican, big money or big influence, it's here somewhere. Jesus, Hacker, this is where they decided to make Reagan president. It's where they pulled together the finance for the atom bomb. Some people even say it's where they fixed things with Gorby's people to break up the Soviet Union.'

'So we're going to do some business?'

'Make the contacts, maybe. Do some serious drinking. Piss on some redwoods, listen to the music, watch the play. Take it slowly, it's meant to be fun. You'll get the idea when you see the Cremation of Care tonight. That's awesome.'

Up a side road the true forest began, and through a complex of gateways, security checks and baggage-handling docks, where attentive camp servants swarmed around the trunk of the limo, they passed through the guarded perimeter and entered the cathedral cover of the giant redwoods and the extraordinary, private world of the Bohemian Grove.

In the evening, the redwoods soared two or three hundred feet into darkness. The smell of wood fires and barbecues mixed with the left-over sappy warmth of the forest and the brief tang of urine from the soaked circle of mossy leaf-mould at the base of each of the surrounding trees. For the past two hours, while Teddy caught up on old acquaintances among the log cabins and tents of Bone Yard camp, its gateway guarded by a full-size dinosaur skeleton, Hacker had been meandering through the Grove, weaving between the hordes of men – only men – who were all clutching glasses, slapping backs and doing the corporate macho things that Grove customs called for. At the end of the long River Road, bordered by the camps – Cliff Dwellers, Silverado Squatters, Isle of Aves, Wild Oats and all the rest – he had come out of the trees at the Russian River where naked, overweight, white backs and buttocks were visible splashing from the swimming float in ungainly crawls.

Now, however, there was an expectant stillness among the hundreds of men ranged around the lake in the dark. Soon after nine o'clock, absolute silence fell. Even the belching and the trickling of urine stopped as a torchlight procession of hooded, robed figures, druids in orange and red, emerged from the trees bearing a covered figure on a litter. They quenched their torches in the water, and in the sudden darkness a burst of singing switched his attention to the end of the lake where a crescendo of floodlights revealed a forty-foot statue of an owl, now surrounded by more robed priests and acolytes.

Teddy nudged him and whispered, 'The figure they're carrying, that's Care. Watch.'

The bier was laid in a black gondola, and the boat made its way slowly across the lake, poled by a tall figure all in black, while dry ice sent smoke billowing across the surface of the water and a faint electronic ululation seemed to fly high above their heads from treetop to treetop. As the gondola approached the shrine, the funeral pall was pulled from the figure showing a grotesque body with a withered and ancient mask for a face. It was lifted from the boat on to the shore and placed on a pile of timber in front of the giant owl. The forest was silent.

Just as the priests advanced on the pyre with their torches, a high cackling laugh from way up the slope in the towering trees sent shivers down Hacker's spine. There was a sudden exhalation of breath from the hundreds of men all around him. In the topmost branches of a redwood, a green, shimmering hologram appeared: the figure of Care, moving, writhing. Its mouth opened and an enormous voice declaimed, 'Fools, fools. When will ye learn that me ye cannot slay? Year after year ye burn me in this Grove, lifting your shouts of triumph to the pitying stars, but when again ye turn your feet toward the marketplace, am I not waiting for you as of old? Fools, to dream you conquer Care!'

The torches went out, but now something was happening to the face of the great owl. With a deep voice that sounded like

Ronald Reagan, its features flickering into life with help from a hidden projector, it said, 'Fellow Bohemians, I, the great Owl of Bohemia, give ye counsel. Rekindle your torches from the Flame of Fellowship. Thus shall ye banish Care from this our sacred Grove.'

The High Priest emerged from the throng around the owl. 'Our Flame of Fellowship shall damn thee for a space, Care. Thy malevolence shall lose its power beneath these friendly trees, and in the flames that eat thy effigy we'll see the signs that, once again, midsummer sets us free.'

As the flames sprang up around the effigy of Care, loud cheers sounded from the crowds among the trees, rockets whooshed from launchers across the lake to explode with multi-coloured thunderclaps, and a band launched itself into 'There'll be a Hot Time in the Old Town Tonight'.

'Phew,' said Teddy. 'OK, Hacker. What did you make of that?'

Not a lot, Hacker thought. Fake California Shakespeare, ham acting and overdosing on the special effects. 'Very impressive,' he said.

Teddy pointed to a group of robed priests making their way into the crowd. 'See who they are?'

Hacker recognised with incredulity the faces of a Supreme Court Judge, the head of one of the world's biggest electronics groups, and a former US Secretary of State. 'Good God.'

'It's a great honour taking part in the ceremony. That and High Jinks.'

'High Jinks?'

'You'll see it. The Grove play. Serious stuff. One performance only and this year they say it's costing eighty thousand bucks. Can you imagine?'

On the model of the Cremation of Care, he thought he could imagine only too well. They walked slowly down past the open-air dining circle, an array of log tables and benches, and towards Bone Yard camp. There was a large sign on a redwood, a picture of an owl, saying: 'Gentlemen, please! No pee-pee here!'

'Too close to the dining area. Everyone used to piss on it. Damn near killed it,' explained Teddy.

'What now?'

Teddy, who was having trouble walking in a straight line, made a big effort to concentrate. 'Well, with a little slice of luck, now is when you get to see your man, just to get to know the guy. He was in the ceremony, but I had someone invite him over to the camp for a rusty stovebolt after.'

They passed the skeleton and walked on to the wooden platform which jutted over the slope of the hill. Bone Yard was filling up with excited old men, talking about the ceremony they'd clearly seen year after year, just as if it were brand new.

'Whoo. That *voice*. Wasn't that something?'

'I kinda liked the hologram.'

'Yeah. Courtesy of Radtech. Cost twenty-five grand, I heard.'

'Ed! Son of a gun. How yer doin'? C'mon over here and help us out,' called a former attorney general. 'Lewis here reckons his dick is so long he can piss twice as far as I can. I've got a hundred says he cain't. C'mon over and judge.'

Teddy waved. 'Nobody's a bigger dick than Lewis. Back in two shakes, Hacker.' Then he ambled off, giggling.

Left behind, Hacker stood there, taking in the scene. Someone was playing loud honky-tonk piano on one corner of the deck. A huge glass contraption of tubes, pumps and tanks was dispensing the sickly drink in all directions. Rowdy laughter came from all around. He watched it all, distant, disappointed, wanting out, searching the faces and finding no echo of his own feelings, nothing but fleshy, drunken, uncritical enthusiasm. Then his gaze crossed a pair of sober, sardonic eyes, and he felt the sudden flash of meeting a fellow countryman in an alien land. A pencil-thin, elderly man, dressed all in black – shirt, slacks and bootlace tie – was watching him, leaning on the railing. As their eyes met, he nodded slightly then came over.

'Something tells me you're not too impressed, are you?' he said with a southern accent.

'It's all very unusual.'

'You don't have to be polite to me. I'm just a guest. It's a giant frat party for rich guys, getting a kick out of pretending they're in touch with nature. Shit, some of these guys destroy a forest every day of their working lives.'

Hacker looked around. 'Maybe I'm here for the wrong reasons. I thought it was meant to be some kind of powerhouse.'

The other man laughed mockingly. 'Maybe once. Maybe still, but only for the inner circle.' He thrust a hand out. 'I'm Bernard.'

'Right, I'm . . .'

'I know just who you are, buddy. I've been wanting to . . .' That was as far as he got. Teddy reeled back to them from the judging.

'Hacker, your man's over there. Come on.' He registered the other a little late. 'Oh, pardon me.'

'No, that's OK. Catch you later.'

Leaning on the rail at the edge of the platform, a fat, perspiring man of sixty or so, dressed in an orange robe, with the cowl pushed back from his head, was draining a glass and acknowledging the plaudits of passers-by for his performance.

'Great show, Randall. Moving, real moving.'

'Good of you to say so, er . . . Ed.'

'This is my friend, Hacker. He's my guest this year. I wanted you two to meet.'

At that moment, a man with his shirt soaked in the Bone Yard's noxious whisky mixture arrived in their midst with a loud rebel yell, seized Teddy by the arm and danced him off across the platform in a violent waltz which had the other men lurching back out of the way and screeching with laughter. In their wake, the man called Randall mopped his brow, sipped from his glass and blinked in an out-of-focus way. 'Hacker. What's that? First name?'

'No. It's just an old nickname. I'm glad to meet you. I have an interest in some useful prospects on the East Coast and I thought maybe . . .'

A stubby finger jabbed him in the chest. The hand it projected from still held the glass, slopping sticky liquid on to his shirt. 'Whoa there. Out of line. Cut that shit. Weaving spiders come not here.'

'I'm sorry, what's that again?'

'You don't know that, you ain't no Bohemian.'

'Well, I'm just visiting but . . .'

Suddenly he was talking to the rumpled hood at the back of the priest's neck as the man in the robe swung, wobbling on his heel, and made off, bursting into a loud song as he went, 'Bohemia, BOHEEEMIA, thy home is here . . .'

Others joined in, roaring the words.

'Kinda pissed off, aren't you?'

It was the man in black who'd appeared at his elbow.

'You could say that. Maybe I just don't understand the rules.'

'Maybe. Or maybe time's moved on and left these guys behind. That weaving spider crap is their way of saying Bohemia's not for business. That's kind of selective. If they want to do business, they'll do it, but not with guys they don't know. Anyhow, I reckon I know where you're coming from.'

'You do?'

'Let's say you're not the only one who's here with a purpose.' Bernard looked at him appraisingly and Hacker knew he was being weighed up. 'I know who you are. I can guess what you want here. Forget the old fart in the robes. I can deliver it.'

'That's a big promise.'

'I'm part of a big operation and we just love making dreams come true.'

'Look. Excuse me, but should I know you? Who exactly are you?'

Bernard's smile was wide but mirthless. 'Bear with me. Just tell me one thing. Do you happen to recognise this?' He paused, then began to declaim slowly, '"This land has a name today and is marked on maps . . ."'

Surprised, Hacker nodded. 'My favourite movie when I was a kid. Saw it ten times. Spencer Tracy. It's the beginning of *How the West was Won.*'

The smile turned into a broad grin. 'Hot damn. You know it. I think I can offer you something you're going to like.'

'So, who are you exactly?'

'Just think of me as the producer.'

# Tuesday July 16th

The electronic card snicked into its slot and the light glowed green. Thick pile carpet hindered the door's opening with a furry brush of opulence, to release an air-conditioned promise of peace. Three days of Bohemia had been enough for a lifetime and now he simply wanted to wash the wood smoke out of his hair, drink plenty of pure, clean orange juice, watch some TV and forget all about Ed Butzer and his constant introductions. 'Hacker, meet my old pal . . .' LA airport was just five miles away. Tomorrow, he'd catch a plane.

On the table by the bed, next to the little tray of expensive Swiss truffles, was a white envelope with his name on it. Expecting some bland assurance of good service from the hotel manager, he opened it to reveal a simple card, bordered in gold. In brilliant red lettering it said, 'Following our brief meeting amongst the redwoods, I extend to you the chance to go one step further. A car will be at the door at 7p.m. Please join us.' It was signed, 'The Producer.' There was no number, no address, and he stared at it with a mixture of excitement and mistrust.

Four hours later, the mistrust was outranking the excitement. He knew he'd broken his own golden rule: never go in when you can't see the way out. The car wasn't what he expected. No limo this, but a small bus. The driver wore a cowboy hat and shades and said nothing, just handed him another letter. 'Glad you could make it,' was all it said.

The bus was silver-grey with dark windows. He could see nothing within, until the driver pressed a button and stepped aside for him as the side door whirred back. Inside were two plush semi-circular couches, a table, deep carpets and, in the corner, a TV screen. He stepped in, sat down on the nearest couch, and the door closed again. Only then did it dawn on him that usually one could see out of tinted windows even when it was impossible to see in. Not with these – the outside world was almost invisible. The driver too was closed off by a smoked glass partition. The bus started off smoothly and

Hacker looked quickly at the door. There was no sign of any opening mechanism on the inside.

A few familiar guitar notes sounded from speakers all around the compartment. He recognized it immediately; one of his favourite country songs, Randy Travis's 'Deeper then the Holler'. The bus glided smoothly along. Unseen streets passed outside and he sat back in limbo, listening and wondering. The song ended and another began. He smiled in surprise to hear the pounding intro to another old favourite, Steve Earle's 'Copperhead Road', but when it was followed by the Adagio from Bach's Concerto for Three Harpsichords in C major, the smile faded. Three in a row was beyond the law of averages. The fourth song clinched it; Led Zeppelin's 'Stairway to Heaven'. He began to shift in his seat and, pressing his face to the glass, tried unsuccessfully to see where he was. This wasn't muzak, this was a message. Whoever they were, they knew all about him, right down to the little details, and they wanted him to know it. Then the music stopped and the TV came to life. On it was a still picture; cowboys on the left, buffalo on the right, and, across the middle, words spelled out in gold letters; *How the West was Won*. Over it came a voice that he'd last heard at Bohemian Grove. The man in the black clothes, Bernard the Producer.

'Good Evening,' it said. 'I'm real glad you decided to come along. I took the liberty of checking out your taste in music to make you feel at home. Now just to set you in the right frame of mind for the time your journey will take, here are some edited highlights of a movie we both know and love.'

A cowboy choir sang a few bars of 'I am Bound for the Promised Land', faded smartly into 'Shenandoah', then dipped below Spencer Tracy's dust-and-whisky invocation; 'This land has a name today and is marked on maps – but the names and the marks and the land had to be won; won from nature and from primitive man.'

It was ingrained in Hacker to watch for weakness and points of advantage in the knife-fight of life, where nothing was to be taken at face value. But this was a puzzle he could not unravel. Someone had gone to a great deal of trouble to produce this edited version of the movie and show it to him in the back of this blacked-out bus going who knows where. There were all the famous scenes. Karl Malden drowning as his raft hits the rapids, James Stewart with his furs as mountain man, Linus Rawlings meeting and falling for Eve. The dialogue wasn't quite as familiar to him as the Producer might have assumed. It was many years since he'd seen it last, and it was only his prodigious memory which had trawled back those opening lines at the Grove, but echoes of it were very familiar when he heard it again: 'I never been kissed permanent before'; 'By God, you're a strong-minded woman. I reckon I seed that varmint for the last time.'

Hacker watched on through the riverboat gamblers, the civil war with the tragedy of the battle of Shiloh, and John Wayne's appearance as Sherman. Then the building of the railroads, Indian attacks, the battles between the sheep farmers and the cattle barons, and Spencer Tracy's voice again; 'If man's life was held cheaper than grass, it was considered a casualty of war, not a crime; and in all this, the man with the star was only one against many.'

Despite his disquiet, the film was peeling back the layers of the years, bringing with it the memory of the flickering, unreliable projector in the small cinema of his youth. He'd lived in a tiny farming town in the back end of beyond, and the cinema was little more than a tin roof over weatherboard walls, with enough knot holes that if you couldn't buy the ticket, you could glimpse a quarter of the screen by standing on a box outside with your face pressed to the sun-warmed, splintery wood. No three-screen Cinerama there, just improvised sheets each side of the screen to take the overspill of the picture. He could fill in the missing scenes between the episodes served up before him.

The finale arrived sooner than he'd expected. Over the great, wide shots of prairie, mountain and lake which turned to modern cities and six-lane highways, Tracy spoke again in vintage form.

'The West that was won by its pioneers, settlers, adventurers, is long gone now – yet it is theirs for ever, for they left tracks in history that will never be eroded by wind or rain, never ploughed under by tractors, never buried in the compost of events. Out of the hard simplicity of their lives, out of their vitality, their hopes and their sorrows, grew legends of courage and pride to inspire their children and their children's children. From soil enriched by their blood, out of their fever to explore and build, came lakes where once were burning deserts – came the goods of the earth, mines and wheat fields, orchards and great lumber mills – all the sinews of a growing country. Out of their rude settlements, their crude trading posts, came cities to rank among the great ones of the world. All the heritage of a people free to dream, free to act, free to mould their own destinies.'

It was only now, in adult maturity, that it struck him for the first time as absurd that the final words coincided with an aerial shot of what seemed to be the mother and father of all traffic jams.

Two things happened then. The screen went black and the bus stopped. Just as it struck Hacker that this video had been very carefully tailor-made to fit his particular journey, the door swooshed open and he was looking down the main street of a cowboy town of the old West.

The bus sat there with the door open, and he sat inside it looking down the dusty street at the rows of timber building; a cliché Western street, bank, sheriff's office, store, hotel, undertaker and saloon. Three men in cowboy clothes carrying Winchester rifles stood at different points on the wooden sidewalks. Beyond the end of the buildings and the hitching rails, the desert started. He didn't feel like moving.

Then the saloon doors swung open and a familiar figure dressed in black appeared, relieved now by a scarlet bandanna round his neck. He waved a welcome. 'Good to see you. Come on in.'

Hacker got to his feet, climbed out of the bus and looked back beyond it. The road trailed across the desert, coming out of the low evening sun. Out there on the fringe of his vision there was the glint of a wire fence. He walked across the dusty, rough roadway, up creaking steps, and was ushered into the saloon. There were two other men inside. One was a relative youngster of thirty or so whom he didn't recognise. He looked at the other man and with a shock saw a face that he had only encountered before on the cover of *Business Week* or in the pages of the *Financial Times*.

'Martin Blunden,' he said. 'Now there's a surprise.'

The president and chief stockholder of one of the world's biggest electronics combines had started to smile, but then looked faintly embarrassed and glanced at the Producer.

'Oh, I'm sorry,' said the man in black, 'I haven't had an opportunity yet to explain our rules.' He turned to the newcomer. 'We haven't had occasion to welcome an outsider in quite this way before. We have a way of doing things here. You check in your real name at the gate. This isn't quite the real world, it's somewhere else, and when you're in here, you're someone else. Our members take their *noms de guerre* from the cast list of *How the West was Won*. I'd like to introduce you to Carleton Young,' the younger man nodded, 'and Lee J. Cobb.'

'And me? Who does that make me?' Hacker said with a noticeable touch of asperity.

'You could be Gregory Peck. We have a vacancy.'

'Look, I thought we understood each other at Bohemian Grove. I don't much like fantasy worlds.'

The Producer opened his mouth but the older man waved him to silence. 'We know that. Just bear with it. It's our only indulgence and it serves a good purpose. If you go along with us you'll very soon see we're extremely serious. I guess you know my reputation. I wouldn't be in this if it were any other way. The names and the style, well, they're a little bit of protection, but they're kind of more than that. They remind us where this country's been and what's had to be done in the past in the name of freedom.'

Hacker looked around at the saloon. No tacky temporary film set this; someone had gone to a lot of trouble and expense. 'I'm not too concerned where this country's been. I'm more concerned about whether I do well out of where it's going next.'

Martin Blunden – or Lee J. Cobb, whichever he was being –

reached into a document case and pulled out a folder which he slid across the table. 'That's your answer.'

Hacker picked it up, looking at Blunden, then started to flick through it, but froze, transfixed by the second page. It was a near duplicate of his own most secret business plan. The only difference was it went further. The anomalies in the figures shouted at him. It assumed far deeper West Coast and southern states penetration than he had ever dared build in to his own sums. Then he read the list of assumptions underneath and looked up in disbelief. 'You can't deliver this.'

'We can and we will if you decide to become one of us.'

Hacker put the folder down on the table. 'What do I have to do?'

'We picked you because you have things we need. A bit of money, a bit of influence, a lot of knowledge in the right places. Every one of us puts something of what he's got in the pot. When you've done enough for us, we'll do all this . . .' He waved a hand at the folder. '. . . for you.'

'So, who are you?'

'We call ourselves Freedom's Friends. If you're with us, I'll tell you more.'

It took him a few seconds. Then, as they'd known he would from the detailed psychological profiles they'd prepared, he nodded his head. 'Go on.'

'Come upstairs.'

It was a wide wooden staircase, the sort gunfighters fall down, that curved up to a big landing with just two doors, one at each end. He was ushered towards the nearer one, guarded by two more cowboy-clad men with rifles.

The first thing he noticed when the door opened was the hum of modern electronics. The room had a discreet air-conditioned chill but visually it belonged to the same era as the rest of the building; thick velvet curtains, gracious old-West armchairs, spindly tables, and gas lights on brackets on the walls.

Next to each armchair stood a tall, ornamented mahogany box with doors. Most were closed but, further up the room, four men were sitting at adjoining tables, intent on the green screens that showed through the open doors of their boxes. They took no notice of each other, nor the new arrivals.

Blunden made no move to join them, but took Hacker over to the nearest table and opened the doors. The screen came to life by itself. 'This is the world's most sophisticated communications and data intercept device. I know because I make it, and the gear I sell to the CIA is a year behind this.'

Hacker raised a polite eyebrow. 'So what can it do?'

'OK. Let's see. Pick a major corporation.'

Hacker thought of a few obvious ones, rejected them, and veered deliberately off-beat. 'Disney.'

'Fine. Choose one of their operations.'

'EuroDisney.'

'Tell me what you want to know.'

'Gate receipts for yesterday.'

Blunden sat and typed hard. Hacker filled the time by looking around. He liked the calm air of professional concentration. Liquor had no place in this room. These men would piss in privacy, not against the trees, and they'd carefully wash their hands afterwards.

'There you are,' said Blunden.

Hacker turned to look at a screen full of figures. 'These are yesterday's?'

'Well, no, as it happens. Today's just came in.'

The Producer was watching Hacker's face, smiling. 'Decision time. Are you in?'

Hacker looked at the screen and felt a buzz of pure excitement. 'You know I am.'

'So be it. Then, welcome Gregory.' They both shook his hand, then Blunden indicated the men sitting further down the room.

'It's game night tonight. We set aside a few hours every week for a game. We pick one particular problem that's bothering us and try to put a bit of a spin on it – come up with some lateral thinking to see if we can give the world a little nudge in the right direction.'

Hacker looked down the room. 'Four players?'

'Oh heck, no. The rest are on line. We only get together

here for the big ones. First thing we do is give you a special terminal and a modem, then you just hook in from wherever you happen to be.'

'That's secure?'

'Straight from my R. & D. labs,' said Blunden. 'You never saw anything so secure in all your born days.'

'How many of you are there?'

'You? Make that *us*. There's the Producer here, then there's three directors just like in the movie, then there's sixteen big-name stars and another twenty who have to be bit-part players until there's a vacancy.'

'So how do I get to come in as Gregory Peck and not some Red Indian?'

The Producer looked at Hacker through half-closed eyes. 'You're a big name and you fit. We have a need. You'll see.' He pressed buttons on the keyboard. Coloured blocks of text appeared, scrolling up the screen. 'Let's see now. We're playing Game Twenty-Nine again tonight. We keep coming back to that one. It's what we call a reward game, to give one of our members a boost for the level of assistance he's rendered us in the general games.'

'What's it about?'

'This one's for Robert Preston. You'd recognize him. Let's just say he's very big in the tobacco business. Game Twenty-Nine is about devising strategies for limiting further controls on advertising and marketing cigarettes.' He jabbed a finger at the screen. 'Each player is allocated a colour. See that purple print? That's Jimmy Stewart.'

Hacker bent to the screen. A block of yellow text was scrolling off the screen. Only the end was still visible. It read: '. . . PROMISE ENDOWMENT FOR FURTHER RESEARCH PROJECT ON THOSE LINES CONCENTRATING ON LOW SUGARS.' Under it, the purple text said, 'I'D THINK TWICE BEFORE I CALLED YOU A LIAR.'

Blunden laughed. 'That's a bit more of our style. It's a line from the movie – implies the truth is being stretched a bit too far. Anytime you can use a quote, you rack up a few more points with the other players.'

Hacker forgot the cowboy fakery, the names. The smell of power came through clearly. The other two watched him, guessing what was going on in his mind. That was, after all, what all their pre-planning had told them. Blunden's presence had been carefully weighed.

'There's something we'd like to do,' said the Producer, 'just to help you understand. There's a game we played a few years back that still has some loose ends that need tying up. Interesting for you and very educational. We store it all, every stage of every game. You can work through it and see what we do. Then maybe you can come up with a few solutions.'

Hacker looked back at the screen. Purple was on again, Jimmy Stewart. 'JIM ARNER, SURGEON GENERAL'S OFFICE, IS STILL OUR BIGGEST OPPONENT. ARNER'S WIFE HAS LOW LEVER CANCER. CAUSING HIM STRESS. EARLY RETIREMENT POSSIBLE. HOME LIFE DIFFICULT, DEPENDENT SCHIZOPHRENIC SON.'

Green italics replied, 'SUGGEST ARNER'S WIFE GETS WORSE OR SON PERFORMS VIOLENT ACT.'

He raised an eyebrow and looked at the Producer. 'How long ago was this other game?'

'Four or five years maybe, back in our early days. Let's see now, I think it was Game Ten.'

# Chapter Two

## Monday July 8th

At National TV, they hadn't the slightest idea that Paul Wade was dead, but the simple fact of his disappearance was causing enough trouble.

'I don't know why you're so bothered, Harry. You never have a good word to say about the bastard when he's here. He's been AWOL two weeks now. Last time it was only a day and you wanted his guts for garters. What's the big deal about getting shot of him?'

Harry Chaplin's defence against the world's recent cruelty was a range of facial expressions which varied only from the amused to the cynical, but just for a moment there was a look of genuine disquiet. The truth was that in the absence of Paul to explain himself, he thought the action was unfair, but he wasn't about to expose a chink in the well-polished armour he showed the world, so he raised an eyebrow instead. 'You might stir up the union stuff all over again.'

'No chance. The union's not coming in here.'

'You could be giving them cause, sacking someone like that.'

'Harry, where have you been? OK, I'm an Aussie. This is your country. You're the guys who changed the rules. How many times have you elected this Government? Democracy, Harry. This is the New Britain you keep voting for. Don't give me that bleeding heart routine.'

'Just seems like a waste of a good reporter to me, Herman. I know he's an airhead, but he's got a sharp eye for a story. It'll take an age to train up someone else. Leaves me carrying the load, that's all.'

Herman Dent's large face was suddenly in suppressed motion; cheeks shaking, bald crown heliographing the reflection of the overhead light. Harry watched him morosely, recognizing the usual signs that Herman had kept something up his sleeve, and that there was no guarantee he was going to like it.

He looked out of the window waiting until Herman, disappointed by his lack of reaction, let him in on it. Outside, the half-finished roads of the Maynards Way Industrial Estate depressed him and gave the lie to Tabard House's grandiose title. Desmond Gilligan, fresh from Melbourne with his little pack of TV buddies, had picked it up for a song towards the end of the property slump. Now National TV pumped out its programmes from Hounslow, just under the Heathrow flight path, with all the expensive sound-proofing problems that had entailed in keeping the noise of low-flying Jumbo jets off the air.

'Harry?' said Herman.

'I hate it when you coo like that.'

'Oh come on. You're going to love this one.'

'Who is it then? You've got someone up your sleeve, haven't you?'

For an answer, Herman pushed his chair back from the desk and lumbered round to the open patch of floor beside it. He stood there, holding an imaginary microphone in front of him with one hand, swaying and dodging slightly with an intense look on his face. In a fake falsetto he declaimed, 'And from the middle of the fighting – whoops that one nearly got me, never mind it's only a flesh wound – this is the battlefield bombshell handing you back to the studio.'

Harry stared at him, horrified. 'Claire Merrick? Herman, tell me it isn't true, please?'

Herman sat down on the edge of the desk and looked puzzled. 'Course it's true. Bloody brilliant, I call it. What are you wingeing about? You wanted someone with experience. I just got you the Rolls Royce of reporters to work with.'

'It's done? You've signed her up and you haven't even asked me?'

'Come off it, Harry. You don't let chances like that slip away.'

He looked defensive. 'Anyway, it was out of my hands. Gilligan signed her.'

'Gilligan? What's Gilligan doing messing around picking staff? He's meant to be a tycoon not an office manager.'

'Listen, Harry. He's hands-on when it comes to National. You should know that by now. It's his big one. His newspapers don't matter a toss compared to this because he's sniffing blood. The poor old BBC's on the slippery slope, the ITV companies are drowning in red ink. Murdoch broke the ice. There's five million dishes out there now. There's another three million homes hooked up to cable and more going on every week. Don't knock it. Gilligan's got his hands on a superstar, and he's going to make the most of it.'

Harry was still having trouble taking it in. 'Claire bloody Merrick. She's a news reporter. Always has been. Why would she want to come and work on a cruddy little crime show?'

'Same reason you did. Because it's been the boom sector of the whole media for the last ten years. Because they can't get enough of it. Because every channel's got one and we've got a few extra wrinkles on top.'

'Give me a break. That's just PR bullshit.'

'Yeah. I have to agree. Matter of fact it was what you put in your job application, word for word.'

Harry's mouth tightened. 'Well that was last year.' That was when I needed a job, he thought. He looked sourly at Herman. 'I wasn't reckoning on Claire Merrick.'

'You wouldn't be scared of her, would you?'

'No, I wouldn't.' But he was. 'We'd better go and start the meeting, hadn't we?'

Herman looked at his watch. 'Time marches on. I'm going to tell them all about it, by the way.'

'Hold on. I've got a few more things to say about it first. Why so fast?'

'Because, Harry, whether you like it or not, she's starting a week today and even our little team of no-hopers might just recognize her and wonder what she's doing here if she turns up out of the blue, don't you think?'

\*    \*    \*

Charlotte wasn't looking at him. She was sitting next to gormless Gary, which was fine by him. Harry tried to concentrate on what the editor was saying. It was a stupid thing to have done. Shouldn't have had a fling with a secretary.

Jane was winding up. 'So to sum it up: we're leading with Harry's story about the Bournemouth bank raid; then there's the Newcastle murders, which in Paul's continuing absence, Judy's going to pull together. Richard, you'll be doing the Euro spot with all that Belgian gang-war stuff and the forged French notes. Then there's Crime America. That's being shipped in this evening. Angela, come and see me about that. It's all cut, just needs revoicing. Apparently it's got this great sequence taped by a security camera where one of the robbers gets his gun caught in the door on the way out of the bank and blows his own foot off.'

There was a groan.

'Two more things,' she said. 'On the wide shot last week you could tell there weren't any calls coming in for the first half of the show, because all the police were just sitting there with their arms folded. We must make sure they look busy, OK? And the other thing is for God's sake don't let them wander off for a beer at the end of the show. The whole point is that they're meant to take the incoming calls, otherwise what's the point? The programme staff were the only ones answering any of them by half past ten last week.' She stopped and picked up her papers, but Herman cleared his throat and she remembered. 'Oh, before you all go, the Director of Programmes has something to say.'

There was an expectant stir as Herman stood up and belched slightly. 'Yeah,' he said, 'just a quickie. Paul Wade has removed himself from our employment. Woman called Merrick is replacing him. You probably know as much about her as I do.'

Jane was looking astonished. '*Claire* Merrick?' she said.

'Yup, that's the one.'

Good God, thought Harry, never mind the poor bloody reporter. Herman didn't even tell the editor.

# Monday July 15th

Claire Merrick woke from a subconscious that was still full of luxury and status into the threadbare reality of a back room in Stockwell, and was ambushed immediately by a fluttery feeling of despair. Ann's spare room. Ann's step-ladder against the wall, Ann's boxes piled in the corner, nothing of her own except suitcases. The sight of it hurt more and more as she woke fully in the narrow bed, and she closed her eyes to slits to blur the distressing impact of it. Returning to consciousness only confirmed the feeling. Professionally, materially and emotionally her life had lurched over the top of fortune's big-dipper with no visible end in sight to the stomach-churning descent on the far side.

Where formerly she would have walked blithely from the huge round bed through thick woollen carpets to the neighbouring jacuzzi with its penthouse view across the Thames, she now looked down at a single Habitat rug on bare boards, and heard from the roar of the gas heater that Ann was already using the bathroom. It was in her nature to defeat depression by doses of focused anger, so she concentrated on Jerome, trying to put the evil eye on him, hoping that whoever was getting out of his bed now had just given him something infectious to remember her by.

If bad things happen in threes, two had been quite enough for her. First the bitter humiliation of the trap which derailed her career; then Jerome's sudden, wounding indifference. Damn him, she thought. Damn his success, his smooth Bostonian ways, and the interest that faded when I was no longer the famous face on the box. The pain of the ending and the descent to this temporary, demeaning imposition on Ann's infinite good nature, blurred together so she wasn't quite sure what she was missing, the man or his money. She looked at the clock and sat up. She was short on time for her next bite of life's bowl of rotten cherries.

To Claire, Hounslow was just a name on the way to Heathrow. Just a boring signpost on the way to the next check-in – not a place of work. Tabard House greeted her with all the appeal of an out-of-town discount DIY store. She turned in at the gate and the security man bent to the window.

'My name's Claire Merrick,' she said. 'I'm coming to work here.'

She expected the flash of recognition that would have greeted her at any other TV station in the land, but the Tabard House security staff weren't given to watching the news, and there weren't many media superstars passing through those gates.

He was a callow youth and he didn't much like the job. 'Haven't got you on the list,' he said.

'Well, your list is wrong then, isn't it?' she said, moderately sweetly with a wide smile designed mostly to show what a serious bite she could inflict if it came to it.

He had been about to let her through, being a decent looking tart, but though he was by no means quick-witted, he had an idea she was being sarcastic and he wasn't having that. 'You'll have to park outside,' he said. 'Can't let you in if you're not on the list. I'll phone.'

'Well why don't you phone now, so I can drive in?' she suggested.

'Can't do that,' he said with a lofty air of initiation into security mysteries she could only guess at. 'Procedures. Now if you wouldn't mind moving your car . . .'

So she, Claire Merrick, accustomed to reserved parking places in the TV centres of the world and the recognition of flunkies, parked her car against a rough concrete kerb in a sea of mud, got out into a puddle, and looked morosely at her new place of work.

Everyone in the Crookbusters production office knew she was coming. Everybody in the whole building probably knew, but only in that office was it a matter of such intense interest. From the secretaries to the researchers and producers, it was a question of a new hierarchy; of how Jane as editor and Harry as *de facto* chief reporter would deal with this cuckoo in their nest, because no one had failed to notice how Herman's announcement had gone down the previous week.

The first sighting was by Charlotte, who happened to be

passing through reception when Claire arrived at the desk. She raced back to the office to spread the news round the secretaries.

'She's taller than you'd think from the telly, and she's ever so nice looking.' That didn't seem quite right, so Charlotte tried again. 'Well, I mean, she would be if she dressed a bit more feminine. Bit tough looking, and she's got some lines below her eyes like she frowns a lot.'

'Doesn't sound like Harry's sort then,' said Charlotte's friend Ginny.

Among the secretaries, Charlotte was the undisputed authority on Harry Chaplin, since their brief fling which had started on a drunken Thursday night, when Harry had been feeling more than usually nihilistic, and ended abruptly four days later when she tried to take him shopping at Brent Cross. For the first weekend, her thin, athletic body, fake Julia Roberts's looks and uncomplicated enthusiasm for trying out every possible sexual variation had kept him more or less occupied. By Monday he was craving someone who could smash his verbal barbs back at him across the net, instead of just saying, 'Come again?' in a slightly puzzled way. Charlotte preferred to let it be thought that she had ditched him, hinting at some strangely deviant sexual behaviour. This however had merely increased Ginny's and several of the other secretaries' interest in him.

Claire had met Jane Bernstein, the editor of Crookbusters, in Herman's office. No contest, she decided instantly, the legend had served her well. Jane, slightly younger, handled her like a time-bomb.

'Let's go see the office,' said Herman, 'then you can meet Harry too.'

'Harry?'

'Harry Chaplin. The other reporter.' He sounded less than certain, a chemist charged with the task of mingling two dangerous elements.

The arrival of the little entourage through the double doors into the production office had the effect of the bad guy walking into a Western saloon. Conversation died away in an instant

and every head swivelled. Claire took in the standard urban
open-plan; grey cubicles, grey desks, grey word-processors.
Most of the faces that turned her way had expectant half-smiles.
She looked round and some of the eyes dropped. At the far end
of the room were two larger cubicles. Both were empty.

'This is yours, Claire,' said Jane, indicating the one on the
right. 'Harry's next to you. He should be here.' She looked
around the room. 'Anyone know where Harry's gone?'

Heads were shaken. 'Never mind,' said Jane. 'We'll find him
later. Come and have a chat in my office. I'll fill you in on
the show.'

Claire stood for a moment, looking down at the desk and
the bookshelf in the cubicle, still festooned with someone else's
photos, calendar and sticky yellow notelets on every available
surface. Oh God, she thought, what the hell am I doing here?
She turned and followed Jane and Herman back through the
room, avoiding meeting any of the eyes trained on her.

Jane's 'office' was nothing more than a glass box in the
corner. Herman made his excuses and the two women sat
down. Jane looked a little embarrassed. 'Claire, we're all really
excited that you're here. It's, er . . . a great surprise.'

'You mean no one asked you if you wanted me?'

Jane waved one hand in dismissal. 'Of course I would have
said yes. I imagine Desmond Gilligan wanted to move fast.'

Claire raised an eyebrow. 'I don't know about that. I
happened to meet him at some reception and he offered me
a job. I thought it would be in news. I didn't know anything
about Crimebusters until his letter arrived, but I said I'd give
it a try.' Not that I had much choice, she thought to herself.

'It's Crookbusters.'

'Sorry?'

'Crookbusters. You said Crimebusters.' Jane's voice showed
it mattered. 'I expect you'd like to know a bit about the show.
You've seen it, I suppose?'

Once Claire might have pretended. As it was, she just shook
her head. 'No, I'm not on cable and I don't have a dish.'

'Ah. Well, you can see some tapes later. You know all about
the crime show boom. Crookbusters broke new ground because

it gave rewards. That was Gilligan's big new angle. Up to a thousand pounds for the most useful information on each of the stories. At least ten thousand for the tip-off of the week. Then on top we run some international crime as well, Europe and America.'

Claire looked puzzled. 'America? There can't be many American crooks running round Britain. What's the point?'

'Ah well, of course there's the entertainment angle. Some of the pictures we get are amazing.'

'So it's not really about catching crooks at all?'

'Oh, I didn't say that. It's just that we like to mix the two.'

'And you get a cheap supply of foreign items to fill up the show?'

Jane, seeing that she was a little out of her depth against her seasoned opponent, changed the direction of the conversation. 'Anyway, just while you get into it, I thought you might like to pick up the threads of a story Paul was covering. He was your predecessor. It would be a shame to let it all go to waste.'

'Yes, I wanted to ask you. What happened to him?'

'Paul Wade? He wasn't very reliable, and one day he simply didn't show up. He'd got half way through a story and I'd like you to pick it up. I'll fill you in on it later.'

Claire Merrick – heroine of the Holborn Tube bomb, thorn in the side of Prime Ministers and Dictators, driven by the devils in her past – looked at the earnest girl facing her and thought, well that's it, the pits, taking over some snotty-nosed kid's half-assed, half-done story in a Hounslow industrial unit.

'Well, I'll think about it,' she said, 'and by the way, I'll need to get the desk changed around a bit.'

Jane had never had one of her staff tell her she'd think about an assignment before, and wasn't quite sure how to respond. Someone came through the doors into the production office outside and she looked up gratefully through the glass, grabbing the excuse. She jumped to her feet, banged on the glass and beckoned. 'Oh look, there's Harry now. I'll get him in.'

Claire had time to watch him approaching. About her age, long brown hair which flopped over his forehead, pale skin and the look of a man used to inspecting the teeth of gift horses.

Intelligent but detached from his surroundings. Then he opened the door and leant into the office, keeping his feet outside and looking at Jane rather than Claire with an expression of polite enquiry.

'Yes Jane,' he said. 'Was there something?'

'I just wanted you to meet Claire,' said Jane. 'Claire Merrick, this is Harry Chaplin.'

Now he did look at her, and for a second she met a pair of intelligent eyes before they hooded into some pre-determined posture of reserve. He came right inside and she stuck out a hand. This, at least, was a grown-up.

'Hallo Harry,' she said.

He took her hand after a momentary delay. 'Claire Merrick,' he said and nodded, looking at her closely. 'Oh yes, of course.' Then just as she began to let her face relax into a smile, he went on. 'You must tell me. I've always wanted to know why ITN fired you.'

The partition between the two cubicles shook violently, dislodging a photocopy of next week's shooting schedule at which Harry had been staring glumly. He stuck his head round the side to look at Claire but all he could see was her backside sticking out from under the desk, and a pair of feet.

'Mind my wall,' he said. 'If you break the building you have to buy a new one. Gilligan's rules.' They were the first words he'd spoken to her since their brief introduction.

She crawled out backwards, colliding with the partition again as she did, and sat up, pushing her hand through the heavy bob of shining dark hair. It had a touch of purple in it, he thought. She looked at him coolly and he looked back. It struck him that she had an old-fashioned and wholly English face, somewhat literary, with its high forehead and straight nose. Her eyes were wide-set, greenish brown, and only the fullness of her wide mouth softened the determination of her chin. This wasn't the two-dimensional image he was used to. 'Have you lost something?' he said.

'No, I've found a whole heap of rubbish which I would have thought someone might have cleared out before I arrived.' She was bone-weary with depression and her voice took on the harsh buzz-saw edge for which she was famous. He mistook it for aggression and his eyebrows rose in surprise that looked like cynicism and they were off into a closed loop of mutual hostility.

'If you want to help,' she said, 'tell me where I can find a secretary or someone to get rid of it all.'

'Ah . . . Herman didn't tell you we're a low-overhead operation, then?' She looked at him impassively. 'I mean, we're expected to do things like that ourselves.' He got up from his chair and looked at the pile of stuff she'd emptied out of the drawers on to the desk. 'Hey, careful what you throw away. That's Paul's stuff. If you find any white powder, I'll have it.'

She shook her head and rubbed her forehead with both hands. 'Never mind. I'll manage.'

'Don't be like that. I can help. Really.'

'Yes? How?'

'I saw a big cardboard box out by the kitchens. You go out of the door over there and . . .'

Claire turned her back on him and collapsed back into her seat. He smiled to himself. She sat there, sick at heart, aware of surreptitious looks from around the big room. The phone buzzed.

'Claire? It's Jane Bernstein. Are you free for a few minutes to pop in to my office?'

She was free. She'd done nothing all day except rearrange paperclips and try to look busy, trapped in her claustrophobic box under all the inspecting eyes. As she went to the editor's office she would have given anything for the financial freedom to go straight past, to get out of the building and never return.

Jane looked at her with trepidation. This was a very unhappy woman who shouldn't have been left hanging around. Herman's advice came back to her. Give her something to do. Get her out and about. She's a warhorse, not a riding-school nag.

Jane reached into her drawer and took out a folder. 'Here's some stuff on the story Paul Wade was doing. This is a progress report I asked for three weeks ago, before he went off.'

Claire took it and skimmed through. 'It's just a grotty little story about car theft,' she said incredulously, looking up. 'Is it really worth it?'

Jane tried a smile on her but it died. 'Well, yes. It's not that little. This is the latest crime wave. Nicking hot hatchbacks is dying out, the insurance companies saw to that. Now the joyriders are getting in to "offing". You've heard about it in the papers, I expect?'

'I haven't taken that much notice. It's stealing Range Rovers, isn't it?'

'Well, any four-wheel drive off-roader. The latest thing is to see how far off the road they can get before they abandon them, then they usually burn them. Paul said they've got all kinds of unpleasant little habits, like supergluing razor blades to the door handles so when the fire brigade come they get their hands slashed trying to get inside. Oh, and they leave hypodermic needles sticking out of the seat upholstery.'

Claire refused to become enmeshed in Jane's attempt at titillation. 'Not very interesting, surely?'

Jane thought of asking Herman to come and remind Claire she'd signed a contract, but she gritted her teeth and persevered. 'Perhaps not, but Paul went a bit further. The crime wave has meant it's suddenly much more expensive to insure the things. That's knocked a hole in their second-hand values, and a lot of owners are having trouble selling them. So they're burning them themselves and pretending they've been stolen. Paul said he'd found a scrapyard where you can go and pay them a few quid and they'll arrange to steal your car, take it apart for spares and put the rest through the crusher. He was planning to go and have a look at it.'

Claire suddenly leant forward with an intent look on her face. 'You don't think that's why he disappeared, do you?'

Jane laughed and shook her head. 'You don't need a conspiracy theory to explain Paul Wade vanishing. If you'd met him, you'd know. He'll blow in one of these days and be surprised to find he's been fired.'

'I hope he does. I seem to have half his possessions in my desk still.'

'Oh dear.'

'So, is there anything in the progress report which might tell me where to start?'

'Not really, but he used to talk to Harry about what he was doing.'

'Ah, well. That's another thing.'

'Yes?' said Jane, warily looking at the set of Claire's jaw.

'Harry. He obviously feels threatened or something. He's not making himself very pleasant.'

Jane sighed. 'Harry's all right when you get to know him. He just puts on this world-weary act. Give it a few days. Please? I tell you what, I'll call him in. It might make it a bit easier if I ask him to help you out on this.'

Harry came into the room full of fake *bonhomie* and exaggerated politeness to Jane, ignoring Claire entirely.

'Harry, I'm briefing Claire on Paul's story. We need a bit of help.'

Harry turned a wide-eyed, innocent stare to Claire. 'Help? From me? I'm flattered.'

# Chapter Three

## Friday July 19th

The police arrived in a minibus, wandered into the conference room, and set about the sandwiches. Claire sat out of the way in a corner, ignoring their surreptitious looks, and went through the briefing notes for the show. It was three hours before transmission time and the TV monitors scattered around the walls of the room were showing videofit pictures of desperate men. The last pieces were being put together in the studio for the recorded sections, which would be dropped like reliable cherries into the unreliable cocktail of the live show.

Studio sound was coming through on the speakers. Harry was in full flow, putting a voice track on one of the taped reconstructions.

'So what we want to know is whether you have seen this man. He's also wanted for another attempted rape in Bognor. Six foot one, heavily built, with distinctive orange hair and a fringe beard. He . . .'

'Hold on, Harry,' said Jane Bernstein's disembodied voice, 'he hasn't got orange hair. Why don't you stick to the script?'

'He's got orange hair in the picture I'm looking at.'

'That's just bad colour on the photofit. It says light brown in the description.'

'Well, what's the use of showing a photofit with orange bloody hair then?'

'Just stick to the words. Anyway, he certainly looks like a rapist.'

'Jane, everyone we've ever shown on this show looks like a rapist. If we showed a photofit of St Francis of Assisi, he'd come out looking like a rapist. Mind you, if I lived in Bognor, I'd probably be a rapist.'

There were a few sniggers from around the room and Claire turned her attention back to the police. They seemed to carry with them a heavy weight, from which a rugby club sense of humour occasionally surfaced like dark gouts of diesel oil from a sunken submarine. Sitting just a few chairs away was Chief Inspector Derek Palmer, the show's resident policeman who, with a glamorous WPC, did the regular introductions to the 'Where are they?' sections, short clips of mugshots, videofits and security camera glimpses of the ungodly. A year on the show had turned him into some sort of hybrid; already a quarter media person.

She looked around again. The man nearest her, shiny dark blue suit, white shirt, dark blue tie, short dark hair, was talking to his neighbour, whose marginally less shiny suit was the only difference in appearance between the two. She cocked an ear, hoping for an extra insight.

'Done this before, have you?'

'Not this one. I've done Crimewatch and that one they do in Birmingham.'

'Worth it?'

'You get chicken legs at the BBC.'

'See that thing they did on the telly last night? The one about the undertaker?'

'Yeah.'

'Know what I always say?'

'What?'

'Show me a woman with lots of diamond rings and I'll show you an undertaker's wife.'

Jane Bernstein walked into the room, followed by Harry and the show's anchorman, Russell Mackay, a silver-haired ex-game show host fallen on thin times, now working hard on being taken seriously as the concerned crime fighter for the two days a week in his contract.

'Good evening, everybody. Welcome to National and to Crookbusters for those who haven't been before, which, looking around, is most of you,' Jane said. 'We've got a lot to run through tonight. Just before we start, I'd like to introduce you all to our new reporter . . .'

Oh no, Claire groaned to herself, why does she have to do this?

'. . . who I'm sure you will all recognize. Claire Merrick, who's just joined us after a prominent career in television news.'

There was a buzz of whispered conversation of the 'I said that's who it was' variety, as they all turned to grin at her.

'We've got three reconstructions tonight,' Jane went on. 'The ram raid and murder in Solihull, the bank manager hostage story from Wigan and the very much delayed story on the Swansea abduction and rape. We've had to hold it over for four weeks now, so thanks very much to the Swansea team for their patience and I'm glad we can finally run it tonight.'

There had been a lot of heart-searching over whether it was acceptable to run Paul Wade's old story, with its less than satisfactory voice track. They couldn't re-edit it because his face appeared in three pieces to camera. Without Wade there, the only alternative was the expensive one – sending someone else to re-shoot it from scratch. Herman had vetoed that.

A researcher came into the room, looked around, then walked over to Chief Inspector Palmer. 'Telephone,' she said, 'outside.'

He got up and followed her.

Jane went on with the business of the day. 'Can I just make a point to you all,' she said. 'Remember, when we're on the air, you can be seen a lot of the time. You're there in the background, sitting at the desks. Please try and look busy. There won't be any phone calls to start with, so just pretend you're answering the phone if you have to. Quite a lot of the early calls will be nutters. I know they can be very funny but if you're all rocking with laughter and sharing a joke in the background, it doesn't look too good if the audience can see you grinning like idiots while we're telling a tragic story, right?' She looked around. 'Now, remember you're each here because you've been working on one of the stories, but the incoming calls come through unsorted, so you need to know about all the cases. Let's go through them, so you all know what to do. I'll hand you over to Chief Inspector Palmer to talk us through the Swansea story, because Paul Wade's no longer employed by us.' She looked around. 'Where's Derek?'

Palmer came back at that moment, went to the front of the room and spoke quietly in Jane's ear. She started and looked at him with her mouth open, then nodded and sat down in a chair as if pole-axed. Claire's interest quickened.

Tony Proctor had taken all possible precautions. He didn't know whether he was really allowed to be there, or whether the owners would have had him for trespassing if they'd known. Mostly, he didn't want other passers-by to see him getting out of the car, the container in his hand, and entering the wood. That way, someone might guess what he was up to.

He had parked the car, as usual, behind the bushes on the other side of the road, and looked carefully in both directions to satisfy himself there was nothing coming. Only then did he get the container out and cross over, but before he could climb the wall, he heard the rising note of a wailing engine, and a figure crouched over the tank of a big motorbike appeared round the bend a hundred yards ahead. Tony chucked the container over the wall where it couldn't be seen and turned to saunter along the verge, bending down to inspect and pick some perfectly harmless weed until the biker was out of sight, then he was up and over the wall in an instant, picking up the box and scurrying into the concealing gloom between the long avenues of trees.

The light made it difficult, crouching under the spiky lower branches and peering carefully left and right all the time, eyes checking, twitching incessantly. There was a sudden noise off to one side, deeper into the trees, and he froze. He was always expecting to be challenged, but perhaps it was only an animal dislodging a stone over by the badger burrows. There was a big reward for all this stealth, so long as no one else knew he was there.

There, off to the left, a gleam of sunlight touched a bulbous, felty, yellow-brown shape, and he knew even at twenty yards it was the first find of the day. He went over and knelt cheerfully to feel down through the pine needles for the fat stem, turning and twisting it to lift it out of the deep cup-like impression left behind. It was a perfect boletus edulis, a cep mushroom, eight ounces at least of the best and just about the most expensive edible fungus in Britain. Ten yards off was another and, as ever, he was relieved and delighted that no one else had found his secret place in the week since his last visit.

By the time he reached the badgers' setts, their mounds always startling on the otherwise flat floor of the woodland, the big basket, with its racks to stop the mushrooms damaging each other, was just about full to the brim. He'd get twenty quid at least for this lot in town. The deli always sold out his stock within a day. The setts weren't worth much of a look – the earth was too disturbed for the fragile spores to take root – but he'd found some chanterelles there once or twice so he always gave them a quick scan and he did so now.

There was something right in the entrance to one of the great holes, a small white domed fungus just sticking up through the mulch that filled this hole, clearly abandoned, almost full of pine needles. He bent to look at it. If the habitat hadn't been wrong he would have said it was an ink-cap mushroom, slightly blue-purple in its whiteness. He grasped it and twisted, registering that it seemed oddly solid just as he felt the hard shape of the toe-nail and saw the whole, dead, discoloured foot come rearing up out of the covering pine needles.

He let go and stumbled, falling backwards as his scream echoed around the wood and a pigeon blundered off, crashing through the high branches. There was dead silence; then, fearfully, he sat up and looked again, a little sideways as though that could diminish the horror. Two legs, leading down to the rest, mercifully hidden in the set. His first unworthy thought was that if he told the police, the secret of the ceps' wood would be out. His second was that didn't matter at all because nothing would ever induce him to come here again.

Derek Palmer looked around the room.

'I'm sorry to say,' he began slowly, 'that I've just been

informed that the body of Paul Wade was discovered this morning in woodland outside Sevenoaks. It would appear he had been there for some time.' His words had little effect on the police but there were horrified gasps from the production staff, and then a babble of voices. Harry looked at Jane who continued to sit there, then got to his feet. He held up his hands for silence. 'Could the DCI from Solihull please brief on the ram raids? While that's going on we'll just have a quick get-together in the ante-room for the production team.'

The detective came forward and began as the team filed out, 'Er, thank you. It happened on the eighteenth of last month. As you'll see from the dope sheet, but obviously not for broadcast, we're holding two men for another similar blag, Jimmy Marriage and Pat Woods. We're pretty certain they're down for this one too so any mention of those names will be very useful. Do particularly be aware that we're not in the business of framing anybody, so do be even handed. Don't encourage anyone to say more than they would in case we fall short in court.' He spoilt the effect by grinning and winking.

The last of the production staff had gone out, and Claire decided to follow. She found a dismayed group of men and women in the other room, all talking at once. Jane had got back in control.

'Look,' she said, 'first things first. We're all shocked, but there'll be time to talk about it after the show.'

'Jane,' said Harry, 'we can't run the Swansea package, can we?'

'I suppose we can't,' she said.

'It's got Paul's face all over it. That's right out of order.'

'Yes, but there's nothing else on the shelf is there? What do we do?'

'Eric, the inflatable escort?' suggested Harry.

'What, live in studio?' said Jane doubtfully.

'It's all we've got.'

'Who'd do it?'

Claire, listening without understanding, wondered why Harry was suddenly looking at her.

\* \* \*

Three hours later, after a desperate rush to get to grips with the way Crookbusters did things, Claire understood perfectly well, and she was cursing Harry with every fibre of her being. Her first bloody appearance on National and it had to be *this*. She was standing in a hastily-rearranged corner of the studio with an ill-fitting earpiece. There had only been time to practise it once. It was all set to go very badly wrong. Even if it went right, it would still look pretty silly.

She heard Russell Mackay's florid handover from his perch on one of the desks at the other end of the set, then the floor manager just to one side of the camera gave her the signal and, for better or worse, she was on.

'Few women,' she said, 'feel totally safe these days, even within the apparent security of their cars. A number of crimes, some featured on this programme, have involved abductions and rape when someone has forced entrance into a car at traffic lights or road junctions . . .' And so it went on, through a series of video clips from past crime reconstructions, to spin the appalling thing out until the moment she had to turn to the car seat beside her and the figure strapped to it. '. . . So meet Eric the Escort, billed as the solution to the single woman's problems.' She walked round the back of the chair as the camera zoomed in on the plastic inflatable figure. It was surprisingly realistic, with some furry substance sprayed on to simulate the clothes and a moulded face, looking slightly saturnine, like a 1930s' film star. She held up another one, uninflated in a small plastic pack. 'Eric stows away in a little bag when not needed, and you can blow him up in a couple of minutes.' At least they hadn't asked her to do that. 'He comes in a variety of styles and faces and will be available at most car accessory shops at £19.99; and he looks convincingly like a real passenger, so when you're by yourself, just bring out Eric and there you are.'

Claire handed back to Russell with relief and walked off the set as soon as she could, feeling a cold and distant fury arising within her at the absurdity, the lack of dignity of it. The end of the show came, but the job didn't stop there. For another hour they had to help man the phones while the policemen took short breaks to smoke and piss. Sitting down, headphones on and one of the log forms ready in front of her, she felt for the first time that evening a tingle of excitement, waiting for whatever might come. The light flashed and she stabbed the button. 'Crookbusters. Can I help you?'

Whatever she expected, it wasn't this. A cultured, old, drawly voice said, 'Oh, good evening, this is Lord Kilgorman.'

'Yes?' she said in surprise.

'That chappie you showed. The one in the raid, you know?'

'The one in Solihull?'

'Yes, that's it. Know the blighter well. Robinson.'

'Really,' she said, pulse quickening.

'Yes. Served under me in the regiment. Haven't seen him since, but I'd know the beggar anywhere.'

'When was this?' she asked cautiously.

'Oh, let me see. Forty-two, possibly forty-three.'

She thought back to the videofit image of a man in his early twenties. 'I don't think that can be the same man, I'm afraid. Your Mr Robinson would be, what, seventy years old now?'

There was a short silence. 'Suppose he would. Yes. Well then there was the man in the other story. Might have seen him yesterday . . .'

Claire hung up as soon as she could.

An hour and a half later the police had gone, taking the last can of Carlsberg from the hospitality table on the way, and the debrief meeting was under way.

'Thank you, everybody,' said Jane. 'Smooth show considering the circumstances. Thank you Claire for filling in at such short notice.'

'You made a beautiful couple,' Harry put in, and someone tittered. Claire glared at him.

'I think we'll dispense with the usual debrief under the circumstances. We've all had a shock,' said Jane. 'You can go. I'd like Russell, Claire and Harry to stay behind.' The room emptied rapidly, but through the outgoing tidestream of staff came the bulky figure of Herman Dent, dancing attendance on a slimmer and more powerful middle-aged man. Claire had met him once before, on the day when he'd summoned her so unexpectedly to meet him in a London hotel, then offered her a job. It was Desmond Gilligan, the owner of National TV.

They stared at him. He nodded at Jane, then at Claire and stood in the middle of the room looking around.

'I watched the show,' he said, and the Australian accent came through strongly. 'It was dull.' Jane flinched, but he ignored her and went on. 'I know you had some problems tonight. I've heard from Herman about this guy Paul Wade, but I think you missed an opportunity. This is a crime show. There's your own man, dead, someone who's had his face on the show for the last year, ever since we started. You could have made a helluva story out of it instead of wasting all this expensive talent . . .' he waved at Claire, 'on some kind of sex-shop inflatable.'

Bad taste, thought Claire to herself. How could we have done that? Jane looked as though she was going through the same thought process, but knew better than to fight her proprietor on those kind of grounds.

'All we know is he's dead, Mr Gilligan. He had . . . let's say, various dangerous habits. He probably just overdosed on something.'

Gilligan shook his head grimly. 'One phone call would have told you. It takes a very determined doper to overdose then crawl head first down a hole in the ground and cover himself completely with pine needles.' He pointed at Claire. 'I've got you the best reporter you're ever likely to have. Put her to work on it.' With that he swung about, jerked his head to Herman and left the office with his Director of Programmes in tow.

In the swirling vacuum of his departure, Harry gave a sour smile. 'There you are, teacher's pet,' he said to Claire. 'Best reporter, eh? Better get to work.'

'After the weekend,' she said tightly. She went to the washroom before she left the building, then came back to pick up the sailing bag she'd left behind. In the car, heading for the marina on the Hamble, she cursed Harry loudly and repeatedly, and Gilligan too for good measure. The familiar journey drained some of the tension, but it wasn't until she'd walked down the pontoon, sniffing the evening sea, unlocked *Tiger Kitten*'s hatch, and swung down the steps into that familiar cosy cabin that the prospect of a weekend by herself out on the pure, living water took the taste completely away.

Then she unpacked her bag and found that Harry had had the last laugh. There was an unfamiliar packet stuffed in the top, and she undid it to find Eric the Escort with a note stuck to it.

'Your ideal man?' it said.

# Chapter Four

## Saturday July 20th

At eight o'clock in the morning, Claire woke late and Harry woke early. She looked out of the hatchway at a blue sky, pursed her lips at missing half an hour of the tide, and began to get ready for sea. He flailed around with one hand until it connected with the telephone and knocked over a glass of water, splashing soggily on the pillow and his hair.

'Who is it?' he growled.

'Sorry, Harry. Did I wake you? It's Jane.'

'You did. It's Saturday.'

'I know. Look, could you possibly do me a favour?'

'No.'

'Don't be like that. This is important.'

'What?'

'Derek Palmer's going down to Sevenoaks this morning to see about Paul Wade. You couldn't go with him, could you?'

Harry took the receiver away from his ear, looked at it in feigned astonishment, playing to an invisible audience, then brought it up again. 'Hold on. I thought you'd put your new super-reporter on it. I don't work weekends.'

'I called her. She's not at home. Her flatmate says she's away for the weekend. Not contactable.'

'Flatmate?' said Harry. 'What does he sound like?'

'It's a she not a he.'

'Well, well.'

'Oh come on, Harry.'

'Jane, it's her story, Gilligan said so. Get off my back.'

'Look, Gilligan's on *my* back. Claire didn't know this would come up.'

'Gilligan's rattling your cage, is he?'

'Well . . . he's been on the phone, yes.'

'He's set up this little trip with Palmer?'

'I think so.'

He looked out through the bedroom door into the studio beyond, thought of the Paul Wade he knew and Claire bloody Merrick didn't, and sighed at the loss of the day he'd promised himself. There was Steffie to think about too and for a moment he thought, well, maybe Steffie won't mind, but he pushed that thought savagely away. He'd get back in time. 'OK Jane, but only if Palmer picks me up and brings me back,' he said reluctantly.

Derek Palmer's usual patch was Notting Hill. He got a day and a half free every week for his work on the show, and he thought the teasing he got from some of his men for his TV appearances was a worthwhile price to pay. He liked Harry and didn't mind the small diversion to Wandsworth to pick him up. Palmer drove through London in a precise, legal way which Harry found slightly uncanny. Each touch of the brakes, gear change, or turn of the steering-wheel was done as if by computer and Harry felt awed and undermined that life could be lived so deliberately.

'Are you still enjoying doing the show?' Harry said, to take his mind off it.

'Certainly,' Palmer replied. 'Gets me out of the office. I just hope they let me go on with it.'

'They? You mean National?'

Palmer laughed. 'No. I mean the Met Public Affairs people and my boss.'

'Aren't they happy?'

'Well, between you and me, some of them think it's a waste of time. National's not big enough yet. Doesn't get the response, though it's getting better. These rewards cause more trouble than they're worth. Any good defence lawyer can make mincemeat out of a witness who stands to make ten grand from a TV station for what they're saying.'

'So they might pull you off?'

'No, I don't think so. They just moan a lot. There's a bit more to it than just results. If you can't turn on any channel without seeing villains' mug shots leering at you, it helps in all kinds of funny ways. Gives the villains the idea it's harder to get away with it than it used to be, now that everyone's watching out for them.'

'It glorifies the police a bit, doesn't it? Sounds like *Nineteen Eighty-Four*.'

Palmer looked at him curiously. 'What happened in 1984?'

'It's a book, you know? Big brother is watching you?'

'Oh, got you. That's the whole beauty of it; the way it slips in to the living room. It's up there with the game shows. The public loves it, so there's no problem.'

They drove on for a while in silence, then Palmer cleared his throat. 'Something I wanted to ask you.'

'Yeah?'

'What is it with you and Claire Merrick?'

With anyone else, Harry might have tried deflecting the question with a joke, but in the car with this professional observer, he knew he couldn't. 'I don't think much of her, that's all.'

'She's a nice-looking girl.'

'If you like that sort.'

'Meant to be a good reporter, surely?'

'I think she's used to being a superstar.'

'Well, she's done a lot. She's famous. She's made it in a man's world.'

'Past tense, Derek. She made it. Then she blew it.'

'I can't say I know much about that.'

'No one knows much about it, mate. One of the best-kept secrets of broadcasting. The word was she started to become a bit of a liability. She got bigger than the stories she was covering, and there was a screw-up. That's why Gilligan was able to get her.' He looked sideways at his driver. 'I know what it is. You thought you were going to have *her* along in the passenger seat this morning, didn't you? I'm sorry if I'm a disappointment.'

\*    \*    \*

On arrival at Sevenoaks they were kept waiting for some time, to Derek Palmer's mostly, but not entirely, concealed irritation, then shown into an office where a heavy-jowled man with receding hair, ostentatiously studying some paperwork, looked up at them discouragingly. He got up and stretched out an unwelcoming hand to Palmer.

'Terry Slatter,' he said. 'DI.'

'Chief Inspector Palmer,' said the other with a slight stress on the 'Chief', 'and this is my colleague, Harry Chaplin.'

Good on you, thought Harry, making it sound like I'm a copper too, but it wasn't to be.

'Yes. Seen you on that show of yours,' said Slatter. 'Now, what do you want exactly?'

'Just the form on Paul Wade,' said Palmer, and got a lugubrious look in exchange which contained a great deal of unspoken antipathy.

Slatter continued looking at them. 'The thing is, gentlemen, I don't quite know how I'm meant to be taking you.'

Palmer raised his eyebrows. 'Meaning?'

'Well, is this an official enquiry? Am I simply being asked for information by a brother officer in the normal way, or are you being TV coppers? Because if it's that, I'll have to go through channels, through the press office and all that.'

'Ah, I see,' said Palmer. 'Let's be quite clear then. I'm here because I knew Wade well and I'm interested. Mr Chaplin is here for the same reason. He's well used to confidentiality if it's necessary.'

Slatter nodded slowly, excused himself and left the room.

'What was all that about?' Harry asked.

Palmer exhaled. 'Just a bit of bullshit. Don't bother your head. There's a lot more like him who get on their high horse because of the TV. They think I must be getting away with something.'

Slatter came back in and passed Palmer a sheet of paper. 'Not that much to say. Cause of death is clear enough. Heroin OD by injection. Traces of other substances found in his blood including cocaine and a compound that was probably Ecstasy. Found by someone trespassing after mushrooms. I take it he did have a drug habit?' He looked at Palmer, and Palmer looked at Harry, who replied curtly.

'He messed around with drugs, yes.'

'Well, that's obviously how he got there.'

'Head first down a hole covered with pine needles?'

'He didn't get there by himself. My guess is he was with someone else when he OD'd, and they panicked because they were smacked up as well, so they bunged him down the hole.'

Harry looked up from the bit of paper. 'Where did you find his car?'

'What car would that be? We haven't found any car.'

'He would have driven down there.'

Slatter's face took on a slight smirk. 'I wouldn't let yourselves get carried away by the drama of it, gents. If there was a car, it'll show up.'

# Sunday July 21st

There was enough wind to test Claire, single-handed, to occupy her fully and keep the lurking devils hiding at the back of her mind. *Tiger Kitten* was twenty-eight feet overall, GRP hull for all the advantages of low maintenance, but a wooden deck and wooden mast which, with the panelling down below, gave her all the feel of an older boat. There were signs of a season's neglect wherever she looked, and on the long reach back from the Needles she started making lists of jobs to be done during the winter lay-up. Damn Jerome, she said to the boat, he even made me neglect you.

Superstitiously, she looked around in case the big Jeanneau 47 should be out on the water, but she knew it wasn't likely. They'd met at the Royal Lymington Yacht Club, so it was boats that had brought them together, but he'd never been able to come to terms with the discovery that she was a far better sailor than he would ever be. Their sailing trips had become fewer and fewer as his role as skipper had become harder to maintain. Gradually his flashy boat had become just another marina cocktail cabinet and Jerome's idea of a sailing weekend had been a party for a few of his friends, then a sexual marathon in the big double bunk. That was why he wouldn't come out in *Tiger Kitten*.

'Single bunks?' he had said. 'Single bunks in that tiny little boat? It'll be banging against the pontoon so hard everyone'll know exactly what we're doing. Might as well do it out on the dock.'

That trapped her in violent, disturbing memories and took her mind off her helming. There were boats racing to windward, a line of quarter-tonners with spinnakers flying approaching to starboard, and she came further off the wind to give them a wide berth, untypically failing to register the committee boat and the buoy marking their finishing line. She wasn't in their way, passing it to starboard just as the first of the fleet crossed the line on the other side, but the wind, and her proximity, sent the crash of the finishing gun unexpectedly erupting into her head, just as that other shot from an AK47 had done before, and she put both hands to her head and started to scream as if she would never stop. With no hand on the tiller, the boat came close to gybing, but it steadied on a dead run as if it alone were there to look after her. Gradually the sobbing figure in the cockpit, away from all onlookers, got herself back under control and set course for home.

An hour later, sails stowed and *Tiger Kitten* made fast, she loaded her sailing bag in the Golf's boot, with Eric the inflatable escort packed in the bottom for a suitable revenge, some day soon, on Harry. It was a warm evening and she thought about taking the hood down, but her nerves were still jangling, and the dark cocoon of the interior seemed more comforting. The bad visibility with the hood up, plus her red and swollen eyes, fooled her into backing out of her space into the path of a Jaguar that was speeding down the gravel of the marina car park. Those eyes were the first thing the other driver noticed when the noise died away and he got out, ready to start shouting. Long channels in the gravel told of his attempt to stop. The deep dent in the rear quarter of the Golf told of his failure. The Jaguar's bumper was unmarked.

He looked at her, the words dying on his lips. 'Hey, I know you. You're Jeremy Hackman's bird, aren't you?'

'Jerome. And no, I'm not any more.' The implied possessiveness irritated her beyond measure, but she couldn't find a form of denial which took it on board.

'Course, it's Claire Merrick. How could I forget? I'm Murray O'Keefe, remember? We had a drink on the boat a couple of times.' He'd been looking at the car, but now turned back to her again. 'You look a bit upset. Don't worry, love, it's only a knock. I fix these every day. Lucky I wasn't in the Ferrari.'

She remembered then; a body repair centre, something like that, fixing fancy cars. Medallion man, open shirts and flashy gold watch.

'The Jag's OK,' he said, 'sorry about yours. I didn't have a chance. Here's a card. I've got hydraulic rams that will pull that straight in a tick.' He looked at her again. 'Spot of lunch or dinner into the bargain, if you fancy it?'

The Golf drove perfectly well and there was no sign of Ann when she got back to the flat, just a note saying: 'Gone out. Back soon. Message from Desmond Gilligan. Call him at once.'

# Chapter Five

## Sunday July 21st

The desk-top terminal had been coupled up the previous evening by a man who arrived and left in a miasma of unremarkable self-effacement. Hacker couldn't have described him to save his life. The monitor sat inside a collapsible shield because, however secure the rest of it was, emissions from the screen display could be read within a limited range by relatively simple equipment. Up here on the sixth floor, Hacker couldn't take that danger seriously, but he went along with it.

In the presence of Freedom's Friends he had smelt the hard, iron scent of money and power. Away from them, deep inside, he was still unsure they could really give him what he wanted and equally unsure that he could provide any real service. Now was the time to start to find out. The machine had been coupled up to the modem since yesterday and the first file should have come in during the night. He poured a glass of orange juice, looking out over the river, and turned up the brightness on the screen display.

It was there. 'GOOD MORNING, GREGORY,' it said in bold red letters. 'THIS GAME IS STILL ACTIVE, THEREFORE WHAT FOLLOWS IS AN UNEDITED VERSION. WHEN COMPLETE, THE GAME WILL BE ARCHIVED WITH ONLY RELEVANT INPUTS RETAINED. EACH PLAYER'S CONTRIBUTIONS CAN BE IDENTIFIED BY A COMBINATION OF TEN COLOURS AND FOUR PRINT STYLES: UPPER CASE, LOWER CASE, ITALIC, OR CURSIVE. PLEASE REFER TO

YOUR GUIDE. YOU HAVE BEEN ALLOCATED ORANGE ITALIC.'

He reached for the document and looked at it again, then put it aside. What use was it to know that green capitals meant George Peppard and brown cursive was Debby Reynolds when he had no idea – apart from Lee J. Cobb – who any of them were in real life.

He hit the return key, and the image on the screen changed to a glowing technicolour rendering of the familiar painting of cowboys and buffalo, but where the title of the film should have been, letters of the same style said 'GAME TEN'. He hit the key again and the screen filled up with words:

GAME TEN.
INAUGURATION DATE: DECEMBER 3, 1991.
QUORUM: IN PLACE. 22 PRESENT.
PROPOSERS: DIRECTOR 1, DIRECTOR 2, JOHN WAYNE, CARROLL BAKER.
SUMMARY OF PURPOSE: PRESERVATION OF IMPROVED GLOBAL SECURITY AND TRADE OPPORTUNITIES AFFORDED BY RECENT POLITICAL DEVELOPMENTS IN EASTERN BLOC.

That hit him between the eyes. He'd been expecting something on a smaller scale, maybe about liquor sales in Mississippi or fighting pollution requirements for automobile manufacturers. He read on with heightened interest.

BRIEF BACKGROUND: COLLAPSE OF USSR ENDS STATIC BALANCE OF RIVAL SUPERPOWERS. DISAPPEARANCE OF IRON CURTAIN INCREASES POSSIBILITY OF VASTLY EXPANDED EUROPEAN COMMUNITY EXTENDING TO BALKANS ONCE GERMAN REUNIFICATION IS COMPLETE. MEDIUM TERM HAZARDS, ESPECIALLY BALKAN WARS, WILL SLOW DOWN PROCESS, BUT BRUSSELS-LED MOVES TOWARDS UNITED EUROPE POINT TO LONG-TERM GROWTH OF EUROPE AS FRESH SUPERPOWER.

FOR EXTENDED ANALYSIS SEE FULL BACKGROUND
FILE E/91/172.

SPECIFIC GAME FOCUS: CONSTRUCTIVE INTERVENTION
IN EUROPEAN POLITICAL/ECONOMIC PROCESSES TO
RESTRAIN MOVEMENT TOWARDS UNITED EUROPE. HIS-
TORY OF PAST FIFTY YEARS SHOWS MAXIMUM WORLD
SECURITY EXPERIENCED IN IMMEDIATE POST-WORLD
WAR TWO PERIOD WHEN US WAS SOLE SUPERPOWER,
PRE-ACQUISITION BY USSR OF A-BOMB. MAXIMUM
WORLD INSECURITY FOLLOWED DURING PERIOD OF
SUPERPOWER RIVALRY.

DEMOCRACY OVERVIEW: SINGLE SUPERPOWER IS
SAFER FOR WHOLE WORLD. EUROPEAN POPULA-
TIONS ARE BEING PUSHED FASTER THAN THEY WISH
BY LEADERSHIPS TOWARDS INTEGRATION WITH NO
FULL AWARENESS OF CONSEQUENCES (FILE REF-
ERENCES E/91/96–99). DEMOCRATIC REQUIREMENTS
NOT BEING FULFILLED. INTERVENTION JUSTIFIED.

RESOURCE ALLOCATION: MAXIMUM. DIRECTORS
HAVE APPROVED LEVEL 7.

One of our old games, they'd said. A game to nip in the bud
the looming European superpower. Just a game. He pressed
return again and the screen filled with coloured blocks of
type. The game had begun. The opening contributions were
conversational, short, jaunty.

'THEY CALL IT THE BELGIAN EMPIRE,' said the first.
'DELORS IS THE EMPEROR, HONEY-TRAP? CATCH HIM
WITH HIS PANTS DOWN.' That was in yellow lower case, a
reply came winging back in black italic: 'IT'S EUROPE, NOT
UTAH. THEY'D LOVE HIM FOR IT. GO FOR THE MONEY.
GET THEM BY THE PURSE STRINGS.' Someone else came
in with light blue capitals: 'FOLLOW THAT UP. HOW?'
The answer came. 'BUST UP THEIR CURRENCY SYSTEM.
SCREW THE EUROPEAN MONETARY SYSTEM. PICK ON

THE WEAKEST CURRENCIES AND BLOW THEM OUT OF THE WATER.' The query came, 'COST?' and the answer, 'NO COST. BIG PROFIT IF IT'S DONE RIGHT.'

Now something new happened. A box appeared on the screen. 'DIRECTOR'S INTERVENTION,' it said. 'GOOD IDEA. FILE IT FOR SUB-GAME TO BE PURSUED BY FINANCE GROUP. STICK WITH THE BLUE-SKY THINKING.'

They kept coming: some wild and wacky, replacing Delors by a look-alike; some notably racist including one which advocated financing feature films specially written round World War Two plots heightening German brutality. Then, in brown capitals which he hadn't seen before, just nine words. 'PICK A SMALL COUNTRY AND UNLOCK THE FLOOD-GATES.' Mister Brown Capitals had clout. The reply was a respectful, 'AMPLIFY PLEASE.'

The response to that was a long one. 'A FOREST FIRE CAN BE STARTED BY ONE SINGLE TINY SPARK. FIND ONE EUROPEAN COUNTRY WHERE THEY'RE NOT SO SURE. NOT THE POLITICIANS, THE PEOPLE. PICK THE MOMENT TO LET THEM HAVE THEIR SAY AND DO WHAT WE CAN TO DELIVER THE RIGHT RESULT. THEN WATCH THE WALLS COME TUMBLING DOWN. ONCE ONE HAS DARED, THE REST WILL FOLLOW. IT SHOULD NOT BE HARD TO FIND THE RIGHT PRESSURE POINT AND THE RIGHT COUNTRY. THAT WILL BE THE FUL-CRUM. WE WILL PROVIDE THE LEVER. WITH THAT WE CAN MOVE EUROPE.'

'WHAT SORT OF FULCRUM?' someone asked.

'VOTING. WHEN THEY HAVE TO GO TO THE PEOPLE. REFERENDUMS AND ELECTIONS.'

Hacker read on, fascinated. At the end was a note addressed personally to him.

'GREGORY,' it said, 'AT THIS STAGE THE SESSION ENDED AND THE DIRECTORS WERE CHARGED WITH ANALYZING AND ENHANCING THROUGH THE USE OF OUR DATABASE, IN ORDER TO PRESENT A FORMAL-IZED STARTING POINT FOR THE FOLLOWING SESSION. THIS YOU WILL BE ABLE TO READ NEXT TIME. NOW,

TO SHOW FAITH, WE ARE ABLE TO PROVIDE YOU WITH
INFORMATION WHICH MAY HELP YOU IN YOUR PRES-
ENT COMMERCIAL OPERATIONS.' What followed had him
glued to the screen.

# Chapter Six

## Sunday July 21st

Claire's phone call to Desmond Gilligan was short and to the point. 'Claire Merrick,' she said, 'you called me.'

She had his full attention immediately.

'That's right,' he said. 'I want to see you. Breakfast tomorrow. I've got to fly at nine-thirty. Can you make Heathrow, Terminal 4 by eight?'

As she put the phone down, she heard the front door open. 'Ann?' she called.

'Hallo. Good weekend?'

Claire got up and hugged the woman who came in with undiluted affection. Ann Farrow was short, stocky and smiling; the only reliable emotional support in Claire's life for as long as she could remember. Well, not quite as long, she corrected herself mentally as she stepped back and looked at her. It had been Ann's shoulder that first soaked up her childhood tears more than twenty years ago in Dagenham when she arrived, parentless and unwanted, in Aunt Molly's spinster household to find providence had provided a comforter in the form of the older daughter of the couple next door.

Ann wrinkled her nose. 'You smell of the sea. That's what you needed.'

'I did. Just me and the boat.'

'No nightmares?'

'I slept like a log.'

Ann Farrow carried with her the uncomfortable outward appearance of an uncompromising idealist: short hair, round glasses, old clothes. Inside that she was the warmest, most generous person Claire had ever met, the anchor of her turbulent life, always there when anything went wrong, arriving unsummoned as often as not, as though alerted to Claire's distress on some private frequency.

Claire made her a cup of coffee. 'What about you?'

'I've spent the weekend roaming the wide open spaces of the office, gazing out across the beautiful vista of my computer screen, and breathing the intoxicating freshness of the air-conditioning.'

'All of it?'

'Every bit. There's a conference next week and I was way behind on the background papers.'

'Poor you. Have you got it done?'

'All except for five thousand words on the effect of the bankruptcy rules on MPs' eligibility.'

'Doesn't sound very exciting.'

'Oh, but it is. With a majority as thin as this it only needs a few more losses at Lloyds to force an election, unless Conservative Central Office can find some untainted donors to cough up the cash.'

Ann was a senior researcher at a left-wing think-tank in Primrose Hill, the Institute for Policy Evaluation.

'I wish I did what you do.'

Ann smiled at her. 'No, you don't. You need the glamour. It's nothing to be ashamed about.'

'There's no glamour at National.'

'Give it a chance. There's too much hurt going round in your head at the moment. Things will get better. They always do.'

Claire took Ann's hand and squeezed it. 'You've been saying that since I was eight.'

'I've usually been right.'

'Not lately.'

'I can't help it if you choose horrible men.'

'Is there any other sort?'

'Well Jerome Hackman was an extreme example, but you know my views. As for the other thing, that will blow over, you know.' She snapped her fingers. 'Did you get my message to call your boss? He's very keen to talk to you.'

'Gilligan? I've done it. We're having breakfast tomorrow.'

'What does he want?'

'I haven't a clue. Funny. I wouldn't have thought he'd have time to bother with little cogs like me.'

# Monday July 22nd

Bothering was just what Desmond Gilligan was good at. Working out where the little details mattered and then bothering until he got them right. He chose a table which allowed Claire to spot him immediately she walked into the upstairs restaurant. He wore a light-coloured linen suit but everything else about him was dark: the tanned skin, the curly hair, the calm, evaluating eyes. Someone had suggested there was aboriginal blood in his ancestry, but the flattened bridge to his nose could equally have been a rugger injury.

'Thank you for coming,' he said.

She smiled. 'When the owner calls, you don't stop to consider whether you have a choice.'

'OK, OK.' He waved a hand dismissively and she wondered if he was fending off over-familiarity. 'Coffee and croissants?'

'Fine.'

He didn't hang about. 'I just wanted you to know', he said, looking around for a waiter, 'that you're a big part of my plans.'

'I was wondering a bit.'

He looked round sharply at her. 'What does that mean?'

In for a penny in for a pound, she thought. 'I didn't realise when you hired me that I wouldn't be on the news.'

'Don't you like the show?'

'It's not what I'm used to.'

He nodded. 'It's not what I got you for, but it kills two birds with one stone. Later on I want you for the chief correspondent job on the news, doing all the really big stories, but there's one or two things I have to do first.'

Yes, she thought, like get rid of Graham Scott who was

currently holding that position, clearly with no idea that his Australian nemesis was already bearing down on him.

'In the meantime,' he said, 'do me a deal. Put your guts into it for six months, and then I'll fix the switch. OK?'

'OK,' she said. 'Was that all you wanted to say?'

'No.' He looked at her meditatively. 'Crookbusters matters more than you could know. Have you looked at the adverts we run in the centre break?'

'No,' she said truthfully.

'Women in skin-tight Lycra selling the kind of exercise machines you know are going to put you in hospital if you ever manage to assemble the kit. Dubbed from the original Hungarian or something. Cheapjack garbage. It doesn't cover your pay cheque, let alone the rest of the show.' He took a sip of coffee. 'We've got to get audiences up in the three or four million range, then the real advertisers will take it seriously. You can lift that show. I don't think the rest of them have too much of a clue. Play this Paul Wade story as hard as you can. If you run into any editorial trouble, tell me. Here are my numbers. You can file me through the office electronic mail system too. I want big, sexy stories on that show, and I want you doing them.'

'Mr Gilligan,' she said, 'forgive me, but I can't quite work out why you're going to so much trouble over one little show on one little part of your great big empire.'

'It's not one little show,' he said, 'Crookbusters is the leading edge. The rewards we offer are doing more for dish sales and cable hook-ups than anything we've ever done before. My figures show it's put forty per cent on National's audience in the past six months. With you and a lot of publicity that can be a hundred per cent in the next six months. That would take us into profit a year early.'

'Then the banks will be eating out of your hand?'

He allowed himself a small smile. 'Well at least they won't be trying to bite my head off. I want big stories, the bigger the better. I'll tell Herman to make sure they don't use you for the crap. Keep me in touch with what goes on. Claire Merrick and Crookbusters. That's a powerful draw.'

# Tuesday July 23rd

Shipley Green Car Auctions was a flat-roofed concrete building on the edge of a small industrial estate. Behind it was a large wire compound where cars and vans stood in rows on rough, cinder-stiffened earth. The estate roads were choked with cars parked with two wheels on the verges, and more cars were flooding in all the time for the auction. It was half past six in the evening and inside the building a powerful smell of fried onions and hamburger wafted from the queue around the food counter.

Hawk-faced men in waxed cotton waistcoats held mobile phones with hands which had the grey-brown sheen of partly washed grease impregnated in their surface. A big Peugeot was driven in by an old man in glasses wearing a donkey jacket. The car stopped in front of the auctioneer's dais and the dealers fell on it, opening the bonnet, peering in through the driver's window and running their hands over its flanks as though they could read its past by touch. Claire felt out of place, conspicuous even in the shabby clothes she'd picked out. They were country clothes, wrong for here. The few girls who'd come with their men were dressed hard, tarty.

'Peugeot 605. 1993 on an 'L' plate. Ex-Hillgate Finance. Full history with it and only thirty-seven thousand showing. Comes warranted and in good working order. Who'll start me at four and a half for the 605?' Nothing happened, and in feigned exasperation, he tried again, 'Four then? Two and half! You must be joking. Three five, thank you, George. Three six, three seven, three eight.'

The bidding went on by curt nods from the bevy of men hovering round the car. Claire pushed past them and walked out to the yard, past the line of cars queuing to be sold. A speaker carried the progress of the bidding out to her. 'Four seven then, four eight. I'll take a half. Four eight fifty for the first time, four eight fifty for the second time. Can't sell it at that price. Come and see us and we'll phone them for you.'

The Peugeot was driven off at high speed round the outside

and back into the park, where it was slotted into line casually by the old man who got out and walked towards Claire. He stopped and hung the keys on a numbered peg board, then looked around and selected another bunch for the next car in the line. Claire walked up to him.

'Excuse me.'

He turned ponderously and looked at her, chin down, over the top of his glasses. 'Hallo?'

'Can you help me. I'm looking for a man called Monkey Duggan.'

'Best help I can give you is to advise you not to, love.' But then he laughed. 'Monkey's inside. Just saw him.'

'Which one is he?'

'Right by the auctioneer. Wearing a green track suit. Ugly little runt.'

'Thanks very much.'

'My pleasure. You'd be better off with me though, I'm not married, well not very.'

She smiled at him and turned to walk back to the hall.

Monkey Duggan was on the phone to someone, like many of the people around him. 'Trade-in, Joe boy, fifty-five K on the clock, warranted. Two owners. Ticket 'til November and it's a looker. Colour? What the fuck do you care about the colour? White. Rubber's a bit shot at the back but it's got new Firestones at the front. Yeah? Eight hundred. You won't get it at that. Eight fifty maybe. All right.'

He didn't bother to say goodbye, just pressed the 'off' button. Claire, who was standing just behind him, waiting, cleared her throat. 'Mr Duggan?'

A white Ford was being driven in. He craned his head round and looked her up and down with an awkward neck movement. 'Who are you?'

'I work for the same people as Paul Wade.'

'Paul who?' but now bidding had started on the Ford and he was distracted. His hand went up. The auctioneer looked at him and said, 'Seven twenty.'

'Wade.'

'Seven forty,' said the auctioneer.

'Never heard of him,' Duggan said quickly and waved again.

'Seven sixty.'

'He paid you a hundred quid a few weeks ago for some information.'

That got him. Duggan turned and looked straight at her.

'Seven eighty,' said the auctioneer.

'Like fuck he did,' said Duggan.

'Sold,' said the auctioneer and Duggan turned back with a yelp and a curse.

'Shit. Now look what you've done. I've fucking missed it.' He looked back at her and then glanced all around. 'Follow me out back. Not with me. Wait and come on behind.'

She found him out by a Vauxhall, on the phone again. 'Joe boy. Missed that one.' A short silence. 'Too much. Went for nine. Yeah. What about a Carlton?' She waited patiently while he sorted out another long transaction, then he broke off the call, looked all around again and stared at her.

'Look. First things first. Your mate Paul never gave me the dosh, so give me one good reason why I should talk to you.'

She reached into her pocket and produced a wad of notes. She counted them out. 'Here's fifty good reasons for starters.'

He looked at them. 'A hundred it was. Then there'll be another fifty for the trouble.'

'I haven't got it on me.'

'Got a cash card?'

So half an hour later, the Vauxhall purchased, she found herself driving Monkey into the town and searching for a NatWest bank. He'd insisted on walking separately down the road to her car. The machine gave her another hundred pounds and he sat there counting it. She watched him thinking about Paul Wade, the man who'd taken out a cash advance from National TV to pay for information, then somehow forgotten to give it to his source. Monkey put the money in his pocket and looked at her. 'I'll tell you what I told him then, shall I?' he said.

# Chapter Seven

## Wednesday July 24th

Claire pulled off into the rough lane and coasted down with a dead engine, steering round the worst bumps to avoid any unnecessary noise. She nosed the car in behind the sheds where it wouldn't be seen and got out, pushing the door softly shut. The black mesh of the scrapyard fence stood outlined against the dawn sky. She remembered Monkey's words: 'Watch the caravan. That's where the bloke lives, the caveman. Go round the right hand side, and just by the back corner the wire's not so good.'

'Do they have dogs?' she'd asked, not fancying a dawn encounter with a Doberman.

Monkey had sniggered. 'They 'ad one. Alsatian, nasty bugger. Chased a cat through the yard last month, cat ran up a pile of cars. Dog tried to go after it an' a Cortina fell on its 'ead.' Then he'd considered a bit. 'Course the car I told your mate Paul about – Trooper, weren't it? Metallic purple – that's gone.'

'Gone?'

'Well, crushed. It's still there in a manner of speaking. I was down there yesterday, but it's just a square lump.'

Now, with a familiar and not unpleasant tingle of going into action, she moved with immense care round the edge of the fence. Between the jeans, heavy jacket and wellingtons, the high banks of stinging nettles still found spaces she didn't know existed. There was a short section of fence by the corner post where the fixings had been loosened and, with a wriggle, she was able to twist through, wondering as she did whether Paul Wade had been exactly this way before her. If he had, he must have been on the slender side and she paused for a moment, half-way through the wire, feeling the link to this unknown, unseen person who had somehow come to die in the course of all this. The realization came to her then that she was unprotected here, despite the legitimacy of her purpose. She was trespassing and almost anything could happen. It was no worse than the deliberate vulnerability of a trip into a war zone, with the constant, dangerous frustration of never being sure where the action would erupt next; the appetite for the pictures serving as the candle flame drawing the moth closer to the casually lethal bullets.

In the still dim dawn, she surveyed the scene. Ranks of flattened, precarious cars were arranged in rows with muddy alleyways between them, evil with pools of dark, oily liquid, scattered dull crystals of windscreen glass, discarded plastic and bent lances of chromium. To her left stood ranks of engines, piles of wheels and doors stacked upright against the wall of a shed. A forklift truck and a big crane were parked just inside the main gates. Beyond them was the big open-sided shelter where Monkey said the crushed cubes were stacked, waiting for collection. She took a roundabout, concealed route to it, past the empty dog kennel, uneasily aware that just outside the mesh of the gates, she could see the corner of the caravan. There was a wall of metal bales stacked two-deep. It took little more than a minute to determine that one of them showed signs of metallic purple paint, and if more proof were needed, a sharply creased sheet of metal showed black letters, 'ISU', the start of the name of the Trooper's maker, Isuzu.

So it was here, and somewhere inside that crushed bale was the plate with the VIN, the number that would prove either way that this was the car Paul had been tracking. She looked at it with a feeling of hopelessness. It must have weighed almost a ton, and it was beyond her to think up any way of reversing the massive force used to crush it. A movement at the fringe of her vision made her turn, and she looked over the top of the blocks to see that Monkey's information was out of date. The kennel wasn't empty. The yard had a new dog, and it was yawning and stretching as it came slowly out of the kennel, revealed in the increasing light as a very large Alsatian.

She froze behind the blocks. So far it didn't seem aware of her presence and she hoped the rank stench of petrol and old oil rising into the morning air was masking her smell. It stood outside the kennel, hanging its head low and moving it slowly from side to side. Then she saw the hackles go up along its back, and an echoing chill ran down the back of her neck. It took a step or two towards the bales of metal which concealed her, and she took a silent pace back into the sheltering gloom which fetched her up against a solid stack of old car parts. She felt down behind her. They were drive shafts, round steel rods an inch and a half thick. Quietly, staring at the Alsatian from behind her barrier, she wrapped her fingers around one.

The dog growled softly, trying to sort out the confusing scents in the air. It looked young and uncertain. She was now holding the drive shaft in front of her in one hand, and she felt something heavy, round and loose on the end of it: a coupling on greasy splines. Blessing the luck which had stopped it sliding noisily off, she eased it free into her hand and hefted it. The dog came to a decision, growled louder and started to pad towards her, and she lobbed the coupling off to her left with all her power. It made a satisfactory clatter among the stacks of cars and the dog, barking loudly, ran off in that direction. She could see it, only thirty yards away, circling, so she picked up a handful of wheel nuts and hurled them, one at a time, diagonally across the yard. The dog erupted into a crescendo of barking and rushed off. A light came on in the caravan.

She risked one more throw, then ducked behind the pile of metal as a hugely fat man, dressed incongruously in Y-fronts and boots, erupted from the door of the caravan. She heard him fumbling the gates open.

'All right, all right, I'm coming,' he was shouting to the dog, 'just hold the bastard.' But his voice and his footsteps were coming straight towards the end of the pile of metal bales, and her heartbeat began to pound in her head. She was crouching with her head down, but then his legs were right in front of her eyes and all he had to do was look down. She raised her head, slowly, fearfully, but he was stretching away from her, reaching up. There was a click and lights came on all round the yard. She gripped the bar, waiting for his head to turn but he was looking out across the yard, not down at his feet. The dog was still barking and, picking up a heavy wrench, he walked off towards it.

She couldn't risk standing up, so she crept slowly to the end of the stack. From there she could see the front gate. It was closed, but the padlock was hanging on its hasp. She waited, forcing herself to count to twenty to let him get further away, then ran as hard as she could for the gate, not daring to look back into the yard. It was a heavy, iron framed, mesh-covered monster of a gate and over the years the hinges had sagged under the weight so that it rested heavily in the mud. She pulled, and it tilted but dug into the soft ground even harder. She bent her back and strained upwards, the wire cutting into her hands even through the gloves and, gradually, it reluctantly moved, but as it did there was a shout.

'Hey, stop. You! Stop right there.'

A torrent of barking began behind her and she looked over her shoulder to see the dog streaking towards her from fifty yards away, and the man lumbering after it.

She dropped the gate and squeezed through the gap, knowing as she did so that the dog would be through it in a flash. Aghast at the time it was squandering, she struggled to lift the gate again and began to drag it closed. The dog was only feet away and as the gate clanged home it lunged at her fingers which poked through the wire. She pulled free just in time as it snapped and slavered at her from the other side of the wire, but the man was charging like a berserk, puffing steam roller. The seconds burning in her brain, she took the padlock in shaking hands and tried to snap it shut on the hasp. At her first attempt, the loop swung sideways.

'What are you fucking doing?' the man was shouting, the gap now just ten yards. 'Leave that alone. I'll have you.'

She was keeping her face down in case he recognized her, and this time, just as his outstretched hands reached, grasping at the wire, the lock snapped shut. She turned and ran for it, hearing his keys jangling and wondering how long it would take him to open the lock through the wire. She sprinted down the track, swerved round the sheds, dropping and retrieving her ignition key on the ground in her haste, then was into the Golf and hammering it round on full lock to get clear. At the gate, the man stood still, squinting as the back of her car came into view and mouthing the registration number to himself over and over again.

In the car, Claire watched the receding gate in the rear-view mirror, and the distorted, distanced, second-hand image immediately calmed her. It was the same trick that had always worked for her in her job: the camera lens sucking out the horror; twisted, stinking death made manageable by the lens's ability to save just those parts she could cope with. She breathed deeply and slowly until she was back under control. You've been in tighter spots, she said to herself. Steady. You're out of there and you're still in one piece. Ten minutes later, on the main road, she saw a café and decided to stop to gather her thoughts. Over a cup of coffee and a plate of scrambled eggs, she considered her options. The worst of it was the idea of going back to National and having to admit she'd got nowhere with her one, single lead on the story. There were no other loose ends to tease out of the muddle. In the ordinary run of events she would have simply said that's tough, I got nowhere, forget it – but this wasn't ordinary. There was the reputation she carried with her into this tatty, one-horse outfit she'd joined. She knew that reputation would have to stand up to merciless inspection on her first job, and would blow away like smoke in the wind if she screwed up. Then there was Harry, and she could see the expression on his face all too clearly.

So desperation, not logic, had her crouched an hour later on the low, wooded hill above the scrapyard, overlooking the entrance and the shed where the crushed cars were. The dog was now chained up. The fat shape of Monkey's caveman could be seen moving cars with the fork-lift truck, unceremoniously crunching the twin tines through their side windows and feeding them into the jaws of the crusher.

His morning's excitement seemed to have left no lasting impression.

All she could really hope for was to get an idea of the comings and goings of the yard, and what use that would be was less than clear – but it was better than doing nothing. You could call it a hunch, perhaps; she'd always had hunches and over the years she'd done best when she'd paid them due heed. It was a hunch that had taken her to the back door of the Damascus Hilton when the rest of the press corps had been waiting for Clinton's group at the front, and that hunch got her the shots the world had wanted. It was a hunch that had told her to refuse the invitation delivered to her hotel room in Tripoli, and she'd paid dearly for failing to heed that one. Now, once more, whatever it was – luck, intuition or the subconscious processing of all the possibilities – served her well. There was nothing immediately interesting about the lorry that came in through the yard gates, except that it was empty. There had been two others in the past hour, but they had been bringing in old cars, squashed untidily on top of each other. This one was larger and neater. It stopped right by the spot where she had so recently been crouching, and a middle-aged man in blue overalls jumped down from the cab. The caveman walked over to him and there was much nodding and waving of arms, then the fork-lift was started, the lorry backed up a few feet and they began to load the bales of metal on to it.

Claire waited, sitting on a log, her feet deep in rotting leaves, until she saw the recognizable purple sheen of paint on one of the last few bales to be loaded, then she got to her feet, climbed quickly through the trees and down to the car. Navigating from the map on her knee, driving one-handed, she swung through the network of little country roads until she was back on the main road near the yard. Only just in time. The lorry pulled out almost in front of her and passed her going the other way. She read the letters on the door – D. K. K. Smelters, Walsall – then swung round and set off after it.

Walsall, she thought. Somewhere north of Birmingham, surely. She groped for a road atlas, and flicked it open on the passenger seat, glancing down for a second or two at a

time until she got the right page. Probably the M25, then the
M40 or the M1. Her fuel gauge showed three-quarters of a
tank – enough to go the whole way, but then what? They
were only minutes away from the motorway and once they
were on it, she knew there would be no way of stopping the
truck. At the T-junction on to the A22, the truck had to halt
to wait for a gap in the long stream of traffic, and she saw her
chance. She jumped out of the Golf, ran to the driver's door
and reached up to hammer on it with her fist. The window
slid down and the driver looked out at her with surprise on
his face.

'What's the trouble, love?' he asked with a marked Brummy
accent.

'No trouble,' she said. 'I've just got to talk to you.'

'Talk?' he said, surprised. 'Why?'

Horns sounded from the queue of cars forming up behind.
'I've got some money for you,' she said. 'I just need thirty
seconds.'

He craned out of the window and looked behind at the
queue. 'OK,' he said. 'If you say so. Just follow me.'

She went back to her car, out-facing the irritated gaze of the
woman in the car behind, and followed the truck out into the
next gap in the traffic. He drove slowly for another half-mile,
and pulled into a lay-by, jumping down and sauntering back
with a funny look on his face.

She got out and smiled at him.

'You're that reporter – Claire Merrick – aren't you?' he
asked with a friendly note of challenge in his voice.

'Oh no,' she said in a breathily overdone voice. 'No, it's
funny, I'm always being mistaken for her.' She thought quickly.
'My name's Janice Hall. I'm an interior designer. I just saw
those metal things on the back of your truck, and I realized
one of them would be just perfect for the house I'm doing.'
She looked up and pointed. 'That lovely purple one on the
end there. The colour's *so* right. Could I buy it off you, do
you think?'

She fixed big eyes on him and smiled again, and he couldn't
help grinning, though he was shaking his head. 'Not mine

to sell, love. I'm just the driver. Got to deliver the right weight.'

'But no one would ever know, surely, and I would make it worth your while.' She reached into her pocket and pulled out her note case, rifling quickly through and hoping she had enough. 'Sixty-five pounds, that's all I've got on me. Would that do?'

'Well, even if it would,' he said, 'what are you going to do with it, love?'

She looked at the truck. 'You've got that crane thing, couldn't you lift it into the back of my car. I can take the roof off.'

He laughed. 'Probably weighs twelve hundred pounds, that block. Wouldn't do your back seat any good.'

'Oh,' she said, looking at the car and casting around desperately. Her eyes lit on the big dent in the rear wing and an association of ideas started. She dug into her wallet again and found a card. Murray O'Keefe, medallion man with a body-shop on the A3. 'Here,' she said, 'this is a friend of mine. He's not far off. Look, it says: five minutes from Junction 10 on the M25. You're going past it aren't you?'

He looked at his watch and looked doubtful. 'For sixty-five quid?'

'A hundred if you'll take a cheque for the rest?'

He looked at her with a questioning expression, took the card and looked at the address, then gave a short nod. 'OK,' he said, 'but it will have to be quick.'

Murray O'Keefe's place was a large industrial unit with a big, concrete parking area outside. The driver wouldn't hang about, and he got busy straight away, craning the heavy cube of metal off the lorry. She saw it safely on to the ground, gave him the cash and, distracted by the sight of Murray O'Keefe emerging from the doors across the yard, scribbled out a cheque. The driver took it, glanced at it and folded it into his pocket.

'Thank you, Miss Hall. Funny thing, you using Claire Merrick's cheque book.'

She stared at him open-mouthed, but he chuckled, swung up into the cab and drove off, thinking about his return trip

to the scrapyard on the morrow for the remaining bales, and
the strange tale he would have to tell them.

O'Keefe stopped beside her and looked at the block of
metal.

'Claire?'

'Hello, Murray.'

'Well, there's a surprise! Come to get your car fixed? I
thought you'd phone first.'

'No, not exactly.' She nodded at the block. 'It's this I've
come about.'

'When they're that far gone, we don't usually bother.'

They couldn't start until after six when Murray O'Keefe's
staff had gone home and the hammering machinery had
fallen silent. Claire spent a tedious afternoon touring round
Guildford, watching the clock and gloomily anticipating the
pay-off O'Keefe would expect. When she got back, he'd made
a start. The block was sitting on the body-shop floor. Metal
plates had been welded to parts of it and, from those, chains
ran to the hydraulic rams around the edges.

'Stand to the side,' said O'Keefe, 'I'm just about ready.' He
hooked up one final chain, then came over to the control panel
next to her and started a whining compressor. Moving a lever,
a hydraulic piston hissed and the chain tightened. He controlled
it carefully, taking up the tension on the chains all round until
one side of the block began to unfold like a steel flower. Five
minutes later, the block was no longer a block, but neither was
it recognizable as a car. He had to unhook the chains, welding
on new plates, searching for the right purchases to unlock the
3D metal puzzle. Every heave of the hydraulics made it easier
as the metal came undone. Eight thicknesses of metal unfolded
to four, then to two, then finally to one. Within two hours, the
lump in front of them was a hollow rectangle, squashed and
buckled, but identifiable.

Four chains were pulling the roof up and away from the sides,
the window pillars straightening out. 'I think the numbers's
inside, on the cross-member. Could be under the bonnet
though,' O'Keefe said. 'One more heave and we should be
able to tell.'

There was a bang as one chain broke free, and he cut the hydraulic pressure. The rear door, hanging drunkenly from one hinge, broke off and crashed on to the concrete. Something else fell with it: something black, crushed and metallic.

'Wait a minute, Murray,' said Claire, and walked over to look at it. It had once been a box of black, enamelled metal. There were more of them inside the Trooper. She turned it over and found the crumpled lid on the other side. It had been perhaps two feet by a foot and a half, and there were markings on it and the remains of a paper label, but that wasn't what held her attention. What did was the slot in the top of the lid, partly closed by a damaged wax seal, the slot you usually see only briefly when you put your folded ballot paper into it on election day.

It was after eleven when Claire got back to the little terraced house but Ann was still up, sitting in the kitchen, drinking cocoa and making notes on a pile of papers. She poured half her mug into another one, pushed it towards Claire and put some more milk to heat on the cooker.

'What's all this?' Claire asked, looking at the papers.

'A comparative study of referendum systems,' said Ann. 'Somehow, looking at you, I'd say the chances are you've had a more interesting day than I have.'

Claire put on a theatrical expression of disgust. 'I've spent the last two hours fending off heavy-handed invitations to jump into bed with Mr Male Chauvinist himself.'

'Oh, do tell me, I love that sort of thing.'

'Red Ferrari, expensive grotty steakhouse where he tried to order for me, gold Rolex, a full account of his weekend successes as a racing driver designed to set my loins quivering, you know the type.'

'Fortunately, I don't,' said Ann. 'What on earth got you into that?'

'A very strange series of events. Quite scary really.'

She started to tell the story of the scrapyard. It seemed a long time ago, but as she got to the appearance of the dog and the rush to get through the gate in time, the fright came back and her voice showed it.

Ann leaned across to her and gripped her hand. 'It's all right. It's over. You got away.'

Claire smiled ruefully. 'I did my old trick. You would have been so cross. I looked back at them in the car mirror and that made it all OK.'

'You mean you squashed it. Now it's coming back, isn't it?'

'I know, I should deal with it head-on. You try doing that when there's a slavering wolf and a human gorilla chasing you.'

Ann thought back to the traumatized child she had first met; the child who could only face strangers through the safety of a glass barrier, who had needed so much careful coaxing to come out from behind her window and be friends. She got up, stood behind Claire and began gently to massage the tense shoulder muscles.

'Anyway, how did that get you into the clutches of the Ferrari man?'

So Claire told her the rest of the story, and Ann listened carefully as she gradually felt the tension drain away under her fingertips.

'They'd used a welding torch on the numbers. I'll never prove it was the same car.'

'No, but *you* know it was though, don't you? And that means you know your man Wade was on to something.'

'I haven't told you the strangest bit, Ann. There were three boxes in the back of this Trooper thing.'

'What sort of boxes?'

'Well, they'd been flattened, but they looked like ballot boxes.'

Ann stopped massaging. 'What do you mean?'

'Exactly what I say. There were three boxes, all about so big,' she sketched out a shape in the air with her hands, 'black-painted metal and a slit in the top of the lid.'

'Good God, that's extraordinary.'

Claire was surprised at Ann's tone of voice. 'Well, maybe.

Maybe not, though. They could have come from some club or something. Perhaps they just dumped them because they didn't need them any more.'

'Why put them in the back of a car you're going to crush? Particularly a car you're going to be very careful to get shot of because it's a bit sniffy. Anyway, why three? How many clubs would need three ballot boxes? I mean, let's see, something that size, you could get hundreds of votes into one.'

'Well, it could be a trade union, something like that?'

'It could be. Did they have any markings?'

'Some letters and numbers and a sort of seal. The lid was crumpled over, but I wrote down what I could see and we're going to straighten it out a bit more tomorrow night for the cameras.'

Ann looked at the piece of paper. 'Bring those boxes back with you afterwards, love. I smell a very strong smell.'

'What exactly?'

'I don't know.'

# Thursday July 25th

Claire was early in to the office the following morning, unsure of the logistics of booking crews at National, and anxious to make certain she could get what she needed for the evening. She logged on to her terminal to look for any leeway in the day's schedule.

There was a message waiting. It scrolled across the top of the screen. 'To CM, Good day. Please copy any updates on Wade to my file. Any problems, you have my full backing. DCG.'

Gilligan, she thought. That should free up a crew if nothing else does. She saw Jane slip into her office at the other end of the room and went over to the door.

'Hello, Claire. How did it go?'

'It was a bit tricky. There was a dog at the yard and an unfriendly watchman. Anyway the upshot is I need some crew time late this afternoon in Surrey.'

Jane looked at the board on her wall, its squares thick with chinagraph markings. 'Difficult this afternoon. Tomorrow's better if there's no last minute surprises for the show. What is it?'

'Pictures of the car Paul Wade was after, and some other bits and pieces.'

'You found the car?'

'I found its remains, minus the markings, but we can't hang about because it can't stay where it is for long. I only need a couple of hours.'

Jane looked unhappy. 'I'm afraid you'll soon discover we're not well endowed with resources here. We have just enough crew days to make the show. You have to book well in advance.'

Claire looked at the board. 'What's this, then? There's a crew down for a shoot in Aldershot. That's only half an hour at the most from where I need them.'

Jane shook her head. 'That's Harry's crew. He's got them booked all day.'

'So what's the problem? He's only got to finish by half past five and I'll be through with them by seven at the latest.'

'Claire, I have a hard enough time making things stretch without encouraging cat fights between my reporters.'

'Why should Harry mind that?'

'You must have noticed that Harry's feeling a bit threatened by your presence.'

'Threatened? He just doesn't like me, that's all.'

'No, that's not all. He was our ace. Then you come along, a real prime-time famous face. Threatened is the word I'd use.'

'So you can't do it?'

'No, I don't think so. Try and fix it for the day after tomorrow.'

'Jane, I think I should tell you that I had a note from Gilligan this morning. He wants rapid progress on this one. He said he would want to know if I ran into any trouble.'

At 5.30 there was no sign of Harry or his crew at the rendezvous on the A3. She tried to call them on the mobile phone but a recorded voice said the number was temporarily unavailable. Probably switched off, she thought angrily. She paced up and down next to the Golf, and it was after 5.45 when the crew bus appeared, and Harry was in no mood to be repentant.

'You're late,' she said as he got out.

'Would you like to start that again?' he said. 'What about "Hello Harry, how are you? I do hope you don't mind having to rush so I can steal your crew." Didn't you have to be polite at ITN?'

'We had professionals at ITN.'

'I am a professional,' he said with words that grated past his teeth one by one. 'It is not professional to pull rank to get my crew off me just because you and Gilligan have something weird going.'

She felt a small flash of shame but she was too far into this to show it. 'Well that's our editor's decision, I think, don't you?'

'No, somehow I don't think it was.'

'All that matters is that we get a move on. I'll take them. You can go.'

'I don't have a car. I wasn't expecting this. I'm travelling with the crew and I have to be back in Putney by seven, whatever happens.'

'Well, then, you'll just have to come along, won't you?' she said in an insultingly reasonable manner. 'If the crew's any good, we shouldn't be more than an hour. If you don't get in the way that is.'

He turned on his heel and stalked back to the crew bus. They pulled out behind her and followed. Three minutes down the road the phone buzzed.

'Claire, it's Jane Bernstein.'

'Yes, Jane.'

'I've just had Harry on, complaining again.'

'Complaining? That's rich. He was late.'

'Well, he has got a point. Look, would you do us all a big favour and try to sort things out with him? I really don't want this going on in the office. It's very bad news. Have a drink or something on the way back, but for heaven's sake straighten it out.'

'I think you should tell him that, not me.'

'I've already told him.'

It was ten minutes to O'Keefe's place and as they parked in the yard, Claire saw his Ferrari next to the office. It didn't look right. Then she saw the heaps of shiny grey crystals all around it on the tarmac – broken glass, not just the windscreen, but all its windows showed gaping holes. She stared. The others got out of the bus. Harry neglected to introduce the cameraman, so Claire made a big point of going over to him. He was a stocky, grey-haired man with a cheerful grin.

'Hello, I'm Claire Merrick. We haven't met.'

'Jimmy Mitchell. Looks as if someone's having an expensive day,' he said, nodding at the shattered glass. 'What are we doing, anyway?'

'Just three or four quick shots. There's a machine that straightens wrecked cars out and there's an Isuzu Trooper and some black boxes. I'll just find Murray O'Keefe, then I'll show you.'

'What are these boxes then?' asked Harry, but he was looking at her retreating back, so he turned and shrugged at Jimmy. 'Might as well talk to a brick wall, eh?'

Jimmy looked vaguely at him. 'Bit of a smasher, isn't she?'

'Et tu, Brute!' Harry wandered off to get some satisfaction from gloating over the damaged Ferrari.

Claire slid the great doors open enough to slip inside. 'Murray?' she called. There was no answer. She walked in. The Trooper had been moved. There was a damaged Opel where it had been. The boxes had gone too. She stood, listening. There was complete silence. The lights were off in the passageway to O'Keefe's office. She knocked at his door. There was no answer and she pushed it open. He was sitting in his chair behind his desk, staring at her.

'Murray?' she said again, then she saw his face, pale on one side, livid blue and red on the other with bruising. He opened his mouth with what was obviously some effort.

'Fuck off out of here,' he said, 'Get lost. Go away. Don't come back.'

'What happened to you?'

'Nothing.'

'It doesn't look like nothing.'

He pulled himself upright and came round the desk on rubbery legs. 'I told you, get out.'

Claire backed towards the door, but he came on, his voice rising, 'You're bloody trouble, you are. I don't ever want to see you again.'

'OK. Fine, I'm going.'

She went back down the corridor and out of the main door, hearing him lurching after her, shouting, 'Go, go, just go.'

She came out into the evening sunlight of the yard and a frozen tableau of the crew looking at her and at the man behind her. She turned round for a final try. 'Look, I don't know what's been going on, but we just want pictures of the Trooper and those boxes. We won't take long.'

O'Keefe clutched a drain pipe and leaned against it, panting and waving his free hand at her. 'What Trooper? What boxes? There isn't a Trooper, right? There aren't any boxes. There never were. I'm telling you there never bloody were. Now just get off my property. NOW.'

# Chapter Eight

'What the hell was that all about?'

'I don't know. What's it got to do with you?'

'Well quite a lot really. You screw up my story by yanking my crew off me for some big panic, then there's nothing to shoot when we get there. It seems to me I'm entitled to ask.'

'I don't know the answer, OK? I just don't know. I'll tell you when I've worked it out.'

Anger was shimmering between them. Jane's instructions to sort things out had got both of them into Claire's car, but any possible peace treaty had been blown away in the opening seconds. They both stared stonily through the windscreen as the latter half of the rush hour snarled up the road ahead.

'What is it with you?' Harry said. 'You're not going to fit in at National if you keep playing the prima donna. You blew all that, from what I heard. Face it, you're in with the has-beens now.'

'How dare you,' Claire said with pure venom in her voice. 'If you knew . . .'

'Oh, I heard the stories. I know perfectly . . .'

'No you don't. No one else knows what happened. No one. Look, you dickhead, you're jealous because Gilligan hired me. Just face it.'

Harry snorted and looked ahead at the traffic, then at his watch. 'Can't you get a move on? I'm going to be late.'

'So, be late. What can I do about it?'

He was silent, and she looked at him then. He looked strained and distressed and she wondered what could be so pressing. 'I'm sure your girlfriend will wait,' she said in a sarcastic tone.

'It's not a girl friend,' he said, 'and I really don't want to be late.'

'So what is it then? Train spotters' club? Heroin connection? Paedophile self-help group?'

'It's nothing to do with you,' he said.

'Oh fine.' She started to pull in. They were going past Richmond Park. 'I'll just drop you here then, shall I?'

He looked at her in anguish. 'No, please. Are you going through Putney?'

She sighed. 'Yes.'

'I'll tell you where.' From then on, through the stop-start traffic, he sat in silence staring out of the window until, on West Hill, he said, 'This'll do. If you can pull over, I'll walk from here.'

She pulled into a side road and he jumped out. 'That's fine,' he said. 'Goodbye.' He walked off, rapidly.

She wanted to know; it was as simple as that. She didn't like mysteries she couldn't solve, and two in a day was two too many, so she waited a few seconds, locked the car and went after him. A board said 'The Templar Hospital and Home, Putney'. The long, yellow, columned facade was short on entrances, but she caught a glimpse of him fifty yards ahead and saw which doorway he went through. Inside were long corridors with makeshift wooden gates protecting staircases; the smell of a hospital but none of the urgency. She heard his footsteps echoing on the stairs. The first floor had a sign, 'Corunna Ward'. She was in a corridor with a door marked 'Pharmacy' and another saying 'Physio'. Ahead was a brightly decorated dayroom full of wheelchairs, but before that there were small side wards and Claire walked past them, trying to look through the windows in each door. They were made of fluted glass, but one or two were open and showed some sort of intensive care. The people lying in the beds were inert. Tubes trailed from their noses or their throats. She didn't have to look far.

A door on the right was ajar. Through the gap she saw

Harry sitting by a bed. Standing at the foot of the bed was an older man in a white coat, holding a clipboard. He was talking to Harry's back and every now and then Harry would turn his head, say something terse and then look back again. An unexpected and unfamiliar sense of intrusion came over Claire and she turned away. She would have left but before she could, the door was pulled wide open behind her and the doctor was more or less propelled from the room by Harry.

'Look,' Harry was saying, breathing hard, 'I will not have a conversation like that in front of her. If you must talk now, we talk out here.'

'Mr Chaplin,' the doctor said in a reasonable but pained tone, 'she can't hear us, I assure you. That's the point I'm trying to make. She is in what we call a persistent vegetative state. She doesn't know anything about her surroundings.'

'That's crap,' said Harry, then suddenly broke off as he caught sight of Claire's back as she tried to edge unobtrusively away. 'Wait a minute,' he said to the doctor and, lunging after Claire, he caught her by the arm.

'What the fucking hell do you think you're doing?' he demanded at the top of his voice. The nurse at the desk turned to look and made shushing noises.

'I'm sorry,' said Claire, 'I shouldn't be here.'

'Look, Mr Chaplin,' said the doctor, 'I have to go. Perhaps we should continue this another time.'

'No, we won't,' said Harry, then turning back to Claire, he hissed, 'Sit down. Stay there. Don't bloody move. I want to talk to you.'

It felt like weakness to retreat, though she could think of no reason he would accept for her presence. Plain curiosity didn't seem enough but she stayed, watching the suppressed violence of his conversation with the doctor over by the desk, a conversation which ended with the doctor shaking his head and a sudden sag of despair in every line of Harry's body. The doctor left and Harry stood there for a while, watching him go, then turned back to Claire with the light of battle in his eyes.

'I would really like to know', he said, 'what right you think you have to follow me up here.'

'None,' she said simply. 'I was just curious.'

'CURIOUS?' he shouted, and the nurse shushed him again. 'Curious? Are you for real?'

'Look, Harry,' she said, 'since the first moment we met, every word you've said has been sarcastic. On the way here, I saw something else for the first time. I saw you worried and preoccupied and do you know something? It very nearly made you human for just a second or two. I was curious to see why.'

He stared at her, breathing hard and shaking his head. 'Don't try and get inside my head. I don't want you there. Understand? Now just go.'

He turned abruptly and went back into the room, closing the door firmly behind him. A white card, loose in a small brass frame on the door said, 'Stephanie Chaplin'. She looked through the glass, moving her head so the fluted distortions kept changing, catching broken glimpses of Harry's back bending over the bed and the still figure in it. Then she walked slowly out, looking into the open doors, recognizing the ward for what it was, a hibernation place for a spring that would never come.

A guilty anxiety gripped Claire all the way back to Stockwell, mixed with a horror that wouldn't go away and sparked off by that ward full of death-in-life, made so much worse than straightforward death by the uncertainty of what trapped consciousness might lie the other side of those blank eyes. Outside Ann's house she composed herself, not wanting to take her problems inside to Ann yet again.

For once, Ann might not have noticed. She greeted Claire with suppressed excitement from the middle of another pile of papers. 'I've been waiting for you. Sit down.' She poured a cup of coffee. 'First things first. Did you get the boxes?'

'Boxes? Oh, no, I didn't. In fact, it's all very strange. Someone did over my frightful friend Murray. He was in a real state. He wouldn't let us anywhere near the place.'

Ann looked at her sharply. 'But the boxes are still there?'

'He says not. Claims there never was a Trooper and there never were any boxes.'

Ann banged her fist on the table. 'Damn.' A brief look of alarm crossed her face. 'You must have stirred up something. Well at least that shows we're on the right tracks.'

'What tracks?'

'I know you've always thought I'm a sucker for plot theories,' said Ann.

'Well, I think you put them higher up the list of possibilities than I usually do,' Claire said judiciously.

'Fine, but just stay open-minded for a little while, OK?' She spread out the first sheet of paper. 'The 1992 General Election. You remember, I'm sure. Kinnock was way out in front in the polls day after day. Never looked like losing. Then suddenly, there's last minute cold feet, Major's back in power and everyone's explaining away why the pollsters got it wrong.'

'Of course. They still are.'

'Supposing they didn't get it wrong?'

Claire looked at Ann's expression of excitement and sipped her coffee. 'Meaning?'

'Major had a twenty-one seat majority after the election, right?'

'Right.'

'So it only needed eleven seats to go the other way to have a hung parliament, and that would have meant some sort of Labour coalition with the Lib Dems.'

Claire nodded and Ann went on. 'Do you know how many individual votes in total it took to swing those eleven seats to the Conservatives? Guess.'

'I don't know. Twenty thousand?'

Ann was smiling and shaking her head. 'One thousand, two hundred and forty one, that's all. Call it a big cinema crowd. That's all it took. If only that small number of people in the whole country had voted the other way, there would have been a hung parliament.'

'Yes, hold on though,' Claire objected. 'That's twenty-twenty hindsight, knowing exactly which ones would be the most marginal results.'

Ann held up another sheet of paper. 'Of course. I'm just showing you that you don't need to change millions of votes to swing an election. All it took was point zero zero three five per cent of the voters. That's nothing.'

'What are you saying, that there was some kind of fiddle?'

'Well just suppose there was.'

'That kind of thing doesn't happen here.'

Ann snorted derisively. 'Oh no? Did you know that right through until the seventies, and who knows maybe into the eighties, if you voted for a Communist candidate, there was a good chance your name would go straight on to MI5's computer.'

'How could they know?' Claire objected. 'It's just a cross on a ballot paper. It's secret.'

'It is *not*,' said Ann in exasperation. 'When you go into your polling station, what happens?'

Claire thought. 'You give them your card and they find your name on the electoral register.'

'Yes, and then?'

'They give you a ballot paper.'

'Exactly, *and* they tear that ballot paper off a counterfoil, *and* both the paper and the counterfoil have a number on them, *and* they write your reference number from the electoral roll on the counterfoil.'

'Why?'

'In theory, so they can check up afterwards if there are any allegations of cheating. In practice, they just lock them all away, but there's one big exception.'

'The Communist votes?'

'You got it. After it was all over and the ballot papers were stored away, MI5 would go and sort through the Communist votes, then all they had to do was cross-reference the numbers.'

Claire was silent then, convinced by the bitterness in Ann's tone, and appalled by the sudden mysterious cheapening of an institution she had always taken for granted. Ann was watching her, waiting for her to say something when she looked up. 'All right then, if you know this, others must too. Why doesn't someone write about it?'

'People try from time to time. It doesn't get much attention. There's sort of a general feeling that maybe it was a good idea and, anyway, when the Soviet Union collapsed it probably all stopped.'

'Did it?'

'When did you last see a Communist candidate? On the other hand, who's to say that our broad-minded security service hasn't decided to target the Greens or some outfit like that.'

'Why would they do that?'

'The psychology of intelligence. You put your energy into fighting the biggest threat you know. There's no absolute scale. You're justifying your existence. If everything's ticking over peacefully and all the anarchists have turned into stockbrokers, you look for the extremists, and if all you can find is hunt saboteurs or people spraying graffiti on animal laboratories, then that's who you start zapping.'

Claire shook her head slowly. 'It's hard to take. Surely if there's one thing that's always been sacred in British politics it's democratic elections?'

'NO,' said Ann. 'No, no, no. Politics is crime by consent. You can never assume anything like that. People who are weird enough to want to spend their best years in seedy local committee rooms or shaking hands at garden parties aren't normal. It's not normal at all to lead that sort of life. Being in power is really addictive stuff. Fiddling a handful of marginal seats to stay in power isn't so unlikely.' She slapped a hand on the table. 'Just think of the consequences. Think of all the health service cuts, the privatizations, the whole greed culture, everything that's been justified, in the end, only by the idea that it's what most of Britain voted for. This would change everything.'

'OK. Just supposing someone did fiddle it, they'd stand a good chance of being found out.'

'No. The fact is the Tories lost fewer of the most marginal seats than the less marginal ones. Everyone just shrugged and said marginals are always quirky.'

'Well, where do all the ballot papers go?'

'Into a warehouse at Hayes for a year and a day, then up in smoke.'

'Literally?'

'Absolutely. They go to the North London Waste Authority plant where they're burnt to provide electricity for Tottenham.'

She gave Ann a lift to the tube but when they stopped outside the station, she thought of something.

'Just suppose they did stuff in some extra votes, why would they need to get rid of the ballot boxes?'

'I haven't any idea. It's such a pity we can't get our hands on those boxes. Give me those notes you made of the markings on the box. I'll check them out.'

Claire tore the page from her notebook and gave it to Ann, then she realized something else was bugging her.

'There's still the exit polls. The rest of the polls said Labour would win, but at the end of voting, the exit polls said it would be a hung parliament.'

'A hung parliament – not a Conservative victory.'

Further down, the screen said 'EXIT POLLS'. Hacker was bored by what he was reading – the end of an obscure contribution about swelling anti-monarchy sentiment in Britain to encourage a move towards Republicanism. The Director was clearly bored with it too. A peremptory order appeared, boxed and incontestable.

'DISCONTINUE,' it said. 'UNPROMISING INPUT TO PRESENT GAME. WE BELIEVE PARALLEL ACTION IS BEING TAKEN ELSEWHERE. SEE FOOTNOTE, ASPEN/071. FRESH LINE OF THOUGHT PLEASE.'

One came. 'PROBLEM,' said light blue cursive lettering. 'EXIT POLLS. IF EXIT POLLS CONTINUE TO GIVE UK LABOUR PARTY SUBSTANTIAL LEAD, ANYTHING WE DO IN MARGINAL SEATS WILL LOOK OBVIOUS.'

'NOT NECESSARILY,' replied pink lower case, 'MEDIA TAKES DELIGHT IN POLLSTERS' MISTAKES. THAT WILL BE NATURAL CONCLUSION. EXPLANATIONS WILL BE FOUND.'

Light blue came back: WITHIN LIMITS ONLY. LAND-
SLIDE LABOUR LEAD – SAY 8 PER CENT PLUS – IN
EXIT POLLS WOULD CAST SEVERE DOUBT ON CON-
SERVATIVE PARTY WIN.'

Pink objected, 'IT WILL BE ACCEPTED AT FACE VALUE.
JUSTIFICATION POST-FACTO IS SIMPLE. EXAMPLE:
PEOPLE TELL POLLSTERS THEY'RE UNSELFISH (WILL
VOTE FOR HIGHER PUBLIC SPENDING), BUT IN PRIV-
ACY OF VOTING BOOTH THEY'RE SELFISH (VOTE FOR
LOWER TAXES).'

Green italic chimed in. 'HISTORY IS ON OUR SIDE. POLLS
USUALLY CLOSE UP IN FINAL HOURS.'

Hacker had hardly touched the room-service meal. The
message at the start had promised him all the final instalments
of the game to date. The Director's box came back. 'DECI-
SION POINT. GAME MUST MOVE ON TO LOGISTICS. IS
OVERALL DIRECTION VIABLE? VOTE BY ALL PLAYERS
COMING UP.'

That seemed to be forcing the hands of the objectors, but
it was becoming clear that there was one way at least of
interrupting the Director. Two flashing words appeared
on the screen: 'COMPROMISE PROPOSAL'. Then after
them, in orange capitals, 'GAME CAN BE PREPARED IN
EXPECTATION OF LAST-MINUTE POLLS SHOWING
USUAL CONVERGENCE. GO-AHEAD OR ABORT CAN
BE DECIDED THEN.'

'ACCEPTED,' said light blue.

'ACCEPTED,' said pink.

Hacker pressed the return key. The Director's box filled the
top of the screen. 'LOGISTICS PLANNING, DIVISION OF
RESPONSIBILITIES,' it said, and there followed a long list.
He read on for an hour. On one level it was just glowing
letters; glowing letters on a screen. It was best to keep it like
that, an electronic game of words, just key strokes, nothing
more, simply an abstraction.

He got up and looked out of the hotel window at the Chicago
sunset. He wasn't a demonstrative man and there was no one
with whom he could share the day's success, but he wanted

to shout aloud with glee. A ripe plum had fallen into his lap, a commercial prize beyond price and, until Freedom's Friends came on the scene, beyond reach too. The Federal authorities weren't easy people to put one over, but his sleeve had been stuffed with aces. At eight that morning, his monitor had fed him the latest Federal internal memos briefing his opponents ahead of the meeting. At the lunch break, unexpectedly, a courier had arrived for him with a copy of the half-way résumé they were sending back to their masters, outlining the maximum concessions they were prepared to make. It had been hard to keep a straight face, reading it across the table from the very men who had despatched it with the strictest secrecy just minutes before. It was like shooting fish in a barrel.

He had sent a thank-you message to the Producer when it was all signed and sealed, and in exchange the Producer had sent him the rest of Game Ten. Why me? he thought, not for the first time. There were so many reasons why he wasn't an obvious choice. He looked down on the crawling dots of street life, closed the curtains on the real world and went back to the electronic game of God.

Game Ten had passed its final hurdle, the exhaustive check through the Tripod software for viability. Small problems had arisen and been dealt with. Control of manpower and logistics had been handed over to the Producer and soon the final button was pressed; three big words in block letters: 'CAMERA, LIGHTS, ACTION!'

But that wasn't the end. The next screen was headed 'CREDITS'. The Producer listed names of all those who had played a part. There were three categories. First came those of Freedom's Friends, listed by their pseudonyms, who had played a significant part in the execution of the game. Points were awarded in proportion to their contribution. Then came outsiders, regarded as controllable, with a list of the rewards or sanctions being used to secure their continuing silence. Then came a list simply headed 'EXTRAS'. There were fourteen names on that list.

The Producer's script then said: 'WE HOLD SHORT-TERM INFLUENCE THROUGH PAYMENTS. THESE KNOW

NOTHING OF THE PURPOSE OF THEIR ACTIONS WHICH WERE, IN ALL CASES, PERIPHERAL, BUT WE CANNOT GUARANTEE LONG-TERM SILENCE. MEMBERS MUST DECIDE WHETHER TO INITIATE STERILIZATION PRECAUTIONS. VOTE NOW. INPUT ONE FOR STERILIZATION, TWO FOR ZERO ACTION, ACCEPTING CONSEQUENT RISK.'

There followed a long list of ones, disembodied thumbs pointing down in this electronic Roman circus. Then, when Hacker was still wondering why Game Ten had not been closed up, another screen appeared and the date on that screen was recent, very recent. 'UNPREDICTED EVENTUALITY,' it began and, as he read, he suddenly knew just why *he* mattered, why the Producer had come specifically to him at Bohemian Grove, and for a moment anger and resentment flared, fanned by the sudden awareness that he'd been played like a fish from the start. But then he thought of the contract nestling in his case, the contract so unexpectedly signed that very afternoon, and he decided, as they had known he would, that whether or not he liked the tune, the piper had been well and truly paid.

# Chapter Nine

## Friday July 26th

Ann Farrow stopped outside the tube station and gave Peter the Poet his usual fifty pence. She waited, smiling while he recited the day's text. It was a verse of 'Daffodils' again, as it usually was when the sun was shining, but she didn't mind. This time though, as he sat back down on his pile of old blankets, surrounded by his carrier bags, she went on her way with a hard edge of purpose replacing the hopeless pity she usually felt at his plight and that of the other homeless people who increasingly thronged the London streets. A suspicion had been forming in her mind since Wednesday night, a suspicion which if it were provable, could change everything.

She was first in at the Institute, half an hour early, so she could do what she wanted in her own time. Sitting down at her desk, she took out the piece of paper on which Claire had written the scanty details from the ballot box's torn label. The letters 'DGE' on the top line, 'EN' on the second, and number '73' on the third. She reached for a guide to Parliamentary constituencies and got to work. By the time she reached the end of the book she had a list of sixteen constituencies with 'dge' in their name, and she had underlined the seven that had those letters right at the end. They were Beaconsbridge, Cambridge, Devon West and Torridge, Halesowen and Stourbridge, Teignbridge, Tyne Bridge, and Uxbridge. She then had to go to the Institute's library. Elections were its very lifeblood, and she soon found a box file of sheets listing the wards which made up each constituency. That narrowed it down to three which had wards ending in the letters 'en'. She didn't bother to look at the other two. The number seventy-three was shouting at her from the sheet of paper in front of her. Polling station seventy-three was in the Gribben ward of the constituency of Beaconsbridge.

Being sure was one thing, being certain was quite another, and she was suddenly very frightened at the implications. She picked up the phone and asked for Claire at National, but the voice which answered the phone said she was in a programme meeting.

The meeting was boring until Jane asked Claire for an update on the Paul Wade affair. Harry had simply ignored her, and Jane had looked moderately satisfied with the apparent truce. A little too early in the proceedings for Claire's comfort, before she had decided exactly what to say, Jane turned to her.

'Claire, we're all agog. Tell us what you got yesterday.'

'It's complicated. Jane, I'd like to talk to you afterwards.'

'Don't worry. We have no secrets from each other in this office. Everyone knows the importance of keeping it within these walls.'

Like it or not, she had to go ahead. 'One of Paul Wade's sources put me on to a particular car Paul had been tracking. It had already been through a scrapyard crusher. I got someone to straighten it out but when we went back to take pictures, he'd been beaten up and he denied all knowledge of it.' She decided not to mention the boxes. It already sounded too much like fantasy.

There was a silence in which everyone else seemed to be looking at Harry, who put on a little dumb-show of restrained amusement. Anger flashed up inside her.

'Whatever some may think,' she said with a hard edge in her voice, 'I wasn't imagining it. There's something here that needs a bit more investigation.'

'Of course, of course,' Harry said in an infuriatingly reasonable voice, and one of the producers giggled.

Jane stepped in. 'That's extraordinary. Have you any more ideas?' Claire shook her head. 'OK,' Jane went on. 'Well I think we need to find you something else to do in that case. We'll talk about it later.'

Back in Claire's little cubicle, a sticky yellow square of message had been slapped, slightly askew, on the monitor screen of her terminal. 'Someone rang from America. Will call back at noon. Didn't get the name.' It wasn't signed.

Helpful, she thought, not to say typical of the secretarial quality National seemed to have attracted; then she did a quick sum in her head and puzzled over it. Noon was 7a.m. on the Eastern seaboard. Whoever it was must have rung the first time at 6.30a.m. local time. Someone was going to a lot of trouble to talk to her. She looked at her watch. Twenty-five minutes to twelve. She flicked on the computer screen and it came alive with another message for her from the internal system. It simply said 'Progress?', and it was from Desmond Gilligan. She began to compose an answer in the terse language of computer mail. 'I found a crushed car Wade was looking for. Proved to contain ballot boxes. Car and boxes were then removed by unknown party. The editor thinks we should leave it there. I don't. Might need your support.' It sounded melodramatic. She sent it anyway.

The next message was from Jane, addressed to both CM and HC. It said, 'Remember what I said. Not impressed by first products of cease-fire.'

The phone buzzed just before twelve o'clock and she picked it up, wondering whether it might be her unknown American caller.

'Claire? It's Ann.'

'Hello. I thought you might be someone else.'

'Well, I'm not. Are you OK to talk?'

'Yes, course.'

'Can anyone else hear? You're not on a speaker or anything are you?'

'No,' she said, stiffening a little. 'It's just me.'

'Those letters. On the box.'

'You've got something?'

'Looks like it. Claire . . .' Her voice sounded faint, out of range of the mouthpiece, then came back stronger. 'Sorry. Someone's here. I think I'd better save this. What time are you going to be home this evening?'

'It's the show tonight.'

'Damn, I forgot.'

'Want to come in and see it? We can talk beforehand.'

'Oh, well . . . Why not? OK.'

Claire gave her directions and put the phone down. It rang again almost immediately and she could tell before anyone said a word from the sudden degraded hissing on the line that it was her American caller. 'Claire Merrick.'

'Hello Claire,' said a voice she had no wish to hear. 'It's Jerome.'

There was a silence. 'What makes you think I want to talk to you?' she said steadily. 'Anyway, how the hell did you find out I was here?'

'No secret, honey,' he said, 'saw you on that show with the rubber man last . . .'

'Don't "honey" me, shithead,' she snapped and, seeing heads lifting around the room, she knew she'd spoken too loudly. From the way the eyes all switched away from her to the next cubicle, and the way two of the secretaries began to giggle, she guessed Harry was doing a comedy routine at her expense.

'OK, OK,' said Jerome in his best, soft, persuasive Bostonian tone, 'just trying to help.'

'Help how?'

'I had to call my old pal Murray,' he said, and suddenly she was listening hard.

'Yes?'

'He said you'd been round.'

'Well?'

'C'mon, give me a break, I'm only trying to help.'

'Try harder then. How did you come to be calling your "old pal"? I thought he was just a man we used to meet on the boat.'

'No, no. He's fixing a car for me while I'm away. That was why I called him, but he gave me some tale about straightening out some junker for you. Is that right?'

'Perhaps.'

'Said he had a truckload of trouble fall on him after you went and maybe you got the wrong idea. Want to tell me what it's all about?'

'No, I don't.'

'I was just calling to kind of warn you. That guy Murray has some strange friends. He said they thumped him around a bit because he was late on some loan repayments. They took away some of his gear with them. He's worried you're gonna make a big mystery out of it and bring the cameras back, then he'll just get thumped some more. That's all. Just thought I'd better tell you.'

'Why couldn't he tell me himself?'

'Yeah, well, masculine pride. He's the macho type. Maybe he would have done, but I said I'd call you anyway. Why don't you tell me about it and I'll find out what you want to know?'

'I can manage, thanks.'

He paused for a moment. 'I hear you've found your true lifestyle at last.'

'What do you mean by that?'

'I heard you'd moved in with a dyke.'

'I'm staying with a friend, that's all. Whether she's gay, straight or a fucking stamp collector is nothing to do with it or with you, got that?'

Maddeningly, he was laughing. 'Come on. I just wanted to know how things were with you.'

'Well, all I want to know is that you're having a really shitty time, Jerome. I hope you rot.' She slammed the receiver down and every pair of eyes in the office looked away from her as she swept the room with a challenging stare.

The show was about to start when Ann was shown into the gallery with a pressing purpose in her mind and a sheet of paper dynamite in her pocket. So completely was Claire a creature of television that it didn't occur to her for a moment that Ann might have an agenda of her own. National TV might have looked like a spare parts warehouse from the outside, but in the dark techno-buzz of the gallery, Claire could have been in any studio, and a live programme commands total attention from those with the addiction, regardless of its ancestry.

Standing at the back, with nothing to do until the second half of the programme, Claire beckoned Ann, who crept clumsily along the narrow gap behind the row of seats, bumping into some of them in the gloom.

'Hello,' she said, 'I've got an incredible . . .'

'Quiet in the gallery,' called the director who, flanked by his vision-mixer and all the other electronic acolytes, was in a state of murderously-controlled panic. 'Soon as you can please, studio. I need you all in place. We must have a go at the opening again.'

They'd tried twice, with a hitch each time, and there was only five minutes left to showtime. The director dipped his head, eyes still on the monitor bank in front of him, and spoke into the mike that snaked out of the desk on a flexible stalk.

'That shot just doesn't work, Peter. We'll have to come in over the top. Lose the man on the left. Spread them out along the table to make a gap.' The floor manager scuttled into view on one of the monitors to tell one of the policemen that, for the sake of art, he was surplus to requirements, and ushered him off the set.

'Russell. Left just a teeny bit. OK. Stand by VT 'A'. Stand by for the lighting change. VTs running. This the final rehearsal.'

This time it more or less worked. The girl to the director's left called out, 'Three minutes to air. Three minutes to air.'

There were one or two surreptitious glances at Ann, and Claire realised that those who'd overheard Jerome's phone call hadn't been slow to spread stories about her sexual proclivities. She didn't care. Harry was on the monitor, the camera zooming in and out. He was looking down, unaware he was being observed, looking natural, almost childlike. She pushed the thought away and glanced at Ann who didn't look at all impressed by the tension building in the gallery towards the climax of going on air.

'One minute,' said the programme assistant. The director ran through a readiness check with all the video tape operators in their remote lairs, getting a loud buzz back from each in confirmation. The monitors were suddenly the only reality and, in the usual manner of studios before presenters uncurl into their final positions and launch themselves, surfing on the wave of the autocue, nothing looked quite ready.

The girl finished a countdown from ten to zero. '. . . three, two, one. We're on the air. The director launched into a rapid-fire series of commands using his voice as a conductor's baton, pacing each micro-second.

'Stand by lighting change. Four, zoom on Russell. Twenty seconds music left; count me out. Lighting change *now*. Dip sound, mix and cue Russell. Run 'A'. Zoom to full face. Stand by Harry with voice-over. Stand by VT 'B' and mix, run VT 'B'. Stand by Russell and cue Russell. Camera Two and Harry back to first position . . .'

Two minutes in, they launched into the first taped report and in the six minutes of leeway this provided, the Gallery relaxed marginally. Ann leaned towards Claire and whispered, 'Do you have to stay here or can we talk somewhere.'

Claire looked at the studio clock. It was fifteen minutes before she had to be on the set. Her make-up was done. She led the way and Ann followed her quietly out of the gallery and into the corridor behind.

'What's the rush?' Claire asked.

Ann delved into her pocket. 'Look at this list,' she said. 'It's the seats the Conservatives just held. I took a three-thousand vote majority as the cut-off.'

She passed the sheet across and Claire scanned it quickly. It showed thirty-five seats where the Conservatives had narrowly beaten Labour.

'Those letters on the label you saw,' said Ann.

'Yes?'

'It was 'DGE' on the top line, then 'EN' below it and a number, '73'.'

'That's right.'

'You said it was the right hand side, with the left side of the label torn off?'

Claire screwed up her eyes and brought back the mental picture of the box. 'Yes.'

Ann nodded. 'OK,' she said. 'I tracked it down. It's a ward of a constituency north of Birmingham, Beaconsbridge.'

Claire looked down at the first sheet. 'That's on this list of marginals.'

Ann looked at her soberly. 'You've got it. Beaconsbridge has a ward called Gribben, which gives you the 'en', and the polling station number for Gribben Ward is seventy-three.'

Ten minutes later Claire was still thinking about it, standing in front of the camera when the floor manager cued her, and she stumbled over the opening line. It was someone else's story, she was just the face and the voice, but it was a nasty tale of rape, and someone had decided it would sound better coming from a woman.

'Jacqueline Bradst . . . er, Bradfield was driving home from work on the twenty-ninth of June,' she began reading from the prompter. 'She had stayed at the office later than usual to finish preparing for a presentation she had to give the following day. Her car was in the usual place in the underground car park . . .' Annoyingly, the autocue operator wasn't quite keeping up. She was having to read off the bottom line all the time just as it came into view. '. . . And she drove off, looking forward to an evening with her boyfriend; but when she'd gone no more than a quarter of a mile, she heard a sound from the back seat . . .' In her ear-piece, she heard the gallery counting down towards the video tape cue, and slowed her delivery slightly to hit the zero perfectly. '. . . And before she could even look round, a man's voice told her he had a knife.'

The camera's red light blinked off, her image disappeared from the monitor and in its place came the taped reconstruction on which her voice track had been recorded earlier. It ran for only two minutes, then the voice in her ear-piece said, 'Coming back to you, Claire, in ten. Tighter please Camera Two,' and the floor manager crouching beside the camera gave her a silent countdown with his fingers until the red light came on again.

'Do you recognize this photofit picture?' she said. 'Did someone *you* know come back that night with blood on their clothing, smelling strongly of petrol? Have you seen, or lost, a pocket-knife that fits the description and, above all, did you see Jacqueline's car between ten o'clock that night and the following Monday, when it was recovered by police from a car park in Wimbledon? If so, our lines are open now and remember, if you're our Crookbuster of the night, you could win our huge cash reward.'

She came off the set again, knowing it wasn't the sort of television she'd ever expected or wanted to do, and found Ann where she'd left her, watching the show through one of the gaps in the back-drops. They watched the next live section, then when the next tape started they went out of the studio together.

Russell Mackay had nothing immediate to do. The anchor-man took a quick look at the short summary of the best incoming calls on the desk monitor, then wandered over to where Harry stood waiting for his next piece. Mackay nodded after Claire. 'Didn't think much of that opening, did you? I thought she was meant to be a pro.'

Harry shook his head, wondering what the two women were talking about so urgently. 'Fluffed a bit, didn't she?'

Mackay gave a coarse laugh. 'I suppose having her girlfriend here put her off. Waste of a cute pussy, I call it. Difficult to imagine a girl that looks that way with that crop-haired bull dyke.'

'Very,' Harry said.

Back in the corridor, Claire was objecting. 'We don't know, do we? Maybe they sold off old boxes for scrap. It could be quite legit.'

'We *do* know,' Ann said defiantly. 'I'm not dumb. The first thing I did was ring the returning officer there. I told him I was selling a new line in ballot boxes and we might be prepared to provide them on free trial. He said they didn't need any, so I asked him when he last changed them. He said they hadn't bought any for at least ten years and he thought they'd certainly do for another ten.'

# Chapter Ten

## Tuesday July 30th

A lot of little things contributed to Claire's unease: there wasn't a tape in the car that she hadn't heard a thousand times; 'Gardener's Question Time' was on the radio and she was not – nor ever had she been – a gardener; the traffic was as bad as ever on the M1, and the occasional drizzle had forced her to leave the roof up which gave her a feeling of mild claustrophobia. Most of all, she knew that with every mile she drove further from London, and every minute that she wasn't putting in time at the office, there was a price to be paid. She'd seen that in the hardening line of Jane's jaw when she'd reluctantly produced her trump card.

'I've got Gilligan's backing for this, Jane. He wants me to go ahead.'

'He's the owner, Claire, but I'm the editor. He doesn't have to run this show. Anyway, you haven't even explained why you're going.'

So she'd told her about the boxes, and won herself a tiny bit of reluctant latitude.

'You know very well we're under-staffed, Claire. I need you for at least one big report a week otherwise the programme doesn't get filled. It's no good doing all this unless it gets some sort of result we can put on the air.'

'Jane, just supposing we could do a story that showed there had been interference, criminal interference, with the results of the last general election?'

But Jane's mind ran on the minutiae of robberies, rapes and murders, and she couldn't see it happening. 'That's something else, Claire. That's a big documentary with lots of resources for the networks. It's not National, is it?'

'Why the hell not?'

That had been the day before. Now it was Tuesday and the returning officer's secretary had made her an appointment for eleven. She groped her way through the north Birmingham hinterland to Beaconsbridge with time enough in hand to buy a pallid sandwich in a plastic triangular shell, which the sandwich seemed as reluctant to leave as a hermit crab, emerging as disconnected slices and leaving much of its damp, industrial mayonnaise filling behind in the angle of the plastic. The High Street was a pedestrian precinct full of the usual chain-store shop-fronts. There was nothing interesting or local to be seen anywhere in sight.

The Council offices were in a dreary, sixties block with litter-strewn lawns around and tatty blue and white signs identifying each department. A Gorgon in a twin-set made her wait for ten minutes on a hard chair in a room with only a NALGO poster and a pamphlet on head lice to help pass the time. The Gorgon returned.

'Mr Dickey's in a meeting,' she said. 'Scheduled urgently. I'm afraid, with a man in his position you have to expect that sort of thing. It'll be a while. Perhaps you could come back tomorrow?'

'I've driven up from London, I'm afraid,' replied Claire. 'I'll wait.'

'I don't think waiting will do you much good, dear. He's got Ways and Means after that, then Finance B Committee. He's in demand, is Mr Dickey.'

'Yes, I'm quite busy too,' said Claire. 'I did make an appointment before I came.'

'I know you did,' said the woman in an affronted voice. 'It was me you made it with, but you just can't expect things like that to be written in stone, you know.'

'Well, I'll stay all the same. Perhaps you could tell him I only need ten minutes of his time.'

The Gorgon went away muttering, and was back in a very

short time. 'You're in luck,' she said. 'Mr Dickey can't see you, but his assistant, Mr Sheard, can give you a few minutes.' Her expression told Claire she thought this was most generous and entirely unnecessary. Mr Sheard was in a small office that looked like an ante-room. A door stood slightly open beyond his desk. He was young, gangly and awkward, knocking a file on the floor as he stood up from his desk, and unsure whether to shake her hand or simply wave her to a chair. He did something in between the two.

'Miss Merrick,' he said, 'nice to see you. What brings you here?'

She gave him a big smile. Recognition was on her side. National might still be a relative backwater, but her days in mainstream TV weren't so long ago. 'Just a bit of research,' she said. 'I'm doing a story about election procedures.'

He looked politely puzzled. 'How can we help?' he asked.

She got out her notebook. 'For a start, how do you seal your ballot boxes when voting's finished?'

'You mean general elections or council elections?'

'Is there a difference?'

'Well, not now, but there was. We've switched over. Last general election we still used the old sealing wax method. Now we're on one-time plastic seals, tamper-proof.'

'Meaning the old way wasn't?'

He laughed nervously. 'No, just that we have to move with the times.'

'What about security? How do you get the boxes from the polling stations to the count?'

'No mystery about that. We have a couple of vans that go round and pick them up. Why?'

She hid behind vagueness. 'I'm sorry, I don't really know. I've just been given a list of questions by my researcher. So no one goes with them?'

'I'm not sure,' he said. 'I think the person in charge of the first polling station on the route goes along in the van to show the driver where to go. I heard someone saying that in the old days, up until the eighties, a policeman used to escort the boxes to the count.' He laughed. 'They haven't got the manpower to do that sort of thing these days. I can just imagine it.'

'How do you identify your ballot boxes?'

'Paper label,' he said. 'Stuck on.'

'What would it say?'

'Oh, it would say Beaconsbridge, then the ward name, then the number of the polling station.'

'Could I see one?'

'Well, I suppose so.' He got up and rooted around in a cupboard, coming back with a square label. She looked at it and felt a giant shout of certainty inside her head. It was the twin of the one whose remains had been on the crushed box.

'I couldn't see the boxes themselves, could I?'

He looked at his watch. 'Well, I don't know.' Then he thought of himself showing Claire Merrick – *the* Claire Merrick – round the basement. Just the two of them. The story it would make in the pub. He shrugged. 'Yes, I don't see why not. They're locked up downstairs.' He ushered her out.

Half-way down the corridor there was a call from behind. 'Mr Sheard, just a moment.'

The Gorgon was standing in the doorway.

'I'm sorry. Won't be a sec,' Sheard said, and walked back. He soon returned, looking a little hang-dog.

'I'm so sorry. Mrs Barker says we need permission to do that. It would have to go through the press office.'

'Oh. Well, could we give them a call?'

He looked back at Mrs Barker. 'There's no one there today.'

Later, when Claire had gone, he went back into his office.

'Robert,' called an older man's voice from the inner office through the open door, 'Can you come in a minute?'

'Yes, Mr Dickey,' he said.

The journey back to London passed faster than the journey up, because Claire's brain was awhirl with all the possibilities. The label swung it. The label and the appearance of Mrs Barker. Mrs Barker hadn't been in hearing range of their conversation. Only someone in the inner office could have known where they were going – someone who had pretended not to be there and put his junior on to the job of dealing with Claire. Someone who hadn't liked what he'd heard.

She was back by three and filed a tight summary on the computer for Gilligan's benefit, phrasing it obliquely.

She left the office at seven. The Golf was as far away from the building as it could be. That was the price of not getting to the office first thing. It was parked on the verge of the car park exit, two wheels up on the grass. When she got in, the windows were misted up so she began wiping the inside of the windscreen clean. She started the engine to finish off the demisting and as she did, a man's voice hissed in her ear.

'Don't look behind you,' it said. 'Drive slowly out of the car park and do exactly what I say, otherwise I will have to hurt you.'

Her skin went ice-cold and she reached stealthily for the door handle, but a blade cut a tiny sharp pain across the back of her neck and she jerked her hand back. Then she thought of the story she'd done on Jacqueline Bradfield, and she thought of all she had ever heard about copy-cat crimes, and an involuntary shiver ran through her.

'Drive off. NOW,' the voice commanded.

# Chapter Eleven

The shot sent a small mess of blood and hair tumbling over and over on to the road. The other gate guard, checking them in, grinned as Hacker jumped.

'Don't pay no mind to Juan, he's just working on his reflexes.'

Hacker looked past him at the remains of the far-off rabbit, wondering whether it was intended as a little reminder that the guns were real. This time, it had been an ordinary car with windows he could see through and there was no longer any mystery about where Freedom's Friends' cowboy town was located: an hour and a half out of Los Angeles towards China Lake. That confirmed he was all the way in, and it was far too late to argue about the particular rules by which they played their game, especially as he'd already started to share fully from the benefits.

There was no one downstairs in the saloon, but the Producer hailed him from the landing and he climbed the stairs. Before they went in, he looked at the other door.

'What's in there?'

'Trophy room.'

'What kind of trophies?'

'Just memorials to past successes.'

'Can I see it?'

'Soon, soon.'

The room they entered was full of people and Hacker registered with surprise that this had to be a big occasion for Freedom's Friends to gather physically in such strength.

The Producer spoke to him quietly. 'All but six here, and they're on line. Special dispensation for pressing business.'

Three men sat in a row at the end table. 'The Directors,' he said. 'Take a seat. There's some business we have to get through first.'

Hacker looked around him. Half way up the room he saw Martin Blunden, bent busily over a screen, then he registered some of the other faces and it took all his control to stop an involuntary exclamation of amazement. He was in high company.

The Producer took him to a vacant seat and switched on the monitor in front of him. The man at the next table turned and gave him a hard stare, followed by a short nod. He knew him at once: Hugh Douglas, the British former cabinet minister who had walked out of the Government in the aftermath of the Iraqi arms enquiry, just before he was fired. Extremely wealthy, now on the board of some very serious weapons' makers, Douglas looked away as the Producer walked to the Directors' table and held up a hand. The quiet buzz of conversation stopped immediately.

'Friends,' the producer said, 'you all know that Gregory Peck died last month. Last week, we played his memorial game for the benefit of his associates and his family. I am pleased to be able to tell you that Tripod has given the game approval for viability and as of today I am charged to start shooting it, with Henry Hathaway as Director. But the Friends move on. You will know that we decided to invite a new player into our circle. Most of you have not yet met him. Friends, Gregory Peck is dead, long live Gregory Peck,' and he waved a hand towards Hacker, who stood and acknowledged a round of applause.

The lights dimmed, curtains slid apart at the end of the room to reveal a screen, and Spencer Tracy's sonorous twang swept the room from the speakers. 'Those who struck it rich wanted all the pleasures money could buy . . .' The riverboat gambler scene, with the song in the background, 'Come, come, there's a wondrous land, where I'll build you a home in the meadow'. They watched Peck meeting up with his girl again. 'Lily, how'd you like to hook up with a no-good gambler?' Then as a finale,

Peck in close up, but it wasn't Peck any more. Some electronic wizardry had put Hacker's own face on Peck's body up there on the screen.

There was another burst of applause and the lights came up. The Producer stood up again. 'Gentlemen, tonight we must set in train the final stage of Game Ten, which recently suffered unforeseen intervention. With particular help from two members we have it back under control. On your screens you will see the scenario we have devised which is currently shooting. We request your input for the concluding stage. First, I would like to present a brief summing-up of the motivations and weaknesses of the present target of the game, Miss Claire Merrick.'

Claire was terrified, so scared that her pants and the seat were wet with an involuntary release of urine. She'd lived for years with the theoretical danger of random bullets and bombs, but the sharp reality of the blade and the trickle of blood down the back of her neck got through all her defences.

'You don't have to do that,' she said in a shaky voice. 'I'll do whatever you want. You can put the knife away.'

She thought furiously of all the advice she had ever heard about dealing with rapists. Be submissive, or was it don't be too submissive? They need the thrill of overcoming you. Was that it?

The voice said, 'Turn right.'

It wasn't the sort of voice she expected. More cultured? There was something deliberately obscured in it. How the bloody hell had he got into the car? That was the trouble with a convertible. The hood was old and a bit loose. Cars surrounded her on all sides. She prayed for one of them to notice something but the Golf's hood was like a black cavern, surrounding the back seat with impenetrable gloom.

'Second left.'

She deliberately braked too hard before she turned, hoping the car behind would hit her, but the driver's reactions were too good and all that happened was that tyres screeched and a horn blared at her. She was in a narrow, bumpy lane.

'Careful,' said the man reprovingly. 'Not clever. Now turn right through the gates and into the shed.'

It looked like a builder's yard. She could see no one around. It occurred to her that this was very well planned.

'Stop here,' said the man. 'Now stay exactly where you are while I get out. Push the back of the other seat forward and open the passenger door.'

The Golf was a two-door car, and getting out of the back would be awkward for him. She did what he said and then, in the instant when he was bent double and climbing with difficulty out of the passenger door, she opened her own door and tried to make a break for it. Instantly she realised her belt was done up. Her fingers scrabbled for the catch as his own hands made a grab for her. Then she was out, slipping on the ground for a crucial moment and then racing for the gate. He was too quick for her, cutting her off and turning with legs splayed wide and arms out to each side, bobbing and jinking like a goalkeeper. He wore a green combat jacket and a black Balaclava with only his eyes and mouth showing, and he held a knife in one hand.

She turned and ran the other way, down the side of the sheds, the cut on her neck stinging and driving her on. It was a narrow alley and at the end it opened into a yard, piled with bricks. All around was high wire netting. The double doors to the shed were padlocked. She picked up a brick and turned to face the man who was walking calmly after her. He put the knife in his pocket and came nearer, wary. She waited for her moment, panting hard, and swung the brick at his head, but she found herself caught fast in an unexpected grip and swung off-balance through the air to land, cushioned by his arm, on the ground with his whole weight on top of her.

She stared into his eyes, three inches from hers. He was wiry, twenty-five to thirty, she thought.

'I told you,' she gasped, 'do what the hell you like with me. There's no need for all this.'

He shook his head. 'Don't think I don't appreciate it, but you've got the wrong idea.'

His weight on top of her receded, and he let her up, holding on to her arm in a painful grip behind her back. He pushed her ahead of him back down the alley and in through a door in the front of the shed. They were in a small office.

'Sit down there,' he said, and she slumped into a chair, wondering.

He locked the door and sat opposite her. There was an envelope already on the table. 'I've brought you here to tell you a story,' he said. 'I just had to be sure you would listen.'

'Jesus Christ,' she said, not believing him. 'You could have just asked me to meet you . . .'

'Just shut up, or I might change my mind,' he said, and she knew she was right. There was a definite touch of Oxbridge to that voice. 'You have no idea what a risk I'm taking. I do it my way. I control the timing, the place, the whole thing. One peep out of you, one tiny little mention to a friend, and the whole sky could fall on my head.'

He's one of those public school SAS types, she thought, doing the dirty bits for MI5. This is what he regards as a normal way to stage a meeting.

'You've been doing some funny things,' he said. 'The scrapyard? Then your trip this morning?'

She felt the wind taken out of her and could only stare.

He shook his head. 'You don't know what you're getting into, I tell you.'

'Who are you?'

'You should be able to work that out. Someone with access to a lot of information about you.'

'A spook? MI5? MI6?'

'Your words, not mine. Now just button your lip. I don't have very much time.' He sat, as though considering where to start. 'You were in Libya. You know quite a lot about Lockerbie.'

It was the last thing she had expected to hear, and it brought with it a lot of unwelcome baggage. She stared at him, mind racing back, afraid of what might be coming next. '*Lockerbie?* All this is to do with Lockerbie?'

'Do I understand correctly? You do know the real story?'

She was getting her breath back, getting to grips with this surreal scene, images bursting unbidden into her head. The flaming crater in the little Scottish town; the collapsed cabin section of the Pan-Am Jumbo lying on its side in a field; and the explosion of an AK47 next to her head in the Libyan desert. 'I know what I think is the real story.'

'Tell me. Just so I know I'm not wasting my time.'

So she told him, and at the end he nodded as if she had passed a test. 'Close enough.'

Now the fright was going and the adrenaline had drained she felt tired and increasingly angry. 'Surely you didn't put me through all this shit for the sake of a history lesson.'

'No.' He pushed his chair back and looked at her hard through the Balaclava's eyeholes. 'You have to understand. In my organisation there are some of us who hold, let's say, unconventional views.'

'In MI5, you mean?'

'Whatever. I was one of the token liberals they signed up in the seventies. Moving with the times, it was called. Not a good idea, at least from their point of view. They had some slip-ups. Whistle blowers, people that changed sides.'

'So, you're the odd man out?' she asked sourly.

'Well, it swung back the other way. They went back to recruiting a whole load of ex-army, ex-navy types; older, right-wingers to a man. Anyway, its highly compartmentalized, my organisation. Bits do things that other bits never hear anything about.'

She nodded impatiently and he went on. 'I was given a new brief. It included checking up on you. That's given me access to some things I didn't know about before and I don't much like them, so I decided to tell you.'

'What?'

'I can only point you in the right direction. Should you ever claim this meeting happened, I have an absolutely unbreakable chain of witnesses who will swear I spent all day somewhere a hundred miles away from here. Got it?'

She nodded again, her blood quickening.

He looked at her, but with only his eyes to go on she couldn't read his expression. 'You're on the right lines. The poll was rigged. Just enough to give it a good prod. It happened in twenty constituencies. In all twenty, there were just a few polling clerks in a few polling stations who agreed to let it be done.'

Avid to understand, she leant forward. 'But why? What's that got to do with Lockerbie?'

'You haven't understood what I've been saying. Think back. The '92 general election was months *before* the US presidential election. Bush had a disaster plan, a military strike against Libya for popularity. Major knew all about it. He was probably hoping it would take place from British airfields before his own election. After all, Maggie had showed how a bit of well-placed blood-thirstiness can help stroke the polls along with the Falklands. Imagine what it would have meant if Kinnock had won. He would have found out in no time what had been going on, wouldn't he? As soon as he got his hands on the files he would have blown the whistle on the whole damned thing. They couldn't have that.'

She sat back and let the immensity of it wash over her, then practicality intervened. 'It's a hell of a story,' she said. 'How on earth do I prove it?'

'It had to be deniable. It was coordinated by a foreigner. Someone who needed our protection, someone who would help muddy the trail if anything went wrong. In that envelope are photocopies of the bank statements of all the polling clerks who cooperated. You will see that in each case there is a payment in to their accounts of £50,000 on the same day, the day after polling day. There is also a photo of the man who coordinated it. I think you'll know him.'

She opened the envelope and slid out a glossy 6″ by 4″ photograph of a fat man with a double chin and a ragged little moustache. He smelt of camphor, which he was for ever rubbing on his chest. The photo didn't tell her that. Her memory did; a memory from a dark night, deep in the desert, when he threatened her life and destroyed her career.

# Chapter Twelve

Claire's captor disappeared almost as abruptly as he had arrived, telling her to wait five minutes before going back to her car. She hadn't the strength left to do anything but obey, but when she went back outside to the Golf some deep sense of unease made her go through a Belfast check procedure on it, crouching to peer underneath, looking in the wheel arches, inside the bonnet and the boot, and finally going right through the interior. There was nothing and she felt a little embarrassed at her paranoia.

She drove out of the yard but her hands started shaking. Ann was away, there was no comfort to be had at home. She was passing a park so she pulled over and walked to a bench, all by itself in the long grass, and there she let her mind roam back. Tripoli, and the mad politics of Middle East reprisals, in the baking heat. It started with a twitchy finger on a US Navy missile-firing button and the fireball that destroyed an Iranian Airbus full of passengers over the Gulf. The Iranians had planned a pay-back. An eye for an eye, a plane for a plane; but Iranian politics weren't simple. Some quite reasonable people were getting back into power. The madder Mullahs couldn't have things all their own way. It had to be deniable, so in the end they gave the contract to some Syrians to make sure they could distance themselves. That didn't work either.

The Syrian government was trying to build bridges to the Americans so it got passed on again, this time to a Libyan spook. He was freelancing. Gaddafi hadn't known. Then, afterwards, when the CIA and the FBI put everything they had into the investigation, they finally arrested two Libyan's who, if they were guilty of anything, were at worst bag-men who'd carried the Semtex that went in the cassette-radio. Juniors, but juniors who pointed the finger at Libya if you didn't know better.

Everyone in the business knew it wasn't really a Libyan plot. MI5, the CIA, Mossad for sure, but the Gulf War got in the way of politics, that and the US presidential election. The war changed everything round. Iran and Syria were the West's allies, heroes through and through. It was too confusing to tell the American public that these new allies were responsible for one of the biggest terrorist outrages against Uncle Sam in human history. Bush needed someone to blame and the evidence against Libya helped. He had a disaster scenario up his sleeve. If he looked like losing the '92 presidential election, he could zap Gaddafi all over again, just like April '86, and send his popularity shooting back up the scale. The only reason it didn't happen was that the Pentagon laid the risks on thick, and the Saudis were against it.

She thought about what she'd just been told. It was all on the boil right up to the British general election. Bush still had his own election to come then. He needed Britain on his side in case he pressed the button, and that meant the Conservatives had to win. Bush believed he wouldn't get the cooperation for his violent charade from Kinnock.

She took out the contents of the envelope. She held up the photo of the fat man but then, despite herself, despite the Englishness of the park, the far-off shouts of children and the buzz of a mower, the smell of camphor flooded out from her memory, up her nose and into her head, infecting her with direct and present pain. Ibn Azogi. When they'd collided he'd been working for Gaddafi, but the Americans must have recognized the qualities they needed in him.

Ibn Azogi.

Libya. Everything green and white. Blinding sun and the stylized pictures of Gaddafi in his shades. The signs of surprising wealth everywhere, mixed with the stench of rotting rubbish piles decaying amongst the building sites. She'd been there like the rest of them, waiting for the American deadline to run out, waiting for the air strike, packing the El Khabir hotel. The wires were humming with the growing threat from Washington. It was a funny business this, hoping for a story, hoping to be within camera-range if the US jets suddenly returned in the night, hoping to be just so close and no closer, two hundred yards, maybe, from a rocket strike, but not part of the smoking, stinking mess in the bottom of the crater.

Moving slowly through the hotel lobby for the first time, she had tried to read in the seasoned faces around her confirmation of her innermost, fluttering fear that all these people knew so much more; had so many good contacts where she had so few. That man from the *Observer*, going out of the door, must certainly be heading for the exclusive private briefing which would set the phones alight from London with aggrieved complaints that she'd been shown up, lagging badly behind the pack. She didn't know, but they all felt it, at least all the ones that were any good. The only thing that time, experience and self-knowledge gave them was the ability to tuck that fear away in a safe, hidden place where it didn't get in the way.

For all that – after four days of frustration, drinking lurid, reconstituted orange juice, swapping stale stories with her crew and wandering the streets dominated by the ever-present multiple images of the Colonel – it was Claire who seemed suddenly to have hit the bullseye. A large envelope of grey, coarse paper had been pushed under her door. This wasn't one of the hotel's little white squares which so often contained vague approximations of incoming messages from London. It contained a piece of slightly discoloured, deckle-edged card, as if it were a cheap wedding invitation. Printed on it in laborious capitals it said, 'Miss Merrick is commanded please to attend at the door of her hotel at 5p.m. for transportation to her briefing. This is directed to her person only and should be secretly maintained.' It was signed with initials only, followed by the inscription, 'In the name of our brother Colonel and the mass democratic movement of the Libyan Arab Jamahiriya.'

Something had bothered her and her first instinct was to call the office, but as her hand strayed to the phone, caution changed her mind. Anyone might be listening. It could be that she had this to herself. The wording, such as it was, seemed to indicate that. Maybe even the Colonel himself, who knows? There'd be time to tell them when there was something to tell.

She walked down the corridor and knocked on Brian's door. Her cameraman shouted 'Enter!' He was lying on the bed, reading *Middlemarch*. Brian was a reserved, academic man, well outside the normal run of tough extroverts that made up the ranks of cameramen. He knew as much of the background to most stories as she did, and often corrected her grammar, in the mildest way, when recording pieces to camera.

He looked at her over his book, reading her body language correctly, knowing immediately this was no summons to action.

'You want me?'

'Only to say . . .' To say what? That she had a non-specific invitation to a car-ride? 'I'm going to be out for a while.'

'For how long?'

'Not sure. A couple of hours maybe.'

'What about the death watch?' They had been spending the evenings and part of each night on the balcony of her room, staring out to sea for the first signs of any triple-A barrage against incoming US jets.

'I should be back by seven. You'd better start without me.'

'Where are you if anyone asks?'

She could have told him. She trusted him completely. She could have, but she didn't, not wanting to prejudice by too much anticipation the unknown potential in whatever was to come. That small decision helped project her headlong down a road along which she had no wish to travel. 'Just be vague,' she said.

The car that picked her up was a small Eastern-bloc attempt at an old Fiat. She was disappointed. She noticed that her departure was marked by the small group of hacks still in the lobby. If it had only been one of the official green Chevrolets, word would have spread straight away that Claire Merrick had been picked up by the Colonel's boys.

The driver wore dark glasses, though the sun was diminishing, and a black, plastic-looking jacket. 'Merrick?' was all he said.

'Yes.'

He indicated the back door and she got in to the narrow back seat, its brittle covering split and outward-curling.

'Where are we going?'

He shook his head.

She tried it in French, then in Italian. The response was the same, so she gave up, sat back and watched. She had expected a short trip across town to some sort of government building but instead, and to her growing unease, they rattled out of Tripoli on one of the great highways that oil money had built into the desert. The coastal sprawl gave way to sporadic villages, then to nothing: scrub, dunes and a dull, heavy horizon of brown shading to grey in the advancing evening.

The journey went on and on and Claire's anxiety grew greater as half an hour became an hour, then an hour and a half. She had kept trying to get the driver to say something – anything – but he wouldn't. She looked back through the window in the direction of Tripoli, half-expecting to see flashes in the sky, signs of the attack, of the story she might well be missing.

It was three hours and a refuelling stop before the drone of the engine altered, the driver slowing, changing jerkily to third, then second, and they swung off left on to a bumpier tarmac road, swept by drifts of sand. Another five minutes of this and they were at a checkpoint where they were waved onwards through a forest of barbed wire and into a large compound filled with ranks of low concrete huts. Taking nothing for granted, Claire stayed in the car, wary and watchful, until the driver got out, opened her door and beckoned her to come.

He led her to the door of the nearest hut, opened it so that harsh fluorescent light spilled out and, when she paused, pushed her with the flat of his hand.

'Don't do that,' she said, and her voice was higher than she would have liked, then a man's voice from inside said, 'Come in,' in English.

It was a small ante-room and the man was sitting at a desk. He was in stained battledress with no insignia, glossy-haired and still young.

'Passport please,' he said.

'Passport? You lot brought me here. What do you want my passport for?' she said, irritated.

'Just to check,' he replied evenly.

Claire dug into her shoulder bag and gave it to him. He flicked through it with the practised ease of an immigration official, which he clearly was not, looked her up and down, then said 'You permit?', and gestured for her to raise her arms to each side.

She did so and he frisked her quickly and impersonally, then nodded and opened the inner door. She went through into a room filled with rows of assorted chairs, some padded, some plain, facing a blackboard and a series of charts. There was a man leaning back against the end table, a man of great bulk, peering at the contents of a folder. He turned towards her and she took in the small, deeply recessed eyes, with a fleshy waterfall of seamed bags below them. His nose was as fat as the rest of him, and below it a ragged little moustache topped rubbery, purple lips hanging wetly below.

'Miss Merrick,' he said in a basso profundo American drawl, 'how good of you to come.' Her nostrils wrinkled at the strong scent of camphor that came with him.

'And you are?' she asked, aware of the aura of power around him, mind racing to take it all in.

'Ibn Azogi,' he said. 'Your own fairy godfather with the story of a lifetime for you. Why don't you sit down?' He waved at a chair.

'Mr Azogi,' she said, 'while I am, I think, pleased to be here, I could be missing the story of a lifetime in Tripoli. I didn't realise I was going on a mystery tour. Supposing the Americans choose tonight?'

He waved his hand dismissively. 'Nothing is happening in Tripoli.' He spoke slowly as though to reach that grating depth, his vocal cords, vibrating less fast, had to take his sentences at a steadier pace. 'Nothing is happening. Radar picked up one contact an hour ago, eighty-five miles out to sea, but it was a small corporate jet. There was a minor incident at anti-aircraft battery number eleven twenty minutes ago when a shell was discharged negligently, but all else is quiet. I tell you. You are missing nothing, and in any case we will be the first to know.'

'All right,' she said, 'I'm all ears.'

Azogi looked at her in mild surprise for a moment, taking in the vernacular. 'I am not *of* the Libyan Government,' he said, 'but I am asked through my connections with a close relation of the Colonel to advise and represent them on certain matters from time to time. This is one of those times.'

He held out a file to her. 'In this file is contained all that you may need to know of the background to the position in which this country now finds itself. There is, in here, the detailed documentary proof that it was not this country that was responsible for the Pan-American bomb.'

Claire reached out a hand for the file, but he pulled it back. 'Not yet,' he said. 'Our interests lie in the saving of lives. The lives of all those who may be killed if Bush presses ahead with his attack. You can perhaps help us to stop that.'

'How?'

'By telling the story on your news tomorrow.'

She waved a hand at the folder. 'That story?'

'Yes.'

'Mr Azogi, I am sure you will appreciate it takes time to go through documents. I will have to check whatever you have in there. Tomorrow is much too soon.'

He stared at her gloomily. 'Tomorrow may not be soon enough for Tripoli if the American bombers come again. We have made it easier. I have prepared the outline of a script for you and an extract of the information so that you can see for yourself what is undeniably true.'

She stared at him, and she still thought that he was simply a funny old fat man who didn't understand the business. 'No, I'm sorry. It doesn't work like that. By all means give me the file. I'll look at it, but I can't guarantee what will get on the air or when. It will all have to be corroborated.'

He went on looking glum, then he barked out a sudden loud order and five men with assault rifles crashed in through the door.

Claire's heart lurched. She was forced back into her chair.

Both her arms were gripped just below the shoulder. The men were bellowing at her, at the fat man, and at each other. There was violence and rank sweat in the air, plus the tang of gun oil. Buff-coloured camouflage jackets crowded both sides of her vision. Straight in front of her another of them stood, pale-skinned, a dark birthmark staining the drawn cheek under his right eye. His teeth, bared at her, were bad, brown and crooked. He held an AK47, the scattered seed of many years of eastern armaments, cradled across his body. Then he raised it slowly, levelling it at her so the muzzle was pointing straight at her eyes. The men let go of her arms and stepped aside. Crude intimidation, she thought, but her lips dried on her and she found herself swallowing hard. The muzzle circled round her face, inches away from her mouth, her chin, then up to her forehead, the brown teeth grinning all the time. Over to one ear, then back past her nose to the other.

It was hypnotic. The whole room was under its spell, apart from Azogi who was rubbing camphor on his chest between the undone buttons of his shirt. Then she saw the trigger finger moving fractionally, whitening, and her eyes locked on that finger. She went on telling herself it was a bluff, right up to the microsecond when the trigger punched the firing pin forward and the muzzle, three inches from her left ear, erupted in shocking, blasting sound, sending her body twisting in an involuntary spasm off the chair and crashing hard to the floor.

Through the shock Claire realized she was not hurt, apart from the ringing in her ear and the scorched muzzle flash on the side of her head, but there was no comfort in that. Of far greater weight was the realization that the boundaries of normal civilized behaviour had been left behind somewhere way back on the road from Tripoli, and that she had not come equipped with the tactics needed for this raw, new way of behaving.

They watched as she picked herself up off the floor, then the fat man spoke once more, in exactly the same voice, the same reasonable tone.

'Miss Merrick. I ask you again. There is no reason for you to make it hard for yourself. All the information here is true. You just have to believe me and broadcast it. Then there will be no problem for you. There will even be a little prize.'

She looked into herself for an answer and found only wounded dignity and proud anger. 'You cannot treat me like this,' she spat. 'It may work in your country but I am *English*.' She turned on her heel as haughtily as she could and stalked towards the hut door, head high. Somewhat to her surprise, it wasn't locked. No one moved to stop her, which surprised her even more. The desert air outside was cooling fast in the darkness and she took twelve or fifteen steps before she faltered to a halt.

She looked around. They hadn't even come after her. Clever, she thought. I'm inside a heavily-guarded camp, maybe a hundred and fifty miles from Tripoli. No transport, no food, no water, no friends even if I could get past the wire. Great flouncing, Claire, but next time make sure there's somewhere to flounce to. The hut door opened behind her and a trace of camphor reached her on the night breeze as a slow, deep voice said, 'Won't you come back in, Miss Merrick?'

She agreed because she had to, because it seemed the only way of getting out of there. Azogi was unimpressed. He had the measure of her and her agreement and she knew it. He was no gambler. He was a chess player who was moving into the endgame, five pieces ahead and looking only for the most certain route to a quick checkmate.

'When you return to the hotel tonight,' he said, 'you will find that there is a rumour circulating about you.'

Claire stiffened, and his eyes wrinkled shut in their pouches for a moment as his vast face displayed enjoyment. 'The rumour will be that you and a woman were sighted together, enjoying each other's charms. The woman is well-known in Tripoli for her beauty and her perverse tastes. She is a lesbian and she makes no secret of it. Her behaviour is frowned upon but she has made herself useful to my brother the Colonel's cause. She will, if need be, confirm it or, indeed, deny it. That will depend on what you broadcast.'

Claire stared at him. 'No one would believe it.'

He tossed her a sheet of paper and chuckled. 'On the contrary.'

It was in English, clearly intended for her to be able to read. 'Merrick Profile' was printed across the top. Her eye went straight to a paragraph half-way down which was highlighted in pink. 'More than half those asked said CM's private life was a mystery to them, and speculated on possible gay relationships.'

Azogi snatched it back before she could read more. 'That is just a little taste for you of the homework we have done and the pressure we can apply. But then, you have said you will cooperate, and I know an English lady should always be taken at her word.' He got to his feet. 'Go! Go back to your hotel. Read the file. Tomorrow, do the story. You will be telling the truth, you will be saving lives, and also, Miss Merrick, you will be saving yourself a very great deal of trouble.'

They left her in a room by herself until the same car came to take her back. The return journey seemed to take even longer, time for her to brood on an impossible situation. She was mortified and furious. The profile had been in perfect English. Who had written it? Who had been talking about her? Just because she kept her life with Jerome to herself, who would jump to that sort of conclusion? By the dim interior light she looked through the contents of the file and it had the smell of truth about it. Telephone intercepts, interrogation transcripts, but even if it all looked gold-plated she knew there was no way she could broadcast it without weeks of checking and cross-checking something that in the end might well prove uncheckable.

At one in the morning she opened her bedroom door. In the darkness of her room she felt the breeze of the open window and smelt the faint tang of Brian's cigar smoke. There was no one on the balcony, not even the camera tripod which normally stood there, ready, through the night. That surprised her. They usually kept the death watch going well into the early hours. She paced uncertainly round the room, then went to knock on Brian's door. No one answered. She went down to the front desk to see if they knew anything, but the night staff were overcome by the complexities of it all and she was unable to establish the most basic understanding. She tried to phone London but there were, as so often, no lines. In the end, extremely bothered, she went to bed.

The first slap woke her abruptly, her cheek stinging, to a bright daylit room full of people. Two more slaps followed, rocking her head from side to side. She sat up, squirming away from the hand, grabbing at the sheet as it slipped down over her bare breasts. Azogi was leaning over her, glaring. His men were around the bed.

'You cheated me,' he said. 'Your crew has gone. You knew.'

'I didn't,' she said. 'What's happened? Leave me alone. Get the hell out of my room, all of you.'

Azogi shook his head and she started to shout louder and louder. 'Get out! GET OUT!' But a hand came over her mouth from the side, and as she tried to bite it her head was forced painfully back. Her neck hurt and the tears started to come.

The memory was vivid, terrible and total, and a very English voice said, 'Are you all right, ducks?'

She opened her eyes, wet with tears, to find herself on the park bench with an old woman, bent-backed, shopping trolley tilted behind her, staring, worried and kindly.

'Is there anything I can do to help?' the woman said.

# Chapter Thirteen

## Wednesday July 31st

Claire hadn't handled it well, she knew that, but there was too much pain and history invested in this to be completely cool and rational. Jane didn't see it Claire's way at all. Jane's own Tuesday night had been spent sorting her CD collection into alphabetical order and worrying about a lump she had discovered on the cat's leg. She walked through the office door to be confronted by her most daunting member of staff in full cry and overdosing on adrenaline. When Claire slowed down enough for her to pick up individual words like hijack, knife and intelligence, Jane's brain went into overload.

Ten minutes later they were sitting in Herman Dent's office, just the three of them, with a very uneasy test of strength under way. Herman had called Gilligan as soon as Jane requested the meeting, hoping to find out exactly how far his boss's backing for his latest recruit extended. Gilligan had listened in silence as Herman outlined the problem, and then told him exactly how to resolve it. Herman still had no idea whether Claire's status should be allowed to override Jane's editorial position. Herman's lack of subtlety was renowned and he regularly trod on his staff's sensibilities without even wiping the debris off his soles, but he was a litmus paper for signalling Gilligan's intentions. He was enjoying one of the few fat salaries at National exactly because he was always his master's faithful servant, a human speaking tube. For once he was at a loss, inclined to believe this unlikely story was a symptom of the desperation of a failed legend, struggling to crawl back on to her pedestal.

He sat back in his chair, making horrible faces as though the electric processes of thought had to be generated by the dynamo of his fleshy cheeks and jaw. He left them each in the isolation of their own threatened thoughts for a clear two minutes, before falling back – for want of anything better – on Gilligan's suggestion.

Jane had one more go. 'Harry's out of the office until the show. I must have Claire. I've got one more story still to shoot.'

Herman stopped chewing. 'Where's Harry?'

'He's doing the Southampton story as a live inject into the show, remember?'

'Oh, yeah,' said Herman vaguely.

Claire broke in. 'This is the biggest story we're ever likely to get. It's got to be checked. We can't just sit on it. I need the time to make sure it all stands up.'

Herman shot her a hard look. 'And you don't think it's a waste of time?'

'God Almighty. No!'

Time for Gilligan's solution, Herman thought. 'It's a hell of a yarn if it stands up.' He looked at Claire. 'Let's give you some back-up. Jane needs you for another story. You want to press on with this one. OK, best of both worlds. We put a producer on it, just to start stirring it around, do some of the leg-work for you. While it's getting off the ground, you go and spend two days shooting Jane's story for her, then we meet up again and see what we've got.'

Claire had a small triumphant smile as she left the office and Jane, noticing it, stayed behind, rounding on Herman as soon as the door was shut.

'How could you do that?' she said. 'I haven't got any producers to spare. She's just hyping it up. There's no way that story will stand up, you know that.'

'Maybe, maybe,' he said, flapping a hand and turning slightly away. 'That's the test, isn't it? Put someone good on it. Tell 'em to look for the holes. If she's fucking around, that way you get to know and – bingo – problem solved.'

'Oh,' said Jane, deflated. 'Right. Let me see . . .' and she left the office reviewing her producers, looking for a hatchet man.

Sheilas, thought Herman as he stared into space, they almost spoil your appetite.

Simon Seawright had no time for Claire and had let everybody else except Claire know that ever since she arrived. National was as close to proper TV as he'd been able to get. He put that down to the uncompromising nature of the critique of broadcast journalism, which had been the subject of the thesis for his Master's degree from the University of Nottingham. Those who turned him down and weren't even aware of the existence of his thesis did so because of his know-it-all air and his shifty looks. Claire had only been vaguely aware of him in her short time at National, but now he put that right.

'I hear I'm to have a look at this story of yours,' he said, looming up by her cubicle and leaning in on her with irritating familiarity.

'You are, are you?' she said with a hint of frost, looking up to see a very white faced thirty-year-old with a pink sheen of irritated dampness around his eyes, nostrils and mouth.

'That's right. Want to try it on me?' His words invested the project with built-in disbelief.

She studied him for a moment, tight-lipped, then took a dossier out of her drawer. She took out the photo without looking at it and passed it across.

'Ibn Azogi. Formerly of Tripoli, now apparently living some-where in London. Centrally involved in the negotiations with Libya which followed the Lockerbie bombing. Closely linked to Gaddafi's cousin.' She stopped and looked at him. 'Shouldn't you be making notes?'

He shook his head carelessly. 'What matters, sticks. If it doesn't I can always ask you again, can't I?'

'No, you can't. If you can't be bothered to write it down, I can't be bothered to tell you.'

She kept her temper, more or less, walked him slowly through the story, made photocopies of the bank statements and the supporting paperwork and handed it all to him.

He said little throughout, making sporadic notes of pointed elaborateness, asking unnecessarily for spellings.

'That's it then,' she said in the end. 'That's about all I've got. It should be enough for you to get started.'

He picked up the stack of papers and shrugged. 'I'll let you know Friday.'

She looked at him, trying to probe his meaning, and got a blank stare back. 'Let me know what?' she asked.

'Let you know whether I think there's anything to it, of course,' he said casually.

Her eyes narrowed. 'Simon, I don't give a shit whether you think there's anything to it or not. As I understand it, your job is to start putting it into effect, right? What I want from you on Friday is a few of the blanks filled in, such as where we find Azogi, plus some ideas on how we start shooting it. Understood?'

'Look, that may be the way things used to be when you were . . .'

The blast stopped him in his tracks and had every head in the office swinging round. 'Listen, you little tosser. Don't push it. You just sod off and get on with your job and I'll get on with mine.'

It was late Thursday afternoon, after a day and a half of humdrum shooting around Building Society branches in Southwark, before Claire walked back into the office. She was irritated to see Simon Seawright on the phone, talking quietly and shielding his mouth with his hand rather obviously as she went by. She ignored him and got down to work in an edit suite, putting together another weary crime package, differentiated from all the others she had ever seen only by the colour of the Ford Sierra in which they'd made their getaway, and the fact that their Balaclavas were lemon yellow. By the time the last shots were added to her four minutes of cut video, and she'd spoken the last few lines of commentary into the mike, she couldn't wait to get out of the place and was pleased to see lights on when she got back to the flat. Ann was back from her latest conference.

Before she got out of the car, she looked at the front of the little terraced house and the lights that were on inside and thought what a difference they made. The difference between carrying the day's tensions festering in solitude into the night, or spreading them out to be neutralized by the healthy disinfectant of sympathy and laughter.

The curtain in Ann's front window moved. A moment or two and then the door opened and she was beckoning. Claire went in and Ann hugged her.

'Hello. Lovely to see you. What's the rush?'

'Hurry up,' said Ann. 'I've put the kettle on. I've got something amazing for you.'

She was in full cry. Claire barely had time to hang up her coat and put down her briefcase before Ann was ushering her into a chair by the kitchen table and spreading bits of paper in front of her. Only then did she really look at Claire. 'Are you all right?' she asked in a worried voice.

'Just about. A lot has been going on. Tell me your news first and I'll tell you all about it.'

'OK,' said Ann, looking at her doubtfully, but then as she turned back to the papers her voice lifted with excitement again. 'I had a bit of time on my hands at the conference – well, a lot really. Harrogate's OK but there's a limit on how much you can do there. Anyway, I had my laptop with me so I went back to my lists, you know – the constituencies.' She was shuffling bits of paper. 'I started thinking about it the other way round. I assumed someone really had been stuffing in extra votes and then I thought about how it would show up. I looked at all the seats the Tories just managed to hold on to from Labour. Now what would the giveaway signs be?'

Claire shook her head.

'The swing, for a start,' Ann went on, watching her intently. 'If you're putting extra Conservative votes in the box, the swings from Conservative to Labour would be smaller, right?'

'I see, yes.'

'So,' said Ann, and held up another piece of paper, 'this is what I got. It's all the marginal seats where the Conservatives held on from Labour with a very small majority, fifteen hundred or less, and where the swing was much lower than the average. I took 2 per cent as the cut-off. There are only ten of them. Now this is when things get exciting.'

She paused for a reaction. 'Go on,' said Claire. 'You're way ahead of me.'

'Well, I have this little programme at work. I call it "Conspirator". It's really just a fancy database analyzer. It looks for offbeat correlations I might not spot, so I set it to work and it popped up with a funny thing. It pointed out that these ten seats had a higher than average turnout. Over the whole of the UK the turnout was 77.7 per cent. Almost all of these seats were over 80 per cent, and the average was 81.4.'

Claire thought about it again and shook her head. 'You could explain that away easily enough. Those were the seats that were fought hardest, so you'd expect more people to turn out to vote there, surely?'

'Yes, of course. That's why I ran a check on the equivalent number of seats that Labour won by the smallest margin. You'd expect the same thing to be true there, wouldn't you? I mean those were fought over just as hard.'

'Yes.'

'Well, it's not. The average turnout in those was 78.8 per cent, only just over the national average.'

'Not that much difference is it?'

'Oh yes it is. 2.6 per cent is a big difference.'

'All right, Ann. Spell it out.'

'Well, supposing someone found a way of adding a whole load of votes in the marginal seats to swing it one way. That would make it look like there had been a much higher turnout in those seats, wouldn't it?'

'I see what you mean,' said Claire slowly, 'but it's not proof is it? I mean it could be just a statistical coincidence.'

'Ah, but that's not all.'

'What else?'

'Your paper label is what. Beaconsbridge is one of the ten seats.'

# Chapter Fourteen

## Friday August 2nd

'IF A MAN'S LIFE IS HELD CHEAPER THAN GRASS, IT'S A CASUALTY OF WAR, NOT A CRIME,' said the screen in the colour of someone playing the part of Walter Brennan playing the part of Colonel Hawkins. A direct quote usually won the day if it was anywhere near relevant, but this time someone dared argue. The Karl Malden/Zebulon Prescott character put in a counter-argument.

'WE ARE MOVING TO DESTROY THE TARGET'S CREDIBILITY. STERILIZATION AT THIS STAGE IS UNNECESSARY. REMOVAL OF HER FREEDOM SHOULD SUFFICE.' Details followed.

One player didn't like it. Robert Preston's words – in the persona of wagon-train leader, Roger Morgan – scrolled on to the screen: 'WHEN A SKUNK NEEDS KILLING – WELL, IT AIN'T ENOUGH TO SAY A SKUNK'S A SKUNK.'

The Director came in. 'DECISION TIME. DECISION IS WHETHER TO IMPLEMENT MALDEN PLAN OR INITIATE STERILIZATION. INPUT ONE FOR MALDEN OR TWO FOR STERILIZATION.

It started as a relatively normal Friday. Claire woke from shallow, disturbed sleep and wished she could look forward to the show with anything approaching enthusiam. But it hung limply there in her immediate future like a muddy puddle through which her route must pass. The buzz of live TV wasn't enough by itself. Crookbusters was just a stale pastiche of all the shows which had gone before it. She could already imagine just what sort of day it would be – the script conferences, the last-minute changes to the items that were already in the can, the mind-blurring tedium of it all. She couldn't have been more wrong but, as it turned out, she would rather have been right. There was something in the atmosphere as soon as she walked into the big, open office. Most of the staff simply put their heads down and ignored her. Others, those she regarded as probable enemies, wore looks of interest or satisfaction. Something had clearly been going round.

Her phone buzzed as soon as she sat down. Picking it up, she heard Jane's voice and she could see, across the office, through the glass of the cubicle, Jane turning to look at her.

'Claire? Good morning. I think we ought to get together later for a chat.' The voice showed traces of nervousness.

'Why not now?' Claire said. 'Is there something wrong?'

'Well . . . there's a lot to do today. I'd rather we did it this afternoon when the spadework's been done for the show.'

'Jane,' Claire said in her even, dangerous voice, 'I've just walked through an office that clearly knows something I don't. I'd like to catch up.'

'It's just . . . it's just about your story. Simon's come up with a thing or two we need to discuss.'

A simple and horrid explanation suddenly flashed upon her. Seawright must have talked to ITN. Someone there must have broken their agreement, told him about what happened after Libya. It took the wind out of her sails for a moment. She heard herself faintly agreeing and put the phone down feeling sick at heart.

She sat gazing at her computer screen wondering how to fight the accusation with no proof. What did it matter anyway? A dirty story, a lot of laughs at her expense. It didn't affect the main issue. At least she was prepared. She set her fingers to the keyboard and began to type the story of Tripoli, of everything that happened and especially what happened afterwards in Malta. If necessary, they could all read it. Preparing it before the accusation came seemed, in some tiny way, to strengthen her hand.

\*　　\*　　\*

On the gate, the youth in the ill-fitting security guard's uniform was having an unusually pleasant morning. It wasn't every day that girls in loose T-shirts driving open sports cars asked him for directions and certainly not girls like this one, with the brown skin and the big, wobbly boobs. Even after he admitted he'd never heard of GGP Freight and Leasing, and he didn't believe they were anywhere on this estate, she seemed to want to go on talking. It was the hand stroking his sleeve that held his attention. It held it so well that he didn't see the man in builder's overalls slipping through behind them, the man who walked quickly out of his sight around the back of the building.

Anonymous in his overalls, the man spotted Claire's car straight away. It was parked in a corner bordered by blank walls with no danger at all of being overlooked. He slipped a notched spring steel bar, a thinner version of a foot ruler, down between the driver's window and its rubber seal. No car defied him for long and it took him all of three seconds to find the edge of the locking bar, hook it with the notch and lift it. Once open, he slipped into the back where he could not be seen and took a package from inside his overalls.

The girl in the sports car gave up stroking the guard's arm, agreed a meeting at a pub later on which she had absolutely no intention of keeping, turned round and drove off, waving.

The morning passed slowly for Claire. Her contribution to the show was edited and finished. The introduction was safely stored in the computer. Everything had been checked and double-checked. That part of her which strangers and adversaries often regarded as the whole – the brazen shell which, challenged or threatened, closed over her to push her aggression up to whatever extreme level it took in order to gain the upper hand – was missing. She knew that Azogi's trap still held all its disgusting power even in this second-rate funk hole. Here, more than ever, there were people who would be delighted to believe it. If Simon Seawright had been on hand, she would have forced it out of him, but he was nowhere to be seen. Sitting at her desk, waiting for the showdown, she made a decision. She would handle the accusation with dignity. She would hear them out, then read to them the account of the events in Tripoli and Malta. After that, it all depended on their reaction.

Finally the phone rang and Claire walked steadily to Jane's office. Simon Seawright was already sitting there along with Chief Inspector Derek Palmer. Seawright looked at her without expression. Palmer stood up clumsily.

'Hello, Miss Merrick,' he said, though they'd seen each other already that day.

She assumed he'd just dropped in for a chat with Jane and expected the editor to show him politely out, but he sat down again and it instantly became clear he was meant to be there. That made no sense.

There was silence, then Jane cleared her throat. 'Claire, I thought we ought to have this meeting because Simon, as you know, was working on the various leads you gave him and the results have been a little – well, surprising.'

Here it comes, thought Claire, but the 'it' that came wasn't at all the one she was expecting.

'Derek's here too because Simon asked him for a bit of help to confirm what he'd found. It's about the list of returning officers you gave him.'

Claire thought back in surprise to the list and the bank account numbers. 'Yes?'

'You said you were given that list by a man from . . .'

Claire broke in. 'I told you who he was.' She glanced at Palmer. 'I don't think you need to bring other people in on that.'

'Well . . . Simon's already told Derek, with my permission,' said Jane. 'As you're about to hear, I don't think that matters a jot, really.'

'Why not?' she said, irritated.

Seawright, on Jane's nod, picked up the story in his self-righteous voice. 'Because not a single one of those people exists, that's why.'

'Oh, come on,' Claire said. 'The man told me . . .' but the meaning of what he'd said began to sink in. 'Maybe he's mixed up the names or something,' she finished lamely.

Palmer was a kind man, but he stepped in with the tone of

someone helping a confused old lady to find the right bus. 'I'm afraid it's right,' he said. 'Simon came to me to see if I could find anyone with these names. We've drawn a total blank. Then there's the bank accounts.'

'What about the bank accounts?' she said dully, with neon lights in her mind flashing 'Set Up'.

'The numbers are all wrong. Wrong number of digits, wrong prefix. They aren't British bank account numbers at all.'

There was a dead silence while everyone looked at her, then at some signal from Jane the other two got up and went out, Seawright in silence, Palmer nodding awkwardly.

Jane sat looking down at her hands until the door had shut behind them, then looked up at Claire. 'I don't understand any of this,' she said. 'Would you mind telling me just what is going on?'

'Jane, I'm not sure I really know.'

'Ever since Gilligan dropped you in my lap without even telling me, I've felt like some sort of passenger,' she said, and Claire wondered at the depth of frustration in her voice. 'I've put up with it. I've let you force my hand on all this because I knew he backed you and you'd win if it came to a showdown, and now what have I got? Just a load of BULLSHIT . . .' It came out as a despairing cry; half wail, half shout.

'Look, Jane, I've got to find out what's . . .'

'You haven't got to find out anything. I don't think you know what's true any more. I'm sorry if our crappy little TV station isn't as exciting as what you're used to, but I don't have many resources and I can't afford to have them running round in circles after some half-baked fantasy instead of working on the show.'

'I know, I . . .'

'I don't really want to talk about it any more. You and I are going to meet Herman on Monday morning and decide what to do next.'

Claire, the terror of her bosses throughout her career, had for once nothing to say; nothing at least that was remotely likely to be believed. She looked at the envelope in her hand, the envelope containing her summary of the Tripoli story, and thought for a moment of giving it to Jane but knew in the same instant it would be pushing the bounds of credibility even further. A little relief still lingered that the events in Malta hadn't leaked, but that was swamped by the horrible realization that her professionalism was no longer just on the line but way over it, and that someone was making a very thorough job of destroying her for the second time. She nodded, got up and went out.

Where to go, that was the question. Back to her desk? Unthinkable. Every eye in the office was on her. She turned to the doors, walked quickly down the corridor outside and made for her car.

# Chapter Fifteen

The car seemed to drive itself, with no particular conscious thought on her part. On the surface her mind was whirling with conspiracies and betrayals. Deep down she craved a silent chance to confront something buried far within her. She walked down the corridor to Corunna Ward oddly afraid of being challenged and stopped outside the door marked 'Stephanie Chaplin'. She looked through the fluted glass and could see no one inside, apart from the curved sequence of distorted segments which added up to Stephanie.

She pushed the door open and walked in, eyes fixed on the figure in the bed, starting with the feet and forcing her gaze slowly up to the motionless head. That came as a shock. It was not entirely still, the eyes roamed around, crossing her own unsteady gaze, but sliding off, always sliding off, around and around. Stephanie had been beautiful but the muscles of her puffy, lopsided face now followed the dictates of some random commander. Tubes led into her and tubes led out of her and the quiet bleep of a monitor was the only promise of continuing life.

Claire stood by her and stared, safe from interruption. Harry, she knew, would not be back from Southampton until well after the show. Who was this woman? Harry's wife? No. There was a touch of Harry in that face, undisguised by the ravages of her state. A sister, it had to be a sister, not that it mattered. She was here for herself, not for Stephanie. Her presence made no difference to the figure in the bed. More than twenty years ago, she should have sat at just such a bed. Aunt Molly had persuaded her to go to the hospital where her mother had lain for a year. She had got as far as the door to the ward, as far as the glass window in the door, and she had not been able to go further.

Now she forced herself to ferret out the deeply-buried strands of it all. The little modern house in Colchester. The pale green wallpaper of her parents' bedroom and the brighter blue paint of the bathroom that matched the bath. The bathroom had glass in its door; glass with its clarity obscured, for suburban decency's sake, by great curves and swirls whose thicknesses twisted the light into shapes that had only colour in common with their origin. Red. Bright red. That had been the colour. Red and the noise of her mother's screams and her father's shouts as they had fought, paying no heed to their watching daughter. When she'd run into the blue, blue bathroom, the colour had still been red, but through the protecting glass she couldn't see the details, just a fragmented shape slumping down and another standing, dropping something that thumped on the carpet. It was easy to pretend then that it was all right, until the neighbours came and the police and the ambulance men, and they took away all the shattered parts of her childhood world.

She looked at Stephanie again, seeing instead the imagined face of her mother in the limbo she had passed into, and it all started to be too terribly real for her. She got to her feet, unable to take her eyes off the figure in the bed, moving sideways across the room to open the door and look in through the comforting glass. That was when Harry Chaplin's loud, exasperated voice ambushed her from outside.

'Not again,' he said, 'I just don't believe it.' She jumped out of her skin.

He stared at her. 'What are you doing here?' he said, but his tone was gentler for a moment as he took in the tears. He went in and she followed. He kissed the woman in the bed on the cheek. 'I won't be a moment, Steffie,' he said, then turned back to Claire.

'I . . . I thought you were in Southampton,' she said with an effort.

'It all changed. We recorded . . . Oh, what the hell difference does that make?' He looked at her in complete bafflement. 'This is incredible even by your standards.'

'I'll go.'

'No,' he said firmly. 'I want to know why you're here.'

She shook her head in defeat.

'Wait,' he said, trying to make up his mind, 'just sit down. Pull yourself together. Give me a couple of minutes.'

He bent over the bed and Claire tried not to listen to the low mumble as he told Steffie where he'd been and what he'd been doing.

He stood up and spoke more loudly. 'Sorry, Steffie love, I do have to go. I'll come tomorrow morning. Don't worry.'

Outside the room, he said, 'Is your car here?'

'Yes.'

'Well, why don't you drive me home and on the way you can explain just why the hell you're meddling around in my life.'

They got to the car and she held out the key. 'You drive. I don't feel too good.'

'I don't drive,' he said shortly, and got in the passenger seat.

She drew in her breath, got in and started up.

'I hear you walked out today,' he said.

'I'm sure the juicy details have gone the rounds. Where am I going?'

'Wandsworth. It's not far and it's on your way.'

Neither said a word until they drew up outside Harry's house.

'I still want to know,' he said.

'What?'

'Why you were there. Come inside and tell me.'

He got out and unlocked the front door. She could have driven off but she didn't. She stared at his back, then got out and followed.

They climbed the stairs inside to a top-floor flat, and he pushed the door open into a room of unexpected magic. The afternoon light came in through big skylights on to a room full of pot plants and canvases.

'You paint,' she said in surprise, and turned to a giant half-finished stylized nude, painted in bold, slashing colours with a perspective all of its own, legitimized by its power.

'Gosh, you must be an investigative reporter,' he said in a tone of ironic amazement.

'Shut up, Harry. I was about to pay you a compliment. They're beautiful.'

'How would you know?' he said.

'I'm just telling you what I think. I paint too.'

'Do you really?' he said in a quite different tone; then he seemed to catch himself. 'Look, I insist you tell me why you were there with Steffie.'

'Who is she?'

'She's . . . she's my sister.'

'What's wrong with her?'

'Brain injury. A car accident.'

She guessed it. 'And you were driving?'

'Yes I bloody was,' he replied, and she knew she'd gone too far, too fast. 'But that's my business.'

Her fuse was short too. 'Stop it. I had to go. I had to know how it felt. My mother . . . I wanted to . . .' She was crying and he was staring open-mouthed. 'Oh, you're such a goddam hard man, how would you know? Fuck you.'

'I'd rather fuck you,' he said and the words exploded like depth charges in a vast bubble of sound between them. They both stopped, astonished, and then each simultaneously recognized something previously hidden and now suddenly revealed. He was shaking his head as she came towards him, his hands knotted into fists, but those fists reached out despite himself and touched her shoulders, uncurling to feel the hot electric flesh through the thin cotton. That was the moment of chemical change when the passion of anger turned on its axis with bewildering speed into the passion of lust.

'I don't think . . .' he started, but then their mouths met and opened to each other and her tongue stopped him in mid-sentence. There was no soft preamble. Their fighting had been their foreplay. His hands scooped her shirt from the waist-band of her skirt, sweeping up to cup her breasts and feel her nipples hardening under his fingers. Her hands tugged at his belt, dragging his trousers and pants down to tangle with her skirt on the floor. He kicked them off his feet, groggy with the impact of her and felt her fingers clutching him, one of her legs raised around his hips, guiding him into her. She had left no time to take off her knickers, pushing their wet centre to one side to let him in and then he was holding her buttocks, both her legs up and around him, their mouths still working together while the undulating pile-driver of her pelvis brought them both to a gasping, staggering, rushing climax.

They slid with difficulty, locked together, to the ground, knocking a stack of paintings to one side and lay, Harry on his back, Claire with her head on his chest, appalled by what they'd done.

'Whose idea was that?' Harry said.

'Both of ours?' suggested Claire. 'You're not going to start some post-coital embarrassment trip are you?'

A smart remark would have finished it then and there and one was finely balanced on his lips but he took time to breathe twice and it faded away. 'No,' was all he said, but his hand came up to stroke her hair. He looked down along the brown length of her body, curved against his, and tried to fix it in his mind, knowing it was one of those rare perspectives on which nature held the upper hand over art. By his fingers, just on the inward curve above her hip was a shiny, pressed rose-bud of scar tissue. Remembering the pictures from Sarajevo – how long ago? Three years, maybe – he allowed himself to realize for the first time that her reputation was perhaps deserved. She looked up at him and they gazed at each other, all the barriers between them shattered.

'Where do we start?' he said, 'What happened today?'

They went to bed, because it was more comfortable and there was no reason not to, and once there they talked and talked and found what they had probably known all along, that they were birds of a feather.

She tried to explain why she'd been there in Steffie's ward, and he seemed to understand as she haltingly told him the story of her parents and her mother's long coma and final switching-off.

'That's what one of them would like to do with Steffie,' he said savagely.

'That doctor? The one who was there the first time I came?'

'He's just a prat. He won't believe me. I keep telling him Steffie squeezes my hands. He says it's all reflex actions, says her hands just move like that by chance. He's trying to tell me Steffie's just some sort of vegetable.'

She hugged him.

'Now, what about you and these ballot boxes?' he said.

She told him all she could and then they dressed and went out for pizza. When they came back, Harry stopped her in the studio and reached for his paints and a canvas. An hour later, two pictures were propped side by side by the bed. Hers was a sensitive, accurate water colour, slightly romanticized, of Harry – his hair tousled, sitting askew, his pallet held obliquely to one side like a wine waiter's tray, brush poised in mid-air as he looked at her questioningly. Harry's picture was something else, a time-elapsed canvas making up a sexual trail of small, intense images all in a line. Claire letting her skirt drop; then naked and standing with legs wide as she moved her easel; then one almost like his but all eyes, staring wide at him.

'My eyes aren't that big,' she'd said.

'They were when you were looking at me.'

Then the last two frames: her stalking towards him on hands and knees across the floor, a tigress with a human head, her heavy, bobbed hair swaying and her mouth open as if to tear into him; and lastly, hastily, his own legs wide apart and her mass of hair all that you could see of her head between them. She lay looking at it, remembering the taste of him in her mouth as she teased him with her lips and teeth, determined to stop him painting in a battle that ended when he dropped his pallet with a groan and reached down to stroke her hair with both of his hands.

In bed, he retrieved the pallet and painted her again, using her stomach as his canvas; a miniature picture of her, arms and legs splayed, hair spreading now across the pillow. It would have seemed like sacrilege to wash it off but he didn't given her the chance, the paint squashing stickily between them in another wild coupling which left them with mad, smeared images of paint, reversed and matching, on their damp skin.

Later, in a night broken suddenly by summer lightning, they woke simultaneously in his bed, each wild with their own nightmare, Claire screaming at the muzzle flash of the AK47, Harry lunging away from the stabbing, dazzling headlights. Each thought they were responsible for waking the other, then, realizing, turned with gratitude to the unaccustomed comfort of a fellow sufferer, to hold and heal. Calmer, warm, fuelled by a less explosive hunger, they explored each other slowly.

Afterwards she said, 'I hate mixing work and sex.'

'Me too.'

'So what do we do?'

'Lie,' he said. There was a short silence then she nodded.

# Chapter Sixteen

## Saturday August 3rd

Ann woke, knowing from the feel of the house that Claire hadn't come home and worrying, despite herself. Since the split with Jerome, there'd been no sign of any men in Claire's life to explain an absence like this. She lay rigid for a couple of minutes wondering what to do, but there was no one to turn to and nothing rational she could say, nothing but a half-baked set of statistics based on an old tin box that was no longer there. The boat, she thought, that must be it. She's gone down to the boat without saying anything. An hour later, she was unlocking the office, relishing the chance to catch up on her enormous workload without the distraction of her fellows around her.

The very first job she had to do was to check the list of speakers for the next conference. Peter should have filed it to her. The computer came up with sloppily done, mistyped names, and she sighed. There was one name too few and she couldn't immediately work out who was missing. Peter had also filed the list of delegates attending. Maybe she'd find it there. This was a much longer list, assembled haphazardly, four or five hundred names. What a way to start the day. She went back to the main screen and decided to index the list, but her mind was only half on the job as she did so, still thinking about Claire. That may have been why she selected the wrong file, the last file in her directory, the one with Claire's initials on it. It was only when she pushed the button and that file came up on the screen, neatly rearranged in alphabetical order, that she realized she had indexed the wrong one.

With a noise of mild irritation, she moved her finger to

clear the screen and start again, but then she took in what was in front of her. She took it in but didn't at first believe it; and a double take had her eyes racing back to the start of the list to see if it were really true. She sat for a long time, pole-axed, excitement giving way to a sudden feeling of frightened hopelessness as she saw before her the confirmation of her worst fears.

This should be awkward, Harry thought, breakfast together after a night in bed with the one person you never, ever expected to sleep with; but it wasn't. Each side of the floodgates there had been so much that fitted perfectly, just waiting for the barrier to drop. They'd talked and made love in equal quantities. She'd told him almost everything; the boxes, Libya, Jerome, the man in her car.

'Well,' said Claire over the toast, 'the weekend stretches ahead. What shall we do?'

He liked the implicit assumption that they would do it together. 'What would you do if I wasn't here?'

'I'd go down to the sea.'

'Why?'

'I've got a boat. It's a place I go to be by myself.'

'OK, I'll be by yourself too. My last girlfriend said she never felt more alone than when she was with me.'

'Do you like sailing?'

'Never been.'

'Do you promise to do what I tell you in the boat and not argue?'

'Probably.'

'Well, maybe,' she said, thinking: do I want my sanctuary invaded? Perhaps I do. 'What would you be doing?'

'Painting. Shopping. I must see Steffie, though.'

'We could go on the way.'

He nodded slowly. 'Can you take it?'

'Yes,' she said with confidence.

In the car on the way to the hospital, he was silent for a while and she looked across at him. 'What?' she asked.

'Like it or not, we've both to go back to work on Monday

morning, and they're all going to be sniggering about you and Seawright.'

'No one knows you're involved.'

'No one but me. That's the point. They all come running to me with every little bit of gossip about you because I'm sarcastic, hilarious Harry Chaplin and, as is well known, I hate Claire Merrick.'

'So?' she said, 'Stay that way. We know how it is really.'

In the ward, Harry ushered Claire to the side of the bed.

'Hold her hand,' he said, 'move your head where she can see you.' Then he bent forward. 'Steffie, I've brought someone to see you. She's called Claire.'

Claire jumped. 'She squeezed my hand. I'm sure she did.'

Harry looked like a dog with two tails. 'There, you see? Try talking to her. I know she can hear you.'

She tried. 'Hello, Steffie. I'm Claire. I work with your brother at National TV.' It felt like trying to record a Christmas tape to a little-known relative on the far side of the world.

She was grateful when Harry took over and she sat back, lost in her thoughts. After a while he looked at her. 'What was that about, when I came in yesterday and you had your face pressed against the glass?'

'Oh . . . It's a bit silly. It's just a way I used to deal with things.'

It wasn't much of an explanation, but he seemed to understand. 'Through glass?'

'Yes.'

'Like TV?'

Claire nodded.

'Now,' he said, 'while we're here. You stopped short last night.'

'Did I?' she said smiling.

'Only in the talking. After Tripoli. What happened?'

Her expression showed she wasn't sure she was ready for that. There was a rattling noise from the bed and they turned in unison to look at Steffie, but her breathing soon returned to normal and Harry turned straight back to Claire.

'Go on,' he said. 'I can't help you properly if I don't know it all.'

So there, in that antiseptic room, she began to tell him the tale of violence and intrigue.

'What did you hear about me leaving ITN?'

'Just rumours.'

'What rumours?'

'That you'd screwed up somehow. Something about Malta? No one knew, really.'

She looked at him steadily. 'Are you being nice, or is that really all you heard?'

'I'm not being nice. I think that was all anybody heard.'

'Well, thank God for that at least.'

'You're shaking,' he said, and she looked at him like an old woman facing a long flight of steps.

'Harry,' she said, and the note of despair astonished him, 'it's not easy and if you don't believe me, I don't know what I'll do.'

'I'll believe you,' he said, 'whatever it is.'

She said nothing for a while, just looking at him, picking her words and thinking back. 'I told you the story up to where Azogi and his men came into my hotel room. They gave me an injection. I don't know what it was. It wasn't unpleasant. Heroin maybe? I kept getting these sort of white rushes of pleasure. They flew me to Malta. I was out of it for quite some time. Then Azogi put the boot in.'

'How?'

She shook her head and said nothing.

He pressed her gently. 'You should finish. It'll be better if you do.'

She looked at him dully. 'The police found me in a villa near Sliema. I was . . . with the woman from Tripoli, the same one Azogi's rumours had said I had been with before.'

'*With* her?'

'Well, if you want to know the full details I was in bed with her down between my legs, except I was five miles high and for all I knew I could have been knitting a fucking tea cosy.'

'OK, steady.'

'I'm sorry.'

'And?'

'And the police found everything you could imagine in my bags. Coke, hash, heroin, even loads of currency and detailed notes of how I was fiddling my expenses.'

'And ITN didn't believe you?'

'Would you have done? They got me out of there but it cost them blood and it was full court martial time when I got back. My story sounded completely ridiculous. I didn't have a shred of evidence to back me up.'

'Where had the crew gone?'

'They'd been pulled out. London made up its mind there wasn't going to be any attack, decided Tripoli was a dead duck, and dreamed up something else for them in a big rush which meant they had to drive to Tunisia overnight for a flight. Brian spent two hours searching Tripoli for me, but then someone told him the rumour. I'd been seen behaving fairly disgracefully in public with this sleaze-bag of Azogi's. He didn't want to believe it, but he couldn't track me down anywhere. He'd left messages all over my room but Azogi's men must have found them.'

'I don't see why Azogi didn't just write it off once he knew your crew had gone. He could have left you the stuff and you might have been able to use it.'

'Because he's a puppet-master, Harry. He wants the puppets to do exactly what he wants, when he wants, otherwise he pulls their legs off. That's all he understands. He's an evil bloody . . .' but her voice trailed off into sobs that this time she could not control, and he wrapped his arms round her tightly.

She cried loud and long, getting some little part of the poison of it all out of her system, on and on until suddenly, from the bed next to where they were sitting, came a strangled noise.

It got through to both of them and, tears suddenly forgotten, they swung in amazement to the bed where Steffie, eyes swinging about unfocused, searching for the sound of distress, mouth moving slackly, was mumbling, 'Cry, don' cry, don't cry,' over and over again.

# Chapter Seventeen

## Saturday August 3rd

Ninety minutes after leaving the hospital, they were on the pontoon, and Claire realized as soon as she saw Harry stepping on to the deck, grabbing the mast for support as the boat shifted minutely under his weight, that he really hadn't been sailing before. His were town clothes: leather jacket, shoes with slippery soles, thin shirt.

'There's some old stuff you can wear in the locker there,' she said, 'starboard side, under the quarter-berth.'

He looked completely blank.

She pointed. 'There.'

In a pair of wellingtons and a sweater of Jerome's that she'd been saving for the next time she cleaned the engine, he looked better; but he seemed to have shrunk into himself, watching her bustling around with an uncertain look of apprehension.

'Are you all right?' she said.

'Yes. Of course.'

Sitting out of the way in the cockpit, he watched her transforming the safely-moored hull with bewildering speed into an alien, complicated form of transportation. The rushing of ropes, the flap of canvas and the rapid ratcheting of winches marked her progress. He stood up and narrowly missed banging into the boom which was now hanging at the foot of a slack mainsail.

'I'm ready to cast off,' Claire shouted from the bows. 'Can you just take the tiller while I get the jenny up?'

Rubbing his head, he took a step across the cockpit, catching his foot in the coiled sheets, and took the tiller gingerly in his hand, looking nervously round. At the bow the big sail rose into the sky up the forestay and tightened as Claire winched and cleated it. One of the sheets snagged on an obstruction and the sail cracked into a filled, straining curve, the boat leaning a little and starting to move horrifyingly suddenly. The mainsail swung out to the side and the tiller began to jump in his hand.

'Come off a bit,' called Claire, looking ahead at the next boats in the trot.

'How?' he yelled.

'Pull it towards you,' she said urgently, and a moored boat seemed to shoot past down the left hand side.

She untangled the sheet and their speed fell off, then she was back in the cockpit, sorting it all out with no fuss. He was relieved and delighted to leave it up to her. They were sailing gently out into the open waters of the Solent when he looked up for the first time, and he felt pure terror. The perspective of the great curve of the mainsail above him took him in a short circuit straight back to childhood, and the booby-trap of a nightmare in an innocent picture book.

It had been a pre-war photo of a racing yacht, its narrow, almost insignificant hull leaning crazily to the press of an almighty cloud of a sail, bulging thunderously from a mast of extraordinary height. To a land-locked five-year-old, the picture had a horrifying fascination. All that terrible natural power, controlled so precariously by the twenty tiny human figures lying along the side of the deck below. At that age he had been unable to imagine anything more awful, more certain to end in crashing, drowning disaster, than to be on that deck under that mushroom cloud of barely contained savagery.

'What's the matter?' asked Claire as he sank down on the slatted cockpit seat.

'Just felt a bit dizzy when I looked up, that's all,' he said lamely.

'It might get a bit splashy in a while. We'll have the wind against the tide out through the narrows. There's an oilskin down below if you want it.'

For a few moments, it was reassuring to go below but that rapidly turned to something far less agreeable, as the odd, uncertain motion of the boat and a previously unnoticed tinge of old diesel fumes set his stomach churning. He made for the open air.

Claire at the helm of her boat was a different and less communicative person, locked in some private communion with the waves and the wind, watching the sails and the busy water constantly. It was just the way she *would* relax, Harry decided, forcing everything else out of her mind by taking up all the available space with some demanding activity. The boat shuddered as the bow dropped hard into an oncoming wave.

She glanced at him, hunched in his borrowed clothes, looking miserably around the cockpit for something familiar.

'Would you like to take the helm?' she said.

'Is that a good idea?'

'Why not?'

'We seem to be, well . . . leaning over a lot.'

'Oh no. It's a very gentle wind. Can't be more than force four. You really can't come to any harm.'

So, under her tutelage, he learnt roughly how to helm, though a nervousness which she could not understand had him bringing the bows up too sharply into the wind at frequent intervals when he felt the boat was heeling too far. She tried to get him to relax, but he wasn't really happy until she freed the sheets off, and she was forced to be content with sailing rather slowly in more or less the right direction, hoping no one she knew would see her in such uncharacteristic trim.

It was early evening when they went back in and, though he'd got more or less used to it, Harry didn't start to enjoy himself thoroughly again until they were tied up alongside the pontoon.

Claire smiled. 'I'll get some food going. Would you like a drink?' She pointed to a locker. 'There's some wine in there somewhere. Why don't you get it out?'

She opened tins, lit the gas and started stirring up the sort of meal she had always cooked on board *Tiger Kitten*, a basic stew of which all the elements came out of tins, heavily laced with Worcester Sauce, soup powder and sherry for flavour. They sat in the cockpit in the late summer twilight to eat it. He passed her a mug.

'I couldn't find the lead crystal goblets,' he said. 'This one's only got three chips.'

'It doesn't matter on a boat,' she said. 'Nothing like that matters, at least not on this sort of boat.'

Harry nodded to the next pontoon where two rotund men in absurd parodies of naval officer's caps were unloading a cart full of supplies into their forty-foot ketch. A woman – uncertainly poised between the dying days of Sloane Ranger wifedom and the pill-riddled world of haggard divorce – was standing in a defensive posture.

'You must have brought it,' said the taller of the two men in a tone of voice pitched towards public shaming.

'Well I didn't. How was I to know?'

'Come on, Jo-Jo, get your act together. You know I always leave it out in the solarium when we're coming down to the boat. Honestly, do I have to do everything myself?'

'What about that sort of boat?' asked Harry.

'That's not a boat,' said Claire. 'That's a floating bank statement. They come down, shout at each other, mix a lot of drinks, shout at each other some more and maybe motor over to the island for lunch tomorrow if they can remember how to cast off.'

'You mean people like that can't sail?'

'Merchant bankers? Some can. Most of them think it's easy. That's because they haven't seen how suddenly it can get hard. They probably hold cocktail parties back home to raise money for the lifeboats, and one day they'll need one.'

'Aren't you being a shade judgmental?'

She shook her head. 'No. I've been there, done that.'

'You?'

'Not any more.' She pointed across the marina. 'See that mast? The tall one with the radar unit on it? Third in from the end of the last pontoon.'

'Yes.'

'That's *Double or Quits*, owned by a Grade-A shit.'

'This Hackman person?'

'Jerome Hackman. Formerly the man in my life.'

'What ended it?'

'It was after everything else went wrong, Tripoli and all that.'

'You split up because of that?'

She snorted. 'We split up because one day I stopped being a toy.' She put on a Bostonian accent. '"Have you met the lady in my life? I guess you've seen her on the box. This is Claire. Pour the man a drink, Claire. Is the champagne in the ice-box, Claire?"'

'How did you meet?'

'Down here. Sailing. I was in *Tiger Kitten* and he was aground with two clients and some bimbos at the entrance to the Beaulieu River. I helped him get off. He invited me to dinner.'

'And?'

'And . . . he was nice-looking. He was . . . we were good together.'

Harry's hand moved to the inside of her thigh. 'As good as us?'

'Stop it.'

'Well?'

'Too early to tell.'

'What does he do?'

'He's some sort of merchant banker. He wheels and deals.'

'American?'

'Are my impressions that bad? Yes.'

'So, are we likely to bump into him?'

'No. He's always travelling. Anyway, the boat's a toy. He got bored with it. He's a useless sailor.'

The memory came back to her, a weekend off somewhere – Salcombe? No, Dartmouth. 'I'll tell you a story,' she said.

Jerome had called up on the boat's phone and booked a table for dinner at the Carved Angel for the fat Swiss couple he was trying to impress, a potential client and his wife. He took the helm at times like that, even though he was useless when the wind wasn't dead steady. Coming into the entrance past the Castle he'd gone too close in, getting into the wind-shadow under the high ground and the boat had slowed, sails flapping.

Jerome always used his engine as an alternative to seamanship so he'd simply switched on and used the power to point as close to the wind as he could, sails still filling gently. Claire had been watching an extraordinarily decrepit boat coming out of the river towards them for a good couple of minutes before Jerome even noticed it; two masts above a towering, battered black hull, an echo of a much earlier age. She thought it was a ketch when it first came into view, then noticed the square sails on the foremast and thought again, a topsail schooner. Every sail was a different colour, patched and sewn, and the rigging was a mixture of ancient rope and garishly modern blue polypropylene. It was a mess, but someone was sailing it gloriously, battering out on a converging course for the buoy ahead. There was only one person visible on board.

'Have you seen it?' she'd called back to Jerome, pointing.

He'd glanced past the sail and scowled. 'Crappy old thing.'

The distance was closing far too fast for her liking. 'He's got right of way,' she'd said as quietly as she could.

Jerome didn't like being told anything about sailing, ever, especially with clients there.

'Don't be dumb,' he said. 'I'm on starboard tack.'

'You've got the engine on,' she called urgently. 'He's under sail.'

'He can't hear it. We don't want to be late for the table,' Jerome said and laughed. 'He's only a water gypsy. He'll give way,' and he kept resolutely on.

There was a shout of 'Water!' from the deck of the onrushing schooner. Jerome merely glanced at it, shook his head, shouted 'Starboard!' back, pointing to the boom to emphasize his point, and kept to his course. Then he looked again sharply, suddenly seeing the signs of the coming collision, but by that time it was far too late. Claire, getting to her feet in horror, was never sure afterwards whether it was luck or very fine sailing, but the schooner came off the wind just enough to miss all the bits that mattered, sweeping its vast projecting bowsprit past the end of Jerome's sail with an inch to spare, then dipping its bow in a trough to catch and rip away the short flagmast and flashy ensign that projected from Jerome's stern.

Jerome had been beside himself with rage, screaming threats

across the water, and the old boat had turned and followed them back the way it had come into Dartmouth. The scene on deck later, as its skipper came on board, was extraordinary. He was maybe thirty-five with a gypsy darkness about his face, long tightly-curling black hair and a faded tweed jacket with elbow patches. For one who looked like a market trader, his voice came as a shock; a deep, warm voice with a touch of old money in its immaculate vowel sounds.

'There's no damage to me,' he'd said by way of greeting, 'so I'll forget your behaviour.'

'*My* behaviour! I'm holding you to blame for this,' said Jerome.

'You had your engine on. I don't know whether you know this, but power gives way to sail.'

'We were both under sail,' Jerome had said, and perhaps it was the expression on Claire's face that made the newcomer turn to her and say politely, 'Would you agree with that?'

'No,' she had said, judiciously, 'I wouldn't.'

Jerome had clammed up then, insisting they exchange addresses. Charles Golant, Church Passage House, Landrake, Cornwall.

Later, Jerome had gone off to feed his clients in a murderous mood. Claire was down below lying on a bunk when she heard a soft thud on the deck as someone came on board. She crept to the hatch and stuck her head out cautiously. In the evening light, Charles Golant was tying a large piece of cardboard to the boat's wheel. She cleared her throat and he jumped.

'Oh . . . I thought you'd gone.'

'I stayed. What on earth are you doing?'

'Just making my point,' he said. She looked at the card. It had big arrows on it. One pointed upwards and said 'SAIL', the other pointed down and said 'ENGINE'. Underneath, it said, 'JUST SO YOU KNOW WHICH IS WHICH NEXT TIME'.

She giggled. 'He'll hate it.'

'I'd better take it off. He might think it was you. That was brave of you, supporting me,' he'd said. 'Thank you.'

'I'm sorry, he can be appalling,' she'd said and he looked at her appraisingly.

'You're with him?'

She nodded. 'So far.'

'If you need rescuing, just call,' he said, 'I'm very good at damsels in distress. There's plenty of space on my boat. I'm afraid it's not quite up to these standards. I tend to do things my own way.'

She watched him row back out to his coal-black pirate ship, then she went back to her book, lying uneasily on silk.

Harry laughed when she finished, then put on a look of alarm. 'Did being a bad sailor count against Jerome?' he said. 'Because so am I.'

Claire laughed. 'Not so long as you don't start trying to be the skipper.'

Harry shook his head and grinned. 'No, I promise. I'm just here for a bit of weekend domination.'

She stood over him in the cockpit, looking relaxed, sniffing the sea air. 'Is that what turns you on?' She mimed lashing him with a whip and he caught her wrist, pulling her gently towards him so that she collapsed on him, straddling his legs, closing round him, thighs, hands and mouth all focused on enclosing him suddenly with nothing held back.

A burst of laughter from a nearby boat, from some hidden, drunken joke, broke the spell after long seconds, leaving them dizzy with desire but aware how close their neighbours were within their floating plastic shells.

Claire sat back, swept her hand up through her hair and looked around. In a thick voice she said, 'Let's go and pick up a buoy.'

'A boy? What's wrong with me?' he asked.

'With a U,' she said, looking at him with wide, hungry eyes. 'To get away from the crowd.'

He wanted to help as she started the engine and singled up the moorings, but she was several steps ahead of him all the way. She let him cast off the bowline when she was ready, just to make him feel wanted, then they were threading their way out of the marina and into the estuary under the stars. Moored boats glided past in a long line, dim and white in the moonlight, with just the splashy chuffing of the exhaust and the slapping jingle of the rigging to mark their passage.

They went half a mile and then she put the lever into neutral, ran forward to the bow with a boathook and snagged the buoy neatly first time. He stood by the mast, looking up at the stars in the summer night, then around the deck at the small frontiers of their private world.

He turned, and she was standing by the cockpit, arms spread out first to the sky, then to him, and as he went back to her he saw from the starlight on her naked skin that her need was as keen as his.

'No one can see us now,' she said as he reached her. The remnants of the wake of a far-off boat reached them and set *Tiger Kitten* bobbing. He stumbled forward and she slid back against the coach-roof where the half-deflated rubber dinghy made a soft cushion, raising her legs to lock them round his back while their hands fought to remove the barrier of his trousers. No one could hear them either, which was just as well as Claire's wild climaxing cries echoed across the water like an ecstatic night bird.

# Sunday August 4th

Harry woke in a tiny, cramped bunk by himself to the compressed metallic voice of the Radio 4 announcer. 'Wight, Portland, Plymouth, one thousand and three, rising, south-west four, backing southerly five to six later.'

He looked up at Claire's knees where she was leaning against the chart table listening. The kettle began to give out a piercing whistle. She turned it off, splashed the water over coffee granules in two mugs and reached down to touch his face. He pulled her down and kissed her.

'Not very romantic this boat,' he complained, 'Separate bunks.'

'I did try but you kept pushing me out. Anyway the prologue was all right wasn't it?'

He stretched, and his feet and head came into contact with the wooden ends at the same moment. His legs were stiff and one arm was numb. Coffee and baked beans helped, and he washed up in cold, pumped water, wiping the remaining grease from the plates with kitchen roll.

'You don't really want to go out again, do you?' said Claire. 'It's going to be a bit bumpy out there.'

'I suppose you don't feel like a day on dry land, do you?' he said hopefully. He saw she looked disappointed. 'You go. I'd like to go back and see Steffie this afternoon. Just point me at a train.'

She hesitated but he pressed the point. 'I know you want to stay. You want to go and sail the arse off the boat and you'll be a lot better off if I'm not in the way. I'll see you tonight when you get back,' and in the end he had his way.

She took him to the station. Then, racing back to capture as much as she could of the day, she submerged all the troubles and anxieties of the coming Monday in a sea of foam and a symphony of knife-edge sailing. They were both quite glad to have the time to themselves, to let the emotional maelstrom into which they'd fallen quieten just a little.

That evening, tired but content, still refusing to think about her return to work on the morrow, Claire pointed the Golf towards London. Just before the M3, a flight of large bugs splattered in red and white catastrophe across her windscreen and the wipers simply spread the mess more widely. Pulling into a lay-by, she searched the pockets of the car for her box of tissues but they were nowhere to be seen. In the end she got down and slid her hand right under the driver's seat where, instead of the hoped-for angle of a cardboard box, her fingers met an unfamiliar bundle of cloth. She pulled it out with curiosity. It was heavy and there was the heft of cold metal within. She unwrapped it and found inside a shining, oiled, grey automatic pistol.

# Chapter Eighteen

Claire had seen plenty of automatics just like this one over the years, discreetly holstered on the belts of British and NATO forces, or waved in the air by the excitable denizens of Beirut or Sarajevo. There, they were part of the landscape of male confrontation. Here, among her tapes of Mahler and Led Zeppelin, next to her *A to Z of London* and a packet of extra strong mints, the weapon was brutally out of place.

Along the side of the casing it said 'Browning'. She touched it cautiously, then picked it up, not by the grip as if to shoot – that would involve her too much in whatever dangerous masculine game it represented – but by the snub, squared barrel. She pulled the magazine out of the butt and knew by the weight, even before she saw the sheen of the bullets inside, that it was loaded. Cars were going past on their mundane way continuously. Her one urgent thought was to get rid of it. She got out and looked around. A five-barred gate between trees blocked a field entrance. She opened it, walked through, away from the view of the cars, and looked for inspiration. The field was empty, but a scatter of cow pats told of its recent occupants. Fifty yards away was a galvanized iron water trough, and round it a deep lake of mud had formed where the pipe had been leaking and the cows' feet had churned the sodden earth into soup.

It occurred to her that perhaps her mysterious and misleading informant had put the gun there – in case he needed to scare her more when he hijacked her – and then forgotten to take it away. She looked carefully round to see she was not being observed, then plunged it as deeply as she could into the middle of the pool of mud. Her arm went in up to her elbow and she let it go, feeling safety returning as her fingers lost the memory of the cold metal. If it had been put there to be found, let them find it now.

But who was 'them', and above all, why?

She washed the mud off her arm in the trough and walked back to the car, wiping her shoes on the grass before she got in. She still had the piece of cloth, and she left it lying on the passenger seat, mulling it all over as she drove in an abstracted haze, but coming up with nothing. It was nine fifteen when she pulled in to a parking space outside the house in Stockwell.

Nine fifteen in the evening was two fifteen in the afternoon mountain time, where the Producer sat looking at his screen. It was ten fifteen in Frankfurt, where business had taken Hacker. The production team in London, monitoring the developing action, fed their little slugs of observation down the modems into the avid electronic web of screens, and Freedom's Friends, on the edges of their seats across the time zones, watched with bated breath as their trap developed.

Ann erupted into the hall as soon as she heard the front door close, breathless with news. 'Oh good. You're back. I've got something fantastic to tell you, but you've got to go straight out first. I thought you'd miss him. You've still got time . . .'

'Who? Slow down a bit. Time to do what?'

'Your mystery man phoned again. The one who was in the back of the car. At least I'm sure it was him. He said to tell you', she went into verbal quotes, 'he'd met you very recently in unusual circumstances in your car.'

'Why should I want to meet him again? He set me up last time.'

'He said something about circumstances making it necessary to give you only some of the facts before, but now he can clear it all up. He said he had to move very carefully, and with what I've got, I'm sure he's right.'

Claire felt wearied for a moment, almost as if it were better just left to lie; but the drumbeat of a story was already starting to pound deep inside and there was no alternative but to say, 'Tell me.'

'No. Just come straight back and be very careful. You've got to be outside the Kensington Hilton at nine-thirty. Will you make it?'

Claire looked at her watch. 'Just.'

'Do you want me to come too?'

Claire looked at Ann with her worried face and smiled. 'No,' she said. 'You stay in case he phones again.'

'Well, hurry back and make sure you stay somewhere fairly public, I don't trust any of these people. If you're going to be more than an hour, phone me or I'll call the police.'

'Make that two hours.'

Over the bridge, cutting a just-gone-red light and blatting the Golf up the North End Road at well over the limit, Claire reviewed the options. Outside the Hilton sounded safe. He couldn't pull any stunts there and, anyway, if he planned to do her harm, there had been all the opportunity in the world to do it before. Past Olympia, she took the short-cut up Russell Road and accelerated out into Holland Road in front of a taxi, which blared its horn in complaint. The lights before the roundabout were against her, but not for long, and she swung into the crescent opposite the hotel with a minute in hand.

Claire looked carefully across at the hotel before she crossed the road, but there was just the usual knot of baffled American tourists gazing towards Shepherd's Bush, wondering where central London had got to, as they waited for cabs to take them somewhere recognizable. She reached the front of the building and looked around. No one took any notice of her. She walked into the lobby and round into the open-plan bar. Nobody. She went outside again and a beaten-up Kawasaki, covered in panniers and couriers stickers, howling down from Notting Hill, cut in and stopped, brake pads screeching, in the taxi bay. The rider flicked out the stand, looked around and walked towards her without hesitation. He was clad in black leather from head to foot, a smoked, impenetrable visor fronting the full-face helmet. She felt a chill of alarm and looked quickly around her. There was no one else nearby.

He stopped in front of Claire, reached a hand inside his jacket and, her eyes fixed on it in helpless fascination that had given up on action, pulled out nothing more threatening than a sheet of paper. She took it with a slightly shaking hand. A muffled voice from behind the visor said, 'Now. Go there. Right now.'

Then he was back on the bike and gone, leaving Claire staring at a photocopy of a page from an *A to Z of London*. A pink highlighter had marked a street somewhere behind Lancaster Gate, and '15A' was circled in the same pink in the margin. There was yellow on the page too – a route to the street – but it clearly didn't apply as it came in from the north.

No option, Claire thought, as she crossed back to the Golf. No option and there never has been. If you play this game you either have to go all the way or pack it in and take up knitting. If I leave it now, I'll always wonder; and she knew that was literally true. She joined the traffic again, through Notting Hill and on past Queensway. She had to check the map at Lancaster Gate, round the one-way system. Second right, third left, first right, she kept repeating. The idea of a house didn't appeal. 15A must be the number of a flat, a flat where she would ring a bell and be drawn into a hidden place by a remote-controlled door. That wasn't the action of a cautious person. Ann's voice inside her head said 'no' very firmly.

She turned into the end of the road and her pulse started to race. Number Fifteen was three quarters of the way down on the left. There was nowhere obvious to park, and a car was coming up behind her. She indicated left and pulled in as far as she could to let the other car by, but instead it braked sharply to a halt inches short of her back bumper. Another car, a white Vauxhall, appeared from behind it, came past both of them and cut in, angled across her nose. Then doors were bursting open all around her, men boiling out of parked cars, men surrounding her, yanking both her own doors open. As she turned her head to the right in sick shock, one man appeared close up, holding a large gun in both hands pointed straight at her forehead.

A garishly striped, blue-flashing Rover wailed round the

corner just ahead and slid to a halt at the edge of the chaos around her and, so totally did she misunderstand the situation, that relief bubbled up inside her through the frozen terror. Some little strand of logic, still doggedly trying to do its job inside her brain, suggested the others should now run away, fought off at the last moment by the Fifth Cavalry. It was only when two policemen, climbing out of the Rover, nodded deferentially to the man holding the gun on her that it dawned on her that she was the one apparently on the wrong side of the law.

They got Claire out of the car with no attempt at gentle handling, frisking her roughly for an unnecessarily long time in legitimized indecent assault, then pushed her protesting into the back of the police Rover, the man who'd held the gun next to her. As the car door slammed shut, she tried to argue.

'I'm Claire Merrick, for Christ's sake. You know, from the TV? I'm not whoever you think I am. For God's sake, what's going on?'

The man raised an eyebrow. 'Not who I think you are? You just said you were.'

'What?'

'Claire Merrick, that's just who I think you are. Claire Merrick, armed, off her head, and fixing to settle the hash of the geezer that lives here.'

She stared wildly out of the window at the men crawling all over her Golf, searching in the boot and on hands and knees inside, under the seat, and suddenly knew she had to thank her lucky stars for a bug on the windscreen, a missing box of tissues, and a muddy puddle in a field near the M3.

'Look,' she said, in what she tried to make a very reasonable tone of voice, 'something's gone awfully wrong here. Someone's leading you up the garden path.'

'Not this someone,' he said with the smugness of power behind him. 'This isn't the sort of someone that gets things like that wrong.'

The uniformed policemen got back in the front of the car.

'We're on our way then,' said one of them. 'Paddington Green, the man says.'

'Right you are,' said the man in the back.

159

Paddington Green, thought Claire dully. High security, used for holding terrorists. What on earth do they think I've done?

She was put in an interview room, watched over by a cross-looking policewoman, and left to herself for half an hour. Then a tall man in a suit walked in and nodded at her.

'Miss Merrick. I'm Chief Inspector Marchant.'

'And I'm fed up with being here,' she said looking at him. Young for his rank, well-spoken and clearly intelligent, he had the look of the fast track about him, the sort you get in Serious Crime, Anti-Terrorist or Special Branch. This was no ordinary copper.

He didn't respond to her comment, just sat down opposite her at the table and put a sheet of paper on it.

'Would you care to tell me about this?' he said.

It was the photocopied map.

'Only if you tell me why,' she said bitterly. 'I don't think you have any right to do any of this.'

'Is this yours?' he said.

'I was given it this evening.'

'Who by?'

'A motorcycle messenger, as it happens.'

'Why?'

'It was a message from someone; a rendezvous to meet them.'

'At 15A?'

'I assumed that was what it meant, yes,' she said with exasperation.

'Who was the person you were meeting?'

'I don't know his name.'

Then he stumped her. 'So you don't know Mr Ibn Azogi?' he said.

She couldn't cover her astonishment. 'Azogi? Yes, I . . . Why?'

'You were approaching his house. You had a photocopied map with his address written on it. Isn't that reason enough?'

His address. Dear Lord, what did this mean? She tried to answer and it sounded – even to her – like blustering.

'I had no idea he lived there. The man who gave me the map didn't say anything about that.'

'So who did you think you were meeting?'

'A man. Does it matter?'

'Yes, it certainly matters. A man whose name you don't know. That's not very helpful, is it?'

'I've had about enough of this,' she snapped. 'You've hauled me in off the streets in full view of anyone passing like a three-ring circus. You have absolutely no reason to keep me here and I intend to make a lot of noise about it. You're not dealing with just anyone, you know. Then to cap it all, you have some goon pointing a gun at me. I'm not going to answer any more of your questions until you tell me what's going on.'

'What's going on, Miss Merrick,' he said with sarcastic politeness, 'is that we are acting on information received that you were heading for Mr Azogi's residence, with a firearm in your possession, intent on causing him harm. The map would appear to support that, and it appears to have an escape route marked on it too.'

There was no whistleblower, her mind shrieked the confirmation at her, just another elaborate trap – and if the gun had still been there, undisturbed under her seat, she would now be caught deeply within it.

'What firearm?' she asked. 'And information from whom?'

'Let's just stay on the subject of Mr Azogi. You do know him?'

'I once met someone of that name.'

'I believe it's true to say you hold a grudge against him?'

'A man called Azogi caused me a lot of trouble. However, I repeat; I didn't know that anyone called Azogi lived at that house, and I don't have a gun. If you are going to keep on with this, then I want to call my solicitor right now.'

There was a knock at the door and the Chief Inspector was summoned out to the corridor. The policewoman stayed. Outside, where Claire couldn't hear, his sergeant had bad news for him.

'We've been right through the car, sir. Nothing at all. There's a piece of rag that Fred reckons smells of gun oil, but that's about as shaky as they come.'

The Chief Inspector considered. 'So . . . we've got no gun, one photocopied map, and a very angry TV reporter. We'd better go back to the tip-off.'

The number he rang, on a secure phone, was a number that he hadn't had to call since his time in Special Branch. There was a procedure to follow and it shouldn't have been him doing it, but time and a potentially explosive Claire Merrick were pressing. It was answered immediately by a careful, precise voice which simply identified itself by repeating the number dialled.

'Duty Officer, please. This is Chief Inspector Marchant, Paddington Green.'

Another voice came on. A Security Service desk officer. 'Can I help you?'

'I hope so. We're holding Miss Claire Merrick in connection with her intended attack on your Mr Azogi.'

He paused, expecting a response, but there was silence.

'We detained her and we're holding her here, but there's no sign of any firearm in the car. I'd like to know whether you have any further information which would give us grounds for holding her?'

The voice was languid, puzzled. 'I'm not quite with you.'

'Well, you messaged us this evening with the tip-off.'

'We did? What time?'

'Er, soon after nine.'

'Some mistake, Chief Inspector. Nothing from here, I promise you. I've been in the hot seat since seven. Sounds like someone got their wires crossed. Claire Merrick, you said. Not *the* Claire Merrick, surely?'

The Chief Inspector put the phone down in baffled annoyance. The message had come from somewhere. The ident was the right one. Someone had screwed up, but it wasn't him. He was prepared to bet that, come the morning, someone at Five would be on the blower checking they were still holding the woman. That didn't help him now, not with an angry journalist and no evidence. Some humble pie would have to be eaten and he started rehearsing the words in his head as he walked back down the corridor.

The screens could buzz in several different ways. The emergency call was an ululating bleep on the tones, rising and descending. It brought all the players out of their seats and staring at the letters unfolding, black inside a fire-red box.

'FAILURE. FAILURE. MERRICK NOW LEAVING POLICE STATION. REQUEST INSTRUCTIONS.'

The Producer was on the ball. Within fifteen seconds he was all over the screen throwing out possibilities, checking the contingency plans, trawling for their ideas.

'ASSUME SHE'S GOING HOME. THEY DIDN'T FIND THE GUN OR THEY WOULD HAVE KEPT HER. ASSUME SHE FOUND IT BEFORE. QUESTION TO STOCKWELL WATCHERS. IS HER FRIEND STILL THERE?'

'AFFIRMATIVE,' came the reply, 'LIGHTS ON IN UPSTAIRS ROOM.'

The Producer again: 'CANNOT RE-ENTER HOUSE, SO MERRICK WILL FIND PAPERS WE PLANTED IN HER ROOM. PRIORITY IS TO PREVENT THIS. HER TRAVEL-LING TIME HOME IS TWENTY MINUTES. THAT'S ALL WE HAVE.'

Hacker, thinking fast, began to type. 'PROPOSE WE KILL TWO BIRDS WITH ONE STONE.'

The Producer picked up a phone, called another London number, and gave some instructions. Failure was not an experience he wanted to enjoy again. The point had to be made that it wasn't acceptable.

It took Claire more than twenty minutes, and she nearly didn't go home at all. She wanted to see Harry, to feel the security of his willingness to believe. Ann would believe her too, but Ann would want to intellectualize it all, to ask questions to which there weren't any answers. She thought of driving to Harry's place, but stopped to phone him first. From the click and the short silence after the second ring she knew even before the recording started, that only his machine was listening.

'Hello,' she said miserably, 'I'm in a box. The police think I was trying to kill someone. I'm going back to Ann's place. I've got to talk to you. I'll call you when I get there.'

Where the hell was he at this time of night? It was almost

eleven-thirty. Had she but known, he was six feet from the phone, the other side of his door, struggling to get out his front door keys without dropping a slippery foil box of hot Chicken Korma, hearing the machine whirring to a stop.

She drove home, parked close to a seemingly empty small truck, unaware that her every move was not only watched, but was the subject of instant world-wide communication.

She walked up the short path to the front door, set upright two milk bottles which had rolled away from their correct place by the cat-flap, and opened the door. There was a sharp and unfamiliar smell in the hall, and when she flipped on the light she saw bright red splashes on the floor tiles and the walls. She backed towards the door – towards the glass panels – in total horror, and heard the footsteps behind her too late to turn more than half way before the arm came round her neck.

The leader sat in the van, watching the view of the front door on the monitor, fed by the tiny video heads concealed in the van's air vent, and waited for the team in the house to return. After the screw-up with the gun, he badly wanted this to go smoothly. It was the fifth active job since he'd joined, and though he had no idea who his ultimate employer was, the money was far, far too good to risk losing by not doing things perfectly. The van's electronic lock buzzed and the door opened as he turned, surprised, knowing the men certainly hadn't come out of the front door. It was two men, but not the two he was expecting. He relaxed as he saw the bulldog features of his controller, the only senior face he ever had seen.

'Changeover,' said the man in his gruff, Yorkshire voice. 'New plan. I need to brief you.'

The leader slipped out of the seat, making a big point of not looking closely at the man who moved past him to take his place. He got into the passenger seat of the controller's Granada. There was another man in the back seat.

'I think it's going to work well,' the leader said. 'They're a good team.'

The controller, seated at the wheel, held a handkerchief to his face.

'Got a cold?' the leader said, and knew too late it was too ingratiating.

The man behind thrust a small aerosol past his face and he thought perhaps it was an asthma spray, but then he heard it hiss and before he knew it, he had inhaled the wet droplets.

The driver of the Brighton train only had a couple of seconds to register the staggering figure that wandered horrifyingly on to the track in front of him before the thud spattered a red spray over his cab windscreen. It took six months of therapy to make the nightmares go away.

# Chapter Nineteen

Harry, never an elegant eater, took the top off the curry on the hall table, unfolding the pinched-over corners to release the lid, and swearing as a small lava-flow of creamy brown sauce ran down his wrist and soaked into the cuff of his shirt. He took a plastic spoonful while he pushed the replay button on the machine. The stress in Claire's voice made him forget the curry and he dialled her number.

It rang twice and an unfamiliar woman's voice answered.

'Hello,' he said, 'Claire isn't back yet, is she?' He knew she couldn't be.

'No, she isn't. Who are you?'

'It's er . . . My name's Harry.'

There was a coldness in the woman's voice that told him Claire had said something about their old relationship. 'Well, I don't know how long she'll be.'

'She just called me from a phone box. She said she was on the way back.'

'Oh . . . good.'

'I'll come round.'

That puzzled her. 'Well, if you must.'

'I don't know where you live.'

Ann was cautious, worried. 'Perhaps Claire wouldn't want you to.'

'I told you, she rang me.'

'Well, that doesn't necessarily . . .'

'For God's sake. We spent the weekend together. Things have changed.'

'Oh.'

'What is your address?' he said through clenched teeth.

She came to a decision. 'Stockwell. We're number twenty-eight, Burnett . . . and the phone went dead.

They didn't often slip up, but they had this time. The previous leader, killed for a failure that was not possible to anticipate, had made one real error. He should have been monitoring Ann's phone, but they'd plugged into the line next door. By the time they found out, when they disconnected her phone and the line they were listening to went on working, the damage was done. The new leader marked it for his report but had no option but to press on. Through that loophole slipped Harry's phone call.

'HANDWRITING SAMPLE AVAILABLE,' said the screen. 'SUGGESTIONS FOR TEXT NEEDED. PRODUCTION TEAM TO WITHDRAW IMMEDIATELY THIS STAGE COMPLETED.'

Suggestions came in, were amalgamated and refined to remove American idiom. The team in the van were equipped to deal with extra documentation, and the fax link soon provided them with as close a copy of Claire's handwriting as they needed as a basis for the final version.

Harry tried the phone again and got a steady 'out of order' tone. He told himself that telephones went wrong all the time, then he went looking for his street directory. He found it five minutes later under a pile of canvases on the floor. The house was near Stockwell tube, he knew that much, and there it was. Burnett Road, off Lansdowne Way. He went down to the hall and unlocked his mountain bike.

Twenty-five minutes after the phone call, he arrived, panting, in Burnett Road. There was no sign of Claire's car anywhere. Number twenty-eight had been divided into flats. He was quite sure Claire had said it was a little terraced house, but it wasn't anything of the sort. It was a tatty Georgian three-storey job, split into semis and then clearly sub-divided, floor by floor. There were three bells. One said 'Da Costa', another said 'Emmy', and the third had no name. He pushed it. Nothing happened. He pushed it again.

Above his head a window rattled up.

'Who's that?' demanded a man's voice.

Harry stepped back and looked up. A middle-aged black man was looking down.

'Sorry,' he said, 'I must have pressed the wrong bell. I was looking for Ann.'

'Fucking late man. What the fuck you doing ringing my bell?'

'I'm looking for Ann. I'm sorry if I woke you. Do you know which her bell is?'

'No Ann here. Now fuck off.' The window slammed down.

She'd said twenty-eight. She'd definitely said twenty-eight. He got back on his bike and pedalled slowly down the road. He turned left at the end, intending to go round the block, and there, suddenly, on the right hand side, was Claire's Golf. He stopped and looked at it to make sure. Then he saw the road sign next to it, Burnett Gardens. Number twenty-eight fitted the bill much more closely; a narrow two-storey terraced house with empty milk bottles on the doorstep. There were lights on inside. He pushed the bell and heard it buzz but no one came. He pushed it again. Still nothing. He put his eye close to the frosted glass and saw disconcerting fragments of bright colour, then bent down and looked through the letter box. In the harsh light of the hall he saw a vivid red puddle on the tiles with a long smear leading away from it.

He stood up sharply, his skin chilling and the bite of sour stomach acid in his throat, and fought the rising fear while he tried to think. Steeling himself, he looked again. There was blood everywhere, on the walls as well as the floor. He took a deep breath and tried the door handle but it was locked. The neighbours' lights were out. He picked a loose half-brick out of the low wall by the front gate. The noise would probably wake someone and they might call the police. Well, that would only save him the trouble.

There were four small panels of frosted glass in the upper part of the door and he chose the one nearest the lock. When he swung the brick against it the whole pane simply came loose with a tiny noise of splintering wood, and fell dully on to the doormat inside. He reached through and opened the door. Two irrevocable, nervous steps took him into the hall and the strong reek of blood that told of the certain wreck of a human being. He moved with tiny, slow steps, down the hall, past the puddles and into a kitchen, where there was more blood, much more blood, and an empty sack of a once-human thing, twisted like a dummy with its legs sprawled out on the floor. The torso and battered, pulpy head were propped against the fridge door. Had he known, it was all that was left of Ann Farrow.

His first awful feeling was one of relief that it wasn't Claire. The clothes and what little he could see of close-cropped hair showed that. He looked away appalled. There were red footprints on the floor and he followed them out to the stairs and up. The marks on the carpet had tapered off by the top of the stairs, but the second door he opened showed him another body and this time the heavy fall of blue-black hair which hid her face revealed who it was. She was lying on the bed, her hand clutching a hammer, its end caked in drying blood, a strip of skin smeared across the side. On the bed by her was an open, brown plastic bottle. A few loose capsules had rolled down the slope of the bed cover, and rested against her arm.

She couldn't have been there long, he thought, and bent closer, to see with sudden, leaping relief that she was breathing. He turned to go for the phone, but then all the elements came together in his head. Her phone message – 'the police thought I was trying to kill someone' – the hammer, the pills. What had happened to her? He stopped and turned back to her. He tried to pick her up, staggering under the weight, and managed at the second attempt. Her feet banged against the door frame as he hauled her into the bathroom. She moved and made a small noise. Encouraged by that, he draped her over the edge of the bath. There was a shower hose and he tried spraying cold water on her head. She moved a little in response. Then he opened her mouth and stuck his fingers down her throat, and in only a second or two she was noisily, violently sick all over his arm and into the bath.

He cleaned her up with a flannel and then tried to do the same to his shirt where the remains of the curry had now met their match. She was a little less comatose, and when he forced two glasses of water down her she was sick again. For ten minutes he watched over her, talked to her, encouraged her, poured drinks into her and held her while she threw up; then there came a moment when she was able to sit, slumped against the wall, without immediately sliding sideways to the floor, and when she lifted a hand to her head and tried to say something.

The Producer looked at his watch and the minute hand clicked round to the right time. He punched in the execute command for the final phase and across the Atlantic a man, now safely removed from Stockwell, moved to a phone and pressed the nine button three times.

The phone rang twice and an operator answered. 'Emergency services. Which service do you require? Fire, Police or Ambulance?'

'Police, please.' The voice was not his own but he'd practised it well. It was thin, weak, old. The police came on. 'I've heard noises. Screams and blows,' he said. 'Just down the road.'

'Yes sir. Could you just give me your name and address?'

'No. I don't want to be involved, you see. Not round here. Can't you just go and see. I think someone was being killed. It was number twenty-eight. We're in Burnett Gardens. That's Stockwell.'

'Thank you, sir. Just your name, sir. Strictly confidential. Just for our own information.'

'No. I won't. It's those gays you see. They're dykes. I don't want trouble with them.'

The phone clicked down and the sergeant on the other end sighed, looked up at his status board and reached for a microphone.

Harry had Claire's arm round his shoulders and her car keys in his hand. There was no one about in the little street, and her legs were taking some of her weight. He got her into the passenger seat and then remembered his bike. It wouldn't go in the boot, so after puzzling with the mechanism for too long, he got the hood down and lifted it into the back seat.

He had never been a smooth driver, and since Steffie's accident he hadn't driven at all, so the rear lights of the car in front took the brunt of his first attempt to leave the parking space. He took it more carefully the second time and made his way safely round the corner, fifteen seconds ahead of the police car that entered Burnett Gardens from the other end and braked harshly to a halt outside number twenty-eight.

Once the two men inside had seen the kitchen, it was only minutes before the street was full of cars. The PC given the job of locating their informant didn't have to wake any of the residents; the whole street was out in no time, and he found it a little puzzling that no one seemed to want to admit having made the call. It was the first CID man on the scene who noticed what Harry had missed; an envelope on the sitting room table, carrying two dramatic, smudged fingerprints marked out in blood, but then Harry hadn't been in that room.

The officer opened it gingerly, holding it through a disposable plastic glove, read it, and whistled. 'All right. Well, now we know who we're looking for, anyway.' He went to the car to set in motion the nationwide hunt for Claire Merrick.

# Chapter Twenty

## Monday August 5th

'Harry,' said Herman. 'We got shit all over the walls. Grab a chair. You'd better listen to what Derek's got to say.'

Jane Bernstein and Chief Inspector Derek Palmer were already sitting in Herman's office; Jane somewhat white, Palmer looking masonically conspiratorial. Harry kept a look of innocent enquiry on his face.

'Bit of a shocker this one, Harry,' Palmer said. 'Seems Claire Merrick went off her head last night. First she tried to attack some Arab at his house, then she went back to the place where she was staying and did in the other woman who lived there.'

'Christ almighty,' said Harry, letting his jaw go slack. 'Did in? You mean killed?'

'Just that. Used a hammer.'

'What, murdered her?'

'Yup.'

'Good God. So she's locked up, is she?'

'No, she isn't. She'd gone. We'll catch her pretty quick; I mean she's not exactly an unknown face.'

Harry decided a bit more surprise was called for.

'But why? I mean, I didn't have much time for her, OK, but I never thought she was that sort.'

'Read him the letter, Derek,' said Herman.

'Well, keep it to yourself,' said Palmer, and pulled out a photocopied sheet. 'She left this behind. Looks like she was going to do herself in too but she changed her mind. They found pills all over the place. First she broke in the door so it would look like someone else did it, then she wrote this.'

He held it up and read it out in the artificial monotone of an officer giving evidence from his pocket book in a court room.

'I shall be past caring by the time you read this. Don't anyone feel sorry for Ann. She shouldn't have done it. I had to kill the bitch because she stopped me settling things with Azogi. I know it was her who told the police. She's been seeing someone else. I told her what would happen if she wasn't faithful. It's her own fault.'

'Bloody dyke,' said Herman. 'Did you know she was a dyke? I didn't. Anyway, who's Azogi?'

Jane Bernstein gave him a reproving glance but kept quiet.

'Some Arab,' said Palmer. 'Apparently she had it in for him. Thought he'd messed her about once.'

'You're sure she wrote this?' asked Harry, and regretted it immediately when he got surprised looks from all three of them.

'It's her handwriting and her fingerprints,' said Palmer. 'Looks like it to me. Why do you ask?'

'No reason,' said Harry quickly, 'I just thought she used to have a boyfriend.'

'Yes, she did. An American. He's being helpful.'

'Doesn't mean she isn't a dyke really,' said Herman. 'She split up with this bloke. Didn't like it that way, maybe.'

'Umm,' said Harry and looked around at the policeman. 'So, what happens now?'

'Fingers out,' said Palmer. 'It shouldn't be too hard. Frankly I'm surprised we haven't picked her up already. The word's been out since last night. She never said anything to any of you about other special friends or places she stayed, did she?'

'No,' said Herman.

'Me neither,' said Jane, 'and she *hated* Harry so she wouldn't have told you, would she?'

So all Harry had to do was look at her and shrug and forget about being an accessory after the fact or whatever they called it; forget about having the object of all their interest lying in his bed back at his studio. If only they knew, he thought with a feeling somewhere between hysterical humour and despair.

The phone buzzed and Herman's secretary's voice, through the squawk box, said, 'Mr Gilligan for you, Mr Dent.'

'I put a call in,' said Herman. 'I mean, he picked her, not me. We'll have every tabloid in the world on our doorstep when this lot breaks. It's not exactly the best publicity, is it?'

He picked up the phone, switched off the squawk and swivelled round away from them. The other three kept quiet and listened unashamedly.

'Yeah, that's right, Des,' said Herman. 'No question. You've read the stuff I faxed?' He listened a bit more. 'This afternoon? Oh, right. Yup, OK.'

When he put the receiver down it took him a second to recompose his face.

'He's coming in. Says he wants a personal input. He thinks we can turn this one to our advantage. Until then, everyone keep quiet, right? Keep it buttoned up tight.'

Harry had taken four steps down the corridor when Charlotte nabbed him.

'Is it true?'

'What?'

'You know perfectly well what. Is it true Claire Merrick's killed her lesbian lover?'

'Don't ask me.'

'It is then,' said Charlotte with triumphant logic. 'Otherwise you would have looked surprised. I know you, Harry. You can't fool me. Go on, what do you know about it?'

'Sounds as though you know more than I do.'

The office was buzzing and Harry realized that for camouflage he had to join in, so he speculated with the best of them. At lunchtime, he borrowed a producer's car and rushed back across south-west London to his flat. Claire was still in bed, sleeping deeply. He stood looking down at her, his body yearning to climb in next to her and seize the quiet moment, his mind yelling the impossibility of the whole thing, calling the widening odds of them ever sharing that bed in peace again. He wrote a note. 'Don't go out,' it said. 'I'll be back as soon as I can. Don't answer the phone. There's food in the fridge.' He went to check that last claim, came back and inserted the word 'no' before 'food'.

Back at his desk, he tried to concentrate on a script for a murder re-enactment, but in his mind's eye, the body was Ann, the witness was himself and the photofit of the murderer kept shimmering into Claire's face. Jane interrupted him.

'We're wanted in the conference room.'

'Who by?'

'The big boss. Gilligan himself. Herman's in a twitter.'

There was no doubt where the centre of gravity lay in that room. Gilligan had a powerful economy of movement. The slightest turn of those steady, all-seeing eyes, the subliminal nod of acknowledgment at their entrance, left no doubt who's room it was, who's game National was. Harry took the seat indicated by Herman and looked around. Derek Palmer was there, in uniform. Vivien Prest, National's press and publicity officer, sat next to Gilligan. Jane had come in with Harry, and that was it.

'All right,' said Gilligan, and the deep voice harmonized with the seasoned-timber look of the face around the flattened nose. 'Thank you all for coming. We have a unique situation to deal with and we all need to think fast. This show's in danger of turning into a laughing stock. We recruit a top name journo and within three weeks, she's killing people. That kills the show.' He paused to let that sink in, looking round at all of them. 'My fault. I picked her. Now it seems she has a long history of obsessions. She was one of those people who saw conspiracies in all directions. Viewed the other way, it's an incredible opportunity.' He looked around like a schoolmaster hoping for a clever child to guess the right answer.

'It's a unique story. A nationally famous woman reporter murders someone and she's front-of-camera in a crime show. It's huge, and we have the inside track. If she hasn't been caught, we'll go to town on Friday with the biggest manhunt story we've ever had. I want you, er, Chaplin, full-time on it. Hand over anything else you've got. I want half the show on it with the biggest PR blitz we've ever seen from you, Viv, and I want to show just how mad and just how persuasive she was, so that none of it sticks to us.'

He turned to Derek Palmer. 'Mr Palmer. Within these four walls, would you bring us up to date?'

Palmer cleared his throat. 'You'll understand I'm not leading the investigation, but I have been asked to liaise closely because of my own knowledge of Miss Merrick. I can tell you that forensic have established that she apparently took a large overdose of sleeping tablets at the scene, then changed her mind and induced vomiting. Earlier in the evening we'd been tipped off that she intended harm to a gentleman of Arab origin living in West London. She was intercepted near his house.'

'Who was this tip from?' asked Harry, who had been doing a lot of amazed head-shaking, and thought it was time to change the record.

'More than my job's worth to say, Harry. What matters is it would seem she decided it was her flatmate who gave us the tip. We've spoken to a Mr Jerome Hackman, who formerly went out with Miss Merrick. He's not at all surprised to hear that, sexually, perhaps men were not her first choice.'

Harry puzzled over that one. Palmer was still talking. 'Her last employers, ITN, told us she'd claimed this Azogi had been behind a plan to discredit her. They say it was nonsense, just wild accusations. Now, as to where she is, her car was found in New Cross this morning, badly vandalized.'

That's what happens, Harry thought, when you leave a nice Golf Convertible in the middle of Balham with the keys in the ignition.

'She has a boat at a marina near Portsmouth. There's no sign of anyone there, but we're keeping an eye on it, and that's about it.'

Gilligan had been making notes throughout. 'Right, thanks. What about keeping it quiet?'

Palmer looked slightly embarrassed. 'Well, I've done what I can. Our Press Office won't give out her name before tomorrow. That's not to say it won't leak, because her picture's being circulated round all the forces.'

'That's not long. We want a beat on it until Friday,' said Herman.

'No, it's OK. The first posters are going up tomorrow,'

said Gilligan. 'We'll be ahead of the game. Now here's what we do.'

Harry got home at seven-thirty with a plastic bag of groceries slung over his handlebars. He'd followed a deliberately indirect route back, cycling all the way through south London to Waterloo station, where he had a job to do before retracing his steps to Wandsworth. He looked carefully at the house from the outside, but there was nothing to give away Claire's presence. He sang loudly as he unlocked the door so that she would know it was him. She was sitting in the studio looking very frail, small and vulnerable in one of his shirts and a pair of track suit trousers. There was a brush in her hand and a painting on the easel in front of her.

He went to her and held her.

'Are you feeling any better?' he asked.

'Yes, a bit sick, but I slept it out. I've been jumping at every noise. I've had the radio on. There's been no mention.'

'I hope you had it on quietly. These flats have thin walls.'

'Yes. Come on. What's happening?'

He held her, wondering where to start. 'It looks like you're going to be a superstar.'

'What do you mean?'

'Your name's going to be in lights. Gilligan flew in specially.' He was speaking lightly as though it were all a big joke, but there was strain in his voice, detectable if you listened hard. 'If you're not found by Friday, you've got half the show. Not only that but from tomorrow there are going to be billboards all over Britain. They've already booked the sites. Big pictures of you with a slogan. A teaser first of all. "If you see this woman, ring National TV", then on Friday, "National's own killer. The hunt for Claire Merrick. On National Tonight".'

Claire sat down on the chair and Harry looked at her painting. It was him, probably. At least it was a nude male lying on his bed, head turned away. The penis, which definitely looked like his, had wild flowers twined around it, painted with loving detail.

'Nice,' he said.

'I don't know what to do.' Her voice was small, flat.

'Nothing for now. Sit tight. Let me think of a way round this. They'll never believe you if you give yourself up. There's a letter confessing it. Your handwriting.'

'God. Someone's pretty organized.'

'Organized enough to put you out of business if you're in their way. Organized enough to rig an election. Who, though?'

'Harry?'

'Yes.'

'What did you do with my car?'

'Left it for the joyriders to find.'

'Shit.'

'Well the police have got it now. Anyway, it's no use to you until all this is over.'

'Why did you want my cash card?'

'I just laid a little trail. It's just as well you had a gold card. I took out five hundred in one hundred pound lots at five banks leading towards Waterloo Station. By the time the computer spits that out, they'll think you're making a run for it somewhere south.'

She didn't say anything, and he looked at her more closely. She was crying silently. He went to her again, put his arms round her, kissing her forehead, then her cheek, then her mouth, opening, as they took the easy way into escapism. This at least they had, now but maybe not tomorrow. They moved, still kissing, to the bedroom, undressed each other, mouths locked for as much of the time as was possible.

There was nothing slow about their lovemaking. She opened her legs around him as they half fell to the mattress, wet and welcoming around him as the springs, slowing her to a halt, brought him deeply into her. She clung tightly to him, hands, legs and mouth, as they drove at each other, blind and deaf to everything outside the perfectly fitting narrow circle of now and each other. They came at the same moment and were slowing, moving still to hang on to the last vestiges of that draining delight, when the doorbell rang.

Harry froze, moved gently out of her and climbed out of bed. He walked to the window, moved the blind aside and looked diagonally down.

There was a police car in the road outside.

# Chapter Twenty-One

The bell went again. Harry turned and whispered: 'Police.'

Claire sat up sharply. 'Jesus. Why?'

'Don't know. Just stay quiet. They'll go away.'

He went back to the blind, peering obliquely through the tiny gap. He couldn't see down to the front door. A figure approached and turned in at the gate – the ground-floor tenant, Mr Nosey Parker himself, Lesley Strawford, a man with a life-long mission to stick his nose into everyone else's business. Strawford's voice boomed a salutation to whoever was at the door.

'Can I help you at all?'

Harry could hear a voice answering but nothing more than that.

'Top floor. I'm sure he's in. His bike's there. Bell's probably on the blink. Go up and knock on his door.'

Sod it, thought Harry. He put on a dressing-gown quickly. Footsteps could be heard on the stairs.

'Get in the cupboard,' he said. 'Don't come out.'

He scooped her clothes off the floor and pushed them under the bedclothes, then went into the studio and shut the bedroom door. He picked up a Walkman from the bookshelf, stuck the headphones over his ears, then dabbed a paint brush into some old burnt umber which was still on a palette as the knock came on the door.

When he opened it, Derek Palmer was standing there.

'Hello Derek,' he said effusively, taking off his headphones, 'there's a surprise. Sorry, were you ringing?'

'Can I come in?' Palmer asked quietly, looking back down the stairs. 'Your neighbour's hanging about down there with his ears flapping.'

'Er, yeah. Step this way.'

'Am I disturbing you?' said Palmer, looking at the paintbrush and all the canvases stacked around. 'I didn't know you dabbled.'

'Yes. Yes I do.'

There was only one picture out on an easel and Palmer walked around to it with the air of a judge at a flower show. It was Claire's newly-painted nude with the floral penis. Palmer visibly winced and looked askance at Harry, who gave a shrug.

'I hope I'm not disturbing you,' Palmer said. 'I was coming past and I got the driver to wait for me. Just got a call that her card's been used in some cash machines.'

'Oh yeah? Where?'

'Round Waterloo. I reckon that's a blind, though. She's too smart for that.'

'So no firm news?'

'No, but the real reason I came was we need your prints tomorrow.'

Harry's heart missed a beat. 'Oh. Sure. Why?'

'Elimination. I'm told you were in her car coming back from some filming. That's what one of the camera crew said.'

God almighty, thought Harry, the house. There might be prints there.

'That's right,' he said casually. 'She took me back to her place, to try and sort out our differences. Didn't work. We wound up screaming at each other.' Can you tell fresh prints from old ones? he wondered.

Palmer's nose seemed to be flaring a little. Harry wondered if he could smell the spermy scent of lovemaking drifting from the bedroom. Then he saw where the man was looking and he died all over again. His picture of Claire, coming towards him, naked, mouth open.

'Who's that, then?' asked Palmer. 'Looks familiar.'

'A life model,' said Harry quickly. 'Hire her by the hour.'

'Wish I could hire one to do that,' said Palmer enviously, but he kept on looking at it as he got up to go.

Harry shut the door on him and only when he heard the police car drive off did he let his breath go with a sigh.

'It's OK,' he said quietly. 'He's gone.' Claire came cautiously out of the cupboard. 'Did you hear all that?' he said.

She nodded dumbly.

'What you couldn't tell from in there was the way he looked,' Harry said gloomily. 'His whiskers were twitching. He hasn't put it together but I bet he comes back for another look. I should never have left that painting around.'

A grim spark of humour reasserted itself for a moment. 'Shame it's not like your others,' Claire said. 'For once in your life you have to go and paint something recognizable.'

'We've got to get you out,' said Harry. 'We need to buy some time while I try to persuade someone to listen.'

'I could go down to the boat.'

'No you couldn't. They know *all* about that. Your delightful ex-boyfriend's been filling them in.'

'I don't know anywhere else.'

'It's got to be somewhere where your face doesn't show, where there's no one around.' He smacked his fist into his hand. 'Got it.' She raised an eyebrow. 'Steffie's place. Godsblanket. Down on the Cornish border. She bought it to do up. It's all by itself. There's a stack of tinned food there a mile high. No one goes near it except me, once in a long while.'

'How do I get there? Train?'

'With posters at all the mainline stations from tomorrow morning? You'll have to drive.'

'In what? Anyway, how do I get petrol and stuff?'

'Maybe I could hire a car and drive you down.'

'Harry, be sensible. If I'm seen, that's it. If you're seen with me, that's our only chance gone, but I think you're right. I can't stay here another day.'

'I could hire a car in the morning.'

'I'll be seen. They'll be watching out. Anyway, if you don't show up for work tomorrow, Palmer's definitely going to twig that something funny's going on. You're meant to be flat-out on the story.'

The answer came to him in the middle of the night and he woke her gently. 'Hey, can you ride a motorbike?'

She reared out of disturbed dreams, trying to grab on to the question, grunting. 'Wha . . .? Do what . . .?'

'Sorry. Just tell me. Can you ride a motorbike?'

'No. No I can't.'

'It's perfect. With a crash helmet on, no one will know it's you. That's the way to get there.'

'Well, I can't.' She slumped back on the pillow.

One hour was all he had. The place opened at nine and he had to be at National by ten or he'd be missed. He was lurking near the front door when they opened up. The showroom was full of red, white and blue striped mayhem machines, road-racer bikes with moulded grooves in the glass fibre for the human software. At the back were quieter, smaller motorbikes, but they were still far too expensive and, in any case, Harry severely doubted Claire's ability to get one beyond the end of the road. It had to be something second-hand, with plates on, ready to go.

A fat youth in a Kawasaki jacket ambled over. 'Looking for anything in particular?'

'Yes. Something used, just for tootling around on. Got to be easy to ride. Maybe a scooter.'

'Haven't got no scooters, not pre-owned.' He made it sound like an obscenity. 'What did yer want to spend?'

'Not a lot. What's the choice?'

'Got a little Suzuki 125.' He pointed at a mini banshee with a pointed racing tail and exhaust pipes like cannon barrels.

'Nothing else?'

'Not unless you want a moped.'

'Why not?'

'Rather you than me.' He broke off and roared, 'Col! Where are yer?'

Another, smaller, spottier youth appeared through the back door. 'Yeah?'

'Have we still got that moped we PXed?'

'The little Puch? Yeah, it's out the back.'

Five minutes later, Harry was the owner of forty pounds-worth of very old red and silver Puch Maxi moped. He parted with more cash for a one-piece overall and a full-face crash helmet. Against the fat youth's advice, he'd chosen a helmet that was a very tight fit.

They showed him how to start it. He signed a bill of sale in the name of Alan MacIntosh of Albermarle Villas, SW12, and wobbled off. It was certainly simple. It was also extremely uncomfortable and very slow. The tiny speedo on top of the grey plastic headlight would show an uncertain thirty miles an hour, and looked like it was exaggerating.

He left it around the corner from his flat, away from his neighbours' prying eyes, and took the helmet and overalls in to Claire.

She was waiting with the yachting bag which was all he'd been able to rescue from the Golf, stuffed with extra sweaters, shirts and a sleeping bag of his. Strapped to it was his lightweight tent.

'OK,' Harry said. 'It's very easy. No gears, just a twist grip to accelerate and brakes like a bike. You put it up on the stand and pedal it to start. There's a little lever you have to pull at the same time. It's two-stroke. The ratio's on the fuel cap.'

Claire looked blank.

'You have to mix up special oil as well as petrol,' he explained. 'They sell it at petrol stations.'

'I don't know about this,' she said, face set. 'I'm not insured.'

He started to laugh and she looked shocked, then smiled reluctantly. 'If they stop me, I suppose that's the least of my troubles.'

'You've got the map? You'll have to stay off the motorways, obviously. The A303's probably best, but I should find smaller roads if you can.' She nodded. 'You know where the house key is?'

'Yes, and I've got the map you drew.'

'What else? There's food there.'

'I'll call you.'

'OK. There's no time to lose, then. Find a quiet street and practise a bit before you go out on the main roads.'

'Stop fussing,' she said. 'Get to work. I'll make it.'

They had a last, long kiss then she was off. He waited four or five minutes, then took his bicycle and rode round the block. The moped was gone, with just a faint haze of two-stroke fumes drifting in the still air.

Harry squandered money on a taxi to get to work on time. He looked out of the windows, wondering if he might see Claire as she wended her way west. He did see her, but only as a huge black-and-white face, being spread on to a billboard in small sections by a man up a ladder.

The meeting started ten minutes after he got there, just time for Palmer to sit himself down in the chair next to him and say – in a chatty, inconsequential way – 'Hope I wasn't disturbing you last night? It suddenly occurred to me you might have had someone there.'

'Someone there? No, Derek, just the lonely old bachelor. The hooker's only booked for Saturday and Sunday.'

Palmer laughed. Then Gilligan, Herman and Jane came in together and he fell silent.

Gilligan sat down and looked around at the mixed bag of staff.

'Update,' he said. 'As of five minutes ago there was no fresh news of Claire Merrick. Personally I hope it stays that way because if it does, we can put out a show on Friday that will treble our audience in one go. We want to keep this tight. To guard against accidental telephone or fax interception, Claire Merrick will be known for all communication as Mayfly. If any of our info gets into the tabloids, heads here will roll, and that's a promise.'

No one doubted him.

'*All* information will come to the Mayfly team. That's me, Jane, Harry Chaplin and, of course, Derek Palmer, who will be keeping us closely in touch with the police effort. We are employing Jerome Hackman, a former close friend of Claire Merrick's, as an adviser. He knows more about her on a personal level than anyone else here. His view is that she is too unstable to pull off an escape for long. We will assign a team to finish an alternative show in case she is caught before Friday, but I want maximum effort on this one. Now, Jane, you do the details.'

Jane Bernstein, never the most confident of editors, didn't like running a programme meeting under the scrutiny of her proprietor, and fluffed more than usual. Harry had the lead role. He was to pull together the supposed circumstances of Claire's dismissal from ITN and the unfolding events of the night of the Azogi affair and Ann's murder. May God forgive me for what I am about to do, he thought.

At the end, Derek Palmer put up a hand before anyone could leave.

'Just in case Miss Merrick – Mayfly, that is – should get in contact with anyone,' he said, 'there is a procedure to follow. If she telephones, keep her talking for as long as possible while you attract the attention of a colleague to inform me. I'll put round a note to cover all eventualities later this morning.'

There was a more sophisticated version of these developments unfolding across the screens of Freedom's Friends.

'UPDATE,' it said. 'MERRICK LEFT OR WAS REMOVED FROM SCENE BEFORE ARRIVAL OF POLICE. METHOD UNKNOWN. POSSIBLE SHE INDUCED VOMITING. OPERA-TIVE'S ACCOUNT OF HER AS INSENSIBLE WHEN HE LEFT IS TO BE EXAMINED USING WHATEVER COER-CIVE MEANS NECESSARY TO ESTABLISH TRUTH. CASE PREPARED AGAINST HER WILL ALMOST CERTAINLY RENDER HER STORY UNBELIEVABLE SHOULD SHE BE CAUGHT; BUT IT IS PREFERABLE THAT SHE SHOULD BE STERILIZED. MAJOR TRACING EFFORT IS NOW BEING INITIATED. WE HAVE TO ALLOW FOR POSSIBIL-ITY OF UNKNOWN ACCOMPLICE OR ACCOMPLICES. DETAILED INSTRUCTIONS FOLLOW. SHE IS CARRY-ING MOBILE PHONE WITH NUMBER WE KNOW. PRO-CEDURES ARE BEING SET UP TO LOCATE HER SHOULD SHE USE THIS OR RECEIVE CALL. THIS GIVES HIGHEST PROBABILITY OF FINDING HER FIRST.

# Chapter Twenty-Two

## Tuesday August 6th

High above the traffic threading through Chiswick towards the M3 and the M4, a camera pivoted slowly on a bracket bolted to the nineteenth floor of the Murray House office building. A pigeon on the ledge behind it cocked its head as the zoom lens whirred out to its fullest magnification. The drivers leaving London had no idea they could be watched in such detail, not just number-plates but, on a clear day, the features of their faces could be seen. This was a clear day.

From the camera, an antenna took the picture by microwave to a switching centre, from where – with all the other pictures gathered from London's key arterial points – it was transmitted by fibre optic link to the Metropolitan Police control centre. That wasn't the only place it went. During routine upgrading two years before, a new unit in a grey metal case had been added, upstream from the main selector. On the police diagrams it was labelled 'signal amplifier,' which was certainly part of its function. It had to be. If it wasn't amplified right there, someone might notice the loss of power as half of the signal drained away down a second link, which had no right to exist.

Freedom's Friends' unofficial control centre ran with far fewer staff than the police equivalent. A scanner identified cars with only the driver on board, and read their numbers. They were checked directly through the Department of Vehicle Licensing computer at Swansea by another link which would have astonished the authorities. The result went back to their own database, filled with all they knew about Claire, her circle of acquaintances, and the few distant members of her family, looking for even the vaguest correlations. Hire-cars were high on their suspect list. Only then did manpower come into it, as a hopper filled with printouts from the cameras, data superimposed across the top of each picture.

It wasn't by any means perfect, and the controllers knew that. They were putting most of their faith in Benny Arensohn, but it was the next best thing to do; and if they had been looking for a moped, they would have found her.

The saddle was small with a hard lumpy centre, nothing more than a glorified bicycle saddle from which years of pounding had removed most of the springiness. The moped clattered over bumps in the road with the stiffness of an iron bedstead. Nervous at the passing traffic, Claire kept swerving into the gutter, but the violence with which the machine would bounce randomly out again forced her to concentrate on steering a straighter course, further out in the road. That put her in the path of passing cars and trucks, which, even at town speeds, sent her swaying with the wind of their passage.

For the first minute or so, the moped had seemed frighteningly fast. That impression died as soon as she wobbled on to a main road. With the twist grip fully open it could barely keep up with the traffic, and every now and then it would start to fluff, slowing until it cleared its throat with a puff of dirty black smoke and returned shakily to its wavering, hornet-like yowl. Before she was clear of London her wrists and hands were tingling, numb from the constant vibration, and her bottom was a disaster area. On the plus-side, though, she had already passed two police cars and been passed by three more without their occupants paying the slightest attention. Inside the secrecy of her helmet, with its slightly smoked visor, she felt more or less invisible.

She stood it for an hour and a half, buzzing along, her bag lashed to the little rack behind the saddle with bungee cords. She stuck to the A30, through Staines, Sunningdale and Bagshot. Green spaces began to appear between the buildings, then fields. It was warm, and she unzipped the top of the overalls to let some draught in. Between Hook and Basingstoke, she was within sight of the traffic tearing along the M3 to her left, wishing herself inside one of those effortless mile-eaters instead of perched precariously on this glorified food mixer. Just at that moment, it lurched under her, coughed twice and, the hornet buzz dwindling to a rattle, ran down to a chain-lashing halt.

In the moment of stopping she realized fully what the security of motion had meant, a state in which no one could get at her. She got off and looked at it morosely. Putting it up on the stand and pedalling hard to try and restart it made her sweat, and produced little more than three feeble coughs. A passing car hooted at her and she started to push, heading for a lay-by, realizing suddenly and in full how hard it would be to get any outside help without compromising the disguising shell of her motorcycle gear. In the lay-by, she considered. Harry might have an idea. He was just a phone call away. She took out her mobile phone.

Punching out National's number, she put an East London whine into her voice. 'Hello? Could I have Mr Harry Chaplin, please?'

There was a short silence, then a voice said, 'Crookbusters, production office, can I help you?'

Charlotte the secretary. Damn.

'Mr Chaplin, please.' Her voice was disguised almost to the point of incomprehensibility.

'He's in a meeting. Can I take a message?'

'I'll call back.'

She turned round as brakes squeaked in the lay-by behind her, and found herself staring at a police car drawing to a halt not six feet away.

Benny Arensohn was a consultant. This allowed his clear genius in electronic communications to transcend any trifling difficulties there might have been over the holes in his background, if he had ever wanted a high-level staff job in a telecoms company. As it was, he came and went on short and highly-profitable contracts without having to fill in tedious forms which would have involved lying about his brush with the American prison

system, and his three years putting together dirty tricks for a
series of US corporate masters. Having an English mother and
an American father, he had shifted his base of operations to
London and found the explosive growth of mobile communications had created fertile ground for legitimate business. He
was on a big job with one of the main mobile phone companies
so when the phone call came, from his most regular paymaster,
offering so very much money for so very little work, he was in
no doubt he could provide what they wanted.

He was working from home that week, so it was a simple
matter of setting up the computer, tapping in to the master
switching centre and accessing the visitors' location register
which kept track of all the mobiles. The security code system
was a tough one, but there was a back door and he knew how
to use it. He put a checker on to track any calls she made and
sat back, waiting for the thing to go bleep.

He was making a cup of coffee when it did. The coded
information spilling across the screen gave him a cell reference, a
kilometre-wide box. He pulled the map out. East of Basingstoke,
maybe the M3? Then he noted the number she was calling and
picked up the phone.

Three minutes later it was on all their screens.

'PRODUCER'S PRIORITY ALERT. TARGET'S PHONE
ACTIVE. CALL TO NATIONAL TV SWITCHBOARD
NUMBER. DURATION THIRTY SECONDS. LIKELY LOCA-
TION M3 MOTORWAY, SOUTH WEST OF LONDON,
BASINGSTOKE AREA.'

Claire could do a fine Solihull accent, and she put it on now.
The young PC had a friendly and helpful look on his face.

'Got trouble?'

'I dunno,' she said. 'It just packed up.'

It came out muffled, and he looked puzzled so she lifted the
visor a little and repeated it. He knelt down and inspected
the bike.

'Bit ancient, isn't it?' He pressed a little button on the
carburettor with a careful finger. 'There's no fuel coming
through.' Straightening up, he undid the plastic cap on the fuel

tank and rocked the moped from side to side. 'You're almost out,' he said. 'That's what's wrong. Did you try reserve?'

'What's that?'

'Don't you know?' He bent to the fuel tap and twisted it all the way round, then pushed the button again. This time, petrol welled out of a tiny vent. He laughed.

'Have you had it long?' he said condescendingly.

'Not very. Never run it low before.'

'Try it now.'

She did, fumbling under his gaze in her attempt to make it look like she was used to starting it. It fired almost straight away and he laughed again, turning back to the police car and waving.

She flipped the visor right down and took off, wobbling more than she cared to. The car stayed in the lay-by, and she wondered what would come up if he should make a spot-check on the registration number. She hoped the last owner had been a woman. It wasn't too smart having the tent showing on the rack either, that was hardly standard moped luggage. A mile down the road was a petrol station, and she pulled in to refuel. A minute later, the police car came past and went straight on. She watched it go fatalistically. If they were after her, they would soon be back. If not, all to the good. Then she went back to trying to understand the mixing scale on the side of the bottle of two-stroke oil.

She paid for her fuel and collected an array of food. It dawned on her that giant filling stations, with their mini-supermarkets, were a godsend – places where she could buy all she needed to survive without exchanging a word, and without being forced to take off her helmet.

By twelve o'clock she was on the A303, heading for Salisbury Plain. She ate her sandwiches in a field overlooking Stonehenge, rubbing her hands to rid herself of the pain from the constant vibration, then stretching out in the grass to ease her aches and pains. The helmet was stifling, insulating, muffling, and she opened the visor; she would have felt vulnerable had she taken it off.

She wondered about calling Harry again, but the brief brush

with Charlotte had put her off. National didn't run to direct lines for the reporters. In any case, the battery charger was still sitting in Ann's flat, so she had better conserve the phone for an emergency.

Ann's flat. The pressing needs of the past day had locked it all away from her. Dear Ann was dead – horribly, violently dead because of her, because of a bent ballot box in the back of a crushed car. The only one who had ever helped her; had ever really understood. No one to run to again. Harry's face came to her, but Harry was a flame where Ann was a rock, and Claire had never had a flame that didn't go out.

The reality of it all crushed her, and a sudden vivid awareness of the utter ruthlessness of the unknown people stacked up against her made her check, illogically and nervously, all around her at the placid rolling fields on the edge of the plain.

She rode on in fits and starts, stopping whenever the saddle soreness got too much, rubbing the aches which returned so quickly every time she started off again, filling the moped up every hour to be on the safe side. It didn't like running for too long or too hard. On long hills it would lose power and, on three or four occasions, it slowed to a crawl so that she had to pedal awkwardly to help it along.

She reached the signs to Ilminster at 7p.m., utterly exhausted. A Shell station provided her with a bottle of milk, a shrink-wrapped foam-backed pack of unrealistically red apples, and a microwaved 'Traveller's Delight' double-bacon cheeseburger; then she turned off down ever smaller lanes, looking all around her until, sheltered between the steep banks of a long-disused railway cutting, she found a soft, concealed place to pitch her tent. Then, at last, away from human gaze, she took off her helmet and shook the warm, clammy sweat out of her hair.

The burger was still just about warm when she ate it; sweet, dense and not at all like meat. Fretting and nervous, she pushed the moped into the cover of the ruins of an old platelayer's hut, and climbed the embankment to check the surrounding terrain. There was a man walking a dog two fields away, but he was moving obliquely away from her.

In the tent, she unrolled the sleeping bag and lay down. Even in the depths of despair after Tripoli she had never felt less in control of her life. Everything hung on Harry and, when it came to it, what resources did he have to bring to bear? Not a lot when it was stacked up against the power of whatever organization they had stumbled across. She wanted to talk to him and reached for the phone before the same cautious thoughts about the battery intruded. Going in search of a coin-box would have meant leaving the illusion of private security generated by the thin tent. She closed her eyes.

Harry wouldn't have been there anyway. He was trying to be himself – to be wise-cracking, sharp, cynical Harry – while covering up his desperate worry. He was trying to leave when he met Desmond Gilligan in the corridor and found himself arbitrarily summoned into the office that had been commandeered for the boss. It was the first time he'd been alone with Gilligan, and it made him all the more aware that this was the man who paid his wages. Gilligan had the economy of words that told him clearly that time was money and wasting either would be marked down against him.

'Just a word or two,' said Gilligan. 'I picked Claire Merrick, so if there's been any error of judgement, that's down to me. I'm not often wrong about people.' He looked shrewdly at Harry. 'I don't think you've been saying everything that's been on your mind today. Have you got any problems about all this?'

Harry almost told him right there and then; almost took the plunge into the whole unbelievable story, but he'd made a life study of not shooting from the hip and it was too hard to break. 'I'm just a reporter, Mr Gilligan,' he said. 'This is just a story.'

'You're not just a reporter, you're *the* reporter on this one. I think you've got a better nose for a story than the rest of this lot put together.'

Gilligan waved a hand to indicate the complex of buildings through the window. 'You don't know how much difference this story could make to the future of this place, Harry. I'm telling you, because it's no great secret, that National's a highly-geared enterprize. Come to that, so's the whole of my business.'

Harry raised a polite eyebrow. He'd read the articles, but he didn't think this was the moment to appear too knowledgable.

'We've borrowed a lot of money, that's what I mean, and we need to get it back. My bankers give me targets, Harry, audience targets. If I don't reach them, then the money starts walking. Your show's been the biggest draw in building that audience. If we become a laughing stock, it's finished. If we do it right, the sky's the limit. That's why I'm staying here until this business is cleared up, and I want it to be us that clears it up, and that means *you*. You can call me any time you like if you think Jane Bernstein needs her tail tweaking. News-sense, Harry. If you think it'll build an audience, just call me and I'll back you, right?'

Retreating from that one, feeling thoroughly out of his depth but also, to his own annoyance, flattered by the attention, Harry made it to the open air before being hailed from a blue Ford.

'Hello Harry,' said Derek Palmer. 'You on your bike?'

'No, I'm not.'

'Hop in, I'll drop you off. I fancy another look at your paintings.'

Harry checked the flat mentally for giveaway signs. It should be clear, he thought. 'Great. Come back and have a drink.'

It was an apple for breakfast and the rest of the milk. Claire packed the tent up with the dew on it, anxious to get away after a night interrupted by the violent snufflings of an animal which had sounded the size of a wolf, and turned out to be nothing more threatening than a small hedgehog. The sun was up as she struggled to get the moped out of the hut and strapped the bags on once more. It took a very long time to start and, for the first few minutes, until the damp evaporated from the ignition circuit, it would barely top fifteen miles an hour.

On the main road the flow of huge lorries began to increase, some blaring their horns as they passed, the Doppler effect tuning the pitch downwards, rocking her with the blast of their air. The Honiton by-pass was hard work – just staying out of the lorries' way – and the moped was running badly again. When it suddenly cut out on her and puttered to a rapid halt, her heart sank into her boots because this time, having just filled it up, she knew the problem had to be more serious.

It was 10 a.m., and Benny Arensohn punched up the number-check page on his computer, just to see if her phone was still switched off.

# Chapter Twenty-Three

## Wednesday August 7th

'You haven't heard a word I'm saying. This isn't just another story. Dump the rest of the show. Ten minutes on Claire Merrick isn't showbiz. I want the whole bloody show on her, have I made that clear?'

Jane flushed. In front of her presenter and chief reporter this was another blow to her faltering status as editor, but Gilligan was not in a mood to show mercy.

'It's very tight. We don't want to screw up.'

'If you'd listened, it wouldn't be tight. That's why I pay you. It's Wednesday. You've got two days. Do it.'

Russell Mackay had had a few drinks at lunchtime and that had given him a very false idea of his status in Gilligan's eyes as anchorman of Crookbusters. He now lurched in where angels should have feared to tread. 'I'm not sure it's a good idea, Desmond. We don't want a ragged looking show and . . .'

A pair of hard Australian eyes swung on to him like a warship's gun turret finding a new target. 'We won't get a ragged show, and you're not going to be anchoring it. I want Chaplin doing this one.'

Mackay flushed, but Harry's surprised 'What, me?' cut him off.

'Yup, you,' said Gilligan. 'This one's got to look right out of the normal run. I'm told you couldn't stand the sight of her, and I want some real venom in this one.'

'Unless they arrest her first so it's *sub judice*,' Harry said, and Jane looked gratefully at him for using his newly privileged position to say what she didn't dare to.

'Palmer says there's no sign of her,' said Gilligan. 'Anyway, you'll have the fall-back show up your sleeve. We're having wall-to-wall promotion on this one, trails everywhere.' He looked round at their faces. 'The boyfriend's coming in this afternoon. Hackman. Why don't you shoot an interview with him, like a personality profile. You've got lots of shots of her. Stitch them together. Go out to the house where it happened. Take Palmer along and do the place where this Arab lives too.' He didn't seem to notice Jane's stepped-on toes.

'OK,' he said. 'Let's get moving.'

Jane and Russell filed out, but Gilligan stopped Harry.

'Saturday morning, we're taking a plane.'

'A plane?' said Harry, startled. 'Where to?'

'The States,' Gilligan replied. 'We're going to make a real splash out of this. I've got to see some people there. I'll get you on the breakfast TV shows, New York, Monday, then maybe Boston, Chicago; who knows?'

Raising your profile, thought Harry, raising your profile so all those US bankers you're deeply in hock to stay sweet.

'How long for?' he asked.

'A few days,' said Gilligan, then looked at him curiously. 'You complaining?'

'No,' Harry said quickly. 'I've got a sick relative here, that's all.'

Gilligan's lack of interest was visible. The man smelt a big chance and only the cash counted. Harry looked at his watch, calculating, wondering if Claire could have reached the sanctuary of Godsblanket yet. He found an empty cutting room and dialled out, hearing the phone ring on and on.

Claire was pushing the moped and it was very hard work. She had to angle it awkwardly so the pedals didn't catch her ankles. She found it hard to keep it out of the way of the traffic screaming past. The end of the by-pass came and the road funnelled down into a tight S-bend under a narrow bridge. She had to pick her moment, rushing through before she was squeezed into the brick wall by a truck. There was a petrol station ahead. Her hopes were raised when she tried to start the engine again. It fired once, twice, then came raggedly to life for just long enough for her to trickle down on to the garage forecourt before it died once more.

Propping it on its stand, Claire walked over to the office. There was a woman in overalls by the door with a friendly smile. Right next to her was a wire rack of folded newspapers. The *Mirror* was the first one she saw and there, all over the front page, was her picture under a banner headline: 'TV Cop-Show Girl on Run.'

Claire went for the Birmingham accent again. 'Gotta problem with me bike. Is there a mechanic?'

The bottom bar of the full-face helmet muffled her and the woman frowned, trying to follow.

'Not at the moment,' she said. 'Greg's out on a breakdown. He's just gone. Probably be back in an hour. Or there's Honiton, but it's a bit of a way. You can come in and wait, if you like.'

That meant taking off her helmet, taking it off with the woman staring at her and the rack of papers confirming the extent of the hue and cry.

'I'll try Honiton,' she said dully, and turned away.

'Suit yourself, love,' said the woman.

All Claire wanted was to get out of sight so she could stop and think. She pushed the broken down machine another two hundred yards, completely at the mercy of a mechanical malfunction she could not solve, desperately aware that her disguise was only truly valid when in motion. Then, weary and uncertain, she wheeled it off the road into a parking area and sat down on the bank behind it, cradling her helmeted head in her hands. Heavy lorries and holiday makers passed her in noisy slugs of disturbed air and exhaust fumes. She lay back, visor open, staring at the sky through the aperture, and wondered if she could somehow sleep it all off. The clouds were calming.

Ten minutes later she'd had all she could take of clouds. She got up and tried pedalling the little bike into life again, perched on its stand. That just made her hot all over again. She got off, furious, and kicked it. Two motorbikes, passing on the road, slowed sharply, seeing her, swung round in a gap in the traffic and pulled in beside her.

They were white BMWs and, taking in the neatly-dressed, helmeted riders and the reflective stripes on their fairings, she thought for a couple of accelerated heartbeats that they were policemen. Then she saw the German number plates and relaxed. They parked the bikes and came over, taking their helmets off.

'You have troubles?' said the nearer – a serious blond giant with earnest spectacles and a large jaw.

'It won't start,' she said. 'But there's lots of fuel.'

The other man, shorter and red-faced, turned back to the BMWs and pulled a tool roll out of a side pannier. The first man looked at her and grinned. 'We see if we can fix it. Dieter is my name. That is Rolf.'

'I'm Jane,' Claire said, and he grinned at her.

'Are you not hot in there?'

'No,' she said, improvising rapidly. 'I have a sore ear. I try not to take my helmet off too much.'

He shrugged as Rolf came back, then began to poke around the carburettor, unscrewing tiny pipes and blowing through them. They were both intent on what they were doing and Claire sat down. Dieter pulled an electrical lead off something right on top of the engine, then unscrewed a grimy grey-and-white object and laughed.

'Here,' he said. 'This is no wonder. Look at the – what is the word?' He turned to Rolf. '*Zündkerze?*'

'Sparking plug.'

'Yes. Look. All dirt. No gap for the spark.'

Certainly the object he held up to Claire was extremely black and oily at one end.

'What should I do?' she asked.

'Do you have far to travel still?'

'Er, yes.'

'Stop and buy a new plug. See the number is written on it here. You will have to find a motorcycle shop, I think. But for now I will clean this one. It should work for a little more time.'

It did. He put it back in and the engine fired and caught first time sounding more like an angry hornet than ever. Dieter made another raid on his motorcycle's panniers and came up with a jar of grease-remover and some treated tissues which removed from his immaculate hands any sign of the encounter. They packed up, bowed over Claire's hand with gallantry and rode neatly away. Claire took to the moped again with enormous relief and a feeling of strange fondness for the flimsy little device which now seemed noticeably more powerful than before.

At three o'clock that afternoon, she bumped slowly down a deeply-rutted drive between dark, towering trees. Dartmoor was behind her and the crossing of the narrow upper reaches of the Tamar at Gunnislake had been followed by a winding, uncertain trek into the tin mining valleys to the north of Hingston Down. She had been backwards and forwards along the little valley many times before she spotted the rotted and overgrown remains of the sign saying 'Godsblanket'. The gate had a chain holding it closed. Harry hadn't mentioned that, but the screws holding the iron ring on the gate post simply pulled out when she tugged at it. There was a lidded wooden box at the gate, half-full of junk mail, and no sign that anyone had disturbed the mud of the drive beyond for a long time. She went in, wheeling the moped carefully along the edge of the mud to leave as few marks as possible, and replacing the gate's screws in their slimy, oozing screw-holes.

The first clue that she was near the house was the sound of a muffled phone ringing through the trees. Harry, she thought to herself. It must be. She came round the corner and there before her was a most extraordinary building. It was an ancient granite mill, dark and satanic, not pretty. It stood in a dripping clearing littered with rotting shards of wood decomposing in mud of a thousand different textures. The building loomed, four storeys high, with a steep wooded bowl of hillside immediately behind it. Georgian sash windows, their paint peeling, marked off three of its storeys, but the top floor was clad entirely in wooden planking arranged in sections like timber venetian blinds. To the right another building was crumbling away, with the central remains, just an axle and a few spokes, of a large water wheel slumped against the remaining wall. Water was dripping off everything and the predominant colours were greys. Even the green shades contained a chill of dead blueness.

She found the key where Harry had said it would be, in the bowl of an old oil light behind a pile of firewood. The lock was stiff, and inside the evening had come early. She flicked a light switch and nothing happened. There was a dusty telephone on the bare hall floor. She picked it up, thinking to call Harry, but the buzz of the tone continued smoothly as she dialled, the turning of the dial making no impact upon it. Food, she thought, and turned left into the kitchen. Something scuttled under the sink. Dust was everywhere, along with what she hoped were mouse rather than rat droppings. Tons of food, Harry had said. The cupboards produced two small tins of creamed rice, one of artichoke hearts, and some pot noodles. She roamed morosely through the rest of the house. There were only six rooms, two on each floor, and an enormous, dark attic on the top behind the wooden louvres.

In the sitting room, which smelt damp but had three shabby armchairs, she found a treasure trove – a cardboard box of extra supplies; boxes of soup powder; a bottle of sweet sherry; crisps that had been thoroughly gnawed by some rodent; and a jar of olives. There was a bathroom with a bath full of dead spiders, and the rest were bedrooms, only one of which looked at all comfortable. All the windows were set in the front wall. The back, where the house butted into the hill side, was solid; so the effect as she moved from floor to floor past the full-length glass in the central stairwell where once, probably, the mill's loading doors had hung, was curiously theatrical. All there was to see outside was the little clearing in the trees where, it seemed, no one ever came.

Drawn by the thought of hot soup, she found the cooker was as inert as the rest of the electrical system. She called National on the mobile phone. This time she was put through to Harry without a hitch and a wave of pure joy swept through her when she heard his voice.

'When did you first realize she had, er, lesbian tendencies?' Harry said. Jerome Hackman was sitting opposite him in a corner of the production office, and Harry loathed everything about the man. Hackman had the detestably well-groomed look

of the successful banker cum sportsman; the soft richness of
flesh fed on the specialities of showcase restaurants, tempered
and chiselled by visits to the fives, squash and royal tennis courts
that he kept dropping into the conversation.

'Oh, it just fits when I look back,' Hackman said airily. 'I
guess I was just, well, a bit special for her, so she made an
exception.'

You liar, shouted Harry inside his head. Outwardly, he just
said, 'We'll have to cover that obliquely. I mean interviewing
you as a former boyfriend while we're talking about her killing
her girlfriend is a bit confusing.'

'Confused the hell out of me,' said Hackman.

'You don't have any idea where she might have gone?'

'No. I hear your tame policeman says she used some cash
machines, left a trail going south. I guess that means she really
went north. She's smart.'

'Oh, right,' said Harry. 'If you're ready, we'll go and get this
interview in the can.'

'I'm told you hated her guts. You must be kind of seeing
the funny side of all this?' asked Hackman, looking hard
at Harry.

'Yes. It's hilarious. I just love a bit of death,' said Harry,
deadpan. The phone next to him rang. He picked it up and,
with Hackman's eyes boring into his skull, he heard Claire's
quiet, drained voice say simply, 'It's me and I'm here.'

He swapped the receiver to his other ear, further from
Hackman. 'Good to hear your voice,' he said in a carefully
formal tone. 'I'm in the middle of something right now. I'm
just talking to Claire Merrick's boyfriend about her and this
murder business. Don't go away though, we have to talk
about the editing and all that. Can I call you back in half
an hour?'

She picked up on it. 'Yes, I've got a few views on that
interview. You know the number. You can call in but I have
to use the mobile to call out.'

Hackman showed no sign of interest as Harry put the
phone down.

*    *    *

Benny Arensohn called the producer's number.

'I got her again. Down in the boonies. I'll give you the refs. Same thing again, she called National. Too short to be a proper conversation.'

'You gotta find out who she's calling there.'

'I can't, not from here. They haven't got the kind of set-up that lets me dial in and check the routing. Someone on the inside might be able to run it down. Do you have anyone?'

'We'll fix it. Someone on the switchboard?'

'Yes.'

'What about tapping the calls?'

'Give me a scanner somewhere near her, no problem – long as she isn't on the move.'

'Fax me what you need.'

Two minutes later it was on the screens.

'TARGET LOCATED AGAIN. EAST CORNWALL AREA OF ENGLAND. RURAL LOCALITY. GRID SQUARE CONTAINS SEVERAL SMALL VILLAGES. ONLY ONE MAJOR ROAD. LIKELY TO BE STILL MOBILE. SEARCH TEAMS BEING DIRECTED TO MONITOR ALL PROBABLE ROUTES.'

In the next few hours, ten men and four women wasted a lot of their highly-paid time, sitting in cars at road junctions and scanning the drivers of the cars passing. Two more, in the back of a well-equipped van parked on the outskirts of Callington, were poring over a set of large-scale maps of the area; while Benny Arensohn, all his other jobs forgotten in his desire for a bonus on a scale he had never before imagined, stayed glued to his equipment, hoping for just one more call from Claire.

Inside the house at Godsblanket time moved at a crawl. As half an hour expanded numbingly to forty minutes, then forty-five, she began to wonder if the phone really did work for incoming calls, or whether the ringing she had heard on her arrival had been some chance electrical fluke. She reached for her mobile phone once more.

# Chapter Twenty-Four

## Wednesday August 7th

Two things happened at the moment Claire switched on her mobile phone; one that she knew about and one that she didn't. First, the house's own phone on the floor next to her rang with a harsh rattle of internal pieces loosened by age. She switched her phone off, blessing the saving of precious batteries, and picked up the receiver. Harry's voice said, 'Thank goodness for that.'

The other thing happened on Benny Arensohn's computer screen, where a string of codes flashed up, then froze and faded almost immediately. He didn't miss it. His target's phone had come on briefly, and come on, what was more, in the same cell as the last time she'd called. Wherever she was, she wasn't moving.

Ten minutes before, Harry had been half-way through dialling the Godsblanket number when Derek Palmer's uniformed figure had come through the doors and made for him. He put the phone down straight away.

'Hello, Derek. What's doing?'

'This and that. We've got a bit of a steer. I just found out she's got a mobile phone. No one thought to say. We turned up her last bill when we were going through her flat.'

'So?'

'So, she's been using it, hasn't she? Guess where she called?'

'Haven't a clue.'

'Here, that's where.'

Harry looked surprised. 'No. Who did she talk to?'

'Wish I knew. Sounds like she didn't get through to whoever

it was. It was a very short call. Anyway the switchboard doesn't log calls and there were any number coming in.'

'Beats me. What are you going to do about it?'

'Well now we know roughly where she is. Next time she calls, we'll have her location as soon as she presses the tit. She can't realize, or she wouldn't have risked it.'

Harry nearly missed the obvious question. As it was he asked it a second later than he should have done, but quickly enough not to trigger any reaction in Palmer. 'So, where is she?'

'Between ourselves. I mean, *really*.'

'Of course.'

'Cornwall.'

'Just Cornwall?'

'Well, East Cornwall, but we can only tell to the nearest cell on the system and because it's rural, that's quite a big area.'

'It's a start.'

So here Harry was, in a phone box on the far side of National's industrial estate, well out of reach of curious eyes and ears.

'Listen, before anything else. Don't use that mobile again. It tells them where you are. Our friend in blue already knows.'

'Oh God.'

'Not precisely, only to within a few miles.' He was thinking furiously. 'Use this phone. It should be OK.'

'It doesn't bloody well work. I can't dial out.'

'OK, OK. I'll phone you. Just stay there. Stay out of sight.'

'There's no electricity either, and you were wrong about the food. There's not much here. I'll have to go out.'

'I should have told you. The electricity's switched off at the fuse box. Just pull the switch down. It's on the hall wall. I don't know about the food. You can't go into a shop.'

'There's a petrol station on the main road. It's got its own shop. I can keep my helmet on. That's what I've been doing so far.'

'That's a bad idea. God knows how many people could be sniffing around.'

'What are we going to do now, Harry?'

There was a pause in which he realized he hadn't a clue. 'I'm not sure yet,' he said. 'I've got a few ideas. I might go back and start all over again at your scrapyard.'

'There won't be anything there.'

'Well, Beaconsbridge then.'

They were both silent now, jointly accepting the futility of it.

'When I phoned you, were you really talking to Jerome?'

'I certainly was. A real charmer, isn't he? I don't think much of your taste.'

She wasn't seeing the funny side. 'What was he *doing* there?'

'Gilligan's got him in. I'm the anchor for the Friday show. It's all about you. Gilligan's taken personal control. He's really pissed off. Don't go out, right? If you have to get food, go straight there, straight back and don't take the helmet off. I'll keep an eye on the calls we get. No one knows you're on a bike.'

He heard a catch in her voice but then it steadied. 'Can you come down at the weekend?'

'After the weekend,' he said, letting her down as slowly as he could. 'Gilligan's sending me to the States on Saturday. Sort of "I Knew Claire Merrick" lecture tour on primetime. I'll come down as soon as I get back.'

'Three or four days,' she said flatly. 'That means the middle of next week.'

'Well, Thursday probably. I'm sorry. I couldn't really say "no, Claire's expecting me down in Cornwall".'

'Will you be able to phone me from there?'

'Yes of course.'

'Harry?'

'Yes, love?'

'You're all I've got.'

'I know.'

'Do you mind?'

Then, into his half of their halting and hopeless conversation, came blazing a moment of clarity, and he felt a surge of totally unjustifiable optimism. 'Listen, Claire. I want to spend some serious time in bed with you. Out of bed too. There has to be a way, and I have to find it. It's as simple as that, really. Don't lose faith.'

'My knight in shining armour,' she said, and in her voice he heard her wish to believe him.

In the evening, while it was still light, she wrestled the moped into the shed beyond the decrepit mill wheel and pulled the remains of the wooden door closed to hide it. The tent was still strapped on the carrier. Her sailing bag was inside the house. She checked right round the outside, taking care to avoid making give-away footprints in the mud. There was little to see; the tumbledown wheelhouse next to the mill; two small sheds; and the narrowest of gaps behind the building where the blank wall rose parallel to an equally blank cliff a few feet behind it. No one would come from that way, the cliff stopped fifteen feet or so above her and dense trees, growing from its summit, brushed the back of the mill, right up to its guttering, four storeys above.

She wanted no trace left outside of her presence, no reason for anyone to force the locked door, the only door which gave access to the inside of the house. Only the safety of that lock and the invisibility of her presence could quell the jumpiness which had her starting at every creak the old house made. As it got dark, an owl called harshly and abruptly. Although the house couldn't be seen from anywhere except the woods around it, she felt uneasy about having a light on, so she went to bed when it got too dark to read the dog-eared and damp travel guides which were all she could find. She pulled the bed against the blank back wall and away from the window – two floors up in the odd, vertical house, so no one could see in; and she left the curtains open to avoid giving any clue to her presence.

Right up to the moment the pubs closed all fourteen members of the Producer's team were busy. Fake National TV identity cards gave them a reason to flash Claire's photo around. No one had seen her – none of the tourists, none of the locals – though most of them had seen the story that was just starting to run in that morning's papers. Several of the locals they asked were left with a strange indefinable feeling of something amiss.

These muscular, quiet men and down-to-earth women didn't seem quite the stuff of television, but then many of them knew National wasn't your actual BBC. Years of bad reception had led to a wide spread of satellite dishes, so Crookbusters was a show they knew.

'What's the reward?' was the usual reply to the enquiries about Claire.

Two of the team, Anna and Georgy, had a close run-in when an off-duty sergeant in a Gunnislake pub wanted to know exactly why they should think Claire Merrick might be in the area.

'I don't quite know,' said Anna ingenuously, shaking her blonde hair over her shoulder and giving him a big, distracting smile. 'We were down here shooting something else and they just told us to start asking around. That's London for you.'

'It'll be the phone call,' said the sergeant, liking what he saw and anxious to show there was nothing provincial about his beat. 'The trace on the Cellnet phone. That Derek Palmer must have tipped your guys off. Waste of time, I tell you. We've been on it for hours. There's no sign of her anywhere. With a mug like that she's not exactly unnoticeable, is she? I mean everyone knows what she looks like. I've got an idea or two about it, though. Look for a woman friend, that's what I reckon.'

He was disappointed when the big blonde made her excuses and left.

At closing time, the squad retired to the back of the van for instructions. They were well-disciplined, respectful, and in it for the money; jacks of all trades on a big retainer to Freedom's Friends. The controller communicated directly by a modem link with the Producer.

'We'll keep at it,' he said. 'There's no reason to believe she's moved. Tomorrow we'll go on with the house-to-house. The villages and the farms, then the isolated houses and any location where she might be camping out of sight. Here are the lists, teams of two and the same instructions stand.'

He'd worked with them all before and he knew exactly what they could do.

'I want no misunderstandings,' he said. 'If she gets into the hands of the police, that's probably OK, but only probably. There's enough to get her locked away and no one's going to believe her, but you never know what some smart lawyer might turn up. Let's be quite clear. If you see her, the first and only option is to snuff her and snuff her in a way that looks like she did it herself. You've all got a copy of the note to leave. It's a perfect copy of her writing.'

# Thursday August 8th

Right through Thursday, Harry was playing at being 'himself', and he couldn't quite remember how to do it. In the final stages of scripting – when researchers, reporters and editors worked in a frantic huddle to get the words right – he'd always been the master of the glib, heartless one-liner which punctured the tragic heart of a story for the fast explosive humour of his peer group. They expected it of him now. He could tell they were all waiting for him to come up with a genuine, memorable Harryism on the Claire Merrick story to be regaled with delight round the bar when the programme was over. He tried, but it was strain enough doing the script, the awful, mistaken travesty of what had really happened. It was achingly difficult to separate what he was supposed to know from what he did know.

'I'm sorry, guys,' he said at one stage, 'got a headache. I'm a bit slow today.' In the end, he was ruthless, forcing soft, warm recent Claire into a backwater of his brain and concentrating on some fictitious, psychotic pervert of their collective imaginations. The script began to flow, spreading like an incoming tide into the pools between the bits of video they had already shot, cut and voiced.

# Chapter Twenty-Five

## Friday August 9th

The time dawdled by. Claire had dozed her way through
Thursday, barely moving from the bed, eating the occasional
sour, briny artichoke out of the tin. Then she'd had a bad
night's sleep, waking at every strange sound, and she got up
in the morning feeling trapped by the house; a fugitive inside
a display case, moving about behind a front wall that seemed
made of windows. The rational part of her brain told her no one
had been down that muddy front drive for a very long time, but
the same vulnerable, self-destructive, unreasoning part that had
deliberately conjured ghosts into dark childhood nights filled
her imagination with horrors. She cleared the dirty tins and
packets into a bin bag and then sat hunched in an arm chair,
pulled back defensively into a far corner, hoping Harry would
phone again, yet fearing the intrusive, give-away sound of the
telephone bell.

By three o'clock she had won a small battle over herself. It
*was* safe here. Harry's choice had been a good one. If she could
but stick it out, stock up on food and put up with the boredom.
This was the place to buy time, if time was going to be of any use
at all. Up in the first floor sitting room, she sat in an old, dusty
armchair with a hard-wearing cover turned abrasive with the
stiffness of age. She leaned back and looked up, and something
flickered in the reflected light that played on the ceiling.

A fraction of a second later she heard the barest trace of
footsteps slushing in the mud of the driveway below, and a
low, barely discernible murmur of voices.

She froze, concentrating her whole being on the input from

her ears. The voices continued to murmur. One was raised a little, female, questioning. The other, male, sounded non-committal. They could have been casual walkers, trespassing accidentally on a locked, unattended, nearly derelict building. They could have been, until she heard them try the front door.

They rattled it a couple of times, and then she heard the squeak of material on glass as they rubbed at the panes of glass to see in.

'No one there,' the woman's voice now said clearly. 'No tracks, either. We can cross off this one.'

'Not so fast,' said the man, and from just those three words Claire was certain of his American birth.

She heard them both walk off, and because she couldn't sit there – hidden, not knowing – she got down on the floor and squirmed across the boards to the low window sill. She raised herself cautiously until she was looking down sideways at their backs. Youngish, mid-thirties, waxed cotton go-anywhere country jackets, heavy walking boots. There were two shed doors ahead of them. The left one led straight to exposure, the moped sitting behind it, her bag on the back carrier. The man chose the right, and she breathed again but the stay of execution was only temporary, because he reached in and pulled out the black bin bag she had stashed there only hours before. He ripped the tied top open and came up with the empty tin of rice pudding, a tin in which the traces left on the sides were still fresh, moist and white.

He turned, and she ducked back out of sight. There was only one door to the whole house, plumb in the middle of the front, and there was no way out before they got to it. There was no possible concealment in the room and in any case her jacket, helmet and sleeping bag were in the bedroom on the next floor up. They were kicking at the front door and, under cover of the noise, she crept out of the room, shrinking back from the huge glass windows that lit the stairwell. She stole softly up to the next floor and gathered up the helmet and the jacket. The sleeping bag was too bulky. This room too had nowhere to hide and neither did its companion across the landing. They were still raining blows on the door and she crept out again.

It was getting hard to think through the silent, shrieking panic filling her head. There was another door, with a cottage latch on it. She opened it carefully – the stairs to the top floor, the loft. She moved delicately up, shutting the door gently behind her and as she did a loud rending of wood followed by a thud announced the front door had given way.

The loft was huge and mostly dark, the darkness broken by odd stars and lines of daylight from the little gaps in the timber planking of the side walls. At some distant point in the past, they had been panels of wooden louvres, pivoting open to let the wind blow through this, the drying floor, of the old woollen mill. They'd jammed closed years ago and in two places pipework for the stove flue and the lavatory vent had been hacked through them. Round the pipes, white sunlight cut a ring into the darkness. She couldn't switch on the light for fear of what that might bring, but she had little doubt these two, who were so clearly not the police, would be coming to check. There were boxes in plenty, and vaguely-glimpsed lumps of furniture in the gloom; places to hide. Then she looked down at her feet in the bar of light coming through the old louvres, and saw she stood no chance of evading detection. Thick dust covered the floor, and her footsteps beckoned like signposts, leading straight to the feet that made them.

At that point she nearly gave up and sat down meekly to chance her fate, but the memory of Harry's voice rang suddenly in her ears; 'Don't lose faith.'

She went to the wooden louvres that made up the wall and peered through the narrow gap next to the flue pipe. She was looking straight into the branches of a massive tree. This was the back of the house with the trees growing up from the rocks behind it. The wooden louvres were horizontal, pivoted at each end, overlapping each other, each one about four feet long with strong uprights between each set. The wood they were made from was dry, slightly worm-eaten and crumbly looking. She tugged at one and it moved slightly, letting a little extra beam of daylight in. She pulled at the one below it and with a dry cracking noise it gave way at one end. Suddenly light poured in and she was looking down through the gap and the branches outside at a ledge on the cliff a few feet below. She bent to the next louvre and tugged with all her might. It gave way with a crash.

A shout came from below. Throwing stealth to the winds, she kicked out one more of the slats, jammed her helmet on her head, and launched herself violently through the gap as feet pounded up the lower stairs. Part of the tree lashed across her helmet and she fell awkwardly through leaves, grabbing at branches and swinging to a bone-jarring halt on the ledge. It was a sliding scramble from there down through bushy outcrops and cracks in the rock-face, diagonally down a steep ramp of rock to the narrow, level strip along the back wall of the house. She got to it, looked up, and a startled face was thrust out of the gap she'd made at the top, then instantly withdrawn. She ran round the end of the house, wrenched the moped out of the shed into the open air, and with the strength of despair kicked it first time into sputtering, smoky life.

The two of them ran out of the front door, twenty feet away, and the man was reaching inside his jacket and pulling at something seemingly caught up inside. The driveway led past them and they were spreading out to try to block her way as they advanced towards her.

# Chapter Twenty-Six

## Friday August 9th

Harry, Jane and the picture editor looked in horror at what was showing on the monitor. Interiors of an office, Ann's office at the Institute, but interiors with colours you don't often see. Everything was blue, everything, including people's faces.

'Spool through it,' said Harry, and the picture editor twisted the knob to fast forward. It was all like that.

'I'll kill the incompetent bastard,' said Harry.

'Could be a camera fault,' said the picture editor with irritating fairness.

'Like hell,' said Harry, looking at her sourly. 'The lazy bugger forgot to do a white balance, didn't he? Doesn't take a second, does it? Every cameraman knows that, except our useless bloody Bernard. That's why the camera thinks everything's blue.'

'Well, we can't use it,' said Jane with an edge of something that was not quite calmness in her voice. 'So we have to come up with something.'

They were editing the last bit of the special. The programme would be linked live in the studio by Harry throughout, to the continuing fury and discomfiture of Russell Mackay who was predicting disaster to anyone who would listen.

Now there was a three-minute hole in the show, a hole that had looked easy to fill with a portrait of the victim, Ann Farrow, shot at the Institute where she had worked in Primrose Hill, complete with sad tributes from her colleagues. Except that now the entire thirty minute tape of rushes from which it had to be cut was useless. The programme was only five hours away and without something about Ann it would be hobbling along on one leg.

'Get me a different crew, preferably Robbo,' said Harry. 'Call Primrose Hill and tell them we're coming back.'

'I don't think you've got time. I'll send someone else,' Jane said.

'I don't trust anyone else. Whichever "someone else" went last time, they let Bernard screw up. Anyway, half-an-hour to get there, an hour to shoot, half-an-hour back. That still gets us back here by five. Someone else can stand over the edit so I can rehearse. Get Peter to double-check my script. He writes like I do. That's OK.'

Parking wasn't easy, but they were inside the Institute in forty minutes. Behind the Georgian facade lay modern, open-plan offices. Robbo was a big, easy-going man; a veteran who'd honed his skill on a million tough stories, before the BBC, in their curious quest for callow youth, pushed him into very early retirement. He was set up and shooting in no time, arranging the lights to get the right result first time with that nonchalance that only comes with years of experience. He did wide shots of the office and close-ups of Ann's colleagues and the personal detritus, postcards and souvenirs, still spread around her desk. Next, they interviewed Ann's boss, Roanne Small, a sorrowing woman whose voice choked off two or three times during the course of her answers. Then they turned back to Ann's desk.

'Can we do a bit on her unfinished work?' Harry asked. 'Would the computer show what she was doing on it last?'

'Yes, I suppose so. All the files have date and time entries on them in the directory.'

Ann's files were locked with her own code but Mrs Small had an override, and within a minute she was calling up a list of files.

'There you are. She was in on Saturday and Sunday, working on six files.' Her voice broke again and she stopped, pointing silently at the screen. Harry bent forward. The latest time and date entry, Sunday, mid-afternoon, was against three files with the same name. The first was: 'ELECFRCM.003'. The next two had the same title and were numbered 004 and 005.

'Could you call up the first one?' Harry asked, 'then play around with the keyboard, change a few things. We'll only have your hands in shot.'

'So it looks like I'm Ann? Is that what you mean? Oh, no, I don't think I . . . I mean that would be . . .'

'All right,' said Harry quickly, 'I didn't mean to upset you. Maybe one of the secretaries?'

'It's just, you didn't *know* Ann, you never met her.'

A secretary came in and typed meaningless additions to Ann's file with the camera, tight on her hands and the screen, shooting from three different angles.

Harry was standing out of the way, watching, when without conscious thought on his part, 'ELECFRCM' whirled apart in his head and rearranged itself as: 'Election Fraud, Claire Merrick'. He stiffened, forced himself to wait until Robbo had switched off, then looked at the screen again. It was a list of thirty-five marginal seats, the first one Claire had told him about.

'Can you call up this one?' he asked, keeping his voice level and pointing at 004. The secretary did. It was the second list; the ten seats with the low swings and the high turnouts. That's all there was, he thought, that's all Claire told me about but there's still a file to come.

'And the next?'

005 came up, and the pattern of it was completely unfamiliar. He knew he had never seen it before. Sunday. That last Sunday Claire said Ann had discovered something else, something she had never had the time to tell her. He had thought the secret must have died with Ann, but now he knew with a leap of his heart that it hadn't, it was here. He knew he was treading on eggs.

The secretary was looking at him with a touch of curiosity and he guessed he was showing too much interest.

'We could do with an extra shot,' he said, improvising brilliantly. 'Can you print these three files out for us? Just so we can shoot them coming up on the printer?'

Robbo was listening. 'It'll mean relighting it, and you've still got your piece to camera to do outside. Have we got time?'

'Yes,' said Harry curtly, and Robbo raised an eyebrow.

When they were ready, Harry turned to the secretary. 'Let them print up one by one, then take them, would you, so we just see your hand again in shot.'

She pressed buttons on the keyboard and crossed to the printer. It fed the sheets out in seconds and she took them, then stood there irresolutely.

'OK?' Harry asked Robbo.

'Yeah, got it,' he said.

'Thanks,' said Harry, and held out his hand to the woman. Without hesitation she gave him the papers and he folded them into his pocket.

Robbo looked at his watch. 'Better crank it up for the piece to camera.'

'OK. One take, I promise.'

It took two, but that wasn't Harry's fault. A skip lorry roared past half-way through the first one, spoiling the sound. The second one went off perfectly.

'Ann Farrow worked here at the Institute for Policy Evaluation, a Labour Party think-tank on the leafy edges of Regents Park. She left here last Sunday after putting in some overtime, her work unfinished, with no reason to suppose she wouldn't be coming back to continue it on Monday. She went back to the house into which she had taken Claire Merrick, a friend in need. Ann didn't make a big thing of her sexual orientation among her colleagues and they remember her only as a true professional . . .'

While Robbo loaded the gear into the car, Harry grabbed the moment to unfold the paper in his pocket. It disappointed him for a second. There was nothing there after all that hadn't been on the previous list, the same ten key seats, but then he saw the difference: something so obvious, so very obvious that they'd all missed it, all except Ann who had clearly stumbled on it that final day. So simple, a blundering fingerprint that blew the chance of mere statistical coincidence right out of the water. He looked at Robbo, and at the phone box on the street corner.

'Just got to make a quick call,' he said.

'Use the carphone.'

'No, I'll be quick.' He ran up the pavement and dialled the Godsblanket number, confidently expecting Claire would pick it up. It rang and rang and no one answered.

Claire glanced the other way and saw the path continuing through the woods. She twisted the throttle open and, snaking through the mud and kicking at the ground to keep straight, she headed for the shelter of the trees. The barrel of the gun now finally clear in the man's hand lifted towards her back just a fraction of a second too late.

She looked back once and nearly fell as the moped's front wheel dropped into a deep rut. The track widened, with piles of logs stacked to one side. Rooks rose cawing from the trees as the little bike's engine howled at them. There was a gate across the road, but beside it was a gap, part-filled by the curling remains of wire fencing. She barely slowed. Then she was out of the wood and the mud track turned to a military-looking concrete roadway, allowing the moped up to full speed with thick chunks of mud flying off its tyres and spattering away behind her. It joined a lane after half a mile, just below the overgrown remains of a tin-mine engine house, and she stopped for just long enough to pull the helmet straight and buckle it up. Then she was off again, safety in motion, panic turning slowly to fierce adrenaline.

Logic said they must have left their vehicle at the other end of the drive, and the track she had taken wouldn't be passable to a car – so they'd have to find some way round, and she had no idea if that would be easy or hard. They'd know about the moped though, so what next, road-blocks? They're not the police, she told herself again. They're the others, the ones behind this whole thing.

She turned sharply left on to another little road that seemed to take her away from the mill. The sun was over its peak and ahead of her. West, that meant. So be it. She took stock. She still had her sailing bag, some of her clothes, her jacket and the tent. Her sleeping bag had gone and – panic seized her – her money? She took one hand from the handlebars and felt her pockets, finding the big purse with immense relief. Was there anything back there that would tell them for certain who she was? After all, they could only have seen a figure with a crash helmet. She could have been a traveller, a squatter, anyone. Then she realized that the mobile phone, the phone that had caused so much trouble, the phone with her number on it, was still lying next to the arm chair. They couldn't miss that.

Above all, she'd lost her refuge and her disguise. They'd be looking for the moped. How many of them were there? Unanswerable questions went round in a circle. She must simply think about the next stage; stay on the smallest roads, get clear. That got her through Luckett and Stoke Climsland and across the main Launceston road north of Kelly Bray, then the lanes disappeared for a while and she was on a B-road, a far more exposed route than she would have chosen. There were a few cars on it, but soon she found herself approaching a welcoming left turn at Bray Shop. With two hundred yards still to go to relative safety, she glanced over her shoulder and saw a police car coming up at speed behind her.

Fear surged up in her and then, just as quickly, died down. In a moment she would know whether the two at the mill had tipped off the police. They would have had plenty of time to get the search going by now. One way or another, there was nothing she could do. Her answer came as the police car pulled out wide and passed her without a sideways glance from the driver or passenger, but in the anticlimax came a worse thought. These people must be very confident of their own ability to find her.

Back in the narrow lanes again, she found a place of concealment down a tiny track and studied the map. Bodmin Moor lay in her path to the west, its few roads likely to be full of tourists. A ten-mile strip of land separated the moor from the holiday villages of the south coast, Polperro and Looe. Crisscrossing that strip from Liskeard and the main A38 down to the sea was a network of main roads and fairly main B-roads. Directly south looked better, into a maze of lanes around Menheniot, Quethiock, Pillaton and down to Landrake. That name nagged at her. Landrake? She couldn't quite fix it. A barn or an empty house, somewhere to lie up, that would be ideal, but for how long? Nearly a week until Harry came back. She headed south.

Consciously or not, Claire was heading for the water. The river inlets branching west off the Tamar, and the nearby sea coast, produced romantic ideas in her head of abandoned boat-houses. Any barns she passed had long since been converted into holiday cottages. Landrake still lodged somewhere in her mind. Near the hamlet of Blunts, the engine spluttered and she switched to reserve, realizing she would have to find petrol – which called for a main road. It was easier to put off the decision; easier to wheel the moped through a gate into a field whose long grass looked as if it had been undisturbed all summer and, lying down out of the sight of the whole world, let the day's nervous exhaustion drop her into a bone-weary sleep.

The red light on Harry's camera went on at three minutes past eight, after the most lucrative advertisement break ever sold in National's short history. This was the show designed to pull the biggest audience yet, drawn by the biggest publicity. The £50,000 prize on offer for Claire Merrick's capture was a guarantee that the advertisers would see audience figures to justify the cost of the slots they'd bought. Gilligan's future, Harry knew, was riding on all this.

Few people, he thought, have been through this. Few people have had to denounce the woman in their life to millions of people. He'd done the best he could for her within narrow margins. He'd chosen the most flattering, highly made-up and least recognizable shots of her from the choice available, arguing with the rest of the team that glamour should be their watchword. He'd seized a moment when no one was looking to alter the briefing note to the graphics team so her height would come up two inches wrong and her hair colour would say brown instead of black. He could imagine the row afterwards about what would be seen as some researcher's stupid mistake and knew no one would suspect him. That was all he could do. The phone rang unanswered at Godsblanket when he risked calling but there was no news of any arrest and he could only wonder and fear.

*     *     *

Larry Couch was watching the show on the set at the end of his counter. Next to it was the close-circuit screen which showed the pumps in case some punter drove off without paying. But of an evening, when the holiday traffic got a bit quiet, he watched satellite TV. Since the hold-up, he liked a bit of noise around. Anyway, Larry always enjoyed watching the box, and this fifty thousand quid lark was something else. He'd seen the papers, but they hadn't had much yet, nothing about all this lezzy stuff, anyway. What a business, eh? He wished there was some punter there watching it with him so he could have said that: what a business, eh? He wanted to share his disbelief. A famous looker like that Claire Merrick knocking off another bird ... One walked in then, a woman who wanted some fags with her petrol, but he couldn't quite say it to her, could he? Then he saw a little putt-putt moped come in. He kept one eye on the closed-circuit, watching the rider struggling with the two-stroke bottle and the nozzle of the pump. The figure turned and walked towards the door, and that's when Larry started to get shirty.

The door opened and he looked up. 'Here, can't you read?' he said.

The visor went up and a muffled voice said, 'What?' in surprise.

'The sign. On the door. Go and look.'

The rider stood uncertainly for a moment, then did as he was told. Larry could have told him what it said. It was quite new, put there since the hold-up, put there to stop anyone playing that bloody trick again. It said: 'Motorcycle riders must remove crash helmets before entering.' He wasn't the only one, the rep had said, they were going up all over the place these days.

After that the rider just sort of faffed around for a bit outside, then to Larry's intense irritation came back in, still with the bloody helmet on.

'Can't you read?' he said again. 'Get it off. Now. Or do I call the police? It's there for a good reason, that notice.'

So she took it off, because that was when Larry realized she was a she, and she sort of shook her hair around so it fell in front of her face and came to the desk, taking a huge interest in the sweet rack off to one side, reaching out sideways to pay him. There was a moment though when he put her change on the table right in front of him and then she had to look round and down to see where it was.

'Bloody hell,' he said. 'Claire bloody Merrick,' and she was out of the door and on the bike before he could get through the flap in the cash desk. He looked back at the screen in time to see the end titles and the call-in number.

'Fifty grand,' he said out loud. 'Bloody hell.'

# Chapter Twenty-Seven

Fifty grand meant fifty thousand nutters and hopefuls from all over the UK were ringing Crookbusters. The lines were jammed solid from the start of the show, with sightings from Lerwick to Dover. Even that hadn't stopped half the policemen wandering off for a beer. Derek Palmer's briefing before the show had been extremely specific. 'Cornwall,' he had said. 'Cornwall or maybe Devon. We're not saying so on the air in case we tip her off, but unless someone else has got her phone, it's Cornwall. We don't know how she's travelling but we're watching all the main roads and we think that's where she is.'

Very few of the incoming calls were from Cornwall. There was a man who said she'd just been to bed with him in Redruth, but he started to giggle two minutes into the conversation and then began to talk about God in a loud and very angry voice. There was an old lady who was sure she'd seen her polishing the brass in Landulph church that morning, and three or four equally vague contributions from the rest of the peninsula.

It took twelve minutes of constant dialling to an engaged signal for Larry Couch to get through. He never once thought of phoning the local police instead. Fifty thousand pounds saw to that. Finally it rang and he got one of the secretaries who pulled a form in front of her and asked him the stock questions.

At the end she waved a hand vigorously and Harry, who was prowling round the desks, grabbed the form from her. He read it through and gave a forced laugh. 'Come on, Helen. A moped? Hardly likely is it?'

'Derek did say that anything from Cornwall . . .'

'OK,' said Harry, 'I'll put it on the computer for you.'

Messing up this man Couch's phone number wouldn't be too much of a problem, he thought.

'No need,' said Helen, 'Derek's just coming,' and she called out in a loud voice 'Derek? I've got one.'

He was there in no time, taking the form, reading it through, and Harry could do nothing.

'Oh *yes*,' he said. 'This one smells good.'

'Why?' asked Harry feebly.

'Wouldn't take off her helmet, then ran for it. Sounds likely to me.'

Devon and Cornwall Constabulary got his call a minute later and acted on it instantly. A patrol car was within a mile of Larry Couch. Four more went to block her escape on the A38, the A390, the A30 and the B3359, and every panda car they could raise began sweeping the lanes for ten miles around. It was still fully light and the helicopter was sent up to help. It could only be a matter of time, they all thought.

Claire, in a panic, had got lost and come round in an almost complete circle. Hearing her name shouted in that way hadn't been as bad as glancing at the screen and seeing Harry declaiming against a huge back-drop blow-up of her face. She squandered a precious seven minutes of her head start going down a dead-end through St Erney and then back on to a junction which offered her no choice but the main A38 again. A sign pointed along it to Landrake. That name again. She took it. The road went up and down steep hills and there weren't any turnings, so she was forced to stay in the careering traffic for a whole mile. The hills helped in one small way. From a crest, as she rode into a large village, blasted in two halves by the shotgun-hole of the A38 through the middle, she saw a flashing blue light half a mile in front, moving fast down the centre lane in her direction. She noted the village sign: this was Landrake. Then she braked, swung left into a full car park and drove the moped behind a van right at the back.

The police car was nearly there. She saw the blue light reflecting in the windows out by the road, fifteen yards away, and heard its engine. There was a big timber building jutting into the car park and she walked quickly into the gloom at the back of it. What happened next was a pure accident of timing. As she approached the back wall, seeking only to get out of sight of the road, a door opened only three feet away from her. An old man looked out, saw her and moved aside to make space for her to enter, and in that split second in which she could see through to lots of people sitting down in a darkened room, it seemed less obtrusive to simply go on in than to turn away.

She couldn't have been luckier. It was a village hall with old hard chairs drawn up in ranks for a performance, and it was only half full. The heavy curtains were drawn and the lights were low. The back two rows were empty and she moved right to the far end. She could hardly sit there with her helmet on, but in the gloom, taking it off seemed a small risk.

No one took any notice of her arrival because at that same moment a tinny piano had started to play and the curtains opened to reveal a line of assorted teenage girls, incongruously dressed in top hats, swimsuits, gloves and fishnet stockings. It sounded almost like 'In the Mood' played in an unusual key. Someone touched her shoulder and she jumped. The old man who'd ushered her in bent to her ear.

'Do you have a ticket?' he whispered.

She shook her head, feigning rapt attention on the stage, and reached into her pocket.

'Two pounds, please,' he said, and she dropped the coins into his hand, still keeping her face turned to the stage. He thrust a piece of paper at her and went back to his perch by the door.

The piece of paper said this was 'Cornish Capers', presented by the Isabella Troppo School of Dancing. There was a long, long list of dances, but it was warm, hidden and fairly safe. People were still coming in, but the seats at the front proved far more inviting and no one came near her.

The dance starred two girls of startlingly different shape who did most of the moving, while the rest kept up a semi-rhythmic shuffle. One was a young heifer with a slightly curved spine, pushing her slack-mouthed face forward towards the audience and projecting at them a look of intense anxiety. The other was a very tall, stick-like girl who moved like a puppet on a string and had thin lips that stayed clamped together in a white line throughout the routine. It ended and another began; a dozen little girls with identical yellow plastic umbrellas tittupping shyly on to the stage to the tune of 'Singing in the Rain'. And so it went on, number after number with the men in front of Claire shifting from buttock to buttock on the hard seats while their wives, undoubtedly the mothers of the countless performers in front of them, took the acute discomfort with all the proud fortitude of childbirth.

Claire was in a limbo, lulled by the isolated calmness of her position, knowing it would end and she would have to go out into an impossibly hostile world. She looked at the stage and her mind blanked out the painful performance occupying it. Instead there came back a clear memory of the person she had been before, when there had been time in her life for relaxation. She was back in Regents Park on a warm summer evening, with a long-gone lover watching Brecht's *Threepenny Opera*, passing a bottle of wine between them, drinking straight from the neck, arms tight round each other. She mused on that but it faded, and old laughter echoed somewhere in her as a man in Lincoln Green produced a cast of hundreds out of nowhere: Peter Wear's one-man *Robin Hood* at the Campus festival. Laughter seemed a long way away. Then a still evening, by herself in another open-air crowd in front of the Great Hall at Dartington, *Merchant of Venice*. Why that one? A good play, but an unhappy time. That brought back a man's voice to her memory, a voice and a vague shape. Dartington. She'd stopped for an unexpected night on the way back from sailing with Jerome, unexpected because of the row that terminated that trip prematurely. A row sparked off by what?

In her mind, a man's voice spoke again and it came back, all of it. The piratical black ketch, Charles Golant smashing Jerome's flagmast with a well-aimed bowsprit, and the addresses they had exchanged. 'If you need rescuing, just call. I'm very good at damsels in distress,' he'd said. Landrake. That was his address, she searched her memory. Church Passage House, Landrake. Could there be more than one Landrake? Quite possible. Would he help her? God knows. What alternative was there? None.

The Troppo dancing school's performance swung into what looked a finale. At any time, the lights might come up. She rose quickly to her feet, turning to the blank back wall as if the ample aisle between the chairs had to be taken sideways and shuffled for the door in the gloom.

She went to the moped but through the darkness, from up the hill, a blue light was still flashing. Road-block? It was quite likely. She took her sailing bag, pushed the moped even further out of sight, dropping her helmet next to it, and went to chance her luck. The profile of the church stuck up against the darkening sky. It was on her side of the road. She didn't want to risk the pavement with the glare of all the cars' lights, so she climbed a fence at the back of the car park and waded through tall grass along the back of a row of cottages.

There could easily be more than one Landrake in Cornwall, she thought again. They're not very inventive about their names, but the four-square Georgian house beyond the cottages said 'Church Passage House' by the door, and she felt momentarily weak with relief.

He might not be there any more. He could be away on his boat. It's a year ago, she thought. Anyway, he might call the police as soon as he sees me, but no alternative had yet presented itself, so she rapped the knocker, then stood well back in the shadows to see who came.

It was him. He opened the door, looked out in surprise, then up and down. She spoke from the shadows. 'Are you still good at rescuing damsels in distress?'

There was a short silence, then he said, 'At your service,' and there was excitement in his voice.

There'd only been one more question after that.

'Did you kill her?'

'No. I . . .'

'The rest can wait.'

Then it was all action. He opened the back doors of a big van, full of clutter.

'Get in there, under the sacks. I'll put some boxes in front of you. Don't move a muscle. OK?'

'OK.'

He hid her, climbed into the driver's seat and started off. Lying in the dark, she felt the van bump off the kerb and accelerate up the road. Two minutes later it slowed to a stop then moved forward in fits and starts. After some time, she heard that deep voice again, raised in a question, then answering briefly. The road-block. Unbearable tension twisted her as the back doors of the van squeaked open, but only for a second or two, then they banged shut, there was a call of 'Go on then' from the rear, and they were off again.

'We're all right,' called the voice from the front, 'but stay where you are just in case. It won't be long.'

The van twisted and turned, accelerated and braked for maybe ten minutes, then bumped down a long, rough track. It turned sharp right and stopped abruptly, dipping at the front and rolling Claire forwards against the metal partition behind the seats.

'Right,' Charles said, 'we've arrived. Just be very quiet.'

He slid the door open and she climbed out. The first thing that struck her was the instantly familiar sound of rigging slapping against aluminium masts in the gentle wind. It was almost completely dark now but she could see tall masts, massed together as if in a marina, against the fading sky; but there were also trees and a hill side stretching away up to her right and no feeling of nearby water. She followed him through a curving pathway between big sheds and ranks of speedboats on trailers. Bigger boats on cradles were crowded together off to their right. Past a massive self-propelled crane on giant rubber tyres they turned left down a long concrete slipway. She followed now without a second thought. There was no hint of coercion and she had no hint of a choice.

At the bottom, he stepped on to a slippery, floating pontoon which stuck out into a narrow river. Three or four small yachts were moored to it as well as a big Dutch barge with lights showing inside. He raised a finger to his lips and bent to untie the painter of a battered, paint-splattered fibreglass dinghy. A voice from inside the barge called out, 'That you, Charlie?' and he froze.

'Yes Frank, bit of a rush. See you tomorrow.'

There was a grunt from within. They got in, and with economical strokes he turned and rowed them past the pontoon and on down what was more of a creek than a river.

He didn't say a word and, feeling protected by the night, the water and the silence, she sat there watching. Over his shoulder she could see that the creek joined a much wider expanse of river ahead and in the bend at their junction a large boat showed black in the silver light, two thick masts bracketing the moon.

He turned his head briefly for a moment, adjusting his course for the first time since they started, a measure of how many times he must have made this journey. Two quick pulls on the right oar brought them neatly alongside the boat, whose rough, dark-planked sides towered over them. He stood, painter in one hand, her bag over his shoulder, and was up the side like a fly, leaving the dinghy barely rocking, such was his balance. She stood carefully, feeling for her centre of gravity and could see no way up, but there, dimly lit in the moonlight, was a hinged gate cut in the boat's high bulwarks. It was closed and he hadn't bothered to open it, so why should she? She found the gaps in the planking around it and used those for a purchase just as he must have done and with a heave she was over the side and standing on deck by him. He grinned, teeth white in the moonlight, unhooked a door in the cockpit, and beckoned her down rough steps in the darkness. A match flared, then an oil lamp glowed and rose into soft yellow light and she found herself in wonderland.

It was a capacious cabin, walled with rough timbers. Big, overstuffed sofas ran along both sides, old oil paintings in battered gilt frames hung above them. Books were everywhere. Richly-carved columns supporting the deck broke up the space, and a mast like a tree trunk passed through it. A passageway ran aft next to the ladder they had come down. She could see another chamber opening off it to one side with a huge Victorian bath in it. A passageway for'ard showed glimpses of more cabins and velvet hangings. Rich, soft decay was everywhere.

'Do you want a cup of tea?' he said. 'Or would you rather have Scotch?'

'Both,' she said, 'if that's OK.'

She sat in silence on the sofa, while he boiled a kettle.

He sat down opposite her. 'You were lucky you caught me. The house is between tenants, I usually live here. This . . .' he waved an expansive hand around, '. . . is the *Cauchemar*, which you've met before, formerly a French fishing boat, latterly a hulk, until I resurrected her. I know you understand sailing boats. You're an expert sailor, it said so in the papers.'

'You do know you can get a big reward from National for catching me.'

'Money is money,' he said, 'and it just fools you for a while until it goes away again. A damsel in distress is something splendid and that doesn't come your way more than once in a lifetime.'

She shook her head. 'You don't have any way of knowing I didn't do it. All right, you asked me, fine, but I would hardly have admitted it.'

'I see auras,' he said. 'I can see yours. I can tell.'

'What do you mean?'

'You sound almost affronted,' he smiled. 'As soon as I saw you at the house, even in the twilight. I saw you as you are, as you couldn't disguise it. A victim, not a murderer, so I knew I had to help. Are you complaining?'

'No,' she shook her head, trying to get the hang of him. He continued to look amused. 'I'm not complaining.'

'You're exhausted, aren't you?'

'Yes.'

'There's a cabin for'ard on this side. Mine's opposite. There's no door, but don't worry, not only am I saddled by birth with the genes of a perfect gentleman, but I'm staying celibate this year as an experiment. I'll run you a bath.'

The bath was fed by a Heath Robinson geyser, apparently fuelled by a coke fire. He pulled a blanket across the entrance for her sake. Ten minutes later she was fast asleep on a hugely soft, shapeless feather mattress under a pile of blankets.

Claire woke to broad daylight streaming in through a pointed glass dome that stuck down through the deck like the upside-down centre of an orange squeezer. The noise that had woken her was the rattle of chains from above and the flapping of sails.

Laid out on her bed were a pair of faded tan sailcloth trousers, an equally faded blue work shirt, and a sailing smock. She put them on, grateful for the feel of fresh clothes, and went through the main cabin and up on deck.

Charles had three sails up and flapping loose, and was just preparing to let go.

'Good morning,' he said. 'Good timing. Come and take over here, will you? Let go when I shout.'

'Are we going somewhere?'

'Just out for a little breathing space. The wind's from the west, we can trickle all the way down to the Sound on that.'

And so they could. The big old boat, sixty foot long not counting the bowsprit, quietly came to life as he sheeted in the multi-coloured patched sails, and with a gathering splashing from under her stem slipped out into the main river and turned to the east.

'Put this on,' he said when she joined him at the wheel, and handed her a battered sailcloth cap. 'Tuck your hair up underneath it. Just in case anyone's watching.'

'Where exactly are we?'

'This is the Lynher. It joins the Tamar at the Hamoaze opposite Devonport, right by the naval dockyard.'

'And that place last night?'

'Boating Heaven. One of the world's least accessible boatyards. A great place. You can only get to it on the top of the tide, and even then you have to know the channel like the back of your hand. Ideal for people like me because it keeps the plastic people away. It's full of us wooden boat eccentrics.'

He was sitting high up on an old leather armchair which sat in a little cuddy like a garden shed behind the wheel. In front of them the deckhouse had window boxes arranged all around it. Claire looked around, through the tattered rigging. A boxed emergency life raft was lashed to the cabin top. That seemed so out of keeping that she looked more closely. The label said, 'Next service due: 1983.'

He caught her look. 'She doesn't sink often.'

'Often?'

'Well, only once in the last two years.'

'What happened?'

'Oh, nothing much. I raised her and fixed the hole.'

'How?'

'Concrete.'

She laughed for the first time in days.

They loafed along, past Ince Castle on the north bank and Jupiter Point to the south. As the Tamar and Plymouth loomed ahead, there were more boats on the water, trots of thirty-foot weekend cruisers on both sides.

'Charles,' she said.

'Yes?'

A direct question seemed the best. 'I've got a friend who's trying to sort things out. How long can I stay on the boat?'

He was silent for a moment. 'As far as I'm concerned, you can stay as long as you like, but I think we'd better find another answer.'

'Why?'

'Well, people come and see me a lot. They don't ask first, they just turn up. The boat's a bit of a focus for all kinds of funny folk. It's their meeting point. That's why we're sailing now. Weekdays are bad enough, but at the weekends they come in droves. I don't think I could hide you for long.'

Despair seized her so fast that she could only nod dumbly.

'However,' he said, 'I do have a little idea. That's another reason we're here.'

Claire had stayed down below while Charles rowed across to the quay at Saltash. She stuck her head out of the hatch from time to time and when she saw the dinghy returning, she was ready for him, taking the painter and a shopping bag full of beer and hot pasties. He trailed the dinghy astern and secured it.

'Did you call him?' she said anxiously.

'Yes. I'm afraid he'd already left, at least his machine was on. I left a cryptic message saying you were OK.'

'Thanks.'

He looked at her. 'Someone special.' It was a statement.

'Well,' she said, 'under any other circumstances he could have been.' She looked at the nearby hill side, terraced with ranks of houses, and shivered. 'I feel a bit vulnerable here. Can we get under way again?'

'Why not? But first of all, look over there.'

She followed his finger pointing along a line of moored boats stretching back around the curve into the mouth of the Lynher.

'Where?'

'What do you see?'

'Some boats.'

'Use your eyes. Tell me about them.'

She went along with it, unsure of what he might mean. 'There's a nice ketch. Then there's one of those fake plastic Cornish Crabbers. The third one's an old Nicholson, then something very flashy I don't recognize and a couple of Hurleys, then there's what looks like a Contessa 32.'

'Very good. What do you make of the Contessa?'

'Covered in seagull shit. Someone's little dream that they never get round to sailing. It doesn't look as if it's been out in years.'

'That seagull shit, and the contents of my shed, might just be your salvation.'

# Chapter Twenty-Eight

## Saturday August 10th

'We can't have that,' Gilligan had said when he learnt he'd been booked first class and Harry was in economy. 'I'm a republican. I believe in equality.'

It was a disappointment that Gilligan's chosen solution was to downgrade his own ticket instead of upgrading Harry's, but comfort was far down the list of things Harry held important right then. Until they got airborne.

The seat in front of him was far too close, and to add injury to the insult, its occupant had tipped it right back as soon as the seat belt light was switched off, forcing Harry to recline his own seat to avoid being crushed into a right angle by the oncoming hypotenuse and, judging by the grunt of protest from behind, setting off a domino effect right down the ranks of close-packed economy class seats behind him.

Gilligan laughed. 'You shouldn't have such long legs.'

The stewardess gave Harry a Bloody Mary from the drinks trolley and passed a soda water to his boss.

'Don't have too many of those things,' said Gilligan, 'I want you in good condition when you get there. Alcohol dries you out, makes it harder to get over the lag.'

'I think it might help if you told me why we're doing this,' said Harry.

'I thought you would have guessed,' the other man said quietly. 'We're still eating up money. I need the banks to keep the faith until we turn the corner.'

'And the banks are American?'

'Two of them are. I can give them all the paperwork you like and they won't get too stirred up, but a story about National on primetime network TV, that's something else. They'll start believing we're for real.'

Harry nodded. Gilligan looked at him and considered. 'You a discreet sort of guy, Harry?'

'When it matters.'

'The first two stations on the list matter more than the rest. There's just a chance of buying in to them. That's the real reason I came along. It gives me an excuse to take a look round when they've got their guard down.'

'So the rest are a waste of time?'

'For me, not for you. I'll leave you on your own for them.'

It was disconcerting to know he would have to talk to his boss for much of the flight. There was a gulf between them. Harry knew Gilligan's track record and the wide span of his business. He sat in a state of mild panic, rejecting possible conversational openings as too banal to waste the other man's time. There was a short silence, then Gilligan surprised him.

'What's with this sick relative of yours?'

'How do you know about that?'

'You mentioned it on Wednesday. Tell me.'

So Harry, warming to the man, told him as he had told no one else except Claire, and Gilligan was interested and listened carefully to the whole story.

'Are you happy they've done everything they can?' he said finally.

'I don't know.'

'When we've got this out of the way, I'll see what I can do. There are some specialists I know who ought to take a look at her. Would that be all right with you?'

'Oh yes,' said Harry, 'please.'

They ate their food then Gilligan sighed. 'Why do you think Claire Merrick flipped like that?'

It was the moment when Harry could so easily have told him about Ann's sheets of paper burning a hole in his pocket, could so easily have taken them out and talked the whole thing through with the one man who might just have the clout to do something about it. He very nearly did, but it was too early. He was unsure of the way this thoughtful, confident man would take it. He felt a growing understanding between them but it needed more time, so he simply said, 'I really haven't a clue. You're sure the Americans are going to be interested in the story?'

'There'll be some very expensive PR people looking for a new job if they aren't. We've done a lot of promotion on this to stir up their appetite. I want you to really hit the way she fooled us all, how plausible she made all this plot stuff sound. Really go for it. Have you seen the London papers today?' Gilligan took out the *Daily Mail* and unfolded it to find a lead story with a still from the show: Harry in the foreground, Claire's giant picture in the background. 'Hunt for Crookbuster Claire Switches to West,' said the headline.

Harry switched back to the main worry. Where the hell had Claire gone? He had left the show at midnight when the calls finally stopped coming in. By that time the police had confirmed the petrol station sighting in Cornwall. The ten-pound note Claire had left behind without waiting for her change was a new one, and it was one of those issued to the bank cash machine from which Harry had taken the money.

Gilligan had been there throughout, and Jane Bernstein had taken a small revenge by putting a demented Larry Couch on to him. The petrol station man had wanted his fifty thousand and he wanted it now – and he wasn't at all pleased when Gilligan explained that Crookbusters' policy was to pay the reward for information leading to the arrest of the suspect, and Claire Merrick had yet to be arrested. What had happened to Claire was a mystery to all of them, and the police were taking it personally that a woman with no criminal experience and no apparent help could simply vanish. They had the moped, that was something. The helicopter had spotted it in a village hall car park. House to house searches, taking in sheds, barns and anything that could hide a human being had yielded nothing.

New York was very hot. Gilligan's equality seemed not to extend to staying in the same hotel. He arranged a time to pick up Harry for the first interview and left. The first thing Harry did when he'd checked in and gone up to his room, jaded from the long flight, was to get out the precious sheets of paper and looked at them all over again.

Ten seats where the swing had been much lower and the turn-out much higher than the national average. Ten seats where a suspicious mind – starting from the belief that something funny must have happened to make the pre-election polls so wrong – could have found succour for its conspiracy theories. Until then only the ballot boxes and that half-label, tying them to Beaconsbridge, served as any conclusive evidence, and where were they now? Gone, just as Ann Farrow was gone, just as Claire ... Harry pushed that thought aside. Then he turned again to the third sheet, the strangest evidence of all. This, he knew, must have been Ann's final discovery, and death stopped her revealing it.

It was the same ten seats, with the same percentage swings and the same turn-out figures. There was no new fact in it at all, but the figures weren't the important point. The only difference was the order the seats had been put in. The previous list had been arranged in numerical order by the size of the swing. This one was arranged in the simplest way, in alphabetical order. Who knows why Ann had done that? Just to tidy it up, perhaps? Had she suddenly seen the truth and printed it out, or had she printed it out and only then noticed? He couldn't know it had been a simple slip of the finger.

He took another sip of his drink from the mini-bar and looked again at the sheet of paper. Alphabetical order, but only part of the alphabet. The constituencies spanned a range from the North to the Midlands, and on down to one or two of the shire counties. Eight of the ten constituencies on the list started with the letters A, B or C. Even that wasn't the end of the far-fetched alphabetical coincidence. The remaining two started with S and T.

He could see it in his mind's eye; someone, somewhere, going through the book, through all the hundreds of parliamentary seats, looking for the ones they could fix, ticking off the seats they planned to hit one by one, starting at the beginning of the book with A, going through methodically until they had enough, though they were only in the Cs. Then what of the other two?

Maybe they decided they needed a few more for safety. Maybe, towards the end, that unseen hand decided, just to be sure, to flick a bit further ahead in the book. It was surely way beyond the possible bounds of coincidence. It was so careless though, childish almost. But was it? he thought, gazing out of the window. No one else had noticed. You had to go looking for it in a certain way to find it, to find that one careless fingerprint in the middle of a statistical maze.

He stretched across for the phone and dialled England. The Godsblanket number rang and rang to no effect. He then called his own answering machine. When he gave it the command, the tape rewound and an unfamiliar male voice said, 'A message for Harry. Your goddaughter has asked me to tell you she is OK and will be in touch soon.'

He didn't have a goddaughter. It had to be Claire, but who was the voice? He walked to the window, looked out across Fifty-Second Street diagonally towards Fifth Avenue, unsure whether to laugh or scream. He tried both.

# Chapter Twenty-Nine

## Saturday August 10th

Social events for Freedom's Friends weren't all that social. The summer barbecue wasn't the usual type of corporate event where rich old men could compare their latest wives and boastfully introduce precocious children. Members' families weren't invited, because they knew nothing of the organization.

They'd taken a decision not to invite their newest member. There was some dirty washing that was better done in his absence, but all the Friends bar four were there for the annual review of business, and those four would be hooked up on audio links for the main business. It seemed much as usual, the great grills were laden with slabs of best beef, starting to spit over the banks of charcoal. The waiters were gliding through the crowd with their trays of drinks. Two helicopters, one within half a mile, the other far off doing lazy sweeps around the horizon, were insurance against intruders, prepared for any light aircraft that should chance to stray into the area.

What was missing for the Producer as he moved from group to group was the usual feeling of unalloyed success. In past years he had become used to receiving their accolades, and they were men who often expressed their appreciation for his services in tangible form. This time, the discreetly-passed envelopes which turned his fat annual salary into considerable riches were fewer in number, and the conversations were all the same: 'Where are we on Game Ten?'

'Still tracking the Merrick woman.'

'Gotta find her. That's what you're there for.'

Extreme measures were called for, and he knew they wouldn't

accept failure. In one of their corporations, they might retire him early, but not here. There was no early retirement from Freedom's Friends for those who knew what he knew. He sat down on the wooden steps looking across to the corral where the C.E.O. of a steel company was gingerly climbing on a fierce-looking but heavily tranquillized bronco. He saw Martin Blunden approaching, the big man, and groaned inwardly as he sat down beside him. Blunden never minced words.

'The Merrick business,' he said. 'Your butt is on the line. What are you going to do?'

The Producer thought of the loose strands and tried to make it all sound good. 'First, the phone calls,' he said. 'Claire Merrick phoned National's switchboard twice. She has a pal there, someone we don't know about. She'll do it again. We've put someone in, so the switchboard's covered now. If we have to, we'll bug the home phones of every National employee she could conceivably be trying to call. Second, there's this little bike she was riding. We know a man bought it for cash in London with a false name. Find him and we've found her friend, and it's my bet he works at National.'

Blunden nodded, got up and walked off. The gong by the saloon clanged and the Friends looked up from their plates and their mugs with anticipation. As they filed in through the door, the speakers began to play 'Come, come, there's a wondrous land, where I'll build you a home in the meadow . . .' Upstairs in the big room, the Producer gave his notes a last check. The rest of the year's record didn't look so bad. His presentation took ten minutes. Their year's achievements included eight major changes in legislation around the world, the destruction of a long-standing political alliance, the disgrace or early retirement of eight politicians opposed to their interests and the sterilization of twelve individuals. He paused at the end for the usual applause, but instead there was a question.

'You didn't mention Game Ten. I am alarmed at the sloppiness of the recent handling of the game. What are you doing about it and, considering subsequent events, have the game's objectives proved worth it?'

He looked morosely at the man who they called Henry Fonda,

dressed with no hint of levity in a fur hat, as trapper Jethro Stewart.

'We are taking all the action necessary to sterilize Claire Merrick. As for the game's objectives, they were achieved dramatically. You have to take it together with Game Eleven, which you will recall secured the narrow Danish rejection of the referendum on a United Europe, and the sub-game which forced the British pound out of the European Monetary System and then more or less destroyed the system completely.' He clenched his fist. 'No one, gentlemen, no one can say we have not succeeded. Before we acted, Europe was hurtling towards union, and I mean full union, a superpower in the making. Look at it now. Thanks to us, they lost the momentum. Sure, there'll be a form of unity, but nothing like it would have been. The internal split in the British Conservatives helped stall the whole movement towards uniting Europe. Gentlemen, if it had not been for the part played by those games at a pivotal moment, we would now be facing a Brussels-led United States of Europe and a wholly different world trade situation in which all of you would have been the losers.'

He got a round of applause then, but it was soon over.

# Sunday August 11th

Being on the wrong end of an interview was a new experience for Harry. This, he soon found out, was a gladiatorial sport – with him, if he stumbled, as the victim.

The show's presenter was a Barbie doll with a brain extension. She was hooked up by an invisible earpiece to a razor-sharp producer in the gallery, and her main skill lay in making the prompts that were hissing into her ear sound like natural questions she'd dreamed up herself.

'You worked closely with Claire Merrick. Did it never occur to you that she might be capable of a crime of this violence?'

'No, it didn't. As we were both reporters, we tended to work on separate stories.'

'She was what I guess you'd call a celebrity before she came to your channel, wasn't she?'

'Certainly, she was one of the two best known female TV reporters in Britain.'

'You feel a need to make that distinction, Mr Chaplin? Is there something different about *female* reporters in Britain?'

'Well, they're a different shape.' That one went down like a lead balloon. 'No, I suppose it's just there are still fewer of them.'

'So would you say that Claire Merrick has been turned into some kind of a peepshow act because of her sexual orientation?'

For a mad moment he thought of saying, 'No, in fact she's heterosexual, she's my lover and she's been framed to stop her trying to expose the biggest crime against democracy ever foisted on the British public.' He could imagine the uproar that would follow, the men in white coats and then, who knows, the men with the bullets not far behind them. Instead he took a deep breath, thought 'forgive me, Claire', and said, 'No, I think it's because she clubbed another woman to death.'

They broke off to run clips from his film and then came back for the finale.

'To date, Mr Chaplin, the British police still haven't found her although there's a reward offered of getting on for a hundred thousand dollars. How can that be?'

'She's clearly very resourceful,' said Harry.

'If you don't mind my saying so, you don't seem too upset that she's still on the loose. Was she a personal friend of yours?' The question was innocuous.

'No. Anyone at National will tell you we didn't get on. Professional rivalry, they'd probably call it,' and Harry thought to himself; misleading it might be, but every word of that answer is strictly true.

Gilligan was waiting for him afterwards. 'Well done, Harry. You can handle yourself pretty well.'

'Thanks.'

'I'm on my way now. You've got all your tickets?'

'Yes, thanks.'

'I should be back in London before you. Give me a call as soon as you get back. We'll put our heads together.'

# Monday August 12th

Monday morning was Philadelphia, and Harry was too groggy to care, but the answers came pat now. He was already realizing there was practically no such thing as an original question. A limo had picked him up from the hotel, he'd been plied with coffee, made-up, sat down, cross-examined, and now he was one of their used-up empties. He was sitting in make-up having the pancake removed and wondering what to do with the six hours before his Boston flight, when a voice behind said 'Mr Chaplin?', and in the mirror he saw a woman standing there with an envelope.

For a hopeful moment he thought, my God they're paying me; then she said, 'Message for you. A viewer phoned in while you were on the air.'

He took the envelope, puzzled. Someone had gone to all the trouble of typing it out.

'To Mr Harry Chaplin,' it said on the outside, 'Studio Guest'. He opened it. 'Mr Denzil Deruda asks Mr Chaplin as a matter of urgency to call him at the MacIntosh Skandless Project.' It gave a local telephone number. The secretary was still standing there.

'Have you heard of something called the MacIntosh Skandless Project?' he asked.

'Oh sure,' she said. 'That's out on the edge of the city. It's some kind of healthcare place.'

The studio limo had a phone in it and he called on the way back to the hotel. Mr Deruda was put on straight away. 'Mr Chaplin, glad you called,' said a voice that sounded strained. 'Caught your show this morning. I was wondering if you could come and see me?'

'Well, maybe, but why? I have to catch a plane to Boston in a few hours.'

'I have some information for you.'

It has to be a nutter, he thought to himself. In Philadelphia? Information?

'What sort of information?' he asked.

'Information about Claire Merrick and who really killed her friend,' said the voice.

'But everybody says *she* killed her,' he said, trying to keep the sudden excitement out of his voice. Nothing in the story even hinted someone else might have done it. Nutter or source? In Philadelphia, for Christ's sake. It had to be the former.

'Not everybody. Not me, for one,' Deruda answered. 'Why don't you come over and talk to me?'

'Maybe. Can you give me just a hint of what this is about?'

'So you don't waste your time? Well, all right. Here's a name for you. Wade. I think it was Paul Wade. Is that a strong enough hint?'

Harry let out his breath in a long sigh.

'When can I come?' he asked.

'How about right now.'

'Hold on a minute.'

He crawled forward across four feet of grey carpet and slid aside the glass division.

'Yes, sir?' said the chauffeur.

'Could you drop me at the MacIntosh Skandless Project instead of the hotel?'

'Would you have the street name, sir?'

He went back to the phone and got it.

'That's no problem, sir.'

The Project was a grand, untouched late nineteenth-century mansion alone in a sea of modern buildings. The limo driver apologized for the fact that he couldn't wait, but Harry thanked him and waved goodbye. The entrance hall had dramatic stained glass, thick, dark red carpet and Wagner playing from hidden speakers.

A man with close-cropped hair, a moustache and rimless glasses looked up and smiled.

'Well hello, I'm Mark,' he said. 'You would be Mr Chaplin, I expect?'

'That's right.'

'Denzil's expecting you in his room. First floor, number five. Now, you haven't been here before, have you, Mr Chaplin?'

'No.'

'Well, if you wouldn't mind just reading the Project's guidelines?' He handed over a pamphlet.

Harry took it, puzzled, and read. 'HIV is not transferable by normal human contact. You have no need to fear communication by hug or handshake. Our guests thrive on physical attention. Be cheerful but also have regard for the dignity of their illness.' It went on in similar vein.

'This is an AIDS hospice?' he said in surprise.

'Oh, you didn't know? That's not what we call it but, you're from England right? I guess that's about it.'

'And Denzil is a patient?'

'He's a guest here, yes.'

Harry climbed the stairs slowly. The decor was dark, gothic. He stopped on the landing, staring at an old painting of a gigantic eagle, ripping at a horse and rider, against a thunderous sky. A voice spoke from an open door behind him.

'We're going into the darkness, Mr Chaplin, all of us. We want to get ready.'

He turned round, and a young man with dark stains under his eyes was standing, leaning against the doorpost, wearing a dressing gown.

'I'm Denzil Deruda,' he said, but he didn't put his hand out until Harry extended his, and then he smiled. 'I can tell you've read the guidance notes.'

Harry walked into a room that echoed the rest of the building, with a four-poster bed with heavily-embroidered hangings, and deep red wall paper. A heavily-carved dark oak bookcase covered most of one wall. A large television was the only truly modern object.

Deruda got into the bed and waved Harry to a chair next to it. 'I need to know something,' he said. 'Are you only interested in your colleague's guilt or might you be interested in her innocence?'

'I'm interested in her case in every possible way,' said Harry noncommittally.

'That's not much of a reply.'

'If she's innocent, then I'm on her side. Does that help?'

Deruda looked at him and sighed. 'God knows, and who cares anyway?' he said. 'I'll tell you.'

'I'm listening.'

'She followed some guy called Paul Wade to a car wrecker's yard,' said Deruda, and Harry arched upright in his chair staring at him in total astonishment.

'How do you know that?' he said, and Deruda smiled in delight at the effect he had provoked.

'Listen, Harry. Until a short while back I had a job. Best paid job I ever had. I was told it was some kind of a dude ranch to start with, out in the Californian desert. Rich customers, so I had to be vetted, sign agreements, all that shit. Weird place. All these rich men making out they're in some cowboy film, with cowboy names. I started off in the kitchens, then when I'd been there a year, they got me in, asked lots of questions, did some more checks and I made waiter. Then I got the blood test back.' He shrugged. 'I came up positive. I kept it pretty quiet but, well, with some people it takes years. I wasn't so lucky.'

'So you left?'

'They're all rednecks there. I'm bisexual. I'd had to fill in forms saying I was straight, not gay, that kind of thing. They checked, but I'd been very discreet. That's one weird place. It's all Wild West but kind of high-tech at the same time. It has these intercoms all over and I got to know the system pretty well, so sometimes I'd, well . . .'

'Listen in?'

'You could say that. Just to stop it all being such a drag. So anyway, I was clearing the dishes in the dining room and I'd fixed the switches so I could hear what was going on in the big club room, and I heard this guy they call the Producer talking about me. You know what? He'd been reading my mail, listening to my calls. Can you imagine? Me and all the other staff, I guess. That made me mad. Anyway he was talking about "dealing with the Deruda situation". I listened to him and I got scared. He'd read the letter; he knew I had AIDS. He was planning to do something.'

'Fire you?'

'Kill me, I think.'

'Oh come on. Why?'

'It may sound dumb, but I'm sure that was what he meant. "Sterilize" was the word he used. These are pretty serious guys.' Something came over him then, and his expression darkened. 'Look, you don't have to believe me. You can just go now, why don't you?'

'I didn't say I didn't believe you. I'm just a bit new to the idea.'

'Well, I went that same night. I got out through the wire. I should have said – there's like a big compound round this place? I got out in the back of the liquor delivery man's truck. I didn't stop until I got here.'

'So, how does Claire Merrick come into all this?'

'I've listened in on them four times but there's only three times when I could hear much of a conversation. First time I couldn't understand a goddam thing. It was all about some German party called the SDU or the CDU, or something like that. Second time, maybe a week before I left, I heard the Producer talk about a man called Paul Wade and what he'd found in this wrecker's yard, and how if they'd done what they'd been told the Merrick woman – that's what he called her, the Merrick woman – wouldn't have found the boxes. He said they'd have to start moving against her and he thought they had a good plan. He kept talking about London and then he mentioned Farrow and how it would be the perfect set-up. That didn't mean anything until I heard you this morning. It wasn't too easy because the intercom was a long way from where they were so I couldn't get all of it.'

'You got enough. Was that all?'

'I heard someone coming so I had to switch off.'

'What was the other time?'

'Other time?'

'You said you heard three conversations.'

'That wasn't anything to do with Claire Merrick.'

'What was it?'

'I recorded it. Then I wrote it down afterwards. Take a look in the closet over there. The little drawer? Do you see a red Morocco notebook?'

Harry found it and passed it to him. Denzil lay back, suddenly tired, with the book closed in his hand, then turned a few pages with an effort and passed it to him.

'You read it,' he said. 'My throat's bad.'

Harry had to strain to make out the tiny letters. It was written like a script:

PRODUCER: No, of course not. We'll just have to do what we did with the guy in Beaconsbridge.

OTHER MAN: Browning?

PRODUCER: No, Browning wasn't Beaconsbridge. That was somewhere else. Beaconsbridge was the one with the funny name, Lawless, Denton Lawless.

OTHER: Yeah, that's right. That was a good one. How did it go again? 'He never been kissed permanent before.'

PRODUCER: Yeah. He couldn't resist going to see that varmint with the pirate girl.

Harry looked up from the book. 'What does all this "kissed permanent" business mean?'

Denzil's voice was a harsh croak. 'Lines from their film. That old one, *How the West was Won*. They were always using lines from that film.'

'Do you know what it meant?'

'No.'

'This club, or ranch, or whatever. Where was it?'

'Out past Edwards Air Force base. China Lake way. Middle of nowhere.'

'Did it have a name?'

'No.' Deruda's voice cracked and he took a slow sip of water. 'But I know what they called themselves.'

'What?'

'Freedom's Friends.'

'Oh, right.'

'You can take it. Take the book.' The voice was just a whisper now.

Harry looked down at Deruda, nodded, and made one of the worst decisions of his life. 'OK. I'll go away and think about it. I'll call you.'

At the door he looked back. 'I hope you feel better soon,' he said, then felt really stupid and fled down the stairs.

# Chapter Thirty

## Wednesday August 14th

Harry's last talk-show turn was over. There was some of National's money left over from an economy routine of burgers, subways and quiet evenings in hotel rooms. A diversion through Philadelphia on the way back was just possible in the time available.

Until Deruda's bombshell, he had taken it for granted that whatever had happened to Beaconsbridge, to Claire, to Paul Wade, and to Ann Farrow had been a strictly British affair. The American dimension threw him. He'd begged and borrowed time in the TV stations he'd visited to search databases. Freedom's Friends didn't show up anywhere. He searched for right-wing clubs and came up with the Rancheros, the Round-Up Riders and the Bohemian Grove, but they were establishment groups, peddling power not death.

He needed a sworn statement from Deruda. How he was going to cope with the American legal system and the hospice, he didn't know. They must have notaries, but did they do house calls? He'd called Deruda on Tuesday evening. The man told him that by all means he could come and talk. Then, he said, after they'd talked again, he'd decide whether he would put it all down and sign it.

He arrived at the MacIntosh Skandless Project and saw the same face at the reception desk. He searched his memory and came up with the name. 'Marcus? Remember me? Harry Chaplin? I've come to see Denzil Deruda again.'

Marcus's face was impassive but there was a touch of anxiety in his voice. 'Hello, Mr Chaplin. Of course I remember.

I'm sorry to tell you this, but Denzil is no longer with us.'

Harry was aghast, seeing his precious time slipping away. 'But he knew I was coming. Can you tell me where he's gone?'

'Mr Chaplin, I'm afraid that's beyond me to say. I don't think you understood me. Poor Denzil has been gathered up.'

'What do you mean? Where to?'

'Mr Chaplin, Denzil Deruda is dead.'

'Oh come on, I only spoke to him yesterday. How can he be? He sounded . . . well, he wasn't dying anyway.'

'No, Denzil's illness had a long course still to run.'

Harry still didn't want to believe it. 'Well, what happened then?'

Marcus clearly thought the bounds of sensitivity were being transgressed. 'For some people, the burden is too hard. Denzil decided not to continue. We have to accept his solution.'

'He killed himself?'

Marcus let go a gusty sigh. 'That is what I'm trying to tell you.'

'How?'

'I can't see how that matters. Mr Chaplin, I wonder – was there any anxiety your visit might have created for Denzil?'

There had been no anxiety involved in Denzil's death. The overdose had been injected as he woke groggily from sleep in the middle of the night by a white-coated man he had taken to be a new nurse. The note he had apparently left owed nothing to his authorship. The Producer's little clearing-up operation had fallen down in one respect only. He hadn't thought it necessary to have anyone check on Deruda's visitors, and for that, although he didn't know it, Harry had every reason to be very grateful.

Instead, he bowed his head in defeat and left, cursing himself to sleep later, on the flight back, for not getting a statement first time round.

# Thursday August 15th

Harry felt no better back in England seventeen hours later. Philadelphia to Beaconsbridge via JFK and Heathrow was a marathon. There wasn't even a convenient railway station, just a slow bus out of Birmingham. He felt a dry-eyed, heavy exhaustion from the truncated night spent in a cramped Boeing seat, but time was driving him again. No one expected him back in the office straight off the flight, but it would be much harder to get away later. He felt depressed as hell, aware that he'd blown an undeserved chance to unravel the mess. He couldn't afford to screw it up again.

There were seven entries in the phone book under Lawless, none of them with an initial 'D'. Four denied all knowledge of a Denton. One didn't answer, one was disconnected and the final one, a young woman with a crying baby in the background, said she couldn't really help, but hadn't there been something in the papers a while back?

The Reference Library had back issues of the local paper, but twenty minutes searching covered only a few weeks, combing every page for a mention of the name, so he noted down the paper's address, thanked the librarian and took a taxi. The *Examiner* was in a square, brick building with peeling metal-framed windows; a building apparently purpose-built to prevent any of its inhabitants raising their sights higher than births, marriages and deaths or the occasional council meeting. A harassed middle-aged woman came out to see him.

'Hello, can I help you?' she asked.

Harry was not normally averse to being recognized, but this time he was not at all upset when she showed she was clearly no follower of Crookbusters. It seemed far simpler. He was able to keep it vague.

'I'm just doing some local research,' he said. 'I need to check a few names.'

'How far back?' she said.

'Oh, since '92.'

'Well, you see, '92 and '93 are still on the physical file. Since then it's all on the computer so it's faster, like.'

'OK, I'll start with the physical file.'

She showed him to a long, narrow room with a few hard chairs, one table, and ranks of filing cabinets all down one side, lingering unnecessarily to keep an eye on him as he began to go through the files.

There were a series of drawers marked 'Personalities', but whoever Denton Lawless had been, his personality clearly hadn't ranked highly. He tried 'Obits', but found nothing more than fat files of valedictory cuttings on past mayors, shop keepers, and senior council officials. Then he tried 'Accidents' and found his man straight away.

'Local Man in Quarry Death Drop,' ran the headline. 'Denton Harold Lawless, a part-time labourer of 18, Stagmore Road, was found dead at the wheel of his badly-damaged Ford Capri sports car on Thursday morning by workers arriving at A.A. T's Randalls Wood quarry. A police spokesman said it appeared Lawless had lost control while racing other drivers on rough ground at the top of the quarry. The retaining fence had been broken and Lawless's car had fallen some hundred feet to the quarry floor. Mr Daniel Carver, a nearby resident, said the rough ground above the quarry was frequently used by local youths to hold unofficial races late at night and said he had complained to the council and the police on many occasions about the risks of such behaviour.'

It went on in similar vein without adding anything further to the story and Harry sat back and pondered. Why would two men in the California desert have been talking about a 'part-time labourer' in the English Midlands? He noted down the address.

Stagmore Street was a sloping side road running down from a crowded shopping street to an enormous and seemingly abandoned building site. The shops were mostly Asian, and the golden domes of a mosque could just be seen behind them on the high side of the street. The right side of the street had been razed to the ground, and number eighteen was one of only half a dozen houses still standing on the left.

The door was opened by a woman of sixty or so, wearing a nylon housecoat. There was horse-racing on a TV somewhere beyond. She was short and suspicious.

'Yeah?'

'Sorry to bother you. Are you anything to do with the late Denton Lawless?'

'Who's asking?'

Harry chose a name at random. 'Richard Fielding,' then realized it wasn't random at all, but the name of one of the Crookbusters researchers.

'Why d'you wanna know?'

Suddenly locked in to the programme again, Harry came up with what he thought was an inspired answer. 'I'm after information that might lead to a reward. The Crookbusters show on National TV?'

'I don't 'ave satellite,' she said, but the word 'reward' had softened her.

'It's a long shot, but I'm looking for information about the death of Denton Lawless.'

'Denton? You've come to the right place. He was my son, but I dunno why you'd want to know.' She coughed and spat past him on to the path.

She turned and shuffled back inside. As she'd left the door open he assumed he was meant to follow. They went into a dark front room where a frenzied horse-racing commentator was in his orgasmic final seconds. She looked sourly at the result that flashed up on the screen and switched the TV off.

'Denton crashed 'is car.'

'I read the report in the paper.'

'So why are you 'ere? I don't know anything else.'

'Mrs Lawless, did you ever think that somebody might have killed Denton?'

She sat down heavily in the only armchair and, without warning, began to cry.

'I knew it,' she said. 'It was the Pakis, wasn't it? He loved that Capri. Last of them, it was, a Capri 280. He wouldn't have gone racing it like they said. Never.'

'Why would the, er, the Pakistanis have killed him?' Harry asked, floundering.

She led him upstairs.

'This was his room,' she said. 'I 'aven't touched it.'

The most noticeable feature of the room was the collection of posters around the wall. They would not have been out of place in Pretoria or Pietermaritzburg. They had no party identification on them but the imagery was pure National Front; Hitler's anti-Jewish posters with black faces substituted. Mounted in racks on the wall was a collection of guns; an Armalite, an Uzi, and handguns from Smith and Wessons to Lugers.

'Replicas, those are. They ain't real,' said Mrs Lawless. 'This is what I wanted you to see.' She showed him a row of shields and little cups, the type sold by franchise outlets that offer key-cutting and quick heel repairs at the other counter. They were badly engraved but the messages were all similar; 'First in Show. Custom Street Machine. D. Lawless'; and 'Best Ford. Edgbaston Kustom Kar Show. 1990.' A huge colour photo, blown up and mounted on board, dominated the only wall that was free of posters. It showed a crop-haired fat boy, holding one of the cups, sitting on the bonnet of a lowered, wide-wheeled, metal-flake painted Ford Capri.

'There, see?' said the woman. 'He'd be out polishing it if it got wet. Hired a garage, he did. Sixteen quid a week, just to look after it. He'd never drive it through a muddy field like the place they say 'e did. If he'd wanted to race, he would have nicked something.'

Harry nodded. 'So why d'you think it was the Pakistanis, Mrs Lawless?'

'Cos of what he did. He told me they'd be fucking furious if they knew.'

The tears had stopped and she looked sly. 'Anyway, why should I tell you?'

'Like I said, there could be a reward.'

'Hundred quid first. A reward's all very well but I want a hundred quid first.'

Harry opened his wallet with a sense of inevitability. 'I haven't got a hundred quid,' he said. 'I've got sixty-five quid and two twenty dollar bills.'

'American dollars?' she said.

What else? 'Yes,' he answered.

'All right. Give them here.'

'Afterwards. You tell me the story first. I'll give them to you afterwards.'

'No money, no story,' she said.

He handed the money over.

'Denton was in politics round here,' she said. 'He'd go to meetings and that. He had views on employment and, er, rights and that. Quotas, that was his thing. He wanted quotas.'

'What sort of quotas?'

'You know, nig-nogs and all that. We used to tell him, his Dad and I, there didn't used to be a black face round here in the old days. Anyway, there was this Asian, Rajit something, and the Socialists, they put him up as the candidate, see? Well, Denton, he didn't like that. He didn't like the Socialists anyway, and as for Rajit, well what did he know about Beaconsbridge? Only been here a few years. So when this bloke came to see Denton, he said he'd help out, like.'

'Help with what, exactly?'

'I'll tell you. You don't need to keep asking. He wanted Denton to drive this van, see. A van what they were using to go round and pick up all the boxes.'

'Ballot boxes?'

'Yeah, the boxes you put yer vote in, like. They used vans to pick them up. Denton, he had to go round six different places – what do you call them, polling places? – and pick up the boxes, with this geezer in the front with 'im. Anyway, they told him he was doing the country a good turn, cos this Paki had fixed it with all his relatives to get thousands of extra votes in, and so they was just putting it right, making it fair, see?'

'Making it fair? How?'

'Well, on the way, Denton had to nip in the yard of the old Fruit Dessert works, Citrus wotsit, down the end there. Just a quick in-and-out, and while he was there, they whipped the back open and swapped over some of the boxes.'

'What about the man in the front? Who was he?'

'He was some bloke in charge. He agreed with Denton that was only fair seeing as what the Paki was up to.'

'How do you know this?'

'Well, Denton told me, didn't he?'

'He didn't write any of it down, did he?'

'Denton? Write? Gawd almighty, you didn't know Denton.'

'So,' Harry said, 'how come he got killed?'

'Well, stands to reason, doesn't it?' she said. 'The Pakis found out, didn't they? They must've done.'

# Chapter Thirty-One

## Thursday August 15th

The wind was a shade east of south, and had been more or less steady for the whole of the past three days. At 6p.m., Fishguard and the bulging tip of Wales were thirty miles to the east. Land was a double-edged sword – security when the darkness fell and the strain of sailing single-handed told on Claire, but a threat in daylight hours, bringing her under the scrutiny of people, people with telescopes, people who might at any moment be alerted to the fact that a Contessa 32 called *Rubber Duck* was no longer at its moorings on the Tamar. She'd given Land's End a wide berth for that reason, remembering that the coastguard station there was the only place remaining round the whole coast where the lookouts still kept up the old practice of observing passing yachts and logging their sail numbers.

Thanks to Charles Golant, it would take a genius to recognize the boat Claire was now sailing as that same Contessa. They'd been loafing along in *Cauchemar*, off Rame Head, eating freshly-caught mackerel, fried with tarragon culled from the herb garden in the window boxes on deck.

'Time to tell me', Claire had said, 'your idea. You said you had an idea.'

'I do.' Charles had looked at her as if weighing her up. 'But I'm just trying to work out whether there isn't a way of keeping you on board instead. It's not just all my friends, but there's bloody old Frank, the bloke in the barge, he's always poking around. I think he comes on board when I'm not there. We could just stay at sea, but that's a bit of a problem because I'm due to have my kids to . . .'

'Stop,' she said, thinking of Ann. 'I couldn't stay on board. There's nothing but trouble wherever I go. You've already taken a huge risk. Come on, what's your idea?'

She had to press him, but in the end he told her. He was sure no one had sailed the Contessa, *Rubber Duck*, for over a year, and he didn't think anyone would miss her straight away. Not only that, but even if the theft was noticed, he had the means of giving Claire an excellent chance of escape.

'So, where do I go?'

'You're a good sailor, aren't you? Wherever you like. You can stay at sea, you can anchor in out-of-the-way places. It's your choice.'

They had come back into the Sound at eight in the evening, and whiled away the time by dropping anchor in Barn Pool under Mount Edgcumbe and telling each other their life stories. At sunset Charles started the diesel and they plodded round the bend into the entrance of the Lynher and picked up a buoy.

It had been quite dark when the dinghy bumped the side of *Rubber Duck*. The padlock on the hatch lasted less than a minute against Charles's hacksaw blade and they were inside, a burst of mildewed air escaping past them. Charles's torch showed an unloved cabin, but one that seemed to have a full complement of the things you would hope to find.

Charles looked at the array of instruments over the chart table and whistled. 'Look at this. It's got the works; GPS satellite navigation, VHF radio, short wave.'

'It doesn't look like anyone's been using them.'

Claire worked the pump in the sink. 'Water tank's empty, but there's saucepans and everything. There's even bedding in the lockers. D'you think someone died, or what?'

Charles climbed back on deck and she undid the engine cover. There was superficial rust on the diesel inside. He stuck his head back through the hatch. 'The diesel tank's almost full,' he said. 'I've just dipped it. The standing rigging looks fine as far as I can see, and there's all the sheets you need in the cockpit lockers.'

She did a quick check round the forepeak. There are three sail bags here.'

'You won't be needing those,' he'd said.

In the course of a hectic night, two cans of quick-drying deck paint had changed the colour of her decks and cabin roof from yellow to mid-blue. The hull was still white but Claire, feeling her way round by moonlight in the dinghy, had painted a red stripe a couple of inches wide along both sides. The name on the stern had been painted over in white and then relettered, and this was where Charles's brilliant idea had wrought the major change. His boat store was full of things accumulated over many years of scrudging, among them all that was salvageable from a series of badly-damaged boats bought cheaply from their insurers. He was a man who accumulated more easily than he dispersed. Among the treasure trove – and indeed the whole reason he had taken her to see *Rubber Duck* – were the mortal remains of *Sea Witch of Coldrennick*, a Contessa 32 which had ripped out its bottom by missing the narrow exit through the old sea defences at the western side of Plymouth Sound.

Of the batch of miscellaneous bits salvaged from her wreckage, only a few items mattered, but they were crucial. The blue spray-dodgers which were laced along the rails each side of her cockpit carried the words '*Sea Witch*' in large white letters, and the two yellow horseshoe life-preservers had the same name stencilled on them. Above all – and Charles's *pièce de résistance* – in place of *Rubber Duck*'s white sails, she now had a full set of *Sea Witch*'s tan sails with her own sail number.

By daybreak on Sunday morning, after six hours of flat-out effort, *Sea Witch* had been reborn, and *Rubber Duck* was a memory. They'd done the work on a buoy upriver, towing her from her mooring with Charles's dory. To muddy the trail, Charles had unshackled the mooring buoy and let the chain drop to the bottom of the river.

'If anyone notices she's gone, they might think the mooring parted and waste time looking for her,' he'd said. 'This river eats chains for breakfast. They're always breaking.'

He moved *Cauchemar* down river to be near her, and during the day time on Sunday he provisioned her. She still had money, and he stocked up on essential foods at a little village supermarket. There were some of the owner's clothes on board; ornate yachting caps with gold braid, a fake naval jacket, and two good sets of oilskins. Charles added more of his own comfortable cast-offs to the pile. They filled the Contessa's water tank from *Cauchemar's* huge supply, laboriously hand-pumping it through a hose pipe, then used a spare battery to get the diesel going, bleeding the pipes and fiddling for a good half hour before it finally kicked into lumpy life.

Claire hugged him as dawn broke on Monday, before starting up the diesel and butting out past the sleeping dockyards, past Mashford's Yard, the moored Cremyll Ferry and Drake's Island, past the breakwater, until the moment when she could hoist the sails, bear off to the south west and switch off the engine to release the easy, wave-soaring, sea-kindly lightness of the hull under its well-balanced rig. The wind had dropped at sunset and she had spent the first night at anchor in a quiet bay, tucked away round the corner from the crowded Falmouth anchorages, fixing a few bits of rigging which unaccustomed use had found wanting.

The morning had called for a beat to the south-east, then back on the other tack to pass the Lizard until she could ease the sheets and alter course westward towards the Scillies with the wind just aft of the beam. It had been splashy, with the boat plunging diagonally into a swell that rolled in from the Atlantic, funnelling into the Western Approaches to make its dying run on to the holiday beaches of the south Cornish coast. She listened to the radio news from time to time but they seemed to have lost interest in her.

Now another two days had passed, Wales was the nearest land, and the lonely waters of the west coast of Scotland were a simple three-day passage ahead of her. She noted the Radio 4 shipping forecast, which promised more of the same, kept half an ear on the main weather forecast at five to six while she made a cup of tea, then heard Big Ben herald the six o'clock news. Fifteen minutes in to the half-hour broadcast, among the ragbag of bits and pieces that followed the day's four main stories, the announcer paused for the psychological half second to punctuate a new story, and said, 'Police in the West Country have extended the search for missing television personality Claire Merrick to the waters around the coast of

Cornwall and Devon. A yacht has been reported stolen from its moorings near Saltash. Miss Merrick, who is known to be a keen yachtswoman, is wanted for questioning in connection with the murder of her flatmate Ann Farrow. The yacht, a white Contessa 32, carries the name *Rubber Duck*.'

# Chapter Thirty-Two

## Thursday August 15th

'OPERATIVE 28 REPORTS PHONE CALLER (PAY PHONE) TO NATIONAL TV, IDENTIFIED AS MRS DESIREE LAWLESS, MOTHER OF DENTON LAWLESS (FILE 10.109). REQUESTED CONNECTION TO RICHARD FIELDING, RESEARCHER ON CROOKBUSTERS, WAS ASKED FOR DETAILS IN ACCORDANCE WITH INSTRUCTIONS REGARDING ANY UNIDENTIFIED FEMALE CALLER. REPLIED FIELDING HAD BEEN IN CONTACT OFFERING REWARD FOR INFORMATION ON DENTON LAWLESS'S DEATH. CONTINUED: NOW I'VE TOLD HIM ALL ABOUT IT, ABOUT WHAT DENTON DID, I WANT TO KNOW ABOUT THE REWARD. YOU TELL HIM TO CALL ME.' ENQUIRIES REVEAL RICHARD FIELDING CURRENTLY ON LOCATION IN LEEDS, YORKSHIRE. FIELDING TRAVELLED THERE BY CAR. BEACONS-BRIDGE, LAWLESS'S HOME, IS EN ROUTE. ASSESSMENT REQUIRED.'

It didn't call for any great insight to make the connection. The contributions flowed in, mostly one-liners with the same drift: 'HAS TO BE MERRICK'S MAN FRIEND. STERILIZE', and the much-used film quote: 'WHEN A SKUNK NEEDS KILLING . . .'

Richard Fielding was quite pleased with himself. National had hired a local camera crew to save money on the overnight stay and the travelling, and they'd been very good. Crime re-enactments were always tricky. You had to make sure of so many things; passers-by appearing in the shot and getting angry when they saw themselves associated on-screen with some horrible crime, for example. Car number-plates were a no-no, too. They'd got it all in the can though, wrapped late on Thursday afternoon. It was all there: a police interview along the lines of, 'In all my years of service, I've never seen anything like the sheer savagery of this attack', plus a lengthy reconstruction, using a hire car, of the abduction and the drive to the scene of the rape and murder. The actress was called Zazzy, and Richard fancied her and had invited her out for dinner, but she'd started talking about her baby and how her man couldn't stay in all evening looking after him.

The crew had gone back to pack away their gear. In place of Zazzy, he'd arranged to meet them at nine in a restaurant near the centre. He took a bath, changed, and at five to nine, walked out of the hotel and up the main road.

Police Constable Geoff Jenkins was unwrapping his sandwiches when the screens went fuzzy. He picked up the intercom and called the sergeant.

'It's Geoff, Sarge. We've lost the cameras. Yeah, all of them.'

The sergeant came and looked, said he'd never seen a fault like that before, and went to put it in the report book. Leeds traffic monitoring system wouldn't be back in working order for quite some time.

It wasn't subtle, but it was the best they could do. They'd put on a shunt, diverting control as well as signals, so they could steer the cameras and view the output from the truck. They were banking on no one coming to fix it until the morning, listening in to the police headquarters communications to check. By the following day, there'd be nothing to see beyond a missing padlock and a carefully arranged electrocuted mouse across two terminals.

Richard Fielding didn't notice the camera panning with him as he walked down the street. It was way above his line of vision. When he turned the corner, another one took over. The only traffic cameras moving in Leeds that night were following Richard Fielding, and while they monitored his movements three different contingency plans were being stacked up ready, just in case. The choice was down to him in the end. Blind luck was on his side. He chose the right route, ignoring the turnings that would have led him into carefully laid traps.

They all met up in the restaurant for a good meal, the conversation dominated by the subject of Claire Merrick, then the cameraman insisted on driving him back to the door of the hotel. There, Richard waved them a thankful goodbye and went upstairs. He got out of the lift, past the huge gilt-framed print of Leeds in Victorian times and the shoe polishing machine, and saw, sauntering towards him, a vision in a gold lamé top and black slit skirt. She had deep, pouting red lips under a cascade of black curls and she smiled as she saw him.

Hooker, he thought, but what a hooker. Almost makes you want to pay for it, except she must have just turned her trick with someone else.

'Hi,' she said, 'in a hurry?'

'No,' he said, surprised, stopping by his door.

'Just, well, I've been sort of let down and I wondered if you wanted some company?'

She had a voice from a drinking chocolate commercial and she was still smiling. Richard felt mildly panic-stricken and highly aroused at the same time.

She saw his hesitation and the voice went even huskier. 'For free, lover. I already took the other guy's credit card number.'

He got the key into the lock with difficulty and closed it after her.

'For free? I mean, I didn't know that happened. I . . .'

'It's your birthday,' she said. 'I've got nothing else planned.'

She was an erotic fantasy to look at and he had no idea whether to move towards her, undress himself, or what. He sat down on the bed, trying to smile, feeling his jeans uncomfortably tight.

She stood three feet in front of him and lifted one of her long stockinged legs like an elegant stork, arching it with perfect control, impossibly high, then forwards to rest her ankle on his shoulder, the skirt falling open so that before him he could see tight silk knickers, barely covering the mound within. She reached a finger down and drew it once, twice up and down the silk, right before his eyes.

'Touch me there,' she said, and he reached forward with electric, tingling fingers to do as she said, the silk moving aside under his fingertips and the warm, wet flesh opening behind it.

She straightened her leg, pushing him backwards on to the bed with her foot, then stood back and dropped her skirt to the floor, following it with the lamé top, and then the bra beneath so that she stood there in knickers, stockings and suspenders, running her fingers through her hair and her tongue across her lips. He kicked off his shoes, forcing his trousers down, struggling to get out of them, and then she was pushing him back again, crawling slowly over him, breasts jutting down so that the nipples traced little puckering, jumping, twin trails of delight up from his hips past his stomach to his chest. He reached down and cupped her buttocks in his hands, through the silk, urgent to push it aside and lift her on to him, but she brought both feet up on to the bed, crouching over him, and with perfect control, holding the silk to one side, slid him into her, no other part of their bodies touching, using her undulating pelvis so that there was no other sensual reality except that encompassing suction of warm flesh.

She watched him carefully as she moved, because there was a curious need in her too, his eyes fixed on her red lips slowly descending towards his and, just when his face contorted in the first spasm of his climax she brought the slim blade out of her stocking top, twisted it up under his rib cage and rolled off him to avoid the fountain of blood, as his luck and his life ran out.

'MERRICK ASSOCIATE STERILIZED,' was all the message said.

# Chapter Thirty-Three

## Monday August 19th

Harry had been worrying ever since he heard the news on Friday morning. He listened to the details and a sharp memory came back to him unbidden, a memory of using Fielding's name to the woman in Beaconsbridge and at some deep level he knew with complete certainty that whatever the police might say about Fielding's missing wallet and the traces of a woman found in his room, Freedom's Friends had got Richard Fielding and it was his fault. It only took another micro-second to make the connection that if he'd used his own name in Beaconsbridge, it would have been him lying dead somewhere. He'd asked if there was any news of Claire. Jane had been full of it.

'They're pretty certain she's stolen a boat. Some sailing boat's gone missing from Cornwall near where this moped was found. Do you think she'd do that, Harry? Steal a boat?'

'Why not?' he'd said. 'I don't know. Is it difficult?'

'They're starting an air search, all round the coast. We didn't get that in time for the show, but if there's no more news by Wednesday or so, we'll go and shoot a piece in one of the helicopters for next week.'

There had been a message for him on the computer. 'Meeting please, Monday 9a.m. Gilligan.' He'd yawned all day, watched the show go out, with its 'still no news on Claire Merrick' update, and left straight afterwards to head for Putney.

'What do I do, Steffie?' he'd said, but Steffie didn't even give that tiny squeeze to his hand that told him some part of her was still there. It was as if that tiny cry of communication two weeks earlier had burnt something out. The polite disbelief of

267

the hospital staff had been clear when he'd told them. Coming back from America, even the weight of the information he bore with him and his worry about Claire had been overshadowed for a short time by his fear that the doctors might have used his absence to switch Steffie off.

Harry had looked at his sister and thought of her and all the sensible things she'd said over the years when she still had a voice, advice to an older but more reckless sibling. 'Use what you've got,' she would have said. 'Don't waste time and energy wishing things were other than they are. If all you've got is one little stick, use it as a lever. Find the right point and you can move the earth.' Then, just as the clear memory of the voice and the words ended, the hand in his gave a little, fitful squeeze.

He'd spent the weekend painting, laying his plans, and wishing the phone would ring. Monday's post came at eight, while he was drinking his coffee and getting ready to go. An Access bill, a Book Club mail shot, and a letter printed in block letters, postmarked ANGLESEY.

He ripped it open. Claire's writing said; 'Dear Mr Chaplin, You will remember me I hope as an old friend of your mother's. I am writing because your cousin William is coming for a short fishing break in Scotland, starting Wednesday afternoon, and I thought you might like to join him as our guest if you can get away from work. I'm sorry it is such short notice, but I'm sure you will make every effort to come. I will expect you at the guesthouse. Should I not be there, call my husband on board the boat *Sea Witch*, which can be reached on short range VHF in line of sight. Use Channel 16 (monitored by Coastguards) from the A83 in the Macrihanish to Glenbarr area when you arrive. Be prepared for some delay.' It was signed, 'Mrs A. Dunwhiddie.'

Harry read it three times. It was a clear instruction on how to find her. He went looking for a map, then realized he would be late for his meeting with Gilligan, and that meeting was now doubly important.

✳    ✳    ✳

Claire had risked a lot to go ashore on Anglesey two days earlier, leaving the boat at anchor well out of the way and rowing the inflatable dinghy a mile along the coast in the late evening twilight to Amlwch. When she was almost there she saw, with horror, that printed across the rounded airbag which made up the dinghy's stern were the letters, unnoticed until then, 'T/T *Rubber Duck*', tender to a boat which no longer existed. She left it upside down on the beach with sand heaped over the name, and hoped no late evening lovers would decide to use it for a bed in her short absence.

Going ashore cost her dear. Her heart was racing and she felt slightly sick. Her scalp stung from the strong per-oxide solution which Charles Golant had bought for her, which she'd resisted using until now, and she didn't think her newly-bleached hair would fool anyone. There was a post-box near the landing place, but no stamp machine, so she had to risk the centre of the small town, paying close attention to shop windows when anyone came near. She was relieved later to be back in the dinghy, starting the long row back against the tide, and spent the rest of that night at anchor.

Her planned early start the next morning had been foiled by a section of old steel cable on the sea bed which fouled the anchor, and it was only after some strenuous diving that she got it clear. It forced home her complete solitude once again and she was cold and totally exhausted afterwards. It was nine o'clock before she managed to drag herself away. The wind had veered a little to around south west, and the boat scooted out into the Irish Sea on a course which would take her outside the Isle of Man. She'd sorted out the GPS system, so navigation was a simple matter of pressing buttons and watching for way points. Not trusting electronics entirely, she kept a dead reckoning track on the chart just in case. Her other concession to modern sailing had been to take out of its box *Rubber Duck*'s Autohelm, a little electrically-driven arm which clipped to the tiller and, so long as the wind wasn't making too many demands, kept her more or less on a steady course. That allowed her to move round the boat.

She heard the first far-off clatter of rotor blades just after ten o'clock. There were four or five other yachts in sight and, reaching for the binoculars, she saw the helicopter, a big Navy Sea King, approaching one of them three or four miles further inshore. It wheeled around the boat in a slow circle, then she saw it rise again, but it was twenty seconds or more before the sound of the accelerating engines reached her. It dipped its nose for speed and headed for the next boat, and she knew with a sinking heart that it must be looking for her, a lone girl in a Contessa. She fought down the sudden panic.

Lieutenant Jeremy Walton peered down through the side window as the *Sea King* wheeled around, and spoke into his throat mike. 'Sodding great Moody, Ginger. Forget that one, there's a whole football team on board.'

'They must be footballers. They're certainly not sailors, look at the bloody fenders hanging over the side.'

It was their second day at it, and privately they didn't think there was a snowball's chance. The boat could be anywhere. Some other crew from Culdrose or St Mawgan was far more likely to win the magnum of champagne they'd been promised.

They flew towards the next one and his interest picked up a little. Right size. They started to take a slow turn around. That wasn't it either. A man in a yachting jacket was sitting in the cockpit, hand on the helm. He was concentrating on what he was doing as the downwash of the rotor blades blew the boat a few degrees off course.

'Whoops, sorry,' Ginger muttered as he eased the chopper round towards the bow.

'Hey, look at that,' Jeremy's metallic voice roared in Ginger's headphones. 'Phwoorr, nice one.'

A girl, stark naked but for a yachting cap, was diving for modesty's sake down through the forehatch.

'Want another look?' said Ginger, chuckling. 'It could be her.'

'No way, my son. That was a natural blonde. Didn't you see? Come on, I'm sure that's another Contessa ahead.'

Claire listened to them departing from down below. The extra peroxide she'd poured over her pubic hair was stinging parts it should never have been allowed to reach. She sluiced water all over herself, wincing, pulled her clothes back on, and went up into the cockpit to look at the figure at the helm.

When she was quite sure the helicopter had gone, she unthreaded the autohelm from inside the sleeve of the yachting jacket and rearranged the inflatable figure in the corner of the cockpit. For the first time she blessed Harry for the cruel joke which had left the little box containing Eric the Escort lying in the bottom of her sailing bag all that time. Then, with land fading from sight and a long haul to an uncertain rendezvous ahead, the tension and the growing exhaustion of constant fear weakened her defences. A wave of irresistible sadness broke over her and she began to weep.

'I'm very grateful for what you did in America, Harry,' said Gilligan. 'You really got their interest going.'

The more Harry saw of Gilligan, the more he was coming to appreciate the style of the man. He was hard and he drove National on a shoestring, but he was a professional; Harry had spent the weekend coming to the almost inevitable conclusion that Gilligan was the only man who could help Claire now.

'I called you in because we're up a gum tree on the story. We've lost our inside track. If they find her now, everyone will have it at the same time as we do and we're not going to look smart.' He looked at Harry. 'Between you and me, I don't think Jane Bernstein has a single clue where to go from here. She's not good with policemen. We're not getting anything special out of Derek Palmer. It's up to you, Harry. Palmer respects you. Get right alongside him, and if he puts you in the way of something special, you've got Jane's job, right?'

Harry almost said something right then but Gilligan was promising a pay-back and it had to look a little harder earned. He went back to his desk, fiddled around doing other things until three o'clock came, then he knocked on Gilligan's door.

'I might have something,' he said. 'Don't ask me how, but I might have something much bigger than you were hoping for and I need all the help you can give me on this one.'

# Chapter Thirty-Four

Gilligan's quick grasp of the dangers of the situation impressed Harry immensely.

'Stop right there,' he said, 'This *is* about Merrick?'

'Of course it is.'

'Right. Let's get out of here. There's been too many funny things going on; this Fielding guy and all that.'

They left the car park in Gilligan's Jaguar XJS.

'You think Richard Fielding is connected to all this?' Harry asked.

'I don't like the coincidence. Since this thing started two staff members of Crookbusters have been killed and a third one's on the run from a murder charge. That's quite enough reason for nobody else to take risks.'

Harry nodded and kept quiet. He realized he couldn't say he'd been in it from the start, the complications and pitfalls ran too deep. He couldn't even admit to knowing anything about the election plot, but he trusted this confident, purposeful man who was threading through the traffic into West London like Ayrton Senna lapping backmarkers round Monaco. He knew what he wanted from Gilligan was in both their interests, and he'd simply have to weave the right web to get his way.

'Save it until we get to the hotel so I can concentrate,' said Gilligan.

Half an hour later they were in his suite, cold beers poured and feet up. Gilligan had taken off his tie and rolled up his sleeves.

'Right, Harry, you have my complete attention,' he said.

'Claire Merrick sent me a message. The first one was through some man, on my answering machine while I was away,' said Harry, blending half-truths.

'Fielding?'

'Maybe. You really think someone killed him because of all this?'

'She killed her girlfriend. Maybe she killed her boyfriend too.'

The words jolted in Harry's ears, reminding him that this was a man who so far had no reason to believe in Claire's innocence.

'Anyway, now she's sent me another message. She wants to talk.'

'Was this other message on your machine?'

'I'd rather not say. If we want to get close to her, the fewer people that know the better. I've got to do it my own way.'

Gilligan considered and nodded his acceptance. 'Makes sense. Just tell me what you want.'

'She says she's been framed. She says she's got a story to tell that will amaze everybody.'

'Do you have any idea what it is?'

'None whatsoever, and she's not going to tell me, but I think I could get her to tell it for the first time live on Crookbusters.'

Gilligan's feet came off the desk in a galvanic heave as he jack-knifed upright, staring at Harry.

'Jeez. You do that and we're all the way back on top of this one. Can you?'

'There's a good chance, but you need to take a risk and back me on it.'

'What do you need?'

'A lot of rope. The next three days off by myself trying to pull it off, plus the top fifteen minutes of Friday's show left open for a live outside broadcast.'

'From where?'

'Somewhere up north. The deal would have to be that you have an Outside Broadcast crew standing by and I'll give you a location nearer the time.'

'You've got it. You need some money?'

'Certainly. I also need your absolute guarantee that no one but the two of us will know until the show goes on the air. Otherwise she might be arrested before we get it out.'

Gilligan thought for a minute. 'Right,' he said. 'That means no advance publicity, but that's no worry. As soon as this breaks, it'll be wall-to-wall news. Then we can do a special re-run of the show afterwards. What do I tell Jane Bernstein?'

'Almost nothing. Tell her you need me for something. Let her get on with the show, then Friday daytime you can tell her there's something special coming. All she needs is an introduction for Russell Mackay and a duration for the piece. I'll do the rest. Book the Outside Broadcast crew completely separately, not through Crookbusters.'

'Harry, you're a star.' Gilligan was grinning from ear to ear as he picked up the phone and dialled Jane Bernstein's direct number.

'Jane, this is Gilligan . . . Yeah, yeah. Look I just wanted to tell you I need Chaplin for the rest of this week.'

Harry could hear the voice raised in complaint from where he sat and Gilligan raised an eyebrow at him.

'I'm sure you'll find a way. Use one of those smart young researchers you've got. That girl, what's she called, Maria? She looks pretty good on camera.'

The buzz of argument continued.

'Yeah, well, that's the way it has to be. Bye now.'

Harry left the hotel twenty minutes later in a Ford Mondeo hired from the Hertz desk, with two thousand pounds in fifty-pound notes in his pocket and a thrilling feeling that he had a powerful new ally. He went straight to Putney and told Steffie all about it. 'I won't be here for a few days, sis. I hope you don't mind. I'll come as soon as I get back, I promise.' He told the ward sister he'd be back on Saturday – a double-edged superstitious defence against doctors who might take advantage of his absence and against the possibility of his trip going badly wrong – then he drove to Liverpool. He wanted to hole up somewhere right out of the way to think his way through a rough script. He also needed to do some

shopping and he had an idea Liverpool would be a good place
to do it.

So it proved. He checked into the Crest Hotel and went
looking for yacht electronics. Where once there had been
thriving docks, marine nostalgia and marina blight had taken
over. The first yacht chandlery he visited offered the very
thing at £199.99, hand-held, multi-channel, high power. The
salesman showed him how it worked, filled a bag with spare
batteries and said goodbye to him with a slightly startled look.
The hotel room had a small desk and he sat down to write the
script of his life.

On Monday evening, the wind increased and veered erratically
so that at times Claire was beating into a stinging nor'westerly
for half an hour at a time before it would back again to a
broad reach. Aircraft made her jumpy. She'd seen another
helicopter on the horizon the previous evening as she hove
to, exhausted, north-west of the Isle of Man, with the Mull of
Galloway light blinking fitfully at extreme range somewhere
to the east. The boat had wallowed all night and the sound of
fishing boats' diesels thudding through the water from miles
off vibrated the thin hull next to her bunk, and had her
out on deck every fifteen minutes looking wildly around for
threatening lights bearing down. At 3a.m., just as she finally
fell into a deeper sleep, a baulk of soggy timber nudged into
the side of the hull with a deep thud and sent her leaping
up on deck, heart pounding, convinced she would find a
catastrophe.

She took her sleeping bag up into the cockpit then, and
spent the rest of the night on the hard slatted seat, raising
her head to look around every minute or two. This wasn't
the normal Claire who had made many long passages in her
life; now even the sea felt dangerous. She felt she was sailing
north down a long tunnel, with little chance of safety at the
other end. She fell asleep for a full half hour in the grey dawn
and found Harry next to her. She was trying to tell him she
was all right when she woke fully and found it was only her
inflatable man after all.

# Tuesday August 20th

The day should have seen her well up to Kintyre but she was getting sail-fright, altering course to stay well clear of the other vessels that kept appearing. It was a week since she'd talked to anybody, a week of losing faith in anyone's ability to get her out of the hole she was in. What was Harry, after all? Just another journo, fairly small-time at that. He wasn't Superman. It was hard to believe at this range that he cared that much for her. Tenderness had never been a large part of her life and the subtle memory of Harry was too short-lived to survive much exhumation.

# Wednesday August 21st

Harry, kept more firmly on the rails by the varied, headlong rush of human contact, had no such doubts as he charged northward up the M6 in the morning. He was past Carlisle by ten-thirty, caning the car into Scotland, shoving away the demons of Steffie's crash. He pulled off at Abington to look at the map, suddenly realizing what a long haul lay ahead, up and around Loch Fyne, to get into the long southward-stabbing finger of the Mull of Kintyre. Then he noticed the thin black lines that marked the ferry crossing to the Isle of Arran and saw there was a short cut. He was an hour early for the twelve-thirty ferry at Ardrossan, so he ordered a pizza at the Fish and Chip shop to fill the time, only to see the man drop it in the chip fat to deep fry it Scottish-style, before covering it with salt and vinegar. The Caledonian MacBrayne ferry across to the east coast of Arran took just under an hour. The Firth of Clyde and the sky above the island seemed vast, swirling with weather on a scale he found disturbing. The yachts in the Firth seemed so puny that his certainty she would be there began to ebb away.

There was no time to take in the beauty of the coast road

round the island. They'd warned him on the boat that the second ferry took only twelve cars so he drove relentlessly, carving up the tourists slowing to look at the slopes of Goat Fell to their left and the seals on the rocks to their right. All the way down the long valley to Lochranza on the island's northern tip, he could see the ferry, out in the water, creeping nearer. Harry overtook four cars in the last half-mile, passed the square brown castle that guarded the loch, grabbing the last of the marked-off spaces in the queue just as the ferry ran its ramp up the slipway.

The crossing this time was only half an hour, and the bar of land ahead, stretching north to south across his vision, was the last thin strip of Scotland separating him from the island-cluttered Atlantic, that should have held in it a boat called *Sea Witch*.

The ferry disgorged him on another slipway in the middle of nowhere, and a narrow B-road took him across Kintyre on to the fast main road down the west coast, then south with the sea and the island of Gigha to his right. It was three-thirty in the afternoon when he got out of the car at the hamlet of Muasdale, pulled out the long telescopic antenna on the VHF set and selected Channel 16. He heard far off fragments of conversation: '*Ocean Dollar*, Gordon, meet me on Channel 20,' and a broken up, 'Martin ... go ... tomorrow.' He waited until it fell silent and started to call. '*Sea Witch*, *Sea Witch*. Come in *Sea Witch*.' There was no response.

After half an hour's fruitless transmission, he drove further south. Past the Argyll Hotel at Bellochantuy, in a strange scatter of rocks where decaying caravans were tucked in every nook and cranny, he stopped and tried again. '*Sea Witch, Sea Witch*, come in *Sea Witch*.' Nothing. Line of sight, he remembered, you've got to be in line of sight. He began to climb the escarpment inland from the road. At the top, he tried again.

This time there was an immediate response, a crackle and a man's voice in broad Scots: 'Person calling *Sea Witch*. This is *Peninver Lady*, who are you?'

I'd better be a boat, thought Harry, and pressed the button again. 'This is the, er, *African Queen*. Come in *Peninver Lady*.

'Mr Bogart, I presume,' said the voice and laughed. 'You're looking for *Sea Witch*? Would she be a Contessa?'

Harry couldn't remember. 'I think so,' he said.

'She's moored just west of Carrer Island. I passed her two hours back.'

'Thanks, where exactly did . . .

The batteries died on him. He looked down at the car, five minutes down the hill, the car with the other batteries in it, and swore bitterly. Old stock. By the time he'd got down there and put in a fresh set, the *Peninver Lady* was gone. He spread the Ordnance Survey map and began to search it. 'Carrer' had to be Cara Island just south of Gigha. It was eight miles back up the road and three miles out to sea. He started the engine.

So bloody near, so bloody, bloody near. Claire was at the end of her tether, awake all night, sailing north, then north-west, burning up her dwindling reserves of energy and fortitude. She'd gone to sleep in the cockpit once and had a nightmare that turned into a waking horror: lights and a loud engine pounded at her, and she awoke with the boat broaching in a huge bow wave as the vast steel plates of a big freighter rushed past yards away. Freezing, shocking water filled the cockpit, washing right over her and pouring down the open hatch as the boat tipped on to its beam ends, swinging to a violent stop as the sails scooped down into the water. Claire's head cracked into one of the winches and she lay there with the water surging over her as the freighter roared away into the darkness, unseeing. The boat slowly picked itself up – like the rubber duck it had originally been named after – shook its wet sails, and lay low in the water, rolling soggily in the diminishing wash.

When she'd got the sails down, she saw the dinghy had been washed from its position, folded and deflated on the coach roof, and was nowhere to be seen. She opened the cockpit locker and pumped and pumped, warming herself and using herself up at the same time. When her arm muscles were on fire from the awkward stroke of the pump handle, it finally sucked air and the bilges were dry once more. She went below to make hot packet soup and found a dripping scene of devastation. The boat had been knocked down on to her starboard side. That was the side with the electronics, and now the satellite navigation was dripping wet, and as dead as a doornail.

Her sailing bag had stayed in its locker on the port side, above the incoming water, and she changed into dry clothes and drank the soup with shaking hands. In other circumstances, knowing she was at the very end of her reserves of energy and sanity, it would have been tempting to call, to hear the reassuring voice of a coastguard rescue centre, but for her, she knew, there could be no rescue, no comfort except in the outside chance that a man she knew so very slightly would be waiting there at the end of the wet miles ahead, at a landfall that only a huge final effort now could take her to.

There was more to come. Exhaustion undermined her navigation. An unexpected light flashed through the dark morning and it took her precious minutes to identify it. Up on deck she heard breaking waves, smelt not just seaweed, but rotting seaweed, and knew it had to be land. More by luck than anything else in her groggy state, she pulled the helm towards her and bore off downwind, to the east, away from the claws of Rathlin Island, the western sentinel of the fifteen-mile channel between Ireland and the Mull of Kintyre. At least she knew for certain where she was then, and she steered north north-east up the wide sound between Islay and Kintyre.

The wind dropped at dawn and she anchored off Gigha but as soon as she slept, it got up again and a dull rumbling transmitted through the chain into the forepeak told her the boat was dragging its anchor. The effort to haul it up almost finished her. She started the diesel, intending to motor round the south of the island to find shelter on its east coast. The depths on the chart were dancing before her tired eyes; the echo sounder was sopping wet and low, blowing mist completed the impossible barrier in front of her.

She went aground on a falling tide close in to the west side of Cara. A sloping ledge of rock took the boat's bows up at a sharp angle with a dreadful scraping, then dropped it down to wedge the keel in a cleft. The boat settled upright, held tight, and it was no longer a shock. Nothing could be a shock now. She shut off the engine, slumped back into the corner of the cockpit and fell into a half-dreaming, half-waking daze. The sun came up and the tide dropped but nothing came near. She was able to climb down on to the barely-covered dry rocks and see for herself how the boat was wedged. Given the energy she might have found a way to get off, to put out anchors ready to use a winch at high tide, but she was moving and thinking like a sleepwalker now.

At 1p.m., after another fitful doze in the warm sun, she remembered Harry and stumbled to the radio, but the VHF set was also suffering from its immersion, and all she could get were a few crackles. At two, the tide was up around the hull again and the boat looked just as if it were peacefully at anchor. Claire was in her bunk, fighting in a black, despairing dream in which men with no faces were surrounding her, pushing her backwards into a sheer pit which, when she looked back at it, plunged a million miles down. The fishing boat's engines woke her, but it had gone past when she worked out what the noise meant and groped her way up on deck.

'You could bloody help,' she mumbled to the man in the cockpit. The tide was lifting the hull now, banging the keel against the encircling rocks. High tide was soon after five, but she panicked at the thought that Harry might come and go. At four she started the engine, revved it in reverse and tried to back the boat out, but her reflexes were tuned, through tiredness, to her own boat, not this one, and in her boat with its ancient gearbox the prop turned the other way. The paddle-wheel effect of the screw began to swing the stern sideways, towards a sharp projecting rock spur. She mistook it for the effect of the tide and her tired mind told her to rev the engine harder to correct. On her boat it would have worked, on this one it simply drove the rock spur with a splintering finality, straight through the rounded bulge of the hull. She switched off, facing utter defeat.

She tried the radio one last time in complete and justified certainty that it would not work and then, reluctantly, logic clouded by intense fatigue but knowing it was a choice between drowning, hypothermia or simply risking arrest, she went shakily to the end locker, took a flare out of its plastic container and made her slow way up on deck to let it off and put her fate in the hands of others. That was when, from just behind her, Harry's voice said, 'Hello Claire, did you have a good trip?'

# Chapter Thirty-Five

## Wednesday August 21st

Harry had found what he was looking for north of Muasdale, just before the road was separated from the sea by a wedge of green fields. The water was choppy, reflecting grey as a thin layer of cloud scudded over in the fresh breeze. Cara Island's strange silhouette was clear; a flat-topped, almost square hill at the southern end rearing up from its low outline. He switched on the VHF transmitter and started to call, sure this time that her voice would respond, but there was nothing, and after five minutes he switched off, bitterly disappointed.

The cloud passed over and the water before him turned sparkling blue. Distance seemed to change with the brighter light; Cara Island came nearer and the sound between seemed less forbidding. A hundred yards down the road was a cottage, a holiday cottage from the look of the piled-up garden furniture and the rusting chain-store barbecue. In the garden, upside down, was a fibreglass dinghy.

Harry knocked on the door, prepared to spend however much of Gilligan's money it took to borrow the boat. No one came. Through a grimy window, he saw there was very little furniture and a dusty look of neglect. That solved the problem.

The dinghy was heavy and slimy with green mould, but when he lifted it under the stern and heaved it over he found a pair of oars and rowlocks under it. If Harry had known anything about boats he would have known that one should never drag a fibreglass dinghy down an abrasive concrete drive, across an abrasive tarmac road, and over a rocky beach, not if one wanted to go on using it. He did it because there was no other way. The effort made him breathe heavily and wore half-way through the bottom of the boat under the bow where it was scraping along as he dragged it backwards.

Another big cloud came over as he brought the oars to the dinghy. The sound took on a threatening grey colour and Gigha moved twice as far away again. He'd never liked water, and he'd never rowed a boat. He took his shoes and socks off, pushed the boat a short way into the water, and climbed in. His weight promptly embedded the stern on the bottom, whereupon a wave and the wind pivoted the bow and pushed it sideways up the beach again. He got it right on the third try, but only by pushing it out up to his waist and clambering in, soaked through.

Rowing wasn't as easy as it looked, but Harry was possessed by a grim determination. He was extremely lucky that high tide was approaching and the strong south to north flow had slowed to near slackness. He progressed unsteadily, catching the blades awkwardly in the waves and veering from side to side, but he learnt fast and when he realized he could keep a steady course by fixing his eye on a point on the slowly disappearing mainland over the stern, life became much simpler. A competent, fit oarsman could have done it in an hour. Harry did it in an hour and a half with hands that were blistering in agony for the last half of the journey. He passed between Gigha and Cara, and suddenly there it was; a white hull, wreathed in exhaust smoke, with a distant figure bending, looking down over the stern. Then he heard a crunch, the engine stopped, the figure disappeared below and the boat was left cocked oddly at an angle to the water. He was close enough now to read the lettering on the blue panels by her cockpit; *Sea Witch*. He pulled on the right oar to swing towards her, rowing as hard as his hands allowed. He had no idea how to come alongside, and swung around in a circle ten feet from her. Then a head appeared out of the hatchway and he saw Claire – a changed, blonde Claire – pull herself up from below and stand painfully upright, facing away from him with a tube in her hands.

'Hello Claire,' he said. 'Did you have a good trip?'

She turned, looked around her, not seeing him, and bent to

something next to her, a yachting cap on some sort of dummy.
'Shut up,' she said. 'That's not fair.'

'Claire, look round,' he called urgently, 'in the dinghy.
It's me.'

This time she did see him, and gaped at him, shaking her
head, then collapsed back into the cockpit.

He had no idea afterwards how he managed to get out of the
dinghy and up on to the deck, but he had the presence of mind
to take the painter with him and tied a knot of sorts round the
yacht's hand-rail. Then he was in the cockpit with her, trying
to get his arms round her as she strained away from him in a
terrified, huddled ball.

'Claire, it's me. Harry. Come on, you're all right, I'm here.
It's me.' He went on saying it over and over again until he felt
her start to relax, turn a doubtful face to him and then sag into
his arms.

It took much longer to get back. Harry had strips of torn-up
shirt wound round his hands. The dinghy was weighed down
with both of them and what they could salvage of Claire's
clothes. The ebbing tide was setting them down the shore of
the peninsula and Harry, prompted by listless corrections from
Claire, was forced to row crabwise to keep the dinghy clawing
across the tide.

'Tell me what's been happening,' he said, but she shook
her head.

'OK, later. I'll tell you my end, shall I?'

She seemed lethargic now, but she nodded.

'I know who they are; well, the name of their group, anyway.
And I know what they did.' And he told her, in bursts when
he had the breath, in bursts to distract from the sharp pain of
his hands and the duller pain of his arms, shoulders and back.
After a long, long time they grounded, exhausted, and just sat
there in the boat.

'We ought to put it back where it came from,' Harry gasped.
'Leave no trace.'

They carried it, one at each end, three yards at a time between
rests, into the cottage garden, then, arms around each other for

support and comfort, limped down the road to the parked car. In the car, Claire, in a weak but steadier voice, said, 'What do you mean, leave no trace? We've left a bloody great boat out there. Someone's going to see it.'

'We'll muddy the trail a bit,' said Harry, and reached into the back for the VHF set. He found a channel where two boats were talking, waited for a pause, and called out with a slight Irish brogue in his voice, 'This is the *Tipperary Mary*, come in any boat receiving, over.'

A strong reply came booming back. 'This is fishing vessel *Dancer Four*, Dougie MacAllan, go ahead caller.'

'This is the *Tipperary Mary*. I can't select Channel 16 – radio trouble. Could you pass a message to the coastguard?'

'Reading you clearly. What's the message?'

This time Harry thumbed the transmit key a lot and scratched the plastic surface of the mike before replying. 'I've picked up two crew members from the yacht *Sea Witch*. She's aground off Cara Island. They're OK. I'm taking them to . . .' here he made a loud whistling noise and pressed the key rapidly up and down.

'Lost the last part of your message, *Tipperary Mary*, please repeat with names of crew, your destination and whether they need salvage assistance for the boat?'

'Negative the last, arrangements are being made. Crew are David and er, Catherine Pope. Destination is er . . . Sligo.' Oh God, he thought, I haven't got a clue whether Sligo's on the coast, let alone which bit of Ireland it's in.

It clearly puzzled his listener too. 'Repeat destination, please.'

For an answer he made frenzied atmospheric noises into the mike, then clicked it off for good.

Campbeltown was a dour, old-fashioned town, away from the fishing quay, but Harry got what he wanted, leaving Claire tucked away in the car in an out-of-the-way street while he used Gilligan's cash recklessly to hire a holiday apartment. It had a built-in garage underneath, with direct access from the apartment. Harry left Claire soaking and slowly recovering in a hot bath while he went to stock up on food.

He got Gilligan on his carphone.

'It's Harry Chaplin.'

'God, Harry, I've been praying for a call. What have you got?'

'Exactly what I said I'd get.'

'Really? Tell me more.'

'Not on one of these things, if you don't mind. Can you get an outside broadcast truck?'

'The OB's ready and waiting in Manchester. Where do you want it?'

'Move it to Scotland tomorrow. Get them to a place called Tarbert on the west bank of Loch Fyne. Get me a mobile number for them, and I'll call them first thing Friday morning with the final rendezvous.'

'Do you want to give me your number?'

'I haven't got one. I'll call you.'

'Are you with . . . our friend?'

'Yes.'

'Where?'

'No, that was the deal. I can't say.'

'OK, I understand. Just tell me, just so I know if it's good. Has she told you anything yet?'

Harry plugged on with his chosen course. 'Not a thing. She won't. I'll hear it when you do, on the air.'

'What sort of state is she in?'

'I'm working on it.'

'You're a clever boy, Harry. Take care, please.'

The bath, the hot food that followed it, and the huge Scotch Harry poured for her, combined to bring back part of the hard, confrontational Claire that was still wrapped round the depleted inner core. They lay together on a cheap double bed with nylon covers in a room furnished with cheap varnished pine and hung about the walls with cheap Highland scenes. There was no sexual thrill. They were two threatened animals taking primitive physical comfort from huddling together, but their talk was the talk of fighter pilots going into attack against overwhelming odds. There was a quaver in her voice and from time to time she would lose track of her sentence and have to start again.

'What did Lawless actually *do*?'

'This is my best guess. They fixed Beaconsbridge. Maybe not all the different polling stations, maybe only some. Who knows? Anyway they had duplicate ballot boxes prepared. Lawless drove the van into some disused factory and they swapped them and later on, just to make sure nothing leaked, they killed him.'

'Somebody would have noticed.'

'No. It all goes back to the main point. You could drive a bus through election security these days. It's designed to stop one bent candidate doing a low-grade fiddle. We're talking sophistication and *money* here, big money. They would have known the counterfoil numbers issued to each polling station. They would have duplicate ballot papers, identical boxes, identical security seals. For the final check, the polling clerk puts in a list of the total number of votes cast at that station. It goes with the boxes. It's meant to stop anyone adding more votes. I guess they just put in a different list.'

'All right. Loony right-wingers might just have done that, but where do these Americans come in?'

'I have no idea, but there's no doubt these Freedom's Friends people were in there. Who knows, maybe they didn't like Labour's policies.'

'Like what?'

'NATO? US bases? The Balkans? GATT? Europe? God knows.'

'It doesn't help us get out of this.'

'Oh, yes it does. You're going on TV on Friday night and you're going to tell the whole story.'

She looked at him in total disbelief. 'How? From where?'

He told her, and saw a sudden light of purpose in her eyes.

# Thursday August 22nd

The southern tip of the Mull of Kintyre was their considered choice in the morning, a morning which saw yet another change in Claire. She was introverted and angry now, and Harry felt the indirect heat of that anger though he knew it was aimed at a different target, a target that had suddenly taken on a name and a purpose if not yet much of a face. They'd kicked the shit out of her, now it was time to start kicking back.

They made their plan carefully. They wrote a short and enigmatic introduction for Russell Mackay to read in studio which simply said, in effect, 'get ready for something special, over to our outside broadcast team'. Harry could imagine the joint fury Jane Bernstein and Mackay himself would be expressing in London at being kept in the dark. They went over and over the script. It was to be a simple read to camera, delivered slightly awkwardly off a clipboard without an autocue, but Harry knew that didn't matter a damn. Its content would rivet the audience to the screen.

Then they'd gone looking for a location.

Thursday night was a curious experience. Harry had the feeling that if there had been an altar in the apartment, Claire would have spent the night praying before it like Joan of Arc. She drew more and more into herself during the evening, looking cold and pale, and they went to bed like an old married couple, getting in their separate sides. She held his hand in bed, lying on her back and staring at the ceiling, and although he put his arm round her, the stiffness in her body kept him from any further contact.

# Friday August 23rd

Harry met the outside broadcast vehicle and the generator truck at three o'clock on Friday on the outskirts of Campbeltown. They were hired from a Manchester facilities operation and they were out to please. It was clearly their first job for National. He led them down the winding road through the village of Southend, then suddenly, beyond the empty concrete towers of the ruined technical school, the land ended and the waves crashed on to the beach below the low cliffs at the very tip of the Mull.

Johnny, the crew boss, was smiling when they stopped on a wide grass patch above the beach, the narrow road at their back winding away from the sea. 'No problem with a link from here,' he said. 'I was worried when I saw Arran and Goat Fell. If that had been in the way we'd have had a problem. Now, tell me what we're doing exactly.'

'OK. The show's on the air at seven-thirty. We're inserting twelve minutes live starting at seven-thirty-two. Then there might be a two-way with the studio, so we'll need reverse sound and an earpiece.'

Johnny looked around bewildered while behind him men cranked up antennae and ran out cable. 'What exactly is it, though? There's sod all here.'

'Doesn't matter. It's a one-camera job. The reporter's just going to talk to the camera.'

'You're kidding. Twelve minutes straight to camera? No pictures?'

'Johnny, just believe me. You'll understand it all later.'

'So where's the reporter?'

'I'll be bringing ... er, the reporter along at about quarter past.'

'No rehearsal?'

Harry thought about their mobile phones and the possibility one of them might call the police. 'No rehearsal.'

Johnny looked increasingly worried, and let out his breath noisily. 'Be it upon your own head, that's all I can say.'

'It is.'

He left them to get on with it, drove back to Campbeltown and called Gilligan. 'OK, we're ready.'

'How's it going to work?'

'The studio does the intro. I come on and do a very quick link from the OB, then we see Claire walk down the hillside and she comes straight up to the camera and starts talking.'

'Good. I'm going to call just a few of the top journos, say five newspapers, three or four minutes beforehand to tell them to watch.'

'Don't say why.'

'I won't.'

'I'll want to get her away safely afterwards. We'll have to take our chances with the police. I want you to lay on a good lawyer. I think you should come up and meet us somewhere.'

'Campbeltown?'

'How did you know that's where we are?'

'The whole damned office knows. Your crew called in just now for some technical talk, line-up and all that. Bernstein came and told me.'

'Shit.'

'Harry, it doesn't matter. She knows where you are, but I'm the only one that knows why.'

'She'll guess.'

'I'll lead her astray.'

When Harry put the phone down, he rang Putney, just to reassure himself that Steffie was still there. He got the ward sister.

'Oh, Mr Chaplin. Doctor Freeman left a message. He wanted a word. Shall I put you through?'

Freeman, the man who thought Steffie should be switched off like some sort of light. 'No, I'm in a call-box in Scotland. I'm very busy. Tell him I'll call him on Monday.'

He put Claire in the car just after six-thirty. She was made-up, dressed as smartly as the choice of worn yachting clothes allowed, and she was constantly going through the script on the clipboard, off in a world of her own, preparing for the showdown. He dropped her where they'd planned: beside the road where she could cut up the slope of the hill to look down on the OB van.

'Why don't you just sit in the car and wait?' he asked.

'Because if this screws up, I want you at arm's length, Harry. You get too close to it in front of witnesses and you're an accessory. Anyway, I want a walk.'

The crew were jumpy, glad to see him, and full of worries.

'Good signal,' said Johnny. 'Are you really sure it's just one camera, one reporter?'

'Well, two,' said Harry. 'I'll do a quick link. Stay wide so you'll pick up the other person walking down that path over my shoulder while I'm talking. Then she'll take over.'

'She?'

'Yes. From this moment on, no one uses your phone except to call National, right?'

'Right. Why?'

'Because "she" is Claire Merrick.'

He would have liked the luxury of savouring the moment, the look of complete astonishment on Johnny's face.

'But how? You mean she's going to turn herself in?'

'She's going to explain what really happened.'

They had a dish on the roof and a monitor rigged up to feed them the show. Harry rehearsed what he was going to say, checking his watch every two minutes. At seven-twenty he saw her waiting on the slope of the hill at the spot they'd chosen. They'd timed the walk that afternoon. At seven-twenty-eight he waved his arm and she started walking down.

At seven-thirty after the advertisement break, the show's titles rolled. Johnny, acting as floor manager, called, 'Show's on the air, silence. Coming to you in two minutes, Harry.'

In the studio, Russell Mackay, looking less than confident in a mid-shot, ran through a quick menu for the show to camera one, then turned to camera two in close-up. Harry glanced over his shoulder, Claire was thirty yards away, perfect.

His adrenaline level rose with that familiar feeling of a bubble expanding in his chest. Here we go, he thought. Russell Mackay, on the monitor, said, 'But we start today's show with a very unusual item indeed; something quite remarkable in the history of Crookbusters. We're going over now, live, to our reporter on the spot.'

Harry started. 'Thank you, Russell. This is Harry Chaplin in the Highlands of Scotland and I have a sensational revelation for you. Walking down the hillside towards me is the most wanted woman in Britain, Claire Merrick.' He turned and looked. She was only seconds away. 'She is here to tell for the first time . . .' He became aware something odd was happening. Johnny was talking, saying things, another of his crew was rushing for the phone. He tried to plough on, '. . . the real story of what . . .'

But Johnny was waving his arms, stopping him, and then he looked down at the monitor and saw not himself, not the Highlands of Scotland, not Claire coming into shot behind him, but some clunker of a story with Gary the researcher masquerading as a reporter in the cells of some police station.

'Christ almighty, what's going on?' he said. Did we lose the signal?'

Claire reached him, worried, questioning.

'No,' said Johnny. 'I mean, I don't know. It went to black for a second or two, then that came on. It's not us. The signal was fine leaving here. Right up to the end of the intro they were seeing our picture. It must have gone down somewhere at the last moment, just as they switched to us.'

'No, no,' said Claire, backing away from the monitor screen with her hands outstretched as if to fend it off. 'There's something very wrong with all this.'

'Hold on,' Harry said to her urgently, casting around in his mind for a reason. 'Links screw up. You know that. They must have had the other package ready to run as a stand-by.'

'Harry,' she said, swinging on him, 'how long have you been in TV? How long does it take to get another input up and on the screen when your big story falls flat? Have you ever seen it done in two seconds before? Fifteen seconds if you're lucky; thirty if you're not. Someone had that planned. We've been screwed. I'm getting out of here.'

'Wait,' he said. 'Give me a minute to call Gilligan.'

He used the phone in the back of the OB truck, and the National switchboard put him through in seconds.

'Harry. What the hell happened?'

'I don't know. I'm asking you.'

'I'm not in the gallery. I was watching it in my office.'

'Claire's climbing the wall. What do I tell her?'

'Tell her, I'll . . .'

But then an engine roared to life, men started shouting and Harry was out of the door, leaving the phone dangling for Gilligan to deliver his sentence into thin air. He took in two moving vehicles, a brown Land-Rover coming fast down the road from the right, and the generator truck, Claire at the wheel, moving off with half the crew after it. He was much nearer. The driver's window was open and he leapt for it, hanging on to the door frame with one foot on the step.

There were tears pouring down her cheeks and a mad, set expression on her face. 'Get off,' she shouted.

'Stop. I'll drive you in the Ford.'

'Get OFF!' she cried again, beating him with her right hand through the window, 'I'm sorting them out, Harry. By myself. Get off, damn you.'

'NO! Just stop a minute.' The blows were hurting him. He couldn't protect his face against them and he struggled to hold on as the truck bounced over the rough ground. Claire and Steffie, Steffie and Claire, pulling him in opposite directions.

'There's no chance,' she said, and struck him hard on the nose with such force that he let go and fell, tumbling over and over into the heather as the truck, towing broken lengths of electrical cable behind it, charged off.

It bounced on to the road fifty yards ahead of the oncoming Land-Rover and roared away gears crunching. Harry sprinted for the Mondeo. It was parked over a hundred yards away, and the run seemed to take for ever, his chest thrust out, head back, arms flailing in the kind of focused agony he'd not experienced since school sports. By the time he'd found the key and got it started both the other vehicles were out of sight round the bend.

He chased them to the narrow turning that led to the lighthouse and up over the edge of the headland. The lane was narrow and rutted, startled sheep leaping away over the wall. As they climbed he could see down to a sea full of white horses, down over a diving curve of grass. Round a right hander, ahead, in a long slide that had the car bucketing and crashing through the ruts, he straightened up just in time to miss the Land-Rover which had pulled over and stopped beside the road.

A huge feeling of relief came over him. It was nothing, a mere coincidence, bird watchers, fishermen, who cared? Innocent, harmless people who'd happened by and been hugely misunderstood. When Claire saw it was only him behind her she'd stop and all this could still be sorted out. They'd go straight to Gilligan, show him the script, swear an affi . . .

He hit the brakes hard and gazed, aghast, down the hill in front: a curving hill, the track running round a ledge in it, and the grass sloping on down below it, another thirty feet to the cliffs and sea far below. Parked across the track was a second Land-Rover, and standing behind it was a group of men. He saw the truck slow down, a hundred yards short of them. Come back, he thought, reverse. We'll throw them off.

The truck growled louder and accelerated again and he thought he knew what she'd seen. The Land-Rover had been swung across the track facing the sea. There was a two-foot gap between its tail and the uphill bank and the tail would be lighter than the nose with its heavy engine. If she just hit that right she could knock it out of her way. He roared encouragement; he was still roaring when, looking through the plain glass of the truck's windscreen, without any attempt to steer for the gap, Claire bored straight into the middle of the Land-Rover at fifty miles an hour, hurling it like a battering ram at the men who turned too late to run, hurling it and them off the edge of the road, and plunging after them so that the twisting, turning Land-Rover and the heavy generator truck, still trailing its lengths of cable behind, soared off the cliff and hit the just submerged rocks below with the close-spaced double thud of a sonic boom.

Harry ran down to the top of the cliff and stared dully down at the wreckage with the water swirling over it, hearing her voice. Four of them. She'd taken her revenge on four of them. Four what? Foot soldiers? There's no chance, she'd said. What about Harry Chaplin? They'd never let him be, would they? He remembered the Land-Rover behind him, but when he'd turned and gone back the way he came there was no sign of it.

# Sunday September 29th

One month later there was a little initiation ceremony at the ranch. Hacker, also known as Gregory Peck, was being granted access to the Holy of Holies, Freedom's Friends Hall of Honour. They lined the stairs and the landing for him, clapping as Hacker, the Producer and Martin Blunden on either side, was taken to the door and given his own key to unlock it. Down one side of the room were thirty-five ornate marble plaques, memorials on Mammon's church wall. The tenth one was veiled by a square of red silk from which a tassel hung. He glanced at the ones next to it; 'Game 9. Genscher resignation. Game 11. Danish Referendum on Maastricht Treaty, 1992. Game 12. Robert Maxwell. Game 13. Israeli General Election.' There was a lot of bare wall still to fill.

Martin Blunden read from a citation, 'Gregory Peck. In skilfully completing this game you have earned full and permanent membership of Freedom's Friends. You have earned the right to select a benefit game for a purpose of your choice. Now, in recognition of your personal contribution, please unveil the plaque.'

He stepped forward and tugged at the tassel. The silk fell from a tablet which said simply: 'Game 10. British General Election, 1992.'

The Producer gave him a sideways look. 'I suppose we *can* say it's truly finished with Chaplin still around.'

'Chaplin never knew. He was just the tool. Merrick was the one with the story, and she didn't get to tell him. Anyway, he always hated her.'

'Is that enough?'

'I've told him she was crazy, and he trusts me,' said Desmond 'Hacker' Gilligan, turning back to look again at his plaque and dreaming of the rich TV franchises still to come.

# Author's Note

Readers may wish to know what facts lie behind this book. I first became interested in the vulnerability of the British electoral system when I read an account by the Intelligence specialist, James Rusbridger, of the way MI5 have been able to take the secrecy out of the supposedly secret ballot, and record the names of voters who voted for particular candidates whom they perceived as far Left. From that, it began to seem at least thinkable that someone might have decided to go further.

I then began an analysis of the results of the 1992 General Election, looking for any statistical oddities. Adding substantial extra votes in a marginal seat would show up as described, by affecting the swing and the turnout figures. Setting the same criteria described in the book, I came up with a list of nine anomalous seats. Seven of those seats began with the initial letters A, B, or C. The other two began with S and T.

A statistician has estimated the probability of that happening by chance at nearly one in four thousand. I can tell you no more.

It is absurdly easy, however, to buy ballot boxes and obtain security seals for them identical to those used in the election.

The origins of the Lockerbie bomb come from a convincing account I was given by a source who would not wish to be named.

The Bohemian Grove does exist and is portrayed accurately. I have studied it for a long time and I commend to any interested reader the article in the November 1989 issue of the American magazine *Spy*, written by Philip Weiss, who penetrated its security. Two other books on the subject which proved useful to me were *The Greatest Men's Party on Earth* by John van der Zee (Harcourt Brace Jovanovich, 1974), and *The Bohemian Grove and Other Retreats, a Study in Ruling Class Cohesiveness* by G. William Domhoff (Harper and Row, 1974). Special thanks to the inimitable Peter Day, who turned them both up for me in a Los Angeles second-hand book shop.

Of the group who inspired 'Freedom's Friends', there are only rumours.